I0762338

MAP

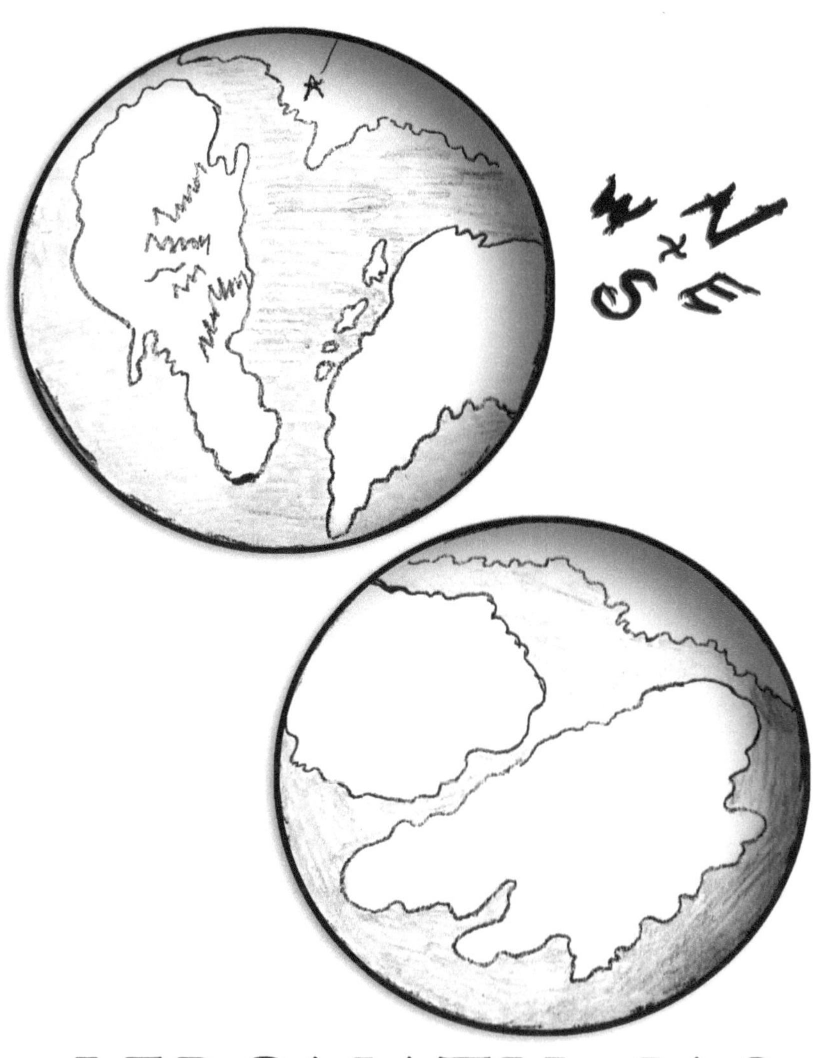

LEBONATH JAS

Look for The Continuation of the Dragonhorse Chronicles:

Dragonhorse Rising (Book 1)

Conscience of the King (Book 2)

Peace on Another's Terms (Book 3)

A Lopsided Colorwax Heart (Book 4) *(Coming Soon)*

Spirit in Motion (Book 5) *(Coming Soon)*

Visit our website at

www.dragonhorserising.com

And for this Author's Peter Aarons Books:

Glory Days (Book 1)

Another Man's Wife ~ A Love Story (Book 2)

Home Again Home Again (Book 3) *(Coming Soon)*

The Converging Objects of the Universe (Book 4) *(Coming Soon)*

Oh, Baby! (Book 5) *(Coming Soon)*

Visit our website at

www.peteraarons.com

Showandah S. Terrill

PEACE ON
ANOTHER'S TERMS

BOOK THREE OF
THE DRAGONHORSE CHRONICLES

This book is a work of fiction, and any references to historical events, real people or real locales are used fictitiously. Other names, places, characters and incidents are products of the author's imagination, and any resemblance to actual events or locales or persons, living or dead, is purely coincidental.

Published 2020 by Short Horse Press.

Original Artwork by Edwin M. Pinson
Book Design and Shorthorse Press Logo Design by Jeremy T. Hanke
The text for this book is set in times New Roman, 11 point
Manufactured in the United States of America
Library of Congress Control Number: 2020921569
ISBN: 978-1-7328052-9-3 (hardcover)
ISBN: 978-1-7342194-0-1 (Paperback)
ISBN: 978-1-7342194-1-8 (eBook)

PEACE ON
ANOTHER'S TERMS

"There is a difference between legislating morality and enforcing civility. A difference between bonds and bondage, religion and faith. A lesson which you are about to learn."

-Ah'krill Ardenai Morning Star

To Ed with love

CHAPTER 1

Ardenai took a deep breath to quiet the butterflies in his stomach. One minute from contact. The Lebonathis knew he was here. Dominus was all they could see on their screens, but he had a fleet behind him just out of range: five Dragonhorse Tactical Cruisers, eight observation vessels from the Seventh Galactic Alliance, including Bonfire Dannis with Belesprit, two big battle wagons from Menorquin, sent to join them as they passed through three days ago, unasked for but appreciated, and because Ulric was their fleet commander, Amberia had sent most of its complement of heavy and midweight cruisers. Corvus and Phylla both had ships on stand-by.

There was no doubt they could win in a war of conquest, but Ardenai wanted a Probative Interposition. Perhaps it was too much to ask. Mostly what he wanted, was Ah'ria Konik Nokota. Ah'davan had said he was there, she could feel him, and he was saying over and over like a litany, don't come alone. Don't come alone. It had set her heart pounding wildly, and Ardenai had been afraid he was going to lose her on the spot.

And here he was, alone. He had made sure Kehailan and the others knew that he only wanted to seem alone for appearances sake, but like an actor as the curtain goes up, he was scared. As many things could go wrong as could go right, so he focused on just one thing – getting Konik into his wife's loving arms before she died.

The planetary capital appeared on the screen in the center of his target area, and Ardenai touched a pad on his console. "This is the Imperial Equi Cruiser Dominus," he said. "I am Ah'krill Ardenai Morning Star, First-lord of Equus, the Thirteenth Dragonhorse."

There was a momentary shimmer and a face appeared on the screen. "I am the Most Wise Lord Eridu," the man said. "Under other circumstances I would welcome you, Dragonhorse, though I find myself doubting your motives at this point. Why are you here, and how do I know it is really you? I have been led to believe you all look pretty much alike."

Ardenai studied the man as he talked, pleased that he was chatty. Plump, pale, with small pink eyes partially hidden by the fatty rolls on his cheeks. A small mouth with creases which told him it turned down more than it turned up. Ring laden hands, soft and unmarred. Others did his work for him. There would be no hand to hand combat with this one. "Surely Halaf or Naram is there with you," Ardenai responded. "They can confirm my identity. As for why I am here, I have the task of returning Anchoress Samarra to you. Unfortunately for her, she is dead."

"It seems an unpleasant habit of yours to return members of my family and government to me in less than pristine condition, Dragonhorse."

"Members of your family and government have a proclivity for trying to kill the people I care about," Ardenai responded. "Samarra tried to kill your daughter, who is a precious gift by the way, and I thank you. Having failed in that attempt, she killed herself. She loved your world and her place in it. I have returned her for that reason. If you do not want the body, I will jettison it into space, return to Amberia for my crew, and go home."

"That seems a rather small ship to have come so far," Eridu remarked. He was sizing up his chances of a capture or a kill, and Ardenai knew it.

"She is extremely fast, well-armed and more than adequate for the task at hand," Ardenai smiled. "Do you want the body or don't you? We don't preserve corpses, and she's beginning to stink."

They looked at each other for a few moments in the way powerful men have of assessing one another. Eridu nodded slowly. "Why are you here, Equi?"

Ardenai had only a second to choose a response or be lost. "I know you have Legate Konik," he shrugged, and Eridu's chin came up. "He who aspires to these armbands of which I have grown rather fond. He is now in command of the Telenir, and I want him. I want to make an example of him so that this whole nonsense with them and their petty incursions will stop. I am willing to give you this aromatic carcass for your women to wail over if you will give me the Legate."

Again Eridu studied him, then leaned just slightly to one side, as though someone were speaking to him from that direction. "I like you," he said, and smiled until his eyes nearly disappeared. "As you can see by the age and condition of the city, we live mostly underground these days, but there is more than adequate room for you to land your ship in the main square. I will meet you. We will dicker over the Telenir, and in any case we will rid you of the Anchoress's body."

"I agree," Ardenai nodded. "Send me the appropriate coordinates so I don't land on anybody."

"Done," Eridu said, "though no one of any import lives on the surface anymore."

Ardenai broke the connection.

Teal, are you yet with me?

Of course I am.

You know I am going to set down?

I do. Kehailan does. Pythos does. Ah'davan does. Be aware that the further underground you go, the more noisy and confusing it becomes, the more difficult it will be for you to communicate, so speak slowly and use small words – think of us as five-year-olds. Be careful. Be quick.

I will.

The coordinates appeared on his console and he allowed the ship to land itself, studying the profile of the continent as it appeared through the orange haze. Equus was mostly water, and cool. Lebonath Jas was primarily land, and hot. He was grateful he'd taken Eridi's advice and worn a summer uniform. Much of the continent he could see was desert, with sealed water pipes snaking between barren hills and occasional orchards which looked on the scanners to be … date palms. Interesting. Herds of caronai, or so he assumed, bunched tight together. He wondered what they found to eat. There were mountains which vanished as the ship got lower, and in a few minutes all he could see was an enormous city below him, its boundaries dwarfing even Thura twice over and then some. The air was thick with dust and smoke, the ground teeming with people, trains and busses. Luckily everything was getting out of his way. No one of import lived on the surface? He heard the landing pods release, and felt a soft bump as the ship touched down.

He ducked his six and a half foot frame to step out, and when he looked up, a row of uniformed men stood at attention on each side of the path he was obviously supposed to walk. Back a respectful distance the square was packed with onlookers, and he could see people in the shade of a huge and quite beautiful government building a few hundred feet away. He had ample time to realize how really kraaling hot it was here before he began his ascent up the steps to greet them.

Eridu was not only in the shade, but under an additional umbrella, and wearing protective eyewear as well. Behind Eridu and to his left stood Halaf with Naram beside him, both wearing evil smiles which boded no pleasant experience. "Ahimsa, I wish thee peace," Ardenai said, gesturing, and Eridu returned the gesture before sticking out his hand, Declivian fashion. "Welcome," he smiled, "I've been looking forward to this." Ardenai shook his hand, and as he did he felt a pinprick in his palm.

I think they just drugged me. Palm of my right hand. If I react now I'll never find Nik.

"My planet can be warm in the summer," he said, casually rubbing his palm as though it itched. Couldn't very well pretend he hadn't felt it. His hands were work-worn, but they weren't impervious. "But this is truly torrid. I'm surprised you've survived as a culture under these conditions." He shot a glance at Eridu. "You have a burr on one of your rings."

"So I do. So I do," Eridu said, pulling his mouth down and making a show of examining his fingers. He shrugged and gestured toward the interior of the building. They began to walk, and the temperature cooled slightly as they went in and then down.

The building had been partially gutted, and in place of rooms there was a wide corridor, slanting down into the darkness. "We began losing the microbes in our soil several generations ago. Our scientists are working on a fix, but mostly we are thinking we will expand our trade and influence with other planets and thrive in that manner."

A reek presented itself and grew more intense. It was getting dimmer, and Ardenai felt his pupils working harder than usual to adapt to the conditions. He was also beginning to feel just the tiniest thump of a headache. What if he was poisoned and not drugged? What if he would soon be joining Samarra and Addur in the burning dust?

Stay calm. Teal's gentle voice. He wasn't alone. *Think only of Ah'davan.*

"We have found it is always better to be able to sustain needs at the local level, then regional, continental, and planetary. It took us awhile to … figure it out." He bit down on a gasp as pain slashed up his back. "So tell me, Eridu, now that you have me where you want me, and since I will soon be in no condition to resist you, what are you going to do with me?"

"Halaf told me you were perspicacious," Eridu chuckled. "No, actually Naram said you were perspicacious. Halaf said you were an arrogant, self-important pain in the ass who would strut into a trap without so much as a moment's consideration, thinking yourself above any sort of subterfuge."

"So there is no Telenir? I know that is not true. I know his kind, and I can smell him."

"Oh, it's true alright," Eridu said, puffing slightly from the exertion of walking. "It is he who wants you, and not the other way around, Dragonhorse. He said if we brought you to him that he would put Telenir boots on the ground to the betterment of our planet and the detriment of yours."

Ardenai stumbled and caught himself against the wall as another pain, this one worse, shot up his legs, his spine and into his already pounding head. "He wanted a corpse? Doesn't seem very smart."

Eridu made an indifferent gesture and a man Ardenai recognized as Brak ducked under his arm to support him as they walked. "No, he wanted to kill you himself, to make an example of you, just as you wanted to make an example of him, and since we are a people who love our sports, we decided to make it by public invitation."

They had come to a set of huge doors which opened in front of them to reveal a space the length of a polo field but wider. At the end closest there was a raised platform perhaps fifty feet in diameter, topped by a pulsing globe and surrounded with livewire. Inside, holding a Yamraj axe, was Konik. If he was thinking anything, Ardenai couldn't fathom it, but then he couldn't fathom much at this point. He was having trouble breathing, his vision was failing, and his muscles were twisting into knots which made him want to scream. "Not … going to be much … of a fight," he grated.

"It's not supposed to be a fight," Eridu laughed. "Our people want to see you writhe and shriek for a while, and then they want to see Konik hack your arms off with that battle axe. After that death should be mercifully quick. Not as quickly as you killed my son – but relatively quick as Lebonathi executions go."

The gate was opened to put Ardenai into the arena, and as Brak came under his arm he whispered, "I can shut that dome off for two seconds, no more, be ready in two minutes," and gave the Firstlord a shove.

Ardenai made a sharp cry of pain as he landed, and the crowd roared its approval. Konik brought the blade of the axe down inches from Ardenai's ear, then dropped to his knees, laughing, his face close to the Firstlord's on the mat.

All praise to the Wisdom Giver, Ardenai! Please tell me you're not here alone. I tried to let you know not to come alone.

No ... not alone. Quick. Lock up. Your head ... to mine. Think ...only of Ah'davan.

What?

Now! I need your ...focus. ... Dying...

You'll only wish you were dead for about two hours. They've given it to me more than once – they like the way it makes you sound.

I can't see! Nik, I can't see! I can't breathe!

Don't panic. It makes the pain worse. Your sight will come back.

Brace yourself, we're going up. Konik pulled Ardenai up onto his knees, which made him cry out again, and again the crowd roared its approval. *Ah'davan,* Konik thought, and even without it being spoken, it was a prayer. He brought his forehead into contact with Ardenai's and made a pretense of grappling with him to buy them time. There was tremendous power in the Firstlord's brain, but very little control and Konik put every ounce of his desperate strength into channeling it. *Ah'davan, Beloved. Addie. I am here. Ah'davan ....*

"Stop them!" Naram screamed over the noise of the crowd. "They're telepaths!"

"Don't be a fool," Eridu scoffed. "Nothing can get through that dome. That's why it was built. Give me some credit."

The dome flickered, then exploded, sending shards of livewire and glastaline into the crowd, piercing and cutting as it went. Eridu ducked, and when he looked up, Ardenai and Konik were gone.

"Seize their ship!" he cried, but it, too, was gone. Only Samarra's corpse was left, baking in the sun. Eridu slumped in a black rage into his plushly padded seat, ignoring the screams of the injured and dying. "How far could they have gotten?" he muttered. "Where did they go? Surely we can catch them. We have a fleet. There are only two of them, with one small ship."

"You're dead wrong," Naram grated. "I have seen their world. He did not come alone. They would not have let him come alone."

Eridu had only to look at him for Naram to blench and step back into the shadows. "Trust me, they will be back here in short order and the sport will continue. He's not strong enough to hold on to our friend Legate Konik for very long."

▲ ▲ ▲ ▲ ▲ ▲ ▲

Konik eased Ardenai onto the scrambleshaft platform as gently as he could. "I've been dosed twice with it, and if there's an antidote I don't know what it is," he said, rising stiffly from his knees. "He'll be cold. Keep him flat, and warm him as best you can. Try not to touch him – it's excruciating. Ice may help his head ..."

"Go," Ardenai whispered. "Ah'davan …"

"Is here?" Konik exclaimed. "She's here? You brought her?"

"We had to," Ah'nis said quietly. "She wanted to see you. Please come quickly with me."

The look on her face told Konik everything he needed to know, and he realized why the Firstlord had thrown caution to the wind. Why he had said, dying. They were out of time. He and Addie, were out of time. He wondered for a brief second as they hurried down the corridor how he looked, how he smelled, but when he saw his wife, saw her smile and reach out to him, he knelt beside her, embracing her as closely as he could and pressing her head against his neck with the palm of his hand.

"Nik," she sighed. "He found you. He promised me he would, and he found you."

"He did," Konik replied, rocking her gently from side to side and kissing her hair, her cheek, and tipping her head back to kiss her lips. "I will not leave you again."

"I have waited so long for you to hold me like this," she whispered. "You smell so good, like you've been working in the gardens all morning when the leaves first tumble."

"A chore I am looking forward to with all my heart," he said.

"We should talk about thinning the rohanth bushes come Aellaeno," she murmured, stroking his cheek, and with a shuddering sigh, she was dead.

Ardenai was freezing to death. He couldn't see for the blinding white light and the pain like someone sticking leather awls in his eyes – ice picks in his ear drums. There was an unbearable shock of pain and though he felt the scream, he couldn't hear it – everything, every thought, every sensation was like shattering glass. Lava, popping, throwing molten globs of fire. He couldn't breathe for the desperate pain in his diaphragm as though it was being twisted on a stick, pulling his ribcage together until it collapsed on itself. Another, lesser shock of pain. His head was going to explode and spray his brains across the wall. His eyes were going to pop out and dangle by their nerves, his teeth were being broken out of his jaw with a hammer.

He couldn't breathe. He couldn't breathe! His legs were being crushed at the knees and ankles. His right arm was being twisted out of its socket, his hand torn from the wrist.

"How can ssuch a tiny wound causse sso much pain?" Pythos hissed, examining the Firstlord's palm.

"Maybe if you swabbed it you could figure out what it is," Eridi suggested, looking with him. "Samarra had antidotes for everything, maybe this has one too."

"Creator Spirit, I hope so," Teal whispered. He'd placed the Firstlord on a raised bed in the sanecere bay, carefully slid his boots off, and covered him with a blanket from the warmer. He could tell that every time they touched the man it increased his agony, because he went from groaning and sobbing to screaming, which told Teal that Ardenai couldn't collect his thoughts enough to get any control over himself. The man might be soft-hearted, but he was no sissy. He wished they could ask Konik. He said they'd done this to him. What kind of monstrous society invented torture like this?

Pythos swabbed the puncture, then bent over Ardenai and flicked him with his tongue. Instead of straightening up slowly as he usually did, instead of seeing the person he was caring for relax, Pythos staggered back and slumped in a coil on the floor. "There are no thoughtss," he managed, and huge tears stood in his yellow eyes. "If I cannot touch hiss thoughtss I cannot touch hiss pain." The tears spilled, and he coiled even tighter, covering his head with his tail to hide them. Into that helplessness, came Ah'davan's last breath, and Konik's anguished cry, and Pythos balled up in utter dejection and despair.

Teal gave him a minute, then squatted on his heels beside the old doctor and said in his slow, quiet voice, "You need to stop that, Pythos. You've run into something new, and you have to deal with it. You can see what it's doing; figure out what it is. Come on, let me help you up. Let's go test that swab. Eladeus only knows who else that man is going to use this on before we're through here. Come on, give me your hands, or do I need to haul you up in coils, because I can and I will."

Pythos looked with one teary eye, realized he was indeed going to be constricted against that massive chest if he didn't do as he was told, and uncoiled a little at a time, finally giving in to Teal's kindly persuasion. The old physician picked up his testing materials and toddled toward the back with Teal, instructing Eridi to watch Ardenai and to fetch them if anything should change.

"My father did this to you," Eridi said, and while it made her angry, it also made her determined. Konik had said ice might help the fire in Ardenai's head, so she looked around until she found a cold box in the pharmic section of the sanecere. If it had medications, it should have medicinal ice packs. She looked. It did. She took two of them and went back to where Ardenai lay gasping in short painful breaths and groaning deep in his belly. He was shaking like a current was running through him, and he had blood in the corners of his mouth, probably from biting his tongue.

Eridi had been to some classes on medicinal herbs, and how the body responded to different kinds of things. She had enjoyed those classes – she enjoyed all of her classes. Ah'din had taught some of them, and her field of expertise fascinated Eridi. She wondered if this terrible thing was chemical, or natural. She thought about something Ah'din had said, and Teal had pretty much said it again just now. 'We can measure the effect of something without knowing what it is.' To Eridi, that was a mind-expanding comment, and contrary to what she'd been taught most of her life. Whatever this was, the effects were terrible. What could she do to help the Dragonhorse?

She thought back to her classes. Ice helped make things numb. The spinal cord sent signals to the rest of the body. As carefully as she could, she slid one of the ice packs behind Ardenai's neck at the base of his skull, and the other where his neck met his shoulders. In a minute or two he was quieter, not much, but some. She went back to the cold box for more ice packs, and when she came out there was a tall, slim Equi in a Dragonhorse uniform, standing in profile looking down at the Firstlord.

"You got him here in time," he was saying. "He got to say goodbye. I hope that helps make up for what you're going through right now."

"Oh, Ah'davan is gone?" Eridi asked, her voice catching a little in her throat, and the young man speaking turned to look at her. He had a typically handsome Equi face, and in that face lived a pair of the most stunning dark brown eyes Eridi had ever seen. He smiled at her, the family dimples asserted themselves in his cheeks, and she knew who he had to be. He had to have been at the banquet that first night. How in the world could she have missed those eyes? That answer was easy. She'd been drugged. She didn't remember anything about her first few days on Equus, not even this absolutely gorgeous creature. For the first time, she realized with a little surge of joy and a prickle of goose bumps, she was a young girl with a sudden crush. A normal, giggly crush.

"Yes, she is gone, but happily," he said, and he had a deep, gentle voice, just like Ardenai's. "Sorry, we haven't formally met. I am Kehailan. The Dragonhorse is my sire."

She wanted to say, and you are the most beautiful thing I have ever seen in my sixteen years of life, but instead she said, "I am Eridi. The Most Wise Lord Eridu is my father, speaking of sorry."

"I thought that's who you were," he said. "The green contacts aren't really much of a disguise if you're trying to hide."

"They do help with the bright lights," she smiled. "I am dismayed by what has happened to your sire, I really am. It was completely unexpected. Teal and Pythos are trying to figure out what to do to help ease the pain."

Kehailan laughed very quietly. "I think my father had a pretty good idea what he was getting into. The thing I've realized about him is that he doesn't care what he has to go through to get what he wants. He hates to involve others, but himself ..." Kehailan made a nonchalant gesture, "not so much. For a long time I thought that was a weakness in him. Now I recognize it as this amazing strength." He looked a little embarrassed as he glanced at her, and she noticed that his dark lashes almost brushed his cheeks when he looked down. "I'm hoping I inherited a little of it myself."

He reached to touch his father's arm, and Eridi put out a hand to stay him, enjoying the little tingle it brought.

"Touching him makes the pain worse," she explained. "Konik says it begins to wear off in about two hours. The ice packs behind his neck seem to be helping a little bit, so I thought I might try a couple more someplace."

"That's a good idea," he said. He paused, tipped his head slightly to one side, nodded as though in response and said, "I have to go. Thank you for taking care of Ardenai. I'm sure I will see you around the ship, though how I've missed you so far is a mystery to me."

"Ah'nis and I were on Dragonhorse Ten until this morning," she grinned. "I'll make sure you see as much of me as you want. I didn't mean that the way it sounded. I meant … oh ..."

"I'll see you at dinner, Princess," he laughed, ducked his head, and was gone.

A few minutes later Teal appeared and said, "Pythos wants you. I'll trade you places."

Eridi looked concerned and Teal give her a reassuring smile. "He says you had a very good idea about swabbing for identification, and he has determined that it is plant based. He says you know more about the plants on your world than he does, simply by being around Samarra, so he's hoping you can help him."

Eridi nodded. "Certainly," she said. "I have been keeping ice packs under the back of his neck, and it seems to help a little bit. I just changed them a minute ago." She excused herself and walked toward the back of the sanecere bay to help Pythos – to offer her expertise. This is what it was like to be part of something as an equal, to contribute with her brain. It was wonderful. She gave herself a little hug as she walked and felt like she was floating. She wondered if Kehailan was seeing anyone, and if he'd mind waiting around for another five years or so.

Ardenai was making a sharp bark in his throat with every painful, panting breath he tried to take. Teal didn't want to touch him and cause him more pain, but he did want to make sure he wasn't cold; Equi lost so much heat through their complex ears. Muscle cramps were even more painful when the muscles were cold. He wondered for a moment if taking him into the hot pool would help him, but that would involve touching him. Teal held his hand just above Ardenai's bare arm, then just beside his ear – no heat coming off him. Teal got a blanket from the warmer and, as gently as he could, added it to the one already over the Firstlord. "Hold on tight," he said, just above a whisper. "Hold on tight, Ardi. I'm right here."

Ardenai groaned, aware of the touch, but he didn't scream, which was of great comfort to Teal. Maybe this was leveling off … or maybe it had driven Ardenai out of his conscious mind. He wished again that he could speak to Konik, but Konik was in no shape to talk to anyone. Teal had looked in a few minutes ago and Konik was still on his knees, rocking Ah'davan's lifeless body in his arms. The thought of it made him want to weep. He knew it would make the Firstlord weep. Pythos had practically had to knock Ardenai out to get Ah'ree's body away from him.

Teal's gloomy thoughts were interrupted by the clumping of boots, and Cornwallis Mettenger was upon them. "Master Captain Teal," he said a little too loudly, and then looked at the spot where Teal had pointed with his chin. "Oh … good … God," he said quietly. "Why didn't someone tell me this had happened?" He plopped into a chair and sucked his teeth. "What did happen? He looks and sounds like he's dying, is he? What a fucking disaster that would be."

Teal told him what had happened, and Cornwallis just sat there shaking his balding head and staring at Ardenai. "You are one crazy son-of-a-bitch," he said admiringly. "Where's the little woman?"

"You mean his wife, the one who is Primuxori of Equus? That little woman?"

Mettenger was unfazed. "Yeah. Why isn't she here with him?"

"She's laying wave cannon platforms on the other side of the planet, or she was a while ago. Pythos says she checks in every fifteen minutes or so. When he starts to come out of it to where he knows anybody, she'll be here, don't worry."

"And yet you're here, and you're … did you know you're now the highest ranking military officer on Equus? Higher than Abeyan? I'll bet that pisses him off, egocentric bastard that he is. You're the only Master Captain. Did you know that?"

Teal smiled in spite of himself. Cornwallis could be such a piece of work. "You know, Wally, I did notice that sometime back. How long has it taken you?"

"Smart ass," Mettenger retorted. He sobered and leaned forward over his thighs to contemplate Teal. "I am assuming that this constitutes enough aggression to declare a campaign of interposition or incursion?"

Teal nodded. "I thought so. Trying to get the Thirteenth Dragonhorse butchered seems pretty aggressive to me, though not unexpected – which is why the little woman, who is quite probably our best strategist across disciplines, is out laying wave cannon platforms and checking out the surface of Lebonath Tras, and why I sent a formal declaration to the SGA an hour ago. You didn't hear it? Everybody else knows it was sent. Where have you been?" Teal didn't add, *eating, or copulating?* But he thought it.

"I've been out and about, so to speak. Did you inform the Lebonathi?"

"No. I only have to do that if I'm declaring war on them, and I'm not. I thought I'd surprise them with a little visit tomorrow, if the Dragonhorse is up for it."

Mettenger looked dubious. "Is he even going to be conscious by tomorrow? He doesn't look like he's going to be back on his feet for weeks. That was the chime for first dinner. Can I bring you something?"

Teal shook his head. "I'll find something later," he said, and Mettenger took his leave. A man had to have his priorities.

Half an hour or so later Pythos and Eridi arrived back in the room, carrying a slender container with several long, thin needles in it. "What if this makes him worse?' Eridi frowned. "I'm not sure he can stand to be in any more pain than he's already in."

"I am reassonably convincced that if it doess not make him better, it will not make him worsse. In any casse I would like to try it, as we may have more cassualties from thiss before we ssee the sstars of home again."

Eridi nodded and stepped aside, and Pythos picked up the first needle. He turned the Firstlord's hand palm up as carefully as he could, and with a quick motion he stuck the needle in the mark Eridu's ring had left, eliciting a hoarse cry of pain. "How long wass it from the time he firsst told uss he'd been drugged until he began to feel the effectss?"

Teal thought about it. "Five minutes, tops."

"Sso, thiss sshould sstart to work in five minutess – perhapss not to any great extent, but we should ssee a change, yess?"

"Yes," Teal nodded.

In a little more than two minutes Ardenai swallowed, and exhaled through his nose as his breathing deepened. Pythos took another needle and made a shallow stick between his eyes, right at the bridge of his nose. Another minute passed and he opened his eyes momentarily, then squeezed them shut, and rolled his head against the pillow. The bark in his throat subsided to a soft moan. When Teal covered Ardenai's hand with his own, it didn't seem to hurt as much. Pythos turned the back the blankets, split Ardenai's tunic up the front, and stuck him a third time at the base of his breast bone. The fourth needle went in his neck at the base of his earlobe, and they sat back and watched.

In a few minutes Ardenai managed to get his eyes open and his breath back at the same time, wincing with the effort. "Well, this is unpleasant," he muttered. "How … is Addie?"

"Sshe is gone," Pythos said, gently flicking him with his tongue. "Sshe died in Konik'ss armss as wass her wissh. In her dying thought, sshe thanked thee."

Ardenai's eyes filled with tears, but they did not spill, which surprised Teal. He was rather annoyed that Pythos had told Ardenai at all. He was limp, still panting for air, still trembling with the pain in every movement. He didn't need heartache as well.

"Is someone with him?"

"Ah'nis," Teal said, coming to stand beside him. "You should be thinking about you right now. I can see that you're cold. How badly do you still hurt?"

There was an exhausted but contemplative silence. "Let's just say that the next time a horse rolls on me I'll think I'm making love to my wife." Again he stopped to catch his breath, watching his left hand as he tried to straighten his fingers. After a few moments' effort he gave up and let his shoulders sag against the pillow. "Nik said this only lasts a couple of hours," he muttered.

"That is not what Nik said," came a rusty voice. He stood in the doorway, eyes swollen, face haggard. He had lost weight at the hands of his captors, and hair that had been a deep, striking silver was now snow white at the temples. He leaned against the wall in a manner which spoke more to exhaustion than nonchalance, and continued. "What I said was, you'll only feel like you're going to die, for about two hours. After that the panic subsides and it's just general agony for a few days"

Ardenai closed his eyes and took a shallow breath. "Pythos," he said, and it was nothing more than a breath. "Gave me something. I'm better."

"I can see that," Konik said. "Best hold still in any case."

By now Teal was beside him, offering a quick embrace and a strong arm. "Come. Sit. This has been a very difficult day for you, Senator. Can I get you something to drink?"

"Thank you," he said, accepting the chair Teal offered. "Water. And if there is any wine on board, especially yours, I could use some of that, as well."

"Let me take care of that," Eridi said. "I will bring refreshments, and then if you will permit, I will go and help Priestess Ah'nis with … whatever she is doing."

At a brief nod from Teal she was gone, Pythos with her, and Konik gave Ardenai a questioning look. "Lebonathi?"

"Um hm," Ardenai replied. "Princess Eridi, the Most Wise Lord Eridu's baby girl. He gave her to me as a fleshgift ..." he was still trying to catch his breath, and stopped with a grunt of annoyance. "... a lifetime or two ago, or so it seems. I'm sure your time with him was no less an eternity. Tell us, my friend, what happened?"

Konik stretched his legs and relaxed his arms in front of him, elbows on the padded armrests, and nodded gratefully as Teal handed him a drink. "Thank you." There was a pause as he sipped tentatively at the water. His eyes closed, and for a moment he looked frighteningly frail. "Their water is filthy," he said, almost in a whisper. "They drink this … foul brew called fermented water." His eyes opened. "I kind of figured that if nothing else got me, either starvation or thirst would. But … you found me. Thank you. You found me."

Teal ventured, "Has Pythos, or someone had a chance to look at you, Nik?"

The response was a silvering eyebrow. "That bad, hm? I'm sure he'll corner me sooner or later. Anyway, I had just figured out that the whole thing with the Telenir was … what's the word?"

"An allegory?" Ardenai offered.

"You figured it out too?"

"I did, with enough help," Ardenai said, squeezing his eyes shut and clamping his teeth down on the pain shooting up his back. "But tell us … your story."

"Stop trying to move," Konik advised. "I was coming in response to a summons I mistakenly thought was from you, when I was caught in a tractor beam between Anguine II and Equus. I tried to send a message, to no avail, and found myself on a Nargawerld ship bound for Lebonath Jas. I'm not sure what the bounty was, but there must have been one. The Lebonathis actually thought I was now the ruler, or at least the commander of the Telenir, which I allowed them to believe to keep myself alive. They were in the process of sending that girl for you. Apparently they'd done that for the Twelfth Dragonhorse as well.

"I told them that if they'd let me go I'd be their ally, bringing my vast resources to their aid. Of course that didn't work, so I convinced them that if they could lure you here for me to kill, I would align my world with theirs for the betterment of their planet. All I could hope for was that sooner or later you would put the puzzle together and realize where I was. I was dismayed when you showed up alone, until I … figured out why you did it …." He paused to collect himself and then looked back up at the Firstlord.

"Thank you. You took a terrible risk."

"She was worth every second of it," Ardenai replied. "Knowing her was an honor I will never forget."

Konik nodded. He caught a tear with his finger just as it spilled, and blinked until they receded before looking up again. "Sorry," he whispered. He looked like he might pass out, and Teal leaned a little closer, just in case.

Ardenai sighed. "I'm sure she was the one who got us out of there, although Brak said he was going to turn off the dome for two seconds."

"He did!" Teal said, still watching Konik. "That must be what happened. Just as the four of us with our heads together managed to find you again and penetrate that dome, it shut off, which is why it exploded. Kehailan had you out of there in less than a second. Amazing tactician, that one. So … Brak shut it off. I hope they don't figure that out before we can get to him."

"We will try to pick him up for interrogation tomorrow," Ardenai said, wincing with the effort to breath. "If they thought you were a powerful ruler, why did they starve you? You look like a wraith. And why did they do … this … to you, and more than once? Precious Equus, how did you live through it?"

"After a while they started to get impatient. They questioned my motives and my story, so they gave me about half a dose of that shit. When I told them the same story again they gave me a whole dose. When I told them the same story a third time they put me in a safe place, some stuffy hole in those ancient buildings somewhere, and brought me out from time to time to 'entertain' me with a banquet or one of their blood sports. They spent the rest of their time planning ridiculous assaults on the AEW and trying to lure you here. As to how I survived it," he sighed, staring into the empty glass, "love, honor and duty make powerful allies. Add hope, and the platform is pretty sturdy on its legs."

A young woman in a Dragonhorse uniform brought a small table and Eridi appeared with a tray holding a bottle of wine, two glasses, and two plates of food. "The kitchen says this should rest gently on a tender stomach," she said shyly, and set Konik's plate in front of him. She excused herself and left just as Pythos appeared with a second tray, which he placed on the bed stand beside Ardenai.

"Please, Nik, eat something," Teal said, uncorking the wine. "Don't stand on formality."

Konik looked at the food, then nodded and carefully, reverently, began to eat. How long had he been eating food that bled when he cut into it? Savage, stinking stuff. He sipped the wine, then took a longer drink. "Another excellent vintage. You really should give up the military and become a vintner."

"Thanks," Teal grinned, looking up from his own dinner. "I've thought about it, but I have to keep my impulsive friend over there out of trouble." He jerked his chin to where Pythos was sitting beside Ardenai, patiently trying to help him swallow some nourishment. "Actually, this is the last of the wine that Gidran put up before he and my mother went to Taraxia, so the compliment is his."

Part way through the meal, when Teal had poured him a second glass of wine, Konik eased himself back for a bit and said, "I'm assuming my seat in the senate has long since been filled and my mythical army has returned to the mists. My beautiful Ah'davan is gone. My daughters have homes and families of their own. I find myself a man without a job … except for thinning the rohanth bushes."

"You probably haven't … had a chance to look at this ship," Ardenai managed. Pythos had raised him up a little, and the pain of being moved was obvious on his face. "It's one of the thirteen Dragonhorse Tactical Cruisers they started building on Andal awhile back."

Konik whistled softly and looked around. "From what I've seen of her, she's a beauty. And she must have some cutting edge technology to have gotten us out of that part of the city like she did. Whose ship is this?"

"Kehailan's," Ardenai replied. "He designed … Pythos, please … flat …" he lay panting and Konik came to stand beside him.

"You have got to lie still. I laid on the floor of that hole they put me in for two days before I could even get my knees under me to crawl to my bed. If one of the guards hadn't taken mercy on me, I'd have died of thirst before I could actually walk again. Are you still having trouble with your kidneys from your jolly stay in the cleomitite mines?" Ardenai nodded slightly. "This will settle there and plague you forever, so don't overstress your back, I mean it. For me, it settled right where that arrow went through my breastbone. I still have trouble breathing from time to time, and my heart rhythm feels a little … off. Probably my imagination."

Kehailan presented himself at that moment, and nodded deeply to Konik. "Senator," he said, "I am so sorry about Ah'davan. She was brave, like my mother. My sire, who is looking much more like he's going to live, has asked me to take you on a tour of the ship, if you are up for it."

"I would like that very much," Konik said, setting aside his glass. "And then, if it is possible, I would like a real bath and fresh clothing, because I'm sure I desperately need them both."

"Let's get those things taken care of first," Kehailan said. "I will show you to your quarters and have someone take you to the bathing pools. A hot soak and a bit of a lie down will help you feel better, and anytime you are ready, I will take you on that tour."

They left together and Teal watched them with a bemused expression which did not escape the Firstlord. "What are you thinking?" he asked.

"That smiling, thoughtful young man who was just here … who did you say that was again?"

"Very funny. Where … is my wife?"

"I was just wondering that," Teal muttered. He got another blanket from the warmer and tucked it around Ardenai as he spoke. "Not that she ever goes looking for trouble, but I think I will check on her whereabouts. I'm sure she's fine. Please try to get some sleep, and I will be back."

▲ ▲ ▲ ▲ ▲ ▲ ▲

Io was not in trouble, but she did find herself in a puzzling place. "Are you positive we're on the right planet?" she asked.

Marion, who was looking around with his forehead furrowed and his mouth slightly ajar, just shrugged. "This be the place," he said.

"This is Lebonath Tras? You're sure?"

"Please don't ask me that again today," he said, "I've answered it at least a dozen times. This is, indeed, Lebonath Tras."

They were standing up to their waists in thick, sharp swamp grass with boggy ground underfoot and a few insects milling languidly about just over their heads. They had been hopping around this particular continent for hours, looking for life signs. They had seen the stone foundations of a small settlement beside a beautiful lake, those of a larger town abandoned near the shore of an inland sea, a third set of stone foundations along a rugged coastline. That was it – no people, and so far, bugs aside, no animals.

"Is this like Lebonath Jas, where everything is underground?"

"All of Belesprit's equipment says no." This from Bonfire Dannis, who was digging with one blue claw in the muck beneath their feet. "The soil here is black, but it's not polluted with anything – no petroleum deposits, no tar. With some drainage this would be good farmland, and this sawgrass is sweet tasting. Make good fodder." She spit out the piece she'd been chewing and reached for another sample.

"So where the hell is everybody?" Marion said, eyeing the insects. The whole top of his head was bald, had been since his twenties, and he wasn't keen on being devoured by sucking beasties. "We did our homework. The Lebonathi speak of their worlds, plural. When they talked about their population I assumed it was spread out over two planets and I thought they thought so too. We've been hopping around all afternoon and I can guarantee you, this continent is empty. From the looks of the air, they're all empty."

Io just shrugged. "Disease?"

Bonfire shook her head. "No sign of bodies, no indication that anything was burned, no mass burials. None of the signs of plague or pestilence."

"War?"

"Definitely not. We'd see it in the soil samples."

"Poisonous bugs? Carried off by insects?" Marion suggested, waving a hand over his head, and the women looked at him in disgust.

"Marion, Sweetie, go back to the ship if you're scared of the bugs," Bonfire said.

Io's transmitter pinged and she looked at it. "It's Teal," she said. "Greetings, what's up?"

Just her tone told him she didn't know what had happened to Ardenai. "Have you talked to your husband today?"

"This morning before he left. Pythos said he got back just fine with Nik and that they were locked up in some meeting." Her tone changed. "Why, is something wrong?"

Ah yes, that was why Pythos had been lying to her. If she thought someone had hurt her beloved Ardenai she'd lose her mind, and she was much more useful and a lot more charming sane. "No. Just didn't want to repeat a lot of information. Platforms in place?"

"Yes. I told Pythos that hours ago. We … as in Marion and Bonfire and I, took Belesprit to survey Lebonath Tras."

"Are they shooting at you?"

"No. We're on the surface and there's nobody here. The planet is verdant, and empty."

"What?"

"Don't ask me. Something has to be wrong with this place, but so far we can't figure out what it is. Please have Ardi get in touch when he's out of his meetings, will you? I'm starting to worry that he's overdoing. And make sure he eats something, will you? I will be back on Dragonhorse in a few hours, unless you need me sooner."

"We'll see you then," Teal said. "Do be careful. I just don't see how that planet can be uninhabited."

"I don't either, but I'm in good company. I'll check in again later."

"Everything all right?" Marion asked as they slogged back to the clipper.

"No," Io said, glancing at him out of the corner of one blue eye. Both she and Marion had those rarest of eyes, blue. That hadn't struck her before. "Something is wrong, but it's under control and they don't want me there. If I go barging in it will just make matters worse somehow. Let's head up to that ridgeline east of us. That is what I see in the distance, isn't it?

Marion squinted through, then under his glasses and saw nothing, but Bonfire's wolfish yellow eyes widened a little, focused, and she nodded. "Looks like a good vantage point," she agreed.

They set the clipper down on a flat spot just under the highest part of the ridge and climbed to the top to survey the country at their feet. The air was clean, and there was a bit of a cool breeze. A beautiful day. On one side they saw the grasslands they'd just covered, bogs shimmering here and there in the humid sunshine, and on the other side, more grass, with trees on the higher slopes, and more water.

"Why, oh why are they living underground in a ruined city in the middle of a desert when they have this next door?" Io mused, scooting herself onto a rock and squinting into the distance. "This makes absolutely no sense. Do they not own this, though they say they do? Are there fierce overlords who sweep down from time to time to make sure nobody is using this place? Is it booby-trapped and we just haven't stepped on one yet? Is everything poisonous? We know that's not true. What is it?"

Bonfire had been scratching around under the edges of rocks and uncovered a store of what looked like nuts. "Must be from those trees down there." She took one of the nuts and cracked it with her fangs, sniffed it, licked it, dug it out of its shell with one of her claws, and popped it in her mouth. "On the bitter side, but edible," she said with a wry face, "and whoever stored them here has to be big enough to carry them here. Some kind of rodent, I'm guessing. Probably the biggest life-form we've come across so far."

Marion pointed toward mountains blue in the distance. "Maybe there's a dragon."

"There is now," Io said. She stood up abruptly and waved the straw she'd been pulling apart. "This is a landrace form of Emmer, or Einkorn. I can't tell which without a lab. It is more nourishing than anything they have on Lebonath Jas, and at some point in time it was planted here, on this planet, not too far away, because I think our rodent friend carried its parent stock up here with the rest of his stash."

"And even though you're curious, you want to leave," Bonfire said quietly.

"I do. I'm sorry. I know it's early, but would it be all right if I dropped you two at your ships and got back? I'm worried that things didn't go well on the surface this morning. Teal's mouth was smiling, but his eyes were really worried. I think something happened to Ardi, or Nik, or both."

"We'll fly over the pole on our way to the ship and I'll take some readings," Bonfire said. "I'll analyze what we've picked up so far, and let you know what I find."

"And I will talk to Eridi," Io said. "Maybe there's a legend that goes with this place. I'll be anxious to get back here and explore some more."

Three hours later her little clipper was in the shunt bay next to Ardenai's big one, and she breathed a sigh of relief. At least he'd made it back – or Dominus had. Having listened to infrequent bits of chatter on the way she knew that Teal, not Ardenai had filed for permission to deploy interposing forces. That Konik had been rescued. That Ah'davan was dead. Any chatter about the Firstlord was conspicuous in its absence.

She hadn't gotten very far when Kehailan came to greet her, nodding respectfully and asking her as they walked how the placing of platforms had gone with Dragonhorse Ten, and the exploration of Lebonath Tras with Belesprit. She would have turned toward the quarters she shared with the Firstlord, but Kehailan took her arm and gently steered her down another corridor.

"Your husband was, as usual, thinking of others rather than himself today, and got himself injured," he said, dropping a hand on her shoulder.

Io felt herself go cold. "Badly?"

"It would have killed me, so … he'll be down a couple days," Kehailan replied with a short laugh. He explained what had happened so Io had a chance to prepare herself before she walked in, but she was still shocked. He was flat on his back and shivering with cold, barely able to breathe, face grey and lined with the pain that had been twisting him for hours.

He gave her a smile that was an effort. "Greetings, wife of mine," he said, working his eyes open, and she realized he'd been dozing. It had probably taken that snake, with whom she was shortly going to have unkind words, a good long time to get Ardenai to sleep in the first place, and now he was awake.

"Hi," she said, sitting beside him. "I understand you had a bit of a dust-up with the neighbor boy downstairs. Other than that, how was your day?"

It made him laugh, and that made him hurt. "Don't be mean to me," he said, trying to get his breath back. "We got Konik here in time to say goodbye to Ah'davan. That means … this has all been … worthwhile. Tell me about Lebonath Tras. Teal says it's empty?"

She told him what they'd found – down to wolf-woman cracking nuts with her teeth, and Marion and his bug phobia – and Ardenai listened, nodding a little from time to time, chuckling a time or two, and when she was through he said, "I will be most interested in seeing what you find on the other continents of Tras."

"I can tell by the tone of your voice that you have a theory as to what we'll find there."

"I do. And mind you it's just a theory. Do you remember the story of the Moons of Cordoba?"

She thought about it. "If I say no, you're going to tell me I was always fooling around in class instead of listening, and if I say yes, you'll ask me for details, and I won't have any. Which would you prefer?"

"I can tell you the legend of the Moons of Cordoba," said Konik's sensuous voice, and Io sprang from her chair and ran to embrace him.

"Nik, I am so glad you're safe!" she exclaimed, hugging him close. "I'm so glad you got here in time to say goodbye to Ah'davan. Did she get a chance to tell you that the rohanth bushes need thinning?"

"She did," he smiled, holding her at arms' length. "You look wonderful, Ah'riodin. Are you healed?"

"I am," she said, leading him to another chair close to the bed. "So, tell me the story of the Moons of Cordoba. Is this anything like the Wind Warriors?"

"Absolutely not," he chuckled, "thank goodness. As I remember the story, Cordoba was a planet very much like Lebonath Jas – hot, crowded – lots of poor people and a very few rich ones. Is this the right story, Ardenai

Teacher?"

"Sounds like it."

"Cordoba had two moons, both of them supposedly uninhabited, but in truth, one of them was verdant and beautiful, and the very richest people on Cordoba kept it as a secret. It was their place to get away and hunt wild game, because all the game on the planet's surface had been hunted to extinction, but on the moon, it was thriving. Correct?"

"Pretty close to perfect, young man." Ardenai closed his eyes and tried not to react to the pain ripping through the nerves and muscles in his lower back. Konik was right about this worsening the weakest part on a person. "I think you might find … something rather like that scenario. Lebonath Tras is much too close for the people of Lebonath Jas never to have been there. Their stories about the planet are too well woven for it to be an unknown. However … the next couple of days may be a little too busy for any exploration."

"I fell asleep for a time after my bath," Konik said, looking a little guilty. "Did the declaration get approval from the SGA?"

"Yes, and you do seem much improved. Which brings me back to the question I asked you a few hours back. Have you seen this ship?"

"I have now," Konik smiled. "What an incredible piece of machinery."

"Think you could fly one like her?"

Konik just stared at him. "What?"

"There are thirteen of these ships coming off the line," Ardenai managed. The pain in his back was getting worse, and it was making him gasp for air, which was embarrassing. He got his left hand to work and pinched himself hard across the bridge of the nose. The pain subsided a little. "There is one ship for each of the affined worlds. My wife, Master Captain Teal and I put your name on the one from Anguine II."

Konik managed to get his jaw hinges to work and sputtered, "I … haven't been a … I'm a test pilot, Dragonhorse. I was never the commander of a huge vessel like this. I … no. Thank you, but no. Who would trust me as a Captain after what I did? Who would follow me? No. Thank you. No."

"Take your time," Ardenai said, closing his eyes, "she's not built yet." His teeth came together hard and his head ground into the pillow. *Pythos, I'm sorry, I need your help.*

In moments the old physician was beside him, caressing him with his hands and his tongue and getting him to take a few sips of something which quieted him and put him back to sleep almost instantly. "He iss worn out," the doctor whispered. "He hass to ssleep." He rolled one draconic yellow eye in Konik's direction and drawled, "And ass for thee, Hatchling, thee iss dangeroussly dehydrated and near collapsse both mentally and physsically. Hass that not yet penetrated with thee?"

Konik hunched up a little and dropped his eyes, which made the old physician hiss with amusement.

"Pythos, I would speak with thee," Io said quietly, and made Ardenai's classic attitude adjustment gesture in the direction of the back of the sanecere bay.

Konik, sensing a row, excused himself to check on Ah'davan, and Pythos followed Io into the other room.

"Yess?"

She had made up her mind she wasn't going to yell and behave like a hothead. He would use that to explain why he hadn't called her, so she made sure of her words and her tone before she opened her mouth. "My husband was badly injured this morning, Pythos. Is there a reason you found it necessary to mislead me about that?"

"Yess," he hissed, "Of coursse there wass, Beautiful One, or I would not have done it. Thy expertisse in the field wass vital to the ssuccess of thiss campaign for which thy hussband hass ssacrificced sso much. Today he did what he doess besst. You did what you do besst. I have sseen thee with him when he iss deliriouss. Thee iss afraid, as thee sshould be as hiss wife, but thee fearss hiss losss too much. Today he wass worsse than deliriouss. Thee would have been helplesss, as were the resst of usss for ssome time, and it would have exhaussted thee, as it exhaussted him. Thy work would have ssuffered and thee could have done abssolutely nothing here."

"It's Calumet all over again, isn't it, Pythos?" she asked quietly. "I wonder how many more Calumets there will be in our life."

"Jusst enough to balancce the joy," the old physician said, chucking her under the chin with his tongue as he had when she was a baby. "Let uss find ssome ssupper and I shall give thee a nicce bath. Ah'niss will ssit with our Dragonhorsse."

By morning Ardenai was pounding the mattress with his fists and cursing under his breath, but his legs were useless, his back an agony of twisted muscles and raw nerves, and sitting up just halfway was all he could manage, even with all Pythos could do to relieve the pain. "Now, I'm really annoyed," he said through his teeth, and Teal laughed in spite of himself. "What?" Ardenai snapped.

"You look like you're ten," Teal responded, still laughing. "Remember when we found that big old vat way in the back of the stone barns at River keep and it was making that interesting hissing, kind of bubbling noise ..."

"Oh, yes – and YOU said, 'If we play around with this long enough it's bound to do something'..."

"So we did, and it exploded and blew us halfway across the barn, and you were lying there with your leg broken, pounding your fists on the ground, saying, and I quote, 'Now I'm really annoyed.'"

Teal was laughing hard by this time and Ardenai began to laugh as well. "And now look at us," he snorted, clutching at his sides, "Still playing around with things we really should probably have left alone, but, like that day, it's too late now. I wanted to get down there today and scare some people."

"Me too," Teal agreed, "Maybe this way we can come up with something even scarier." He pulled up a chair and sat close to the Firstlord. "Can I hand you your tea, Sir?"

"Thank you," Ardenai replied, still chuckling. "I give praise this morning that at least my hands are working and I can swallow. Can you imagine what it must have been like for Nik, lying there all alone hour after hour and day after day? The thought makes me shudder."

Teal was quiet for a moment, blowing on his drink. That had occurred to him, as well. How easy it was to make others suffer when one had no sense of suffering oneself. Perhaps, that would change soon.

"Where did you just go walking?"

"Nowhere," Teal smiled. "I was wondering if your strategy had changed since Lebonath Tras has put in an appearance."

"I think maybe so," Ardenai said, staring at the scenes of Equus going by in the huge frame on the wall. "It has occurred to me, even before yesterday, that if we are going to teach these people how to live with themselves, that we need to remove any means they have for leaving the planet."

"Shouldn't be hard," Teal shrugged. "Their fleet is miniscule and antiquated. They were counting completely on the Telenir, and from what Konik has said about being delivered by the Nargas, that may have been their only window to the outside world. If their ships are Nargawerld technology, or purchased from them, Mahruss and his classmates could build you one in a week."

"Have they figured out we're here?"

"You know, I don't think so. We're high, and our signals are cloaked. They were looking for your ship in the lower atmosphere, and when they couldn't find you, they went back to looking on the surface. None of their towers saw Dominus leave the atmosphere, so they're assuming that is the case."

"Primitive thinking," Ardenai muttered. His brain was working so well he decided he'd try again to bend one knee, and was immediately sorry. He groaned and lay panting. Teal rolled his eyes and reached for Ardenai's cup so he didn't add burns to his list of woes.

"So," Ardenai managed, once again grinding his teeth in frustration, "go snatch something. Let's figure out what they're using."

A short time later it was reported to Eridu that his personal craft had gone missing from its space buoy, and that those responsible for guarding it were being questioned at length. Had the Telenir or the Equi managed to steal the thing? Eridu was beginning to wonder. Just because they hadn't seen Ardenai's clipper leave the atmosphere, did that actually mean it hadn't left? He had been assuming the technology which had freed them from the dome had come from the ship, and that it was the ship to which they had returned, but what if they hadn't? What if the whole thing about going back to Amberia and picking up his crew had been a ruse?

True, there had been no crew aboard the thing, and Eridu had been thrilled at the thought of keeping it, but … if Ardenai had lied and he wasn't one lone ship, what else might be out there? Without the Telenir they were positioned very badly in this, and the Dragonhorse had apparently kidnapped the Telenir as he left. Seemed foolish. Konik was a big man – not as big as the Dragonhorse, but strong, and quick. Ardenai had been helpless. As the Equi had said, it wouldn't have been much of a fight. Two enemies alone on a ship? Maybe the ship had been programmed to pick up the Firstlord after so long, regardless. That made sense. Maybe taking the Telenir as well had been purely accidental. Yes, that's probably what had happened. Eridu felt momentarily better. But ... why hadn't Konik come back? Ardenai would still be curled up in a ball, unable to defend himself for another few days.

Eridu began to get an uneasy feeling in the pit of his stomach. "Naram," he said, waving a languid hand over one shoulder, "What sorts of readings are we getting beyond six hundred miles?"

"Up?"

"Yes, up. What did you think I meant?"

Naram chose not to answer that. "There is nothing beyond the usual meaningless waves and chatter, Most Wise One."

"Send two ships up there to take a look, and come and tell me what they see. Have they buried the Anchoress yet?"

"Yes, My Lord. They unwrapped her first, as you requested. She died as the Dragonhorse said she did, by her own potion, which was found in her mouth, on her hands and in her pocket."

"So he's at least telling us the truth on that matter," Eridu mused. "Get those ships in the air, or out of orbit, or wherever they are and find out if we have visitors."

Naram bowed his way out, and Eridu sank back into his chair, rubbing at the rings on his fingers and wondering if he should be planning a little jaunt somewhere, just in case.

CHAPTER 2

"Narga," Teal groaned, extricating himself from the grease of the ship's engines and twisting at the waist to ease his back. He caught the rag Kehailan tossed him and said, "I am too broad of shoulder and long of leg to be crawling around in there." He turned and looked at his nephew with a frown that was not quite serious. "You couldn't have grabbed something a little bigger than this? For instance, something with an engine compartment one could stand up in?"

"Apologies," Kehailan said, bowing to hide his twinkling eyes. "It is of Narga design, and they are twelve hands tall. It did not occur to me that you would go in yourself, Master Captain. I assumed you'd get that slim, slight senator who loves antiquated spacecraft to slide in there. And I do have several technicians even smaller than Konik."

"If you want something bigger, we have a couple just coming into range," said a disembodied voice – Equi Communications Officer Cutter, borrowed from the shunt bays at the Great House with the promise of quick return thereto. He would have been listening both to the shunt bay and the space chatter as was his job. "They'll be able to see us in about two minutes."

"Good," Teal said. "Captain Kehailan, just as they can see us, pull their crews off, and send a message from their location saying there's nothing up here."

"What about the ships?"

"Blow one of them up, whichever is the older. The newer one, I'd like to check out for speed and armaments. Who is your second in command?"

Kehailan gave him a bemused look. "You," he chuckled. "Maybe Cutter. Seriously, I don't have one right now. All these cruisers are running with skeleton crews, or close to it – command staff is the shortest of all."

Teal pursed his lips in thought. "Why don't you … think about training the alliterative Senator Konik as your second for now? See if he likes the ship. And in the meantime as you pull the Lebonathi crew off, put me on and I'll bring the ship to tractoring range."

"What do you want me to do with the crews?"

Teal thought a moment. "Do you have the coordinates for where Io and company were last on Lebonath Tras yesterday?"

"I can get them from Bonfire very quickly. Is that where you want them set down?"

"I think it's a good spot. No animal life signs to interfere with theirs. Chances are they'll be scared enough to stay bunched together and they won't be underfoot up here. I'll get ready to scramble over there." Kehailan nodded and Teal jogged away.

It didn't take Teal long to be sorry he'd volunteered. Half an hour later his laconic drawl came over the transmitter. "This is the SGA captured vessel Essence of Dead Gaknar requesting a tractor."

Teal heard Kehailan laughing before he could actually hear Kehailan's voice. "Acknowledged, Dead Gaknar. Would you like to come aboard, or should we just scramble you with some foaming rosemary into the nearest body of water?"

"Captain, I made the vile, vomitous mistake of assuming that because we breathe the same mixture of air they do, that this air would be breathable. It really isn't. The second you have this thing in tow, please get me off of here."

Kehailan was quick, and Teal was just as quick to the bathing pools. Twenty minutes later when he stepped into Ardenai's room the Firstlord was already chuckling under his breath. "I've been there. I understand," Ardenai said. "What did you find?"

"Straight Narga technology. I think they could well be the only outside contact the Lebonathis have had. As far as I can tell they've not tried to make any improvements or personalize their vessels in any way, which I find odd."

"Well, have some lunch, if your stomach is up for it, and after lunch I would like you to join Io and her crew on the surface of Lebonath Tras. I also want Kee to start picking crews off ships, sending them to the place you suggested for now, and blowing up the ships, big and small. I want every single thing out of the sky that can leave the atmosphere – civilian, military – everything. I'll talk to Hamar about confinement space."

Ardenai had a particularly cold gleam in his eye which surprised Teal, and then it dawned on him. Ardenai couldn't do anything but lie here, fighting pain, gasping for air, wondering what everybody else was doing. "You know," Teal said, "Instead of watching the pastoral countryside of Viridia go by in that frame, you could probably be helping Io with what she's doing, if we did a little fiddling around with the system."

Ardenai looked immediately brighter. "Could we?"

"I assume so. You designed the system, what can it do?"

"It can surely do that," Ardenai smiled. "Why didn't I think of it?"

Teal bit down on a chuckle. "No idea."

Ardenai flipped a hand. "Be gone with you. Have lunch and find Io. Oh, and take Dominus. I want Eridu to get the idea that I haven't gone anywhere. Make him wonder what I'm up to. Pick off a couple of ships yourself if you feel like it."

Teal nodded, then turned at the door. "Ardi, try to get some sleep. Things are going well. I'll get Kee to tune up your cosmoscope in here and wake you when you can watch us. You might even be able to talk to us."

"Thanks," the Firstlord muttered, blowing on his hands, and Teal added a blanket from the warmer before he left.

Unlike Lebonath Jas, Lebonath Tras appeared to be more water than land, but not by much. A nice distribution of the two, Teal thought. He had been admiring a hundred shades of green, blue and tan for an hour as he skimmed low over the planet. He'd made sure he flew low enough to let the crews of those two ships see him – made sure they saw the seven chevrons and running horse of the Firstlord of Equus. He was tempted to ask one of the SGA ships to scramble food and shelter, then remembered the Lebonathi suspicions about Equi food and called Kehailan to ask that, as the Lebonathi ships were being destroyed, some of their food supplies be transported with their crews. Not a necessity, but nice if possible. He'd also asked that not too many men be dropped in the same place. Spot them around a little, just in case.

He'd swooped over the abandoned villages, taking depth readings for any signs of subterranean habitation and had found nothing bigger than rodents. He picked up speed, hopped across a sea of adequate size, over an ice cap, and followed a long mountainous finger of connecting land bridge to another verdant continent.

As he was doing these things he was chatting with Ardenai from time to time, wishing he could see him so if he drifted off to sleep Teal could let him rest. They'd enjoyed some time together earlier, leaving Dragonhorse Thirteen in a series of dizzying barrel rolls to whiz close to the surface, picking off two small scout shuttles and dropping their crews, squawking with fear, back onto Dragonhorse to be added to the crews already on Lebonath Tras. A light cruiser had fallen to their guns, and then, his thirst for vengeance somewhat assuaged for the moment, Teal had dutifully headed for the surface.

Having reached the approximate coordinates, he pinged a signal off Io's little clipper and found her on a high, blunt nose of land which jutted out into a long, crystal clear lake. He hailed her and set down in the closest spot he could find large enough to support the fifty foot Dominus.

Io was again with Bonfire. Marion had been called back to his ship to start transferring Lebonathi crews and blowing Lebonathi ships out of the air. From the sound of his voice Teal could tell he was disappointed, and he wondered if, when this particular campaign was over, Marion would ask for his beautiful science ship back.

Teal walked in the women's direction, breathing in the warm smell of the water and the surrounding vegetation. The air was fresh, as good as any Equus had to offer, and Teal's abused sense of smell was particularly grateful. He stopped to admire a small plant sprawling in the rocks with hundreds of its fellows. "Evangeline's Carpet," he said aloud, "Or something very much like it." He pinched off a tendril, sniffed it, and realizing he had neither pockets nor a gathering bag, set it on a rock to retrieve on his way back to the clipper.

"Sent by the Dragonhorse to help you in any way I can," he said.

"Good," Io said, shading her eyes against the sun.

At this moment, in this light, Teal realized again how really lovely she had become as an adult. Wonderful smile, huge blue eyes, a bounty of ringlets the color of a fresh, ripe peach. The smattering of freckles on her arms made her look a bit like a flickernick, but …

"Why are you looking at me like that?"

"I'm just realizing that you are a beautiful woman, Ah'riodin. Ardenai is a lucky man."

Io looked at him for a long moment, still shading her eyes. There was not a hint of teasing, not a hint of lechery in the comment. It was simply an observation by a man she'd known and trusted all her life. "Thank you, Teal. He's lucky to have you, too," she said finally. "Do you really want to help us?"

"That's why I'm here." He sat on a rock and bent to study the little patch of earth they were working on. "Checking for insects?"

"Insects and microbes. Sampling the soil, and it's kraaling slow work," Io sighed. "We can't do more than ten square feet of this planet justice in a whole afternoon. Would you mind taking Dominus and skimming above and below the treetops? You can probably get an overview of the whole planet in a few hours. We could really use that information and Belesprit is too high to see much real-world, lower than the trees, three dimensional detail."

"I would be happy to do that," he nodded. "Dragonhorse, do you want to stay with your wife, or go with me?"

Io looked up and smiled. "Hi there, Handsome. I assume you can see us but we can't see you?"

"Correct," he said, the strain in his voice telling them he was working his muscles. "With all due respect to my gorgeous Primuxori, with whom I would gladly spend every waking moment ..."

"Stop being such a male," Io said, making a fending motion. "Go with Teal. And Ardi, stop moving around so much."

"How does she know these things?" Ardenai asked quietly.

"The same way I do." Teal chuckled. He excused himself, retrieved his sample of Evangeline's Carpet, and tipped the big clipper off the outcropping toward the valley below. "Still with me, Dragonhorse?"

"Um hm."

"Can you see what I'm looking at as we fly?"

"Um ... hm."

"Pythos give you one of those little pinsticks for pain just now?" There was no answer. Teal was making complete visual records as he went; there would be time later for the Firstlord to review it.

He got signals back when he pinged the water he was flying over. Some large, some small, some moving, some stationary. Apparently this body of water was alive, but with what? Were they plants, or animals? He flew east, skimmed lower and slowed down. These trees appeared to be in rows. Hoary with age and long untended, yes, but they had been planted. He marked the spot on his map and moved on.

Swinging Dominus in leisurely fashion from one side to the other, he wound his way up a river supported by many tributaries and forming a long lake with a convoluted shoreline. He followed it until it became a river again, and doubled back to explore. In a wide sweep of protected cove he found remnants of a stone wall – a foundation, or a fence of some kind? Some simple rectangles of hewn stone that were definitely foundations. Beautiful spot. He set down on the beach and walked up to take a look. The surfaces were smooth, flat, squared off. Well worked. Hundreds of years old? Thousands? Again he marked the spot for more patient eyes and struck off on foot, following what seemed to be part of a stone pathway that ended where a carefully walled-in spring still bubbled out of the hillside. No animal tracks – not large, not small. No birds. No sound but the wind. How could a planet that felt so alive be so quiet and lifeless?

He was most of the way back when his field boot slipped just enough on a loose stone to stagger him. He grabbed a woody shrub to stop his fall and continued walking. Within a minute the scratch on his wrist felt like it was on fire. He went down to the beach and stuck it in the water, grimacing with pain. He scrubbed it with sand, soaked it again and the burning subsided to a throb which was definitely uncomfortable.

"I wonder, are you part of the potion?" he said, eyeing the small blue scrape. He got a pair of gloves, some nippers and a specimen bag and found his way back to the offending shrub. He took a little more of a sampling than he really needed, and went back to the clipper.

He found two more sites where homes or barns had once stood, then turned east across rough country and over a high mountain hump to a desert which stretched away toward the horizon. Still nothing. Still no fauna. He kept pinging water. Where there was water there should be living things. This was a mature planet. Logically the animal life should have evolved along with the plants. Why had it not done that? Plants and trees abounded around the springs and rills, but no animals. He just shook his head.

The clipper was quiet, but it was obvious. It cast a huge shadow and it disturbed the air it passed through. It could in no way be a natural part of this planet. If they really wanted to see this place it would have to be on foot, which was slow, or on horseback. He tapped the transmission pad on the console.

"Master Captain, how may Equus serve you this day?"

"Officer Cutter. Thank you for agreeing to come with us. Please find out where the nearest horse transport is."

"You are welcome, and I already know the location of one, at least. They were scheduled to leave Equus a day after we did, on route to Calumet."

"Loaded?"

"Yes. Manifest said mostly brood mares to swap out for fresh blood, maybe some retiring geldings or polo stock. I don't remember all the details. They're pretty slow, so they should just now be passing within communications range. Would you like me to contact them?"

"Please. Ask them if they're hauling any good saddle stock, and whose plans will go awry if we turn them aside awhile."

"I'll find them. If they are hauling usable stock, do you want them to divert?"

"Yes. If at all possible. I need horses down here, and I'm going to need horsemen, so alert Tarpan and Abeyan. I will be speaking to them when I return to Dragonhorse."

"I will do that. Enjoy the rest of your flight."

Teal slowed way down and eased over the tallest mountain in a range of jagged peaks as tall as any on Equus. He turned slowly around the top of the mountain, looking down at the snow and scree. A few scrubby plants clung to the sides, and as he completed the loop he spotted a large cave, tall rather than wide, near the top, on a climbable slope. Again he marked the spot. He and Ardenai would come back here, maybe with Marion and Kehailan, or Gideon and Criollo, and see if they could wake whatever mythic denizen slumbered within.

Again he picked up speed and shot out over a large body of water, a sea from the size of the breakers, slowing as he reached the other side. Here, he found dense jungle climbing precipitous slopes to the hips of mountains taller than the ones he'd just left. It would be impossible to see anything without setting down. He slowed down further and looked again, half expecting to see a mighty stone city rising out of the trees, like the ones in picture books. He banked down a long, narrow valley and lifted to the plains beyond – a vast, verdant grassland. He felt like he had come up out of the canyon which had given Canyon keep its name, and discovered the plains of Viridia. Stunning. But empty.

He made a wide loop and headed back down along the shoreline to where the cliffs grew less steep and wide white beaches stretched for miles. He saw what might have been ruins, and set the clipper down in the gleaming sand. Being that he had been following the sun around the planet he still had plenty of daylight. He got out, taking a bottle of water and some pressed bars of dried fruit and nuts mixed with grains and honey. The thought of honey made him think of Ah'din, and for a long minute he ached for the gentle warmth of her head against his shoulder, the feel of her arms around his waist. They had been married for more than half their lives, and sometimes he missed her desperately. She would love this spot. She would take her shoes off and wade in that inviting, crystal water. He was content to swish his hand in it and touch one finger to his tongue before turning to walk toward the trees. "Briny" he said aloud. "But not overly so."

He walked a hundred feet or so from the clipper to a place where he could sit and look into the jungle as well as out into the breakers, took a long drink of water, and munched slowly on his afternoon snack. He realized with a snort of amusement that they couldn't offer him enough to wade out into that water. He didn't have a clue what was in it and he really didn't want to find out at this point. Maybe someday, though. By and large the ocean water on Equus was unpleasantly chilly and rough, except for the currents around Achernar. This water was warm enough to bathe a baby. He set his water bottle on the rock where he'd been sitting and walked further toward the jungle. There had been buildings here – larger than what he'd found so far, but not huge. The foundations were modest, and the scattered stones spoke to the lack of any real size.

Villages. Towns. Farms. No cities evident, and absolutely no life. So, what had stored the nuts Bonfire had found? There were nutrients in the soil. Marion had spoken of bugs the size of shuntcraft, though Marion had a thing for flying insects. Speaking of which, since he'd left the bogs there weren't any of those, either. Maybe everything else was nocturnal. Maybe … everything was nocturnal! He trotted back for his water bottle, fired up the clipper and made a loop back in the direction he'd come.

Being pretty well assured there was nothing to collide with he brought the clipper up to two and a half transonics, and in less than an hour he was back where he'd first entered the atmosphere. He slowed down and skimmed low over the area where they'd been dropping crews. A couple dozen fires spaced a hundred feet or so apart dotted open places on the forest floor, and Teal hoped these people had enough outdoor experience not to let them get away into the trees. He wondered if they'd gotten any supper. He thought again about the fires, and asked for a couple of shuntcraft to hover over the campsites, just in case.

Again he made a loop and started hopping back toward the forested cove, staying behind the sunset, just ahead of the dark, when animals tended to be the most active. He set the clipper down, shut it off, got out and listened. He walked a distance away toward the old stone foundations and just stood with his eyes closed, waiting, opening those amazingly complex Equi ears, with their delicate flutes like the shell of a chambered nautilus, letting them relax and flare back to catch the most tenuous of sounds. Insects. Something scurrying on miniscule feet, the soft chirp of a bird … no … a bat …something with silken nearly silent wings passing overhead. Something rustling leaves in the shrubs along the old stone walkway. Tiny things. All tiny things. Nothing that would leave any carbon footprint at all. Not anymore.

He plopped in the sand where the beach met the old stone path, pulled his knees up to rest his elbows and sat, thumbs on his cheekbones, rubbing his forehead with the tips of his fingers. This planet had been abandoned. Everything. Every man, every woman, every child, every animal big enough to catch and carry, every building, had been removed. Long ago. Long before … what? If they dug deep enough, looked hard enough, would there be roads? Signs of internal combustion? Right now, this was a planet completely at peace. A planet in complete recovery. Teal stood up, raised his hands out over the sea, and in his beautiful, clear tenor he sang the planet a song of cleansing and protection. Then, realizing he was tired and hungry and had no idea how long he'd been gone, he fired up the clipper and headed into the upper atmosphere, keeping an eye out for any remaining Lebonathi ships.

▲ ▲ ▲ ▲ ▲ ▲ ▲

The Most Wise Lord Eridu was in shock. The ships they had sent up early in the day had said nothing was there, and yet they hadn't returned.

The next two ships had reported space debris, and then they had vanished. Four heavily armed contention vessels in formation had left their buoys and proceeded to the area in question, and disappeared. Then nobody else wanted to go up. Small ships were vanishing. Bits of big ships had been spotted drifting around aimlessly in space. Over the course of the day his entire military fleet had apparently vanished into oblivion. Every single ship that could get them off the planet was systematically being destroyed or stolen, or … something. They had tried to get word to the Nargas and had received no reply, lousy allies that they'd turned out to be.

Still Konik had not returned, though the Lebonathi tracking stations insisted that the big clipper had been seen heading for Lebonath Tras. Why would anyone risk damnation to go near that smoldering, Gods-forsaken rock? It made no sense. Ardenai was definitely out of the picture – Eridu had seen to that – so it couldn't have been him in the clipper. Maybe that fool Konik had gone there, trying to escape the wrath of the mighty Eridu, and the witches had burned him alive. It would serve him right.

Several members of the High Council were already bundling up their wives and children and heading out of the city, claiming that the Dragonhorse was going to return and kill every man, woman and child because of what Eridu had done to him. Why, then, had they been in the stands cheering with everyone else while the Telenir grappled with him?

Eridu, when he examined himself closely, knew the answer to that. He wouldn't have listened to them if they'd told him to behave otherwise, and they knew they'd better be in the stands for an event such as this one. He was powerful, and it made him smile, even as he worried. Power always felt good. Power always found a way.

As darkness fell he went out and watched streams of people boarding trains, busses, any conveyance they could find to get out of the city. Naram, who stood beside him, said people who had any, were offering outrageous sums of money for the right to travel. Stores were being raided for water and supplies. Several riots had already broken out as even the people who could afford food realized there wasn't going to be enough, whether they could pay for it or not. Classes were beginning to break down, and it was terrifying.

"Bring me every single member of the delegation who went to Equus, and meet me in my private conference room in an hour," he said, and Naram nodded, stepping back as he did so, knowing Eridu wasn't going to want to hear what he had to say next.

"I will do what I can," he said. "I can find the Secretary General, of course. Halaf would never stray far from your side. And the Standard Bearer, Brak. I know where three or four of the women live, and a half-dozen of the Royal Guard. The others, I cannot get to and probably couldn't find anyway. My guess is, they're among the caronai bawling to get out of the city, or buried too deeply within to even know what's going on."

"Foolish of them," Eridu said quietly. "Find who you can and bring them to me, and plan to stay with them." He thought a minute. "Isn't Brak the one who said he was trying to add power to the dome when it exploded?"

Naram nodded. "We think it was hit with a weapon of some kind."

"Isn't Brak the one who threw the Dragonhorse in with the Telenir?"

Again Naram nodded. "It was. Why do you ask?"

"Just speculating," Eridu mused. He got word to his wives to make sure their food supplies were properly secured and that they had a way out of the city to one of their more secluded estates, and then sent for dinner. There was no point having an unpleasant discussion on an almost empty stomach.

Within the hour, but barely, Halaf and Brak had presented themselves. Hassuna had arrived with her husband and Akadia with hers – both women showed signs of a recent and severe beating – possibly because they'd allowed themselves to be used as whores while away from their husbands. The others straggled in, looking fearful and confused.

"Tell me everything you know about the Equi," Eridu said, "Leave nothing out."

It was the beginning of a long two hours of useless conversation. The Dragonhorse was a pompous ass. No, he wasn't. Yes he was. The Dragonhorse loved children. The Dragonhorse ate children. The Dragonhorse could kill you with his eyes. The Dragonhorse had a beautiful singing voice. The Dragonhorse did not yell or throw things when he was angry. Yes, he did. No, he didn't. The Dragonhorse carried his own dishes to be washed. The Dragonhorse had brainwashed Girsu into defecting. He ate no meat. But he ate children? No, he didn't, yes he did. He frequently spent time with their anchoresses. He had two sons and one wife, who also had a son. He had killed Prince Addur for raping some Equi girl who he claimed was still a child. He had turned Princess Eridi over to the Eloi without having even tasted her fruit, claiming she was a child. He played a very rough game called polo, or pulu, and rode a horse very well. He had given them the freedom of the city and had fed them strangely, but fully. Not true. He had cast them out of comfortable quarters and made them eat dirt. No he hadn't. Yes, he had. He sat at table with everyone alike sharing in the food, which was simple but good. They ate common slop from a common table, none of it worth eating. Not true. True. No one in Thura had any money. He was exceptionally big and frighteningly strong. No argument. He spoke quietly and laughed frequently. His people seemed genuinely to love him and he them. His people were terrified of him. He had killed Prince Addur, but it had not pleased him to do so. He had come that night to tell the Secretary General he regretted the man's loss. So, he was weak, afraid of what he'd done? Yes, probably. Probably not. Oh, and he had spoken once or twice in unguarded moments about finding Konik. He needed to find Konik.

"Needed to find him as in wanting to kill him when he did find him?"

"Just … needed to find him."

"And no one has any money? So they are poor."

"Not at all. They are so rich people in all walks of life just take what they need."

At that point, Eridu began to realize they were lost. He had made an enemy where he should have made a friend. He had allowed pettiness to interpret simplicity as primitiveness. His lands, his titles, his wealth, were about to go into the common coffers of the Equi people. This ridiculous line of thinking plagued him for an hour or so before he began to wonder if he could somehow bluff or bluster his way out of this. But … why should he have to do that? Was he not the Most Wise Lord Eridu? Who would dare to cross the man upon whom the Gods had shed their glory? He smiled and sat back in his chair.

Maybe all of this notion about ships disappearing into the void was a big mistake. Maybe they had lost the ability to transmit and they would appear in the morning. Maybe Legate Konik had not reappeared because he'd killed the Dragonhorse, taken his ship and gone to the Telenir homeworld to fetch his forces. Maybe the Equi were already running for home with the Telenir right behind them. The Dragonhorse had been given drugs that would probably kill him anyway. In any case none of this could be solved tonight, and it wasn't his job to solve things. That, was Naram's job. Naram would figure this out, or pay the price. He sent for a lovely young girl he'd recently met at the home of one of the council members, and asked if she would like to have a late supper.

He was still fondling her the next morning when the earth began to shake.

▲ ▲ ▲ ▲ ▲ ▲ ▲

Teal watched Pythos as he fastened the wide belt around Ardenai's waist, then two around his chest and cinched them down hard, pulling the apparatus tight against the Firstlord's back from kidneys to shoulders. "How doess it feel?"

"Cold," Ardenai gasped, sucking in his breath and running his hands over the smooth surface.

"It iss ssupossed to be cold," the serpent said patiently. "The cold helpss keep thee from feeling where the Jacerei are ssticking into thy miss-erable, sstubborn backsside, my preciouss hatchling."

"I love you, too," he chuckled. "Will they stay in place if I walk or move around much?"

"That, iss a very good quesstion," Pythos said. "Ssome are in one inch, ssome are in half an inch. If they do come loosse, thee will know it in a big hurry, O' Wisse One. Thee will find thysself ssqualling on the paverss."

"I'll catch him," Teal said, but he was worried. Ardenai was on his feet this early morning, boots and britches on and blood in his eye, and now a uniform tunic going on over the only thing keeping him from collapsing in a shrieking puddle on the floor. All of them had tried to talk him out of this, to no avail. The planet below was going into panic mode, and Ardenai wanted to head it off. It was easier to catch wild horses on the plains than in the hills, and he wanted Eridu and the High Council corralled before they had a chance to scatter.

"I think this time we'll take a little bigger presence," he had said, and now Dragonhorses were preparing to enter the atmosphere – the whole herd of them – four preparing to go off in different directions and slowly skim over the cities, just above the rooftops. At eight hundred feet in length they were sleek and relatively small as Equi military vessels went. Still, they were over twenty storeys tall with a main beam two hundred feet across. They expanded to seven hundred and fifty feet with their wings in firing position. The ground was going to shake like grains of wheat jumped on a tabletop when an angry man pounded his fist, and that's what this was – an angry man, pounding his fist. The last ship, Dragonhorse Thirteen, would fit nicely, but snugly in the main square of the city with her wings partially extended.

"Wake 'em up," Ardenai growled, looking at the main viewer, and the Astricting Pulse Cannons began to fire on their platforms – not hard, not fast – just a low, undulating thunder that brought Eridu up out of bed and sent the people of the city screaming out of their underground chambers and into the streets, where they looked up at the bellies of five enormous white ships, each bearing the seven stacked chevrons and the running horse of Equus. Four of the ships peeled off in leisurely fashion and the fifth settled slowly toward the spot where Ardenai's clipper had landed two days before.

Eridu was still in his robe and slippers, his Nuntius d'affaires clothed, but barely as they raced to the surface, fearing the imminent collapse of the buildings around them. Several remaining members of the High Council and their families reached the steps from the government apartments just as Naram and Eridu did, and … stopped. Terrified beyond speech they clung to each other and watched as an enormous ship as tall as most of the buildings, filled the square.

A disembodied male voice which penetrated every crack and crevice in the city said, "By request of the Government of Equus and its Affined

Worlds, by permission of the Seventh Galactic Alliance and consent of the United Galactic Alliance, by order of Ah'krill Ardenai Morning Star, the Arms of Eladeus, Firstlord of Equus, the Thirteenth Dragonhorse, you have come under the rule of Interposing Forces. You are now citizens of Equus, and subject to her laws."

Eridu spun around and would have run, but there were three men standing there, shoulder to shoulder, wearing royal purple dragonhorse uniforms. Two of the men, he knew. The one on the left, was Konik, who gave him a wicked smile. The one in the middle was a stranger, no less terrifying in size and demeanor than the Dragonhorse himself. The one on the right, was Ardenai.

"Going somewhere?" the Firstlord asked, and Eridu stepped back.

Could this be Ardenai? "Are you real?" he asked warily.

"Very," Ardenai said. He stepped forward, poked Eridu once in the chest with his forefinger, brought it up to draw it slowly under his fat chin, and stepped back. "Not what you were expecting?" he hissed.

"And why are you here?" Eridu asked, deciding bluster was as good a plan as any for the moment. The graphically symbolic knife slash had pretty well wiped his mind of anything useful.

"You sought an alliance with the Telenir, remember? You were duped first by a man who thought himself Telenir, and now, at last, you are being taken over by the real Telenir. It is an ancient word and it means, simply, telepaths. You wanted to be allied with the Telenir," Ardenai said quietly, though his voice carried to the city," I give you the Telenir."

There came the rolling thunder of Equi ceremonial drums, and from the ship, walking thirteen abreast an arm-span apart, dressed trimly but modestly in silver-green and white, each with a silver python on the right arm of her tunic, came row, after row, after row of women.

CHAPTER 3

The Eloi," Ardenai breathed, and even he was awestruck. "The Telenir of legend. They who used their intellect to wrest power from the Ninth Dragonhorse, and saved us from our own Time of Calamity... and got their own song, which puzzled me many a long day before I kind of figured it out …" he chuckled, "… and then my High Priestess mother actually explained it to me. Telenir is not just a word that means telepaths. It is a verb, not a noun, and it is feminine."

When they had stopped, Ardenai turned from watching them, to watching Eridu. "There are one hundred and sixty-nine priestesses there, all highly trained and highly educated. They will help you govern, redistribute your wealth to better advantage, control your population, increase your food supply, educate your people, your daughters and sons properly, clean your air, and whatever else needs to be done to make you a happy and productive Equi world. They will not be working alone."

Again he gestured, and again there was a salvo of Equi drums. This time it was men who exited the ship thirteen abreast, wearing the purple uniform of the Thirteenth Dragonhorse. They, too, had a silver python on their right sleeve. Each man stepped up beside a woman until there were thirteen rows of twenty-six.

"These are only symbolic numbers, of course," Ardenai said. "There are many more, but you get the idea."

"You have no right to invade us," Halaf grated. "We have done nothing to you … to your world."

"We are taking over governance of your world, not because of what you have done to us," Ardenai said patiently, "but because of what you have done to your own people. Your air is unbreathable, your path unsustainable, your politics unconscionable, your religion unspeakable. Your people are hungry, though obviously you are not. Your girls are uneducated, though obviously you are not. Your wealth goes to the few, power to fewer yet. The whole SGA wants you reined in – now – before you kill yourselves off or spread your poison into the Alliance. We are here to do that."

"My Gods!" Eridu exclaimed, momentarily forgetting his sneer. "Have you looked at the Nargas? Have you?" He almost took a step forward, but Ardenai's eyes moved him back.

"Eridu, I know this is hard to understand," he said, real sympathy in his voice, "but the Nargas, though they eat some dreadful things, have enough to eat. Everybody gets fed on Nargawerld. Few of them have much education, but all of them have equal access. The women are every bit as savage as the men, and as many are captains, instructors, scientists and world leaders as their male counterparts. The children are trained and cared for equally, though perhaps not in a way we would do it ourselves. They have no religion, so they do not use it as a tool of oppression. They raise what they eat, and they have solid trading partners. You, have almost none of those things. You, were on the brink of planetary disaster. Now you are not quite so close. Now, you are a tribute world of Equus, and you can repair yourselves in safety and peace, and we are going to help you do that. When you have fully recovered, you may choose to become an affined Equi world, or you may choose membership in the SGA."

"And what if we choose neither. What if we choose not to accept your rule?" Naram sneered. "What then, Dragonhorse?"

Ardenai's shoulders twitched. "We will persuade you, and you will not like it." He made a short, sharp bark of laughter, and winced just a little as one of the jacerei bit into the side of his spine. It was nothing more than a slight tightening around the eyes, a quick catch of the breath, but a movement which did not escape Eridu. So, he was in pain. Did that make him more dangerous, or less?

"I want you to realize that nearly everyone on your planet can hear me at this point. We have absolutely no desire to harm you, but we are going to control you, and change you, and try not to destroy your culture in that process. Exactly how much gets destroyed, will largely be up to you, of course, because, much as we do not want to, we can destroy your entire civilization without ever harming a hair on your heads." He looked slightly agitated and shifted his weight from one leg to the other. The man in the middle stepped ever so slightly back and over, the Firstlord's shoulder came ever so slightly to rest against him. Again, not a movement lost on Eridu who was trying to figure out how to use this weakness.

Naram, reading his features, made a slight movement of his head and beckoned Eridu to one side. "Please do not think I am being disrespectful," he whispered, making a subtle, mollifying gesture. "But you have done grievous injury to two of those men, which has angered the third – the Master Captain – who loves the Firstlord like a brother, and who will kill all of us without a moment's compunction. Believe me, I have seen that look."

Eridu raised a disbelieving eyebrow and Naram shook his head in warning, glancing over at the trio of Equi observing them. "Most Wise Lord, I have read their books on war and conquest, and I have come to believe this is not idle boasting. The Equi are telepaths, powerful ones, and they can, and have, used it as a weapon. If their history books are true, they can get inside our heads and make us think anything they want us to, about who we are, what we are, where we have been. They can wipe our minds of one memory, every memory we have ever had, or every sense that we were ever a society. They may well be able to kill all of us in a split second and not harm a single inch of this planet. Do we really want to take that chance?"

Eridu flipped a hand in dismissal and said loudly, "These things are not possible. We are the chosen of the Gods. The Gods would not allow such a thing to happen to us. Your fear embarrasses me, Nuntius. They let you read those books so you would think they have powers they do not, and technology they do not. Can you not see that they are making idle threats?"

He turned back to the others with his snout in the air and Naram resumed his place, his features momentarily registering both disgust and disbelief before falling back into their usual, stoic lines.

The Master Captain put a hand on Ardenai's shoulder and fixed Eridu in his gaze. "You think we're bluffing, don't you. That's too bad. Would you like a more … intense demonstration of the technology which shook you this morning? Or perhaps a personal sampling of what Naram just warned you about? He's right, you know, and you really should listen to him."

"No, thank you," Eridu said. It occurred to him that he was standing here in his robe and slippers in front of thousands of his subjects, squinting until his eyes watered, being humiliated by these savages, with their sharp profiles and their dirty looking skin. It made him feel foolish, and that made him angry. "We know you are Godless," he blustered, playing to the crowd, "you killed our Anchoress, will you kill our precious faith as well? Destroy the flamen who personify the Gods?"

Ardenai shook his head slightly and smiled. "Your Anchoress killed herself," he said. "There is a difference between legislating morality and enforcing civility. A difference between bonds and bondage, religion and faith. A lesson which you are about to learn." He paused, Eridu saw him catch his breath, then recover as Teal's hand closed on his forearm. "We have much to discuss, Most Wise Lord Eridu, and it grows warm out here. In three hours please have ten of your most trusted advisors from across your government meet us in the ship. You, I will expect an hour from now. Again, we have no intention of harming you. You will be our guests, but I do insist that … you come. Do I make myself clear?"

Eridu glanced at Naram, then the face of the Master Captain, and nodded grudgingly. "We will be there," he said. "I will be there."

"We will leave escorts with you to see that you do," Ardenai said. He turned slightly, addressing the council members and the throng behind them. "We are here to invest in you, not destroy you. This evening we will begin to gather people for meetings according to what they do, how much money they have, their education and so on. For now, please go on about your daily business. No one will be harmed unless he brings harm to another. You are now Equi citizens. We are going to help you feed yourselves so that each and every one of you can go to school and get an education, regardless of your age. All of this will be made clearer shortly, but … for now prepare ... yourself for these changes. Master Captain Teal, Senator Konik, I will leave this in your capable hands and return to the ship to prepare for our meeting." The next instant, he was gone.

The man in the middle stepped toward Eridu and extended his hand. "We have not been properly introduced, I am Teal, Master Captain."

Eridu hesitated, knowing this was not a usual Equi greeting, but he dared not refuse the handshake. He accepted the firm grasp, and Teal continued, "The Dragonhorse is a good and kind man, and your people will thrive under his rule. I, on the other hand, am a vengeful bastard, and what you did to my friend and kinsman, was worthy of like payment." He laughed, and gestured in the general direction of Eridu's quarters. "Best get you dressed before your meeting," he said, slapping Eridu on the shoulder just where it met his fat little neck, and Eridu felt the needle go in.

Eridu's eyes grew huge and he clapped his hand over the puncture with a yelp of dismay. "How can I go to a meeting if I am writhing on the floor? Dear Gods, I am not a big man, what if you gave me too much? How did you …?

"Oh, that part was easy," Teal said modestly, "though I probably should have thought to weigh you. Perhaps I would have if you had weighed the Dragonhorse before you stuck him. Anyway, better keep walking. Senator Konik, do come along in case we have to carry this fellow. My wife is a doctor. So am I, actually, though my specialty is horses. They weigh a lot more than people, and I'm used to dosing them. Anyway, while I was out and about yesterday I happened across the plants that go into your magic elixir, and because I've watched my wife so much, making up the ingredients was simple. Of course I'm not sure I got them in exactly the right proportions, but you should be able to tell me that pretty quickly."

Eridu set up a high pitched whine as the sharpened twig Teal had stuck him with began to take effect. "Oh Gods, no! I cannot go through that! I am not a warrior! Please, give me the antidote. I will do anything you want, give you anything you want, just give me the antidote!"

"What antidote?" Teal scoffed. "I barely had time to make up the part where you nearly die. I certainly didn't have time to concoct any antidote. Senator Konik came out of it just fine after a few days, and the Dragonhorse is feeling much better. I'm sure you will too."

"The Dragonhorse, is barely able to stand, and in terrible pain, I could see it in his face! The Telenir survived by a hairsbreadth, and now I wish he hadn't. Oh, Ow!! Curse him! Curse you! The pain in my head is growing unbearable!"

"Well, do you have an antidote for the concoction you gave them? Maybe it will work on this potion as well. Of course you may not have time to find it."

"The Anchoress of the Ancient City. She has the antidote!"

"We'd better hurry and get there, hadn't we?" Teal said, and he and Konik trotted along behind Eridu, who was scurrying down the dim, foul smelling corridors, no longer aware of his slippers and night clothes, groaning with pain and staggering from time to time as he clutched at his neck.

Is he going to collapse on us? Konik asked, *because I do not want to touch that maggot, much less carry him.*

Teal shook his head. *If he does collapse it will be from his own fear and not what I gave him.*

Teal proffered the twig and made a motion for Konik to stick himself with it. He did, and in another minute he looked at his finger and mouthed, *Ow! That hurts!*

Does, doesn't it? But it wears off in half an hour or so, and it doesn't travel very far. I stumbled into it yesterday, and I mean that quite literally. I scratched my arm on the thing, which is how I came to my current level of expertise.

You really are a bastard, Master Captain. I'm impressed.

They turned in at the doorway of a dimly lit shop which smelled of herbs and some other unfamiliar and unpleasant things. There were items that looked like parts of plants and animals, hanging from pegs on the walls and Teal and Konik gave each other an uneasy glance.

If they offer us a snack, don't take it, Konik advised soberly.

"I need the antidote for your damned torture concoction!" Eridu bellowed as he came in the door. He leaned panting against the counter, patting himself over the heart, and a priestess who looked much like Samarra came nodding out of the back. She was younger, but equally bald, clad in black, and sober faced. "Now!" he screeched, and she scurried away.

In a short time she was back, extending a tiny jar. "How much should I give him, in case he is in too much pain to administer it to himself?" Teal asked, politely intercepting the jar, and the woman appeared to see him for the first time.

"One of these for every hundred pounds," she said, handing him a small spoon to go with the jar. "A little more will not hurt, too little will do no good."

Teal had a thought enter his by now suspicious mind and added, "I intend to give some of this to my kinsman, The Dragonhorse, who ..."

In a flash the little jar was out of his hands and back in hers. "I'm glad you said something," she murmured. "You will need a blending slightly different from this."

Another uneasy space passed while they studied the … things … on hooks and shelves, and listened to Eridu moan and curse her, and she was back with an equally tiny jar. "This will work for Our Most Wise Lord, and be safe for your kinsman as well," she said, casually bypassing Eridu to hand the jar to Teal. "A spoonful for every hundred pounds."

"Thank you, Priestess," Teal nodded, and to his surprise she nodded back with a slight smile.

"You are welcome, Master Captain Teal. Welcome to Lebonath Jas." His eyes widened and she chuckled. "This morning's edict would have been hard to miss," she said, turned, and disappeared into the sweltering darkness.

"Well, give me some!" Eridu demanded.

"Let's get back up where it's lighter first," Teal said, and strode away, with Eridu panting along behind begging for the antidote.

When they reached daylight Teal spun around and fixed Eridu with a malevolent gaze. "If you ever dare lift a finger against the Dragonhorse, his family, or any Equi, including those millions who now reside on this planet, I will make sure that you get exactly what Ardenai got, and that you get enough to kill you, but slowly. Do I make myself clear, Most Wise Lord?"

"You do," Eridu gasped. "You do, Master Captain. The antidote."

Teal looked at Konik. "You stuck your finger with that just as hard as I stuck his neck. Does your finger still hurt?"

Konik shrugged. "It throbs a little." He showed the twig to Eridu. "This, is what he stuck you with, Eridu. Your head aches because you're not used to the exercise and your heart is pounding. You don't need that antidote any more than I do."

"Hold out your finger," Teal said. Eridu just looked at him, terrified and angry. "Hold out your finger and I'll give you some of this. Or not. Your choice."

Eridu stuck out his index finger and Teal unscrewed the jar lid, put a heaping spoonful on Eridu's finger, and put the lid back on the jar. Eridu quickly stuck the finger in his mouth, and nodded to Teal, murder in his small, pink eyes.

"Go get dressed, Oh Most Wise Lord Eridu, and decide which ten people you want to attend this first meeting," Teal said. "You have five minutes left before the Dragonhorse expects you. I will give you back that lost time, and we will see you in an hour." Eridu disappeared into the depths of the building, yelling for his Nuntius d' affaires, and Teal took off down the steps at a dogtrot with Konik beside him.

They found Ardenai where Kehailan had assisted him, back on the bed in the sanecere bay. His tunic was off, along with the apparatus he'd been wearing earlier. There was a pillow under his knees and he was sitting partway up, eyes closed, breathing even but shallow, only the slight, involuntary groan in his breath saying he was miserable.

"I know it's early for Celebration of Storms," Teal said, "but I have a little present for you, Brother Mine." Ardenai opened his eyes and Teal held up the jar. "I got this from one of the priestesses in the bowels of that building yonder. She says it's the antidote for what Eridu gave you. Do you want to try it?"

"Oh sure," Ardenai muttered. "It just might work."

"It might," Teal agreed. "How much do you weigh this morning?"

Ardenai thought a moment. "I've lost weight," he said, as though it would surprise anyone. "I'm just under two hundred and twenty pounds."

"So … one of these little spoons for every one hundred pounds ..." Teal said, holding the jar up to the light.

"A little too much is better than not enough," Konik added.

"So … how can we figure a fifth of this tiny thing?" Teal asked, examining the spoon.

"How about two and a quarter?" Konik said.

"How about thee letss me meassure it?" Pythos hissed, hurrying out of the pharma. "Medicationss sshould be kept away from children," he said under his breath. He took the jar and the spoon and toddled back the way he had come. He was gone awhile and when he came back he had an earthenware tumbler in his hand. "Drink thiss," he said, and Ardenai shuddered.

"When you say that, my friend, it bodes no good for me." But he took the tumbler and downed the contents. "Eww."

"Nasty?" Teal asked.

"For the lack of a better word, it's … fleshy," he grimaced, swallowing again in an attempt to keep it down.

Teal decided to spare him his observations in the Anchoresses' pharma. "Doing anything?"

"Not yet," Ardenai sighed. "Maybe it's just ..." His back arched and he caught his breath, coming down with a sharp cry that was half pain, half surprise. His eyes got very wide and he managed between panting breaths to gasp, "Precious Equus, what a jolt!"

"Hold on tight," Teal said, taking his hand, and Ardenai grasped it in a bone crushing grip. "Pythos, have we made a terrible mistake here?"

"I tessted the concoction. It is not poissonouss."

"Yes, well I know a lot of stuff that's technically not poisonous that will knock you on your ass," Teal muttered.

Ardenai released Teal's hand long enough to give it a comforting pat, and in a minute or so his whole body began to relax. He exhaled long and slow, and sagged into the profile of the bed. "Now, it's beginning to work," he sighed. "I feel like they borrowed my bones to build somebody else, but I'm really, really good ..." and he was out.

"Shit!" Teal exclaimed.

"He iss assleep," Pythos chuckled, giving Teal a comforting flick of his tongue. "For how long, remainss to be sseen."

"He has a meeting in fifteen minutes," Teal said, still looking with worry at his friend's face.

"I'll bet he doesn't," Konik observed. "You gave Eridu a spoonful of this on his finger, didn't you?"

"I did, and he's a little fellow compared to Ardenai," Teal agreed. "Maybe he's asleep as well. Let's see if we can find his shadow, Naram, and have him check. After all, if Eridu wakes up and thinks he's missed a meeting, he'll be embarrassed. We don't want to embarrass The Most Wise Lord Eridu."

"I'll go find Naram," Konik said.

"And I'm going to put a blanket over Ardenai. I think he's cold. He should probably be lying flat."

Pythos huffed in annoyance. "Thee did thiss to Criollo when he wass tiny and nearly cooked the poor babe. Go on. Go prepare for your meeting. I will cover thy friend."

Naram, Konik noticed, seemed genuinely worried by Eridu's deep sleep. "You drugged him," he insisted. "You drugged him so that he would not be at that meeting. You are trying to embarrass him, to shame him as you did this morning, to get even with him for what he did to you."

Finally, Konik had had enough. "Eridu is no deeper asleep than is the Dragonhorse. They both took the same concoction, and their one on one meeting is going to be delayed until another day, period. I am here so that Eridu will not be embarrassed by having fallen asleep, don't you get that?"

Naram just glared at him. "We don't want you here," he sneered.

"And I didn't want to be here!" Konik replied hotly. "My wife was dying! All I wanted was to spend what little time we had left, with her, in our home. But no, I spent all but the last five minutes of her life shut in one of your stinking holes, eating your bloody, stinking food and puking it back up again. If your precious Eridu hadn't tried for an alliance through intimidation and torture, none of us would be here right now. You want to blame someone for what is happening? Blame him!"

"We tried to make friends with you," Naram said, still glaring. "We gave the precious gift of the Princess Eridi."

"That's your idea of friendship?" Konik grimaced. "We usually give a box of tea. Listen, Naram, the girl is lovely, but she can't make up for what you're doing to your people. You brought the Dragonhorse a child. He cares for her, but not in the way you were hoping he would. He has said he will not harm you so long as you make an honest effort to change, which is more than any other ruler in this part of the galaxy would have done. And know this," Konik added quietly, "your Most Wise Lord deprived me … of the love of my life … and if I can make him answer for that, I will. Tell him to come with the others." He turned quickly and left, leaving Naram in a state he wasn't used to – thoughtfulness.

Ardenai smiled a little at Teal's gentle prodding and pried open his sleepy eyes. "Good morning," he mumbled, patting around on the bed. "Oh … Teal, where is Ah'ree? Is it time to feed already? I must have really slept in. I'm going to be late for school."

"Oh no," Teal groaned, and Ardenai burst out laughing.

"Sorry. You looked so worried, I thought I'd give you something to worry about."

Teal just shook his head. "You are a piece of flawed flesh. Do you have any idea how lucky you are that I'm married to your sister?"

"I know how lucky she is to be married to you," Ardenai smiled, and sat up to swing his legs over the side of the bed. "Thank you for giving me my life back. How did you get your hands on that antidote?"

"Ah … it involved a certain amount of unpleasantness that Eridu is unlikely to forget or forgive. Let's get you dressed and brushed and I'll tell you while you get ready. We have a meeting with our various counselors in just a few minutes."

"No," Ardenai grimaced, "Teal, I'm starving."

"Put on your tunic while I find you a snack. I'll fix your hair, you eat."

"Deal," Ardenai said, and hopped easily off the bed into his usual, sinuous stance. "Where's my wife?" he asked, stretching his long arms ceilingward and groaning with relief.

"Oh, I know that look. You two can find time together later," he promised. "Right now you need food, and to get to that meeting. She'll be there."

Food wasn't all he needed, but he acquiesced, and ate what Teal brought him while Teal brushed his hair out of its rumpled, three strand overbraid and pulled it from the crown into a clip at the back of his head. "Sorry I don't have time to fix this properly," he said, "but we have exactly one minute to get where we're going." He threw the brush aside and they trotted off to the main conference room on the ship to greet their visitors.

The Lebonathi arrived looking more frightened than angry, and it made Ardenai wonder. These people had such a repressive religion, such a male dominated society. Why were they not more sullen? It merited watching. Eridu was the last to come, accompanied by Halaf and Naram.

"We don't stand on formality here," Ardenai said. "Sit where you are comfortable on this side of the table," he said, gesturing to his left. "I sit at one end because I am left handed, and it tends to get in people's way."

And because you're a God, Eridu thought defensively, but he had the sense not to say it, just in case it turned out to be true. One of the Lebonathi council members stood up and pulled out a chair for Eridu, nodding and bowing him into it, and he sat with a "Harrumph," and looked with hostility around the table. He had ordered ten people to be here. Eight had come besides Naram and Halaf. Two could not be found at meeting time, and it was surmised that they had fled the city. That balanced a little too closely the seven members from the ruling party he had begged, ordered, intimidated into coming with the three members of the minority party to whom he had sent a cursory invitation. They, of course, all showed up. He was going to find out why Aruda and Lagash had decided to defy him. "Get on with it," he said.

Ardenai just smiled at him and nodded graciously to the others, making the ancient Equi gesture of greeting as he spoke. "Ahimsa, I wish thee peace. You know who I am. Teal Master Captain is my kinsman and right hand in all of this, as is the lady sitting next to him, my wife, Ah'riodin. Together, with the cooperation of our people, we hold the reins of Equus and the AEW. Next to my wife is Priestess Ah'nis, who will govern women's affairs, religious affairs, much of female education, I would think. The man who will be the military governor has not yet arrived."

That part wasn't exactly true. Ardenai hadn't been able to decide for sure who to pick for the job. He had one strong candidate he could maybe spare, and that was his father-in-law, who, he knew, would hate the assignment, but take it because of the prestige. That wasn't a very good reason.

"Because you haven't been out and about much as a culture, I thought you might like to meet some of the other races you will be getting to know, so, going down the table on this side, you have the Dragonhorse Captains in no particular order: Marion Eletsky from Terren, Bonfire Dannis from Phylla, Ulric Hamar from Amberia, Cadence Holofernes from Corvus ..."

Eridu's fists came down on the table. "The first has covered himself with filth, the second is a wild animal, the third a mindless savage, and that last one is obviously Sapphic," Eridu grated. "We do not share a table with their kind."

"You do now," Ardenai said blandly, and gestured to the next man in line. "Captain Mecklin is from Calumet. Because we are always careful in the arena of justice, we are not only recording all of this, but we have observers with us – Cornwallis Mettenger from the Seventh Galactic Alliance and Physician Pythos from the Islands of Achernar. You know Senator Konik, who is from Anguine II. Kehailan of Equus, my eldest son, is Captain of this vessel, and I believe you know the young lady sitting next to him, as well."

Eridu squinted at the girl for a few moments in silence. She was Lebonathi, or was she? Her eyes were dark, but her hair and skin were white. She was dressed in the same tunic as the woman introduced as Ah'nis … same filthy sinful snake down her right arm …. She smiled at him, but she also made eye contact, and her meat teeth weren't very sharp, as though they'd been filed. "I do not know her," he said at last.

Eridi had made up her mind that no matter what he said, she wasn't going to react, but the comment hurt more than she'd expected it to, and she was grateful when Kehailan's hand closed momentarily around her forearm.

"I'm not surprised you don't know me. You never saw much of me, being as I was female," she said, paused a heartbeat and found complete control of her voice. "I am a citizen of Equus, but I am also your daughter, Eridi, and I am here to make sure our people are treated fairly."

Eridu just stared at her with his mouth slightly ajar, then said with exaggerated dismay, "I sent a beautiful, innocent young girl to Equus for that ... snake-eyed piece of dirt-eating shit at the head of the table, and this is what comes back to me? A shameless woman who dresses like a whore and who has been given to one of his mongrel whelps to straddle? I am appalled. You have no place at this table."

Eridi put one hand on Kehailan's arm to stay his notion of going over the table at Eridu, raised the other hand and smiled at her father. "I have a lot to learn, I admit, but this I do know, my innocence is better informed than it was, and therefore more precious. You would have had me pregnant by a man I didn't know. Instead, I am being educated, and cherished for who I am, not for what I can do or whom I can please. I am an Equi citizen, and I am dressed like one. It is what you wanted for me, and I have embraced it, as I embrace the man at the head of the table, whom I love and respect and trust with all my heart, as father and friend – as I would have done for you, given the chance. When the time is right, I can choose whomever I want to be with sexually, whelp of the Firstlord or not. It is my hope, my goal, and my mission, that every woman on Lebonath Jas will find herself in this same, 'appalling' position of which you speak." She took a breath and lost her smile, though her face remained pleasant enough. "Where you are most incorrect, is in thinking I have no place at this table. I do, and I will not be yielding it anytime soon, so please be polite about my presence."

"Ah yes," Ardenai said into the stunned silence of the Lebonathi and the mental applause of everyone else, "My world got richer, and your world is about to change, Eridu. Look at your daughter, and see how rich it can become. Please, introduce the members of your council."

From Eridu's point of view the afternoon did not improve. They were introduced to Lornak, some … being … who, from the condition of its clothes and its hands was obviously a peasant and who was treated with a ridiculous amount of respect because it was some kind of authority on dioecious date palms, whatever that meant, and when Eridu couldn't help staring at … it … it smiled, said, "We have five recognized sexes on Equus. I am N-Gen," and gave him an indulgent look, as though he were a child, before nodding to the rest of the dirt-eaters and exiting, while they all grinned and nodded back like performing monkeys. Eridu was sure that thing had been brought in just to taunt them, like the serpent, brought in to terrorize them, and that Sapphic woman – brought in to flaunt the Equi's lack of morality – to belittle Lebonathi beliefs – to show them that what they valued no longer mattered.

Food was served, and they were told that in addition to the dates and mushrooms, foods such as these – seeds, grains, nuts, fruits, cheeses – were on their way to help with critical shortages. Equi nutritionists were working on developing things that were more the taste and texture the Lebonathi were used to, to ease the transition. Much to Eridu's dismay two members of the majority party and every single member of the minority party, actually said thank-you, and then proceeded to try the stuff. When Eridu asked with a sneer why the Equi presumed they knew what the Lebonathi digestive system would and would not tolerate, Ardenai flashed that annoying smile and reminded him that they'd had Lebonathi guests – had sat at table with them, had paid close attention to their nutritional needs – rubbing Eridu's nose in the fact that his people had been forced to eat peasant slop at a common trough. All of it smelled like dirt, or shit, or both, and Eridu gagged graphically, which made Konik laugh; the sound no more pleasant than the look on his face.

Karun, who was going to hear about it later, had the temerity to ask after that traitor Girsu, who as it turned out was now a respected citizen of Equus, and was being approached to teach classes in Lebonathi Culture at the University level.

Eridu began to get truly alarmed when the Firstlord asked who controlled the delivery system for the planetary water supply. He led with a communal shrug and denial of knowledge on the subject, and the members of the council were at least smart enough to follow his example. Ardenai just smiled. Then he requested lists of people who were doctors, teachers, and scientists, along with lists of those who were politicians, lawyers, bankers, or independent due to wealth. Agronomists, farmers, orchardists. Those who managed factories, those who owned businesses.

"Why?" Eridu demanded. "What are you going to do to these people?"

Ardenai just smiled. "I plan to kill the politicians, lawyers, bankers, and the wealthiest, and put the rest in charge of reshaping the planet," he said. "That is the answer you expected, isn't it?"

Eridu just glared.

"Hear me. If we are to even things out and not just start the pendulum of revolution swinging wildly from one faction to the next, we must talk to everybody, Eridu, not just the politicians, or the poor, the teachers or the lawyers. Everyone became who he is for a reason, and I need to know what those reasons are. Does that help allay some of your fears?" Ardenai's comment was greeted with a sullen silence and he worked at hiding his annoyance. "I can tell you just so many times that we are here to fix things, not make them worse. That's why we want to know about your water supply. That's why we want to know who has which job. And, yes – for some of you, that will mean things do get worse from your point of view, but it should under no circumstances mean that anybody has to die. If people start throwing themselves off bridges and under buses, it will be because of the lies you are telling them, not the truth I am telling them. Those who genuinely choose to die for their religion or their politics rather than change their status or their beliefs as they apply equally to all people … them, I cannot help, but I will pray for their souls."

Eridu was beginning to smolder, and Ardenai decided to try for a change of subject. "Let's talk of easier things for a bit," he said, "You speak of being an Autarkhos of two worlds, Lebonath Jas and Lebonath Tras. Is Lebonath Tras represented here today, Eridu?"

"Why do you care, Dragonhorse? Equus is represented. That's all that matters."

"Let's assume it's not all that matters, just for conversation's sake," Ardenai said, and turned to the man Eridu had introduced as Karun. "Your background is in World Affairs. What do you know of Lebonath Tras?"

"It flames in the sky, beckoning the damned. It is the world of witches and the dead," the man said nervously, and Eridu again brought his fist down on the table with a curse.

"You fool!" he spat, "We are two worlds! That is all these people need to know! We are TWO worlds! Lebonath Tras is our sister world, and she is powerful."

"In a better way than you might suspect," Ardenai agreed. "It only looks to be on fire because of the pollution in your atmosphere." He paused and gave Eridu a puzzled look. "Besides, if it is a world of fire and the damned, what makes you think it would ride to your assistance as your sister world? Which is it, a molten ball of fire and condemned souls, or a verdant and powerful sister world? It cannot possibly be both, can it?"

"See?" Karun sighed, "Oh Most Wise Lord Eridu, look at them. Look at their ships. They already know our worlds. They have visited the flames. Trying to lie to them only makes us look foolish. What they do not know is our hearts. In there may yet lie some secrets, but not on our worlds. They know … better than we, what is and is not there."

Eridu rose angrily, shoving his chair backwards and screaming, "This is OVER. We are leaving! Any of you who do not leave with me now, are traitors and will be treated as such!"

"Please sit down," Ardenai said quietly. He pointed a finger at the council members. "Do not move from your seats, gentlemen."

Eridu spun around and looked for something, anything to throw. It was evident in the movement of his hands and eyes. "I will kill you!" he screamed, "I will kill you!"

"You will sit down," Ardenai responded. "I have not said you are a prisoner, but for all intents and purposes you are. The fact that you are threatening me is understandable, but when you threaten those of your own people who are trying to get you to see reason, for them I am concerned. Now sit down, or I will sit you down, and you will not enjoy the manner in which it is done."

Eridu grabbed his chair by both arms and heaved it over his head, but it was weighted for space flight, and he toppled over backwards with it, sprawling comically on his back on the plush maroon carpet. When he looked up Ardenai was standing over him, offering him a hand. Because he was half stunned he took it and found himself upright as though he weighed nothing.

Something snapped inside and he began screaming and swinging hysterically, and Ardenai casually fended him off as though he were a recalcitrant child. "Everyone take a break," Ardenai said over his shoulder, hands out in front of him to push away the blows. "All but you, Wally, and you, Naram. I don't want this little dust-up to go unremarked."

When everyone was out of the room and the door was shut, Ardenai seized Eridu by the front of his luxurious tunic and jerked him up until his feet were dangling and his face was inches from the blazing eyes and the big white teeth, which were clenched in fury. "Now you listen to me," Ardenai snarled, "you stop this tantrum right now or so help me I will snap your neck. Do you hear me?" He gave Eridu a good shake. "Do you hear me? Your people need an example to follow to help them get through this! Now either act like the ruler of a planet, or die like one, but choose, because we are done here." He let go suddenly and Eridu dropped to his back on the floor. "Now get up, and act like we've had a man to man chat."

But Eridu didn't get up. He rolled onto his belly and kicked and screamed and pounded his fists, shrieking obscenities and prayers to the Gods until he was exhausted, and then he began to sob. The three men just sat there and watched him until Mettenger finally said, "Just kill the little fucker. You're going to have to do that sooner or later anyway, and I'm getting hungry."

Ardenai gave Cornwallis a look of utter disgust. "And how would you react if someone bigger and infinitely stronger and more powerful arrived in your life and said they were going to take away everything – your power, your prestige, your money, your respect? If you had known nothing but privilege your whole life, if being physically soft and mentally manipulative was the norm for you, was what was expected of you, and someone suddenly took all of that away from you, how would you react? I'm taking his world away from him. I'm willing to let him thrash around a little if that will help him get a grip on what's happening. If you're hungry, there's the door."

Mettenger looked from Eridu to the door, to Ardenai, who said, "Let me make this easy. Get out." And he did. In a few moments the door opened and Ah'nis settled herself silently between Naram and the Firstlord.

CHAPTER 4

"I couldn't wait to see this place," Ardenai murmured, "And now all I can see is you."

"You could see better if I was on top," Io replied, growling softly with pleasure as his teeth found her neck, and in one of those quick, graceful movements of his, she was looking down rather than up at the underside of his chin.

"Better?"

"Ummm," she said, sitting up and moving languidly just with her hips.

He made a sharp sound and rolled again with her, spreading her legs with his and pushing hard as he began to release. She wrapped her legs around his waist and cried out with him, then her tone changed, and in a split second he was absolutely still on her. "Io," he said quietly, "did I hurt you?"

"No," she quavered, unclasping her legs, but he withdrew and rocked back on his knees in the warm sand to look at her by starlight.

"Then why do you have tears in your eyes?" he persisted, reaching with a forefinger to touch her cheek. "This was too much for you after a long and trying day. I was selfish, and I am sorry."

"You're wonderful and I love you," she whispered, and the tears spilled.

"Aww," he said, "Fledermaus, why do you cry?" He changed positions to sit on the blanket beside her, and gathered her into his arms. "Tell me what's wrong."

"Nothing ..."

"And don't tell me nothing, because that is obviously not true, and it is always a trap. What happened to upset you?"

"Speaking of obviously not true," she said, leaning her head against that wonderful warm spot where his neck met his shoulder. "My stupid body sent me the signal that I'm pregnant, that you just put a baby in me, and we know that's not true because my tubes are tied, and I just wonder if it will ever be true again." She snuggled her head against him and wept, and he rocked her gently and kissed her hair and tried to figure out what he could say to make her feel better.

It had sounded like such a good idea at the time – to take the big clipper, have dinner on board, and go check out that beautiful beach Teal had talked about the night before – where it was so quiet, and there was nothing, nobody to disturb them. It had been so long since they'd been really alone, where they could laugh and cry and scream and chase each other around, and roll together onto the warm earth and make love. And now, here was reality, intruding with its usual impeccable timing.

"Tell me what I should do," he said, kissing the tip of her ear where it persisted in poking itself out through her mass of curls. "I will do anything you want me to do, to make you feel better."

She shrugged a little against him. "We came out here to make love."

"We came out here to be alone," he corrected gently. "If you want to make love, we can do that. If you want to talk, if you just want to lie on your back and look at the stars, we can do that. Tell me what you want."

"I want to make all this go away, and go home and be the wife of a teacher who raises horses for the Great House. I want a garden, and rohanth bushes, and a baby to rock in the swing in the back yard, like Ah'ree used to rock me. Like you used to rock me."

Ardenai took his left arm from around her, picked up a small rock beside the blanket and side-armed it into the water, hearing the distant plunk as it hit. "I cannot have this discussion again," he said. "When I say I would do anything for you, it has to be within the realm of what I can do for you. I am the Thirteenth Dragonhorse, Io. This is what I was bred to do, born to do, and trained to do. You knew that when you married me. I was not a teacher, I was already Firstlord. We promised each other, no surprises, remember?"

"Yes," she sniffed.

"Canyon keep is still there, with the swing and the rohanth bushes. If you want a baby, have the surgery and I will give you one, gladly. I would love a baby with you. But the teaching and the quiet life at home, that's gone, and it's not coming back. You want to stay home with Ah'din and my parents and trim the bushes and rock the baby – and if you don't think you'd be bored to death in a week – do it. Better yet, take our baby and go spend time in our apartments in Thura. Represent me in the Great Council and amongst the Eloi. I would love that. The Equi people would be richer for it. And I will be home just as often as I can to help you. But whatever you do decide, you need to stop trying to make me feel guilty about who I am and what I do just because you can't make peace between who you are and what you want to do. I love you, but I also love who I am becoming. I have said a dozen times that if you are heavy with a baby I can take Wren ..."

"Do not bring her up again," Io snapped, turning away from him. "I know what my job is, and I'm not giving it up to some nubile machine."

"So now our sex life is a job. Perfect." He folded his arms and stared gloomily at the patterns of starlight forming on the surface of the shallows. "And she's not a machine ... exactly. She's a very nice, very intelligent person."

"And you've had some erudite and illuminating discussions with her, I know, you've told me – which just makes it worse, in case you were wondering!"

They sat in a loaded silence for about two minutes before Io leaned back into him and her hand slid down to caress the shaft of his phallus. "I love my job," she murmured.

"I love the way you do your job," he said, and she swung a leg over to straddle him while he sat there, allowing him to swell inside her and leaning back against his updrawn thighs. "That feels so good," he whispered. "Can we just do this awhile and not talk?"

"Mmmmm," she replied, and began shifting her muscular buttocks, first to one side, then the other, squeezing his phallus until he cried out and released himself to her. "Good job," she said, leaning forward to bite his nipples as he dropped his back onto the blanket. "Leave your knees, just like that. I could sit like this forever …."

They had paused for another breather when Io said, "People take babies with them all kinds of places."

"That they do. Ah'Lauren and Rounce take their twins everywhere with them. They were born on a science vessel. I think they're with us on this campaign, as a matter of fact."

"We should think about it," Io mused.

"You tell me what you decide and I will do my share of the carting and changing."

"Maybe we could ..."

"I didn't mean tell me now," Ardenai whispered, nuzzling her breasts. "Right now I'd love it if you got on your forearms and knees for me. I'll make it quick."

"Make it slow and make it twice," she amended, and relaxed into the warmth and the thrusting and the knowledge that he couldn't resist her. She did wonder momentarily if her body was going to continue throwing her false signals. That had been a jolt and a bit of a heartbreak – If Ah'leah had carried she might be showing by now, and Io and Ah'din and Ah'rane would be rushing around getting ready for the delivery. Delightful and fulfilling as the thought of a baby romping the halls of the Great House was, she knew it was a fantasy. She had duties, and there would be no baby for a long, long time, if ever. He peaked, and she pushed back against him, releasing herself to the joy of the moment, knowing neither of them had to worry about a pregnancy or the sex of a child. They had each other, which was more than enough.

It was at their usual pre-dawn meeting that Teal told them there might be horses on Lebonath Tras in a day or two. Ardenai missed the feel of a horse between his legs, and the idea that they could discover the planet more fully if they rode, made a lot of sense to him.

"I'm going to head out to meet the transport this morning," Teal said. "If they don't have any usable saddle stock there's no use in them getting any closer. If they do have horses we can use, they might as well head straight for Lebonath Tras, rather than coming this way first. You look especially refreshed this morning, Dragonhorse, what are you going to do?"

"I am going to go on a treasure hunt for a team of Lebonathi scientists," Ardenai said, picking up his cider and breathing in the warm fragrance. They'd missed the celebrations of High Harvest, and all of them were feeling the let-down. "Rumor has it they have a small facility in the mountains way east of us." He flipped a finger the general direction, still blowing on the cider to cool it.

"How did you find out about them?" Marion asked. "I got the impression that if anybody knew anything about anything, they weren't telling."

"Remember when we finally got back together yesterday and we were talking about Lebonath Tras, the so-called 'witch world', and one of Eridu's High Council members muttered something about the crazy, discredited scientists who still thought there was a verdant world up there at one point?"

"Um hm." Marion nodded. "I thought I saw your ears prick up at that point – literally."

"And that same council member bugged out his eyes and said the people who thought that were witches themselves, remember? He said it was from them – those witches – that the anchoresses got the herbs for their potions, and so on."

"We're waiting," Konik said.

"I'm trying to drag this out so you'll be impressed with my sleuthing," Ardenai laughed, "but have it your way. Teal is pretty sure the sample he collected on Lebonath Tras is part of the concoction Eridu gave me in that needle to the hand the other day. He also said he smelled Evangeline's Carpet in the Anchoresses' pharma yesterday. Nobody is going to Lebonath Tras, we know that, so somebody has those plants here on Lebonath Jas, quite possibly the crazy scientists who think there was a world up there, and who have some of its flora stashed away somewhere safe."

"And you think they're east in the mountains?" Kehailan asked.

"I do. I had Ah'nis and company go and hunt up the friendly anchoress who gave Teal that little jar yesterday, and she admits they are there. Either they will be there or they won't, but from what she said, several of them have been together there for many years, and I'm hoping they have some knowledge about a couple of things that puzzle me."

"Such as?" Kehailan asked between bites of breakfast.

"What do they know about Lebonath Tras, and what do they know about the Kaiein, the Burning Time Girsu talked about. It was at that point that their religion took a turn toward darkness and I'm wondering what the impetus was."

"Good idea," Konik said, "though I think I'd be looking for historians rather than scientists. You do look your old self this morning, Ardenai. Pain pretty well gone?"

"Thanks to you and Teal I'm good as new, except for one spot in the small of my back that's a little twingy."

That'll happen when you spend all night making love to someone fourteen inches shorter than you are instead of getting some much-needed sleep, Teal observed.

Thanks for the tip about the beach. It has been thoroughly ... explored. Ardenai responded, and nodded himself back into the conversation. "I'm sorry, Eridi, what were you saying?"

"I came here instead of to the women's meeting because I was wondering if I could have your permission to go and see my father later this morning. He invited me, and he said he would let me visit with my mother."

Ardenai grimaced without meaning to, and then gave Eridi an apologetic smile. "I worry about your safety. I do. I know he is your sire, but he is also a desperate and dangerous man surrounded by desperate and dangerous people. Which reminds me, has anyone been able to find Brak?"

Kehailan shook his head. "Eridi and I could try to do that as well as visiting her father," he said. "That's my way of saying I do think we should let her see her father, and I don't think we should let her go alone."

"I thought you were meeting with some Lebonathi technicians," Teal observed, crimping a grin. He was also wondering if Kehailan, who seemed at long last smitten, needed to be reminded about this girl's age.

I don't, at least not at this juncture, but she is an interesting child. "We're not meeting with them until this afternoon," Kehailan added aloud, smiling at his uncle, who looked appropriately surprised and impressed. "I'm meeting with technicians, Mecklin with some soil scientists, Konik gets to tell the council members that we're going to have to start getting rid of their meat animals … I have a complete list for you."

"Take the girl to see her father," Ardenai said, "and see if Ah'nis will go with you. Maybe Eridi can take the two of you on a bit of a tour, but be careful, and do try to find Brak. I'm worried that if they find out he helped Konik and me, they'll kill him or worse. Nik, since I assume you're not going to spend the day eating and sleeping as Pythos recommended, what are you doing this morning?"

"Reading, maybe," he said evasively. Everyone knew he spent his spare moments sitting beside Ah'davan's casket, singing quietly to her, or reading her favorite books aloud.

"I like your idea of finding historians, and I want you to do that, but first, would you please go with Kee? I really worry about any of us wandering around the city in less than a phalanx. Since a phalanx is out of the question, a fourlanx will have to do."

When breakfast was over and they were scattering for meetings or other duties, Ardenai called Konik aside and said, "I would speak with you before you head off to do other things. Shall we walk?" Konik nodded and they set off around the mezocourse of the ship, nodding to others who were out running or walking and enjoying the scenes of Equus going by on the walls, floor and ceiling. "Nothing like a stroll in the Oporens countryside," Ardenai noted. Then he made that characteristic huff which told Konik he had something of import on his mind.

“What troubles you, Dragonhorse?”

“You,” Ardenai said, tempering it with a smile. “I have been inconsiderate of you and what you have been through these last seasons, and I wanted to apologize for that. I have been focused on other things, and you have been strong, and because of that, I have ignored your needs.”

Konik shook his head. “From the second I laid eyes on you in that arena until a long and trying meeting yesterday, you were in too much pain to recognize anyone’s needs, Ardenai. Please don’t be concerned.”

“But I am,” he said, “and again, you are kinder than I deserve. When I was watching Eridu kick, scream, cry and curse for over an hour yesterday, it came into my feeble brain that I have given him that courtesy, but not you. I have picked your brain, offered you a ship, heaped responsibility upon your shoulders, and offered you not one minute to recover from your ordeal, to grieve for your wife, or the chance to get on a ship and take her body home. For that I am ashamed. Please forgive me.”

They walked awhile, smelling the breeze, hearing the crunch of leaves under their feet and the sound of hoofbeats as two people seemed to canter by on horseback. “Home is where you create it,” Konik said at last, gesturing out at the projections. “I have spent an eternity imprisoned on the planet below us, worrying about my dying wife, but knowing you were caring for her as you promised you would, because that’s how friendship works. You did what you could. I got to say goodbye. Now I have things to do that keep my mind from the pain that … wells up every so often.”

“You should have had the option,” Ardenai said quietly.

“I don’t want the option,” Konik responded. “Your beloved wife died just like mine did, from the same terrible disease, and instead of letting her go and rest in peace, you clung to her memory like a madman. For two years you were a shadow of yourself. Her physical weakness became yours. You were a weak and weeping man, Dragonhorse. I thank you for showing me what a fruitless exercise that would be.” He smiled to soften the sting of his words and gave Ardenai a pat on his shoulder. “I am not criticizing. You must realize I came at my wife’s death from a very different place than you did. Because Ah'davan was over fifty years my senior, we always assumed she would go first, though there were a few times I nearly preceded her." There was a brief, humorless chuckle and Konik rubbed at the spot where Sarkhan's arrow had shattered his breastbone. "By the time I actually found out how sick she was, it was too late to do anything but just prepare myself for what I knew was coming."

He was quiet for a few paces. He didn't mention that Ardenai had had exactly the same opportunity to prepare himself and had retreated instead into denial. Ardenai felt the implication, grateful that it wasn't voiced. "Anyway, I don't have time to waste doing something that hurts me and does nothing to bring Ah'davan back. She is gone. I will draw on her strength to let her go. But … make absolutely no mistake …if I get the opportunity to take vengeance on the people who kept me from my dying wife, I will do so."

Ardenai nodded, eyes still on the projected country road beneath their feet. "I understand, but I must tell you this. If you are going to move on, move on. That includes putting aside any thoughts of personal vengeance. If you choose to stay here you stay as a representative of Equus, and of the Thirteenth Dragonhorse. You must act accordingly."

"Of course," Konik purred. "As you know all too well, Ardenai, I am a creature of duty."

Ardenai thought about those words as he dropped into the atmosphere and skimmed east in Dominus. He'd considered bringing one of the stubby little eight by twenty foot hoppers each Dragonhorse kept in its shunt-bay for runabouts and shuttling small amounts of material over relatively short distances. They were less obvious, and easier to set down in tight spaces. But Dominus was extremely fast, and she was well armed. At fifty feet with a sixteen foot beam, she also had a splendid array of scientific technology and resources. He just might need some of those things this morning.

He kept one eye on his course and turned his thoughts back to Ah'ria Konik Nokota. The man was strong. He was brilliant. He was thorough. A creature of duty. He was also humble, and deeply kind. Ardenai had been somewhat reluctantly planning to put Abeyan, who could be insensitive and arrogant, or Ah'nis, who was female and a tad abrupt, in the seat of military governor. Now … Ardenai was thinking maybe … Konik? He had been a senator for years, had degrees in the history of governance, maybe political science, one in engineering of some kind, one in music. Extremely well educated man. He already knew something about these people and this place. Paired with Ah'nis they could be a team to be reckoned with.

He had decided one thing for sure, he was going to govern Lebonath Jas separately from Lebonath Tras, and had already filed a Statement of Intent to Initialize Recolonization with the SGA. But to do that, and to do it right, he needed somebody, anybody, who knew what it had been in the first place. Karun and Eridu had just cringed. Their response had been that they were not scientists, but Ardenai figured they were too superstitious at heart to talk about it. He had been left with the definite impression that if you knew what anyone outside your own field was doing, you were a snoop at best and probably a spy. The anchoress had said little, and while she appeared to be friendly to the cause, Ah'nis had said she was also scared to death that she'd be found out and scourged or killed. A whole society based on mistrust, suspicion and punitive response.

He choked back his speed and dropped down to a thousand feet, watching the planet in real-time below him. There were people everywhere. How puzzling. Eridu had said almost no one lived on the planet's surface. They might not live there, but they were surely working there – or were there so many because they were fleeing the urban centers and there was no place for them to go underground? It was too hot for that, and the population too fair skinned. They would die in short order. There was no water. The penalty for tapping into the pipes, was death. Ardenai shuddered.

He would ask Cadence and her wife, Merrilina, to help him assess the situation – Merrilina had the head for charting possibilities and probabilities in any given situation in any given space. He touched the transmitter on his console and spent a few minutes in conversation with Dragonhorse Five.

He slowed again as the mountains came up in front of him, and began to circle down, looking for the marker he'd been told would be there – an almost indiscernible X on a dusty spot on a barren mountainside. Not really big enough to set down on, but for Ardenai that had never been a problem. He was an extraordinary pilot, and he knew it. He tried never to test it unless he had to, and, being who he was, he never mentioned it. It was a gift, like most everything in his life. He came down on all pods, activated the levelers, and ducked out the door into that appalling Lebonathi heat that threatened to suffocate him, even before the sun was up. In seconds, an older man appeared from a crack in the rocks and hailed him.

"Welcome," he called, striding forward with his hands extended. "I am Ashur. I know that our Most Wise Eridu offered you his hand in treachery. Please know that I do not." He stopped just short of arm's length and said, "This is how we greet one another. I turn my palms up, because I am welcoming you. With your palms down, grasp my forearms, my hands under yours because you are in my space. Yes, like that! Welcome, Dragonhorse. I am honored."

"As am I," the Firstlord responded, grasping the man's forearms. "I am Ardenai. Ahimsa, I wish thee peace. How did you know I was coming?"

"Ensharra contacted us," the man said, gesturing toward what looked like a solid wall. Ardenai followed him around a bit of a corner and onto a steep, narrow path between two high pieces of rock that came almost together at the top. An old lava tube. They walked perhaps a hundred feet before it widened out into a small three sided caldera, hidden from sight on all but the sheer side of a cliff, with nothing but jagged cliffs and wilderness beyond, as though the volcano had blown out in that direction. Within the bowl, there was an abundance of life – all of it struggling to survive – but tenderly nurtured. Along with an impressive array of native plants and trees there were several varieties of fruit trees, herbs, vegetables and shrubs, one of which Ardenai recognized as "Teal's Bane." It made him chuckle, and Ashur turned to look at him.

"My kinsman had a run-in with that shrub," Ardenai said. "Who is Ensharra?"

"The anchoress who gave Master Captain Teal the antidote for you yesterday. She is also the one Ah'nis and her friends came to see last night."

Ardenai gave him a searching look and saw relief on his weathered features. He also saw a man who was not albino. Ashur had brown hair turning gray and skin that on an Equi would have been very fair had it not been sunburned, but he had hazel eyes, not pale blue or pink. "You … were hoping we would come, weren't you?" Ardenai asked.

The man gave him a single, acquiescing nod and an enigmatic smile, gesturing him inside a low building set against the side of the bowl to avoid the afternoon sun. It took a moment for his eyes to adjust from the glare of the sand in the bowl to the dim interior of the shed, but when they did adjust he realized the lighter places on the walls were maps – very old – and he walked over to study them.

"I … have seen this place," he murmured, running his forefinger in an arc without touching the ancient paper. "And my kinsman, Teal, recorded this spot right here as he flew over it. These maps are of Lebonath Tras."

"They are," Ashur said, and when Ardenai turned to look at him, he was not alone.

There were three men and two women standing there, still as statues and as quiet, all very thin, none of them albino. One of the men had a piece of cloth tied over the bottom half of his face.

"Ahimsa, I wish thee peace," Ardenai said quickly. "Forgive me. My curiosity overwhelmed the good manners my parents taught me. I am Ardenai."

"You are the Thirteenth Dragonhorse," said the woman who appeared to be the older of the two. "A man of great power, and yet you are here. In this place. May I speak to you?"

"Of course," he said, looking puzzled.

She smiled. "I was asking if a strange woman speaking to you was offensive. I see that it is not, and that the concept is really quite alien to you. I appreciate that. I am Etana."

He gave her a respectful nod, but his eyes were concerned, and Ashur did not miss it. "You do not trust us," he said bluntly.

Ardenai sighed. "I do not mean not to trust you," he said, "but you are very open, and very welcoming, and I have come with Interposing Forces to inflict my government on your world. The fact that it does not seem to concern you, does concern me. The fact that … Ensharra?" Ashur nodded. "…was able to get word to you, means that I just possibly might have walked into a trap."

"You have walked into a trap," the second man said. "I am Isin, and you are trapped here with a group of disenfranchised lunatics who are going to sit you down and fill your head with nonsense about this world we think exists above us – this Lebonath Tras of nightmare – the world of witches where evildoers go to burn."

"Sit," the second woman said with a smile, "that being the important word in Isin's statement. You are suffering from the heat. I am Larsa, and this is my husband, Elam." She gestured toward the man with the cloth over his face. "At least he would be my husband if we had been allowed to marry. Still, we have a babe, and if it is discovered that I made a child with him, our lives will be forfeit."

Ardenai folded gracefully onto a cushion and waited until the others had seated themselves, then said, "Forgive my question, but why weren't you allowed to marry? You are not related, are you?"

"Nuh," Elam said. "Ihaaa a speeet inpedmnt." He dropped his eyes and slowly slid the cloth down so Ardenai could see his disfigured lip.

"You couldn't get married because you have a cleft palate? Why wasn't it fixed?"

"Ah, the question of the wealthy and privileged," Isin said, running an impatient hand through a mane of hair going from brown to grey. "Why didn't you just fix it? Why didn't you just pay to have it fixed? On this world, they don't 'fix' such things, Dragonhorse. They destroy those so afflicted."

His anger made Ardenai cringe inside. "I was thoughtless," he said simply. "On my world such things are fixed immediately and without question. I am your prisoner, tell me about Lebonath Tras."

"No, you tell us," Larsa said. "You said you have been there?"

"Yes. I was there last night with my wife. We … enjoyed the stars." His face colored slightly and Ashur laughed in spite of himself.

"Not a man who is good with secrets, I see," he said, and Ardenai colored more deeply.

"No. I am a simple soul, a fact that is well known and occasionally used to advantage by others. I … hear the baby."

"She is fussy," Larsa said apologetically. "The heat bothers her, and we have very little water."

"We have all we need," Isin said sharply. "Tell us about Lebonath Tras."

Ardenai sized him up, and then gave him a calculating smile. "I think not," he said. "You tell me. As I said, I have little reason to trust even people who seem as genuine as you."

They looked from one to another and Ashur finally said, "What we will speak is heresy. We can be killed for what we are about to tell you."

Ardenai flipped his hands palms up and said, "Who will kill you? I am the only one here."

Etana caught him by the wrist of his right hand and studied the small blue wound on his palm. "If you are who you say you are, and Eridu did this to you, why is he still alive?"

"Because I am who I say I am," Ardenai replied. "Tell me what I came to find out, or I will leave you in peace. This is going nowhere and I have not slept deeply in several days."

"Very well," Etana sighed. "But let us show you, rather than telling you. I promise, no harm will come to you. This is not our secret, but rather a secret we were given to guard, and those who came before us, and others before them. Come with us."

They took him outside in a sober line and marched to a spot on the backside of the caldera where boulders and scree gave scant foothold to scrubby brush. "Here," Isin said, and he, Elam and Ashur began to push on the stones.

"It's actually all one piece," Larsa said helpfully, and Ardenai reached above their heads and pushed it open. Cool air rushed out and all of them hurried inside. "Quickly!" Larsa said, and Ashur swung the door shut.

It was pitch black, and Ardenai felt the hair stand up on the back of his neck. What had he gotten himself into? Then Isin lit a lantern, and beckoned for him to follow along what seemed to be another lava tube. It grew cooler and ever more still until at last they emerged into a cavern perhaps fifty by one hundred and fifty feet, and fifty or more in height. There was the trickling drip of water at the back, and stacked high and neat along the length, rows of glowing containers, clear on their front side. Ardenai went forward very carefully and looked. Animals. Pairs of cryogenically stored animals. Something that looked like a fox. Pink fish with white fins. Small yellow birds with black wings. A Fleeter with backswept horns and dainty hoofs. Ardenai spent half an hour before he ever turned around, and when he did his face was filled with the wonder of a child.

"The animals of Lebonath Tras?" he asked, and Ashur shook his head.

"Not exactly. As far as we know and were told, these are all that is left of the animals on both planets," he said sadly. "And now we will tell you the story you came to hear. But first, let me go and collect the water that has fallen at the back of the cave so the babe can have a drink, and we can offer you one, as well."

They went back up the lava tube and pushed open the door, briefly admitting the painful heat, before shutting the door again with them on the outside.

"Isin," Ardenai said, "If you will walk with me to Dominus I will get all of us something cool to drink. As a matter of fact, you can all come if you wish. I could easily overpower Isin, but not all of you."

Ashur shook his head and smiled. "You are too curious to leave, and we are too trusting to think you would. The rest of us will meet you inside. Larsa is still trying to nurse Umma, and the heat dehydrates her until she has no milk at all."

"I'm sure that's exactly what every man wants to hear," Larsa muttered with some embarrassment, and Ardenai shook his head.

"This one does," he said soothingly. "This planet now belongs to Equus, as do I. Your needs are of primary importance to me. We will meet you inside in a few minutes."

What the Firstlord brought into their home was bountiful beyond anything they had ever seen. Dried fruit, nuts and seeds pressed into sweet bars, a wonderful and fragrant juice, fresh vegetables, crusty bread and cheeses, and water – gallons of water – more than they could remember ever having. He prepared a simple breakfast for them, and served them, explaining in his quiet voice what each food was, and then sat down and took the baby while Larsa ate.

Umma fit easily between his elbows and the cupped palms of his hands, and Ardenai realized she was pathetically thin. She smiled at him and kicked her feet and Ardenai obligingly nibbled her toes to make her laugh. "You're a beautiful girl," he said in his gentle voice, and she fixed her eyes on him.

"You're very good at that," Etana observed. "Do you and your wife have babes?"

"No," Ardenai said. "I have a son who is grown, one who is in his teens, and my wife has a somewhat younger son. Together, we do not have any children yet, though we would like to have one of our own – a little girl like this one would be especially nice."

"We have heard your rule is only two children," Larsa said somewhat accusingly, and Ardenai knew it was directed at him.

"My late wife and I had my oldest son as our only child," He explained. "Io's son is from her marriage to her first husband, who was killed in battle. Gideon doesn't count, since he is adopted, so since Io and I each have only one, technically we can have one more. Does that make sense?"

"Rumor has it you eat children," Ashur said blandly. "And that's how you keep your population down."

"Well of course that's the actual truth of it," he shrugged, "Is there any other way than eating your offspring?" and he nibbled Umma's toes. "You promised me a story. I'm waiting."

"And here it is," Ashur said, "insofar as we know it. There was a time when both these planets were thriving, Jas more urbane and industrial, Tras more primitive and agricultural. But they were never linked as legend would have you believe, because we never perfected space travel to any extent. While we made great strides in industry and technology, and were just short of reasonably safe and comfortable interplanetary travel, we failed to keep up agriculturally and ecologically. Over time we began to polarize, and travel between the planets, always difficult, became less and less frequent. Jas became more polluted, and Tras less and less populated as people were lured to the big cities by promises of wealth and adventure. I guess it's in our nature as Lebonathi to love being packed tightly together, because everyone wanted to live in the city. Nobody wanted to farm. Nobody understood where food actually came from. Food associated with dirt and mud became distasteful, and water became the preferred medium for growth. We came to depend heavily on meat as status food, and stripped Jas to feed the Caronai and other meat animals, most of which are now extinct.

"At some point we lost control of our children – not just our population, but the minds of our young. People who had no ties to education, took over education, and it became about money, and teaching religion rather than science. The wealthy got wealthier, and they began to preach that the Gods had given them this planet for their own use. They hunted to extinction, fished to extinction, cut trees to extinction. The planet got hotter and hotter and as it did the rhetoric surrounding the will of the Gods got hotter with it. What they had said would take centuries, took decades, and we were in ruins.

"People grew more and more hateful and intolerant. There seemed to be more and more of us and we were constantly at war with each other. Even our games were bloody and violent, preparing our young people to kill each other. I suppose it's lucky we did kill each other, because that's the pathetic way in which we controlled our population. To get a job you had to be religious. To be wealthy you had to be religious. And that same faction claimed that the Gods were not going to let anything happen to the planet, that they would swoop down and save us all from ourselves …" He paused and looked forlorn. "This is beginning to sound really crazy, isn't it?"

"It is crazy. And yet it sounds familiar," Ardenai said. "One version or another of this story can be applied to the vast majority of industrialized planets. Most of them managed to arrest that negative motion and save themselves. Some planets actually had to be abandoned. The Potami are just now recolonizing such a planet. A few civilizations blew themselves up or poisoned themselves into oblivion. So far this planet has done neither of those things. Tell me about the animals, and about Lebonath Tras."

Elam relieved Ardenai of the sleeping baby, and the Firstlord sat back with a glass of cold cider first to his forehead and then to his lips. He'd never been so miserably hot in all his life. He had moments where he thought he was either going to pass out or go to sleep, regardless of how interesting the story might be. The fact that a couple of days ago he'd been freezing made him want to laugh out loud.

"Now we are approaching what is called the Kaiein, the Burning Time in our history ..." Ashur began, and Isin broke in, his voice tinged with anger.

"And despite what the politicians say, we're still in it. Religion and politics have become inextricably tangled, opinion has become sin, fear and hatred drives the lower classes, power and corruption those above, and everybody thinks that they're the ones who are right. Everybody hates everybody. Education has ceased to have any prestige, replaced instead by money and inheritance. Even those who still manage to get an education are swayed by religion into believing such things as render their intellect ineffectual." He sighed and looked almost hopeless for a moment, staring at Umma, then shook himself out of it. "Sorry, Ashur, I interrupted you."

Ashur gave him a slight wave as though he were used to it and continued. "Anyway, about the only people left with the ability to think were the few scientists who were still highly trained, and they could see the end of all things coming. They set about gathering up as many of the animals from this planet as they could and putting them into cryogenesis. They went to Lebonath Tras and realized it was nearly pristine, and that when the Lebonathi were ready to start over again on a more sober and prudent path, it would be a place for that new birth. Since the planet had been largely abandoned anyway, they disassembled what was left, made sure most of the craft that could make the trip were destroyed, and since the Lebonathi were by nature suspicious of wilderness, and the world was spiraling downward away from technology and reason, it was easy to keep people off the planet through lack of travel and the invention of some really awful, deeply religious stories about what was up there – hence the world of witches and the dead."

Ardenai sat for a long while sipping his drink and pondering Ashur and Isin's words. Nobody said anything, content to have a full glass of water for each of them while they let him think.

Ardenai just shook his head and stared a hole in the floor. "Then, if Lebonath Tras was pristine, why did they take the animals?"

"Oh, is that what's been bothering you?" Isin asked. "As far as we can tell, there weren't a lot of species up there to begin with, and they brought most of them down here to be hunted."

None of this had made much sense, and Isin's words made no sense at all. Species were species. They developed in a certain order and …usually … exponentially. He shook his head. Too complicated for this particular venue. A trickle of sweat coursed down his back. "Why not go up there to hunt?"

"Good question. My guess is that it wasn't civilized enough, and it was neither safe nor easy to make the trip. Most Lebonathi hunting is, or was, controlled. People drove out, shot a cornered or trapped animal from their vehicle, and went home with bragging rights. There's still a very little of that going on – animals bred for the purpose, of course, or mechanized. Nothing is left in the wild." Isin sighed. "Perhaps I should say, nothing is left of the wild."

"The animals they brought down? Their offspring? Is that what they hunt?"

"Probably not any more, though I don't know for sure. Some died because this was not native habitat, and the rest were killed. Some of the animals out there in stasis are directly from Lebonath Tras, but we don't know which ones. There's probably a record of who came from where, but we don't have it, and I don't think we have all the animals, either."

"I'm sure you don't," Ardenai said sadly. "That planet is empty. The seas are empty. The skies are empty. There are vast grasslands that are completely empty. There are some tiny creatures like insects and rodents, but that's all." He put his hands on his thighs and stood up abruptly. "Field trip," he said. "Get Umma, we're going for a ride."

"We cannot leave here," Ashur said quietly. "We are the guardians. If we are gone, everything will be gone when we get back. Everyone steals from everyone. The animals will be gone."

Ardenai held up one finger. "Give me a minute," he said, then paused. "Forgive me. You have devoted your lives to this, and I was about to do something without your consent. I would like to show you two places today, because I would like your permission before I proceed with recolonization. If I bring some people down here who can absolutely be trusted to guard what you have guarded for so long, will you come with me?"

They looked at each other, then Ashur nodded. "Even if we did not trust you, we cannot resist you in any case. Do what you will."

Just sitting he was drenched with sweat, and walking to the ship in heat like this was more than Ardenai wanted to do in order to contact someone. He closed his eyes and concentrated.

Pythos?

I am here, Sweet Boy. How may I serve thee?

I have something amazing I want you to see. Would you contact Moonsgold and then bring two armed members of the SGA down here along with the two of you?

Thee knows I will do anything to spend time with Doctor Moonsgold.

I do know this. We will wait for thee, Father.

"It will be a bit," Ardenai said, and spent the next half hour studying the maps on the wall, asking questions about Lebonath Tras, and listening to wild stories. By the time Pythos and Moonsgold arrived, Ardenai knew full well how the legend of the Wind Warriors had gotten out of hand. The legend of the witchworld of Lebonath Tras would make any six-year-old wake up screaming.

We are coming down, Pythos said, and Ardenai prepared his hosts for their arrival.

"Pythos is one of the serpent physicians of Achernar, and he has been my doctor and my friend for my entire life. Dr. Moonsgold is Declivian, and the two of them consider themselves a comedy team, so be patient." He opened the door to admit a man and a woman in light summer uniforms, a man with two completely separate chins and brilliant gold eyes, and a huge green sea dragon who bobbed and hissed politely. To their credit, nobody screamed.

"I thought perhaps these two could begin cataloging the species, or checking your catalogs," Ardenai said, hoping normal conversation would relieve some of the tension in the room.

At that point, Umma began to cry, and the old dragon's head snapped around instantly. "A baby!" he hissed. "There iss a baby? Pleasse, bring her here at oncce."

"No!" Larsa cried. "We trusted you and you betrayed us!"

Ardenai looked completely flummoxed. "What?"

It was Moonsgold who burst out laughing. "She thinks the good doctor is going to eat her baby. I'm sorry, I'm sorry, I know you're afraid," he said, gesturing expansively and trying to control his chortling. "My dear girl, we mean you no harm. The only person I know who is more kind and gentle than Ardenai Firstlord, is this being. He just wants to play with the baby. Please indulge him in this or he will yammer until you do."

In a minute or less Pythos had the baby and Larsa's fears had evaporated. He was dancing around with the child in his arms, caressing her face with his tongue and she was laughing and trying to catch it as it flicked in and out of his toothless mouth.

"We must go," Ardenai said, chuckling at Pythos' antics. "I know you're hoping to keep her, but I'm sure her mother will want to take her along. Besides, I have things for you to do while we are gone."

Ardenai showed them the trove of cryogenic cases, posted the guards, who he noticed had fully charged pultronels plus their slingshots, and finally got the five scientists and the baby aboard Dominus. "Have you flown?" he asked.

"Not in anything like this," Ashur said quietly, looking at the gleaming array of controls and equipment. "And you fly this yourself? You didn't have a crew waiting on board?"

"It's a very simple machine. Sit until we are up and away, and I'll take you on a tour," Ardenai smiled. He lifted the ship slowly to minimize the sensation, and peeled slowly off the side of the mountain.

"This is the Imperial Equi Clipper Dominus. I am leaving the planet's surface, destination SEGAS Belesprit. Captain Dannis, do you have coordinates for me?"

"Programming coordinates as we speak. Captain Dannis is on Lebonath Tras with a team. This is Timothy McGill, and for the moment I'm second in command. How are you feeling, Sir?"

"Much better," he smiled. "Tim, do you have an absolutely secure place to store a thousand or so cryogenic cases?"

"Activated?"

"Yes."

"I … think so, yes. Let me check." There was a short break during which Ardenai showed his guests how to use the food replicator and got himself something to eat, and McGill was back.

Dominus, this is Belesprit. Are you there?"

"We are. What can you tell me?"

"We are in the process of shifting some cargo, and when that is done, we will have a secure location for your activated cases."

"I have five scientists with me who have devoted their entire lives to protecting those cases. May we come aboard and inspect the space, just for their peace of mind?"

"Of course," came the prompt reply.

When they were safely in the shuntbay and the main door of the clipper hissed open, Ardenai made a gesture for the scientists to precede him. They did so, and discovered a double line of officers and crew, standing at attention. "They honor you," Ashur said quietly, and Ardenai shook his head and smiled.

"No, Ashur, they honor you. The Affined Equi Worlds reserve their highest accolades for those who sacrifice themselves as scientists and teachers. As I told Eridu yesterday, your world is about to change, and this is just the beginning."

Kehailan stood at a respectful distance, but within earshot for him, appearing to look at other things, and watching Eridi moving restlessly on the lounge under her father's cold scrutiny. The four of them had arrived at Eridu's sumptuous apartments when Eridu had said they were to be there and he had immediately begun caterwauling about those who supposedly came in friendship and then showed up on his doorstep as an armed mob to make sure he couldn't speak to his beloved daughter in private – probably because they feared she would break out of their control and return to his loving arms … or some such nonsense that had made Kehailan want to slap him. Konik and Ah'nis had obligingly stepped just outside the door, but Kehailan had stayed inside – far enough away to maintain their privacy, of course. He stood now, studying a colorful, robotic bird maundering in a cage and wondering if it had ever had a counterpart in the wild.

"Where is my mother?" Eridi said at last. "You promised me I could see her if I came."

"I promised you could see her if you came to visit me," he corrected with a sly smile. "If you came only to see your mother, well then, that wasn't our agreement, was it?"

"Father, I am very happy to see you," she smiled, making her hands relax in her lap. "Gifting me to the Dragonhorse opened up a whole new world for me, very literally, and I am more grateful than you will ever know."

"You must tell me the truth. He did have sex with you, did he not? He would not have handed you off to his whelp over there if he hadn't taken your fruit first. Did you like it?"

"He has never laid a hand on me, much less anything more intimate," Eridi replied, maintaining her smile. "He hasn't handed me off to anyone. You must understand ..."

"You know, I'm tired of people telling me I must understand," Eridu retorted. "That piece of shit who thinks he's taking over said it, and now I'm hearing it from you. I don't like that."

Eridi shrugged and pursed her lips, determined to maintain civility. "I can … sympathize. My first little while after I was taken away from the main delegation and put in the hands of the Eloi, I was afraid and suspicious of everything they did to me and for me. There were medical examinations that were invasive and unpleasant. They changed everything I was eating and wearing. For a while I was kind of stunned. Of course they figured out that Samarra was drugging me, and got her away from me and those drugs out of my system, and things got better very rapidly."

"So he did rape you. They repaired your maidenhead during that examination."

"Don't judge others by what you would do," Eridi said shortly, and took a deep breath. "I am as I was when I left here. What I'm trying to tell you is that you chose well for me. The Equi are good people who want what is best for our people as well as their own. Instead of invading us and killing us, they have added us to their government so they can protect us and guide us toward a more productive and sustainable ..."

"You sound like a fucking parrot!" Eridu snapped, getting to his feet and waving a hand over his head. "They say they are here to help us, and how many ships have we seen? Five, and only one has landed. Five! How can they control a planet, help a planet of who-knows-how-many billions with only five ships?"

"It's not the ships, it's the technology," the girl sighed. "You … we could all be dust in less than a minute, of that I have no doubt. And as to there being just five ships – there are many times five, I assure you. I'm sure if you requested it, they would let you tour some of them."

Eridu ignored the suggestion, leaning close to her ear and rolling his eyes toward Kehailan. "You like him, don't you?" He whispered. "I have something you could give him. He would forget everything in the world but you. He would be yours forever. He would beg you to straddle him. He would wet himself just looking at you. He would jerk himself and coat the ceiling as he lay waiting for you. He would be your slave, Eridi."

"Very tempting," she said in a conspiratorial tone, "I do fancy him, you know. I would like to see that, to see what's under those riding britches. He says I'm a child, but you and I both know better, don't we? What is it you want from me in exchange for this 'something' of which you speak?"

"I want you to help me kill the Dragonhorse. Without him, this whole invasion of his would fall apart and we could get back to our lives."

"You really think so?"

"I know so. I backed him down when we were alone in that room, and he admitted as much to me. His people don't want a war with us. They want him gone as much as we do. His only purpose in life is to impregnate women. He is not a leader, he's just a figurehead with good genes."

"I see. Let me think about it while I visit with she who is your wife. I need to know she will support me in this little insurrection, and then I will fully support you."

Eridu began to growl and straightened suddenly from his whispering stance, realizing he was being played. "I would let you see your mother and gladly," he said, "Unfortunately she met with an accident and is no longer taking visitors, or food, OR BREATH!" He spun around and snarled at Kehailan, "Did you think I would let this whore of yours come in here and entrap me? Did you think I would not protect myself from the likes of you?"

He yanked a nasty little pultronel from his robes and fired at Kehailan, who dodged to one side as Eridi jumped up to grab her father's arm and got his opposing fist in her face. Her head snapped back, she connected with the carved stone table, and by that time Kehailan was nearly on top of them. Eridu stumbled over his own feet and fired again as he went down, leaving a deep, bloody burn from the center of Kehailan's chest to just under his left ear, and then brought his elbow down hard in Eridi's ribcage as he landed. "I will kill you both!" he screamed, kicking the stunned Equi off him and trying to get to his feet to use his weapon again. "I will kill you both!"

At that moment Konik rolled through the door, came up firing, and Eridu ceased to move. Ah'nis ran to Eridi, and Konik pinched the crys-tel around his neck. "We have wounded," he said. "Pick up every life sign in this room, heartbeat or not." In ten seconds they were all on the scramble platform of Dragonhorse.

"Where is Pythos?" he said, trying with his hand to stop the blood running from the side of Kehailan's neck.

"On the surface, helping the Firstlord," Cutter said from his post on the bridge.

"Get him here now. We have two people in critical condition."

At that moment they heard hyper-telepathic Ardenai, panic in his usually calm voice. "What has happened to Kehailan?"

"He's alive, but he's been shot," Konik said. "Where are you?"

"On Belesprit. I'll be right there."

The Firstlord turned to Ashur and the others, eyes wide with alarm. "You will have to trust me," he said. "Timothy, in this order, put me on Dragonhorse, put Pythos and Moonsgold on Dragonhorse. Put the cases on your ship and the plants and the building itself … everything … anything … in any cargo bay that will hold them. Now. You will be safe here ..." and he was gone.

"Keep her very flat," Ah'nis was saying to a pair of corpsmen as Ardenai materialized. "I think her ribs are broken, and she is having trouble breathing. He may have broken her jaw or her teeth."

Ardenai dropped to his knees beside Konik, who was compressing the side of Kehailan's neck. "Can you do that as I pick him up?" Ardenai asked, then looked around in momentarily puzzlement. "Where are Moonsgold and Pythos? They were supposed to be here."

"We're having a little trouble locating their signal. I think they're underground somewhere. I have sent Hunter to find them and get them out in the open," Cutter's voice replied.

"Thank you," Ardenai said, picked Kehailan up as carefully as he could, and together he and Konik carried him to the sanecere bay.

Ardenai took a towel from a stack on the counter, Konik moved his hand, and Ardenai applied pressure to the jagged wound. "You know how to do this, you don't need me," Konik said, taking another towel to wipe his bloody hands as he activated his crys-tel. "Cutter, I don't know whether Eridu is alive or dead, but lock him up, and someone needs to keep an eye on him until I get there."

"Precious Equus ... what happened?" Ardenai winced, pushing the burnt edges of Kehailan's tunic away from the wounds. "What did you two find out there?"

Kehailan's face contorted momentarily and his eyes came open with a gasp and a snarl. "Whatever you think you're after, you're not," his father said, putting a firm hand to his chest. "Hold still. You're losing a lot of blood and thrashing around isn't going to help any."

Kehailan's eyes closed and he took a deep, shuddering breath. "Eridi," he mumbled. "You told me to take care of her ...." To his father's growing consternation he groaned slightly, and went out again.

"Again I ask, what happened, Senator Konik?"

"I'm really not sure," he admitted, "I only got into the room when the shooting started, and Eridu was the one doing it. What got it started, I do not know."

Moonsgold arrived beside the bed and put his hand over Ardenai's to move the towel. "Ouch," he said cheerfully. "You know they're not going to let you two play together anymore after this. Here, let's see if we can get that royal blue blood of yours to stay where it belongs." He went very efficiently about cutting away Kehailan's uniform and cleaning and cauterizing the wounds, and Ardenai stepped to one side and breathed a sigh of relief. Moonsgold had such a way of making things seem less awful. At that point it penetrated his brain that Eridi, too, had been injured, and he came to stand at the foot of her bed. He could see the ragged rise and fall of her chest. He could also see the grim look on Pythos' face. "How is she?" he whispered.

"When Eridu hit her ... he broke her neck," Pythos said quietly.

Ardenai made a fending gesture and managed, "He what?"

"He hit her hard enough to break her neck," Pythos hissed. "Art thou deaf now, too?"

"Sorry, I'll leave you alone," Ardenai said. He took two steps back and put his fist over his mouth. Why had he been in such a hurry to get this fleet in the air? They were short of doctors, they were short of corpsmen, nurses, pharmacists. Ah'nis was crying – helping as best she could while she did, and it made him realize he was doing nothing but annoying Pythos and wringing what the Twelfth Dragonhorse had referred to as his bloodstained little hands. He stopped. *Blaming yourself will do no good,* he told himself firmly, and went back to see if he could help Doctor Moonsgold.

"We're getting all cleaned up here," Moonsgold said, wiping blood away from the furrow the pultronel had ploughed up Kehailan's chest and applying copper integument to help deaden and heal the wound. "We'll just put a kedge here … and another one … here, to help hold things together. Couple more and we'll be done. Tear these off and hand them to me one at a time," he said, handing the Firstlord a roll of tape strips.

Ardenai watched Pythos working on Eridi, trying to save her life – trying to set her neck so she could breathe properly, watched two Medtechs arrive from another ship with more equipment, watched Moonsgold bandaging Kehailan's wounds, hiding the blood and the burns, heard him say, "Cover him, He'll be shocky," as he turned from Kehailan and applied his skill to saving Eridi. And while Ardenai was watching and doing what he was told, sliding his son's field boots off and wrapping a blanket around him, touching his face lightly as he slept away the pain, he was trying to wrap his head around the idea that a man would deliberately hit his child hard enough to break her neck. Eridu, had broken his beautiful, intelligent sixteen-year-old daughter's neck.

He was pretty sure Konik had killed Eridu, and he was pretty sure he didn't care, but he decided he'd go and check. He stepped into the hall and said, "Where did they take him?"

"They're in the brig," Cutter said, knowing who he meant. "How are the Captain and Princess Eridi?"

Ardenai wasn't used to hearing Kehailan referred to as "The Captain," and just for a moment it caught him off guard. Kehailan, had changed these last seasons. He really had. Growing into the role of eldest son of the Firstlord of Equus. He had become this charming, surprising young man, and now somebody had shot him. Why? What had he done?

To his vast surprise and, he admitted, his momentary disappointment, Eridu was alive, groaning on a bunk with Konik sitting on the bunk across from him, watching. "He yet lives," Ardenai remarked with a slight grimace of distaste.

"Only because you told me not to kill him," Konik said, looking up at the Firstlord. "I did shock the shit out of him. How are Kee and Eridi?"

"We don't know yet," Ardenai said. He stood over the bunk and pushed down on Eridu's left shoulder to flatten him onto his back, eliciting a moan of pain. "And here we are again," he said through his teeth. "What happened, Oh Most Wise Lord Eridu? Why did you shoot my boy?"

Eridu put the back of his hand on his forehead and sighed as if it were all too much to bear. "He was trying to rape Eridi. I left them alone to go and get Eridi's mother, and when I came back, he was mounting her. I had to shoot him to save her."

"You must have been horrified indeed," Ardenai said. "So, how did Eridi come to have a broken neck?"

Eridu didn't even react to the news. "Kehailan must have broken it when he tried to subdue her. He will pay for this. The penalty for the rape of a child is death. We are all Equi citizens. He will have to pay the price."

"You're quick, I give you that," Ardenai said, backing away to sit next to Konik. "You shot my son, and you broke your own daughter's neck, Eridu. The print of that ring on your right hand is square in the middle of her poor mouth. You pathetic aberration of a man. You broke your daughter's neck!"

"You broke my son's neck, what is the difference? Your son was raping my daughter. I will swear to it."

Ardenai began to bunch up and snarl deep in his throat. "It's pretty hard to rape someone with your pants on, you lying ..."

"Dragonhorse," Konik said in a warning tone, and his arm came across the Firstlord's chest. *If you come up off this bunk I will stun your ass to save your soul, you know I will.* The voice became audible again. "You have no reason to kill him. Let me rephrase. You have no legal reason to kill him. You now embody the law on this planet, and for all intents and purposes, this planet is now Equus. Take this same situation, set it in the Great House. What are you going to do?"

"Put Bashkir in here with him and turn my back for an hour?"

"Bashkir's not here," Konik said, dropping the same arm around Ardenai's shoulder. "Let's go find Teal instead. Just as big, twice as deadly."

"No," Eridu groaned. "I am an Equi citizen, I have rights."

"I'm glad we're capturing this," Konik said, "that comment will play well on the cosmoscope. I'll lock him down and file the statement he just made. I will also file mine. When either of the two he put in the sanecere bay wakes up, we'll take their statements and find an adjudicator to hear the evidence, or just hold him until the Military Governor gets here."

"I think he's already here," Ardenai said blandly. "I just need to figure out what to bribe him with so he'll take the job."

"What if nobody believes me?" Eridu whispered. "Me, a poor prisoner of war?"

"Then you will be exiled," Ardenai said, "and I have a couple of places in mind that would suit you just fine. I know it would suit me to send you there. Araneans would just love you. Tender and juicy."

Kehailan was waking up when he got back – blinking hard and gasping as he tried to turn his head on his neck. "Hi," he said as his sire bent over him.

"Hi. Can I ask how you feel without getting a smart answer like, 'with my fingers'?"

"You're no fun," Kehailan said, trying to swallow. He was still groggy, and Ardenai supported him enough to get some warm cider down his throat before easing him gently back on the bed and raising the head a little. "As Gideon would say … Thanks, Dad … I like that. Dad. Probably not appropriate for the Thirteenth Dragonhorse. How is Eridi?"

"Both my sons can call me Dad," Ardenai smiled. There was a pause. "It will be awhile yet before we know anything about Eridi. Can you tell me what happened?"

"She's bad, isn't she?" he said, fixing his sire with a rather bleary look.

"Yes, but Pythos is doing his best. Here, drink a little more of this. How did you two end up in this mess?"

"Good question," he said sipping at the warm drink and knitting his brows in an effort to concentrate. He was supposed to be somewhere right now – where was that? "Technicians … I think. Is that my next meeting?"

"Kee? Would you rather just sleep? This can wait." His father eased him back down onto the pillows, and Kehailan waggled a forefinger.

Shaking his head was definitely out.

"No. I'm good. We went to see Eridi's father because he told her ... she told us … he told her she could see her mother. He tried to bribe her with some kind of sex potion … to give me … to get her to kill you. I think." Kehailan paused and closed his eyes for a minute. "I hope this is making sense, I have a kicking headache. Anyway … what did happen? Ah … Eridu told Eridi her mother had met with a fatal accident … I am drawing such a blank … he called Eridi a whore … said we were trying to manipulate him, which she was, of course … something, I forget … whipped out that Narga pultronel and took a shot at me, then punched Eridi because she tried to stop him. He fell somehow, not sure how he did it, and as I lunged for him he shot at me, and this time he hit me … I felt the jolt … and here I am. A full-on failure as a bodyguard. Neither of your sons is a decent bodyguard. Sorry."

"Sounds plausible," Ardenai smiled, then his face hardened. "Eridu says he shot you because you were trying to rape Eridi."

"What?" Kehailan scowled. His father could see the pain pounding behind his eyes as he tried to think. "Oh, of course," he said, and managed a flicker of smile. "Naram or Halaf must have told him that the rape of a child is punished by death. Very clever."

"Very," Ardenai agreed. "You sleep. I abandoned some people rather abruptly on Belesprit … and, by the way, did you find Brak?"

"No. Didn't have a chance. Rat maze down there."

Ardenai patted his shoulder, snugged the blanket around him, and strode off to find Cornwallis Mettenger. Before he put boots on the ground he wanted to make absolutely sure all his documentation was in order. He found Mettenger in the main conference room, coffee in his hand, a slab of pie at his elbow, going over those documents. Ardenai hooked a chair with one foot and sat beside him in a fluid motion that amazed Mettenger. He was convinced and had been for some time that most Equi had no real backbone, that it was more of a heavy, flexible cord. Being able to move like that, proved his point.

Yes, the request to recolonize was here and in good order. Ardenai could proceed at any time. Because of the sterling ecological record Equus could boast, he could proceed in any manner he chose. Blessings of the SGA. Yes, everything was now in order for the full deployment of Interposing Forces, equipment and weapons on Jas. Again, choice of the Thirteenth Dragonhorse. No restrictions.

Mettenger did wonder why Ardenai had gone through all this trouble, jumped through these hoops each in the proper order when he was pretty much the head of the SGA. His word was as close to law as a single entity got, and yet here he was, the obedient servant. And who was he serving? Himself, right? Certainly no one was going to risk crossing him and losing the Affined Worlds as trading partners. The whole idea of the Firstlord made Cornwallis's head hurt, and there he sat in the flesh. The Thirteenth Dragonhorse. An entire civilization was built around the rising of one of these insuperable beings every seven hundred years, and he, Cornwallis Mettenger, could reach out from where he sat and poke one – golden armbands and all. He was almost tempted to try it.

Ardenai took the time to read the documents and make a copy on a crys-tel, which he added to the fine chain he wore around his neck and dropped back inside his sleeveless purple tunic. While he was reading a young man magically appeared with food and something cold for him to drink, and Ardenai said, "Please tell whomever is looking out for me that I appreciate this very much."

"We're all looking out for you," the young man smiled, and was gone.

Mettenger just looked at him. "I don't get it. They would die for you," he said.

Ardenai neither quoted the old platitude nor rolled his eyes. "Strange, I know," he murmured, and gratefully began eating as he worked.

"What is that?" Mettenger asked with a slight grimace of distaste.

Ardenai glanced over and saw the look. "Fresh fruit, raw vegetables, little crispy breads … dressing …." He was no longer looking at Mettenger.

"No, the thick green gunk you're drinking."

"Fresh greens, chilled berries, herbs, spices, a dash of raw honey. You should try some, it's very good. Good for you, good for your stamina and your waistline." The rather pointed comment ended the conversation and Mettenger finished his pie in silence, still watching Ardenai out of the corner of one eye.

Fascinating man. Had four different documents open in front of him, a graph and two maps, plus something Holofernes had sent him just a few minutes ago. At the same time he was talking to someone telepathically, Mettenger could tell by the way he tipped his head slightly to the left, toward his dominant hand, and his eyes lost just a hint of focus. He smiled, so whatever it was, it was good news. A minute and a couple bites of food later he tapped open the transmitter in the center of the table and Ulric Hamar's roached head and tattooed face spun into view.

"Dragonhorse. How does the Dragon-son?"

"He'll be all right with a little rest," Ardenai smiled. "How are things aboard Dragonhorse Amberia?"

"You mean the Dragon's Teeth?" Ulric chuckled. "We all know who got what label. Things are fine here. How may I serve you this day, First-lord?"

"Did you pick up the Lebonathis we set down on Lebonath Tras?"

"We did. They're all accounted for and in good health. I've sent for an Amberian confinement vessel, but for now we've squeezed our troops onto two carriers and we're using the third as a containment center. It seems to be working well."

"So, if you had three carriers to begin with, how many soldiers do you have available?"

"I can put forty-five hundred highly trained troops on the ground at your command. You can have fifty thousand SGA troops in twenty-four hours, and I can have twenty thousand more Amberian troops here in two days."

"I'll take the forty-five hundred for now. I want them in Dragonhorse uniforms, and I want them armed and in light harness underneath. Our documentation is now in order and we're going to start through that city down there from the center out and we are going to figure out exactly what and who is in, over and under it – not by looking at pictures, but by looking into the faces of its citizens."

"Looking for something in particular?"

"Many things, though in the process I am seeking a particular man," Ardenai said, "and I'm afraid … we may not like what we find."

"Sir, when do you want your troops?"

"First light for the city – and I will trust you to put ground commanders in place. You know your troops, I don't. Have them report to Master Captain Teal for my instructions."

"I will. Thank you," Hamar nodded. The image vanished.

Mettenger looked puzzled. "Shooting war?"

Ardenai leaned back in his chair, folding his arms and tapping the nail of his left middle finger against the gold band on his right arm. It made a slight click, click, click, like the tick of a clock, and Mettenger found it unsettling. The man was staring at the table, working his teeth gently against one corner of his lower lip, as he often did. Was he thinking, or was he talking to someone? Was he planning strategy, or plotting mayhem? In any case, he had the keys to the kingdom, two big, golden keys – one imbedded permanently in each arm. Click, click, click. What would it be like to have that kind of power? How tempting would it be?

"The thing that concerns me most," Ardenai said suddenly, reaching for his glass, "is civil war. One faction jockeying for position against another, and how to discern when that is the case and when it is a genuine alliance with us. As Teal says, I need to get a lot more out in the open before I can make any judgments. These people are suspicious. They are used to being used, and being betrayed, and seeing underhanded, secretive and manipulative strategies employed to gain the advantage. I do not want to do any of those things. But large numbers of troops? No. I have firing platforms. We can take out an individual, or an army. True power rests in the arms of trust, and what I need people for, is to make this personal. Someone who feeds them, defends women's rights, sees that children get safely to school. Anyway, excuse me," he said, unwinding out of the chair, "I have a job unfinished that is amongst the most important of all." And he left, taking his dishes with him. Mettenger just sat there, wondering if anybody was going to bring him more pie.

Ardenai did not go directly back to Belesprit. He went first to the sanecere bay and looked in on Kehailan, who was getting a transfusion, Marion Eletsky sitting beside him talking about something that was making both of them chuckle, and then in on Eridi, who still had five people standing around her working and speaking in hushed tones. Ah'nis looked up at him, and he gestured for her to come over. She nodded, excused herself and made it almost all the way to him before she burst into tears and fell into his arms in an exhausted, sobbing heap.

He took her to a spot where they could sit together and just held her and let her cry. For a long time he remembered what color blue the couches were against the white walls, and what kind of flowers were on the table beside them, and the big, exotic plant in the pot in the corner, and that Ah'nis smelled, not of incense, but of nervous sweat. "She's my baby," Ah'nis kept saying, "She's my baby." This woman who had given up having babies to serve Eladeus, was losing the baby Eladeus had given her, and she could not understand. Ardenai could not understand. But he remembered that hour, because he had, for the first time in his life, set his head against that of a mighty priestess and together they had begged for the life of that child. The transcendence of that supplication, beyond anything in the material universe, changed him – changed forever his view of the Eloi and their power, and made him a willing part of who they were.

What time was it? Ardenai couldn't believe it hadn't been days or weeks since he had left Belesprit so abruptly, but it hadn't. It had been four hours and fifteen minutes, exactly, from the time he left, until the time he reappeared on the scramble pads and trotted off to the cargo bay with Timothy McGill beside him. "I feel terrible," he said. "I told these people I would honor their decisions and then did something absolutely radical without even asking."

"I think they understood," Tim said. "Things seem to be fine, though I did kind of … override something you told me to do." He looked apologetically out of the corner of his eye and hunched down comically into his collar.

"Kind of?" Ardenai drawled, looking down at him. Tim was neither very tall, nor particularly sturdy looking, but possessed of striking intelligence and one of the most beautiful smiles Ardenai had ever seen. He and Kehailan were long time working partners, often lovers and always fast friends, and the Firstlord liked him very much. He'd thought, at least until recently, that if Kehailan were to settle down and marry someone, it would be Tim. Ardenai would have approved.

"Well, kind of ... kind of, if you know what I mean," Tim said, and laughed. "I didn't bring up the plants and the shed. I wanted to make sure I'd heard you correctly. I did ask Dragonhorse Five to send down extra personnel to guard everything. I'm sorry. It ... I'm a botanist, you know, and it just seemed, if you'll pardon the term, unwise, to yank everything out of the ground in the heat of the day and hope we could find the right kinds of pots and the right kinds of soil to keep them alive. And why bring up the shed and not the plants? That's why I thought maybe I'd misunderstood, and I didn't want to disturb you until I knew Kee was out of danger."

Ardenai reached out and pulled Tim to him as they walked, giving him an affectionate kiss on top of his head. "Thank you for couching that so politely. I know I was stressed, but I should have been thinking better than that."

Tim slowed down their pace and said quietly, "To see their reaction when I decided to ignore part of what I'd been told to do by the Thirteenth Dragonhorse, just because I thought it was a hasty decision on your part, was very interesting, and very telling."

Ardenai stopped in front of the huge doors to the cargo bay. "How so?"

"They begged me to do what you had told me to do, even though they agreed with me that it was the wrong thing to do. They were afraid for me, of what you would do to me."

"Bless their hearts," Ardenai said softly. "We do have a very long way to go, don't we?"

"And ... they're afraid to leave the cargo bay."

Ardenai just shook his head and chuckled, but he was quailing inside. If he couldn't reach the most intelligent and open of these people, how in the name of the Creator Spirit was he going to reach the rest of them? Everyone was giving him so much credit for being wise, and yet he knew little of suspicion and less of poverty. He had always had unlimited access to economic, social and informational resources, never had to ask what anything cost except in terms of emotion or responsibility. These people weren't even having their most basic needs met. How could one climb a ladder if all the rungs in the middle had been destroyed? How was it even remotely possible to apply force to get people to give up being suspicious? It was an oxymoron which escaped even the Thirteenth Dragonhorse. Most especially the Thirteenth Dragonhorse, he thought glumly.

"Still worried about Kee?" McGill asked, and Ardenai realized they were still arm in arm, still stopped in front of the cargo bay doors.

"No. I am worried about these people," he said, and briefly told Tim what had been going through his mind.

"Not all SGA member planets are wealthy," Tim said reasonably. "Remember what you just said. You have unlimited access to informational resources. Use them."

"Right now let's start with the five people we have in here," Ardenai agreed. "We have someplace we need to be, and we're running out of time." He wheeled McGill back around beside him, and they went through the cargo bay doors together.

"Stress is stress, good or bad, and transition, no matter how welcome, is never easy," Ardenai said, extending his hands in apology. "I asked you to trust me and then abandoned you, and now I must ask that you come with me quickly, as there is something I want you to see, and be a part of," he smiled, gesturing toward the exit. "Doctor McGill is more than capable of taking good care of your work, as he has already demonstrated in the face of my panic. Again, I am sorry. What we suffer willingly ourselves we cannot bear to see our children suffer."

They didn't move a muscle. Didn't say a word. They just sat in a somber row and looked at him.

Ardenai cocked a quizzical eyebrow at Tim, who shrugged. "They're terrified?" he suggested under his breath.

"Perhaps a small assist is in order," Ardenai murmured. *Tim, can you hear me?* McGill looked startled. *I see that you can. Please launch Dominus and then put the six of us on board.* McGill nodded and left, and Ardenai sat down next to Ashur. "Did all the cases arrive in good order?"

"You … haven't killed him yet," Ashur managed, "but you will, when he least expects it."

"Who, Eridu? No, though believe me I wanted to. Broke his own daughter's neck, shot my son for no reason ..."

"Doctor McGill."

Ardenai gave Ashur a full-on look of incredulity. "Precious Equus, why would I kill Timothy?"

"We assume," Isin said, "that since you have what you want, you will kill all of us, and we understand. We are ready. But if you would, please spare Umma."

"This is just ..." and they scrambled. "Crazy," Ardenai finished, stepping to the pilot's seat of Dominus. "Get that look off your faces, you're not hurt. Sit down. Play with the food replicator. Go take a bath. Replicate new clothes. I don't care what you do. I'm going to have a glass of wine and listen to music. I may sing. I may have two glasses of wine. I don't understand you, and I'm rapidly reaching the place where I don't understand me, either. If that happens we will all be in a lot of trouble. Go on, do whatever you want." He made the clicking noise with his tongue that he used to move horses, and flipped his hands forward. "Shoo." He took a deep breath and added, "Larsa, there's a machine in the back that will give you whatever clothing you need for Umma. Just tell it what size." He flipped his hand again. "Go. I need to quiet the voices in my head."

For a while, they just watched him, half expecting a sudden burst of temper, expecting to be jettisoned out into space, for that is where they found themselves. Going where, they did not know, and the big Equi was not speaking. He poured himself something slightly darker than the color of his tunic from a bottle which appeared from a machine when he asked for it, moved a hand and filled the space with unfamiliar but beautiful music and closed his eyes, sipping his drink and following the rhythm with the fingers of his left hand.

Finally, when he did no more than he said he was going to, which included ignoring them, they got up and began to move around. Larsa went to the back of the clipper, because that is where Ardenai had said she would find clothing for Umma, and Umma needed changing. In a few minutes she was back, eyes shining, beckoning to the others. "Come and see this!" They followed her, and stood staring in amazement. There was water. A whole pool of water. There was a sense of trees and rocks, beautiful projections on the walls that made it feel as though they were deep in a forest, the likes of which they had never seen. The water itself was moving, trickling melodiously into the main pool, which was huge, at least six feet wide and ten feet long, enough water for their plants for months.

Is this what he had meant by "take a bath"? He wanted them to get in here? All of them together? They looked at each other. It could be acid that would dissolve them, bones and all. It could be charged, and when they got in they would all be electrocuted. Larsa looked longingly at it. How wonderful it would be to bathe Umma in that clean, sweet smelling stuff. She sighed and looked for a machine that could produce clothing. That seemed unlikely in itself. But he had said it was here.

"Look." And he was there, smiling. His eyes were large, and a beautiful color, but he had pupils like a poisoness snake. It belied the sweet smile and gentle voice. "Over here. Just talk to it. How much does she weigh, how long is she?"

"I'm not sure," Larsa admitted.

Ardenai put out his hands. "Give her to me," he said. He hadn't hurt the baby before. She knew he'd just take her anyway, so she handed Umma over to him. He extended her in his arms. "Twelve pounds, and about six hands – twenty-four inches. Tiny for a babe nearly eight months old." He promptly handed her back, spoke to the replicator, and was gone. In a few moments Umma had clean changing rags and a close-fitting one piece garment that stretched easily and fit her well. Larsa wondered if it would have hurt to give her baby a bath in that wonderful pool.

They had just over an hour to explore this miraculous clipper ship, with its food, its music, its maps and books which appeared at the appropriate motion. Umma had a nice nap on a huge, luxurious bed that was dressed all in white and maroon, with soft pillows and clothes like a breath of cool air.

Ardenai said almost nothing except to give them the occasional instructions on how to get or find something. He spent much of the time with his eyes closed, listening to music as he said he would, only his grip on his wine glass telling them he was awake.

There was a quiet chime, and the ship slowed. The Firstlord sat up straight, set his glass aside, and concentrated on the panel in front of him as a green ball streaked with blue filled the viewing screen. “Lebonath Tras,” he said. “I wanted you to be the first Lebonathi civilians to set foot on her, since you have done so much to preserve what you could of her past. Teal, are you down?”

“Just releasing our pods,” said a somewhat lighter voice. “Are you close?”

“We are. Please give us another ten minutes or so.”

They watched with mingled disbelief and effervescing hope as the planet ceased to be round and gained definition, the sky went from black with stars to clear blue, the landscape ceased to be flat and became mountains, grasslands, forests, lakes – blues and greens of the kind they had only seen in the books they had hidden away. A much larger ship appeared below them and to one side, and they settled close by with a gentle hiss and thump as the landing pods deployed.

Another Equi, Ardenai’s height but thicker of chest and arms hailed them as the door opened. He came to embrace the Firstlord, then turned to them with a beautiful slow smile which lit his eyes. “Ahimsa, I wish thee peace,” he said. “I am Teal, Master Captain. Please, set your feet on the planet you have waited so long to see.”

They crept out like animals released from a cage after long capture, and Teal and Ardenai exchanged a glance. Had these people ever seen a meadow, felt ground that wasn’t burning dust, seen a waterfall, a pool, a river running over rocks? There was a noise from inside the bigger ship and Ashur placed himself in front of the others. "What is in there?" he asked suspiciously.

"Horses," Teal said simply. "Give the baby to the Firstlord."

"Why?" Larsa asked, knowing the answer. They were going to be fed to the … horses … but her daughter was going to be spared. Or was she going to be fed to them first, as some sort of sacrifice?

"Because," Teal said patiently, "When she is a very old woman she will be able to tell her great grandchildren that she was held in the arms of the Thirteenth Dragonhorse, and watched the release of the first horses on Lebonath Tras."

"I see," the woman said, though it was obvious she didn't. She yielded up the child to Ardenai and stepped aside, off the ramp of the clipper and onto the green grass of the planet.

"Are you ready?" Teal asked, and Ardenai nodded.

"I have been ready for days," he said. "I don't think I've ever been so homesick in all my life."

Teal flipped up a hand, the doors on the side of one end of the craft became a ramp, and with a whistle and a shout, two hundred horses poured out four or five abreast, bucking and snorting, chasing each other across the meadow toward the river, being driven by five men on horseback. Some stopped to graze, some to roll, some went for water, and some just kept on running. "Those are the ones we will keep," Teal said, pointing to the runners. "They will get us started, and then help augment the expedition mounts that will come."

Ardenai just stood there, breathing in the smell of horses, enjoying the feel of the earth as it vibrated with hoofbeats. "What do you think, Umma?" he said, looking at the baby, and she looked back with all seriousness. "These animals will be an integral part of your life, and I think we should go and say hello, don't you?" He set her on his hip and walked toward one of the nearer horses, whistling softly and holding out a hand. A black and white mare responded and came whuffling with a soft nose to explore the laughing baby.

Teal turned to look at the five Lebonathi, who were huddled in a cringing knot. Larsa was sobbing and near hysterics, her hands partially extended, pleading to hold her daughter.

"She's in very good hands," he smiled, ignoring their terror. "Those are horses. They are the heart of the Equi people. They are vegetarians and so are we. This is grass. It's soft and it smells good and invites sitting and lying, or walking and looking. That's a river over there. You can hear it over the rocks. It's nice to wade in. Feel free."

Isin straightened his back and made himself look at the Master Captain. "We are obviously not free. What is our fate?" he asked.

Teal felt an annoyance he didn't show. His grandmother used an old saying he remembered. She'd say, 'waiting for the other boot to drop', and that's what these people were doing – these sad, skinny people – waiting for the other boot to drop. How could they be happy when they'd been hunted all their lives? Why be joyous when you know you're the sacrifice? Why get excited about living when you've faced death every day of your life?

"So, why did you have that baby, anyway?" he asked, picking a tall stalk of grass and peeling it as he watched Ardenai and Umma visit with the old mare.

"That's an odd question," Larsa quavered, wiping her eyes and looking up at him.

"How so?" he said, returning the look. "It's not a whit stranger than asking what your fate is going to be when you are being honored as heroes by the Firstlord of Equus, who is exhausted and who has many other things to do. Ten thousand people are clamoring for his time, his help, and he has given his day to you. Now answer my simple question. Why did you have the baby? And don't tell me she was an accident, because that would be cheating." He began to smile, and Larsa burst out laughing.

"Your fate, will be whatever you want it to be, Larsa. The process of that fate will probably go something like this. You will help us survey the planet over the next few seasons. You will begin to waken the animals, and as you do that you will also make sure you have enough reproductive materials – sperm and eggs, DNA, whatever – to assure a viable population.

You will spend time figuring out, based on their chemistry and adaptation, which animals are from which planet, and you will decide whether you want to transplant all of them up here for the time being, or leave those that belong on Lebonath Jas in stasis for another fifty years or so. You will choose where and how you want to live. Do you want to live here with AEW and Lebonathi colonists and have a big garden and raise Umma in an unspoiled paradise while you practice your science, or do you want to live on Lebonath Jas in a secure facility and be part of the sweeping and exciting changes?"

"Forgive our skepticism," Etana said. "We were relieved, even happy when you invaded our world, and we are thrilled to be part of this, but at the same time we have even less than we had this morning. We cannot go back to where we were. Too many people saw this big white ship. They will think we have something worth taking and they will make the effort to climb up the side of that mountain and take it."

"Your home is in no danger for the moment, though I don't want you going back there except to pack." Ardenai said, walking back to the group with the baby and the horse, who was tagging along behind. "Think of it as being between homes. I have a place I want to show you. Or, to be more precise, I want Teal to show you here in the next day or so that I think might be to your liking for now. Might even be a good spot for a research facility, constructed off planet and dropped in place so you can get right to work. You will be joined by many hundreds, even thousands of people from the AEW: farmers, agronomists, orchardists, scientists – because it's going to be your immediate job to feed your sister planet until she can get back on her feet and choose a direction in which to go."

He handed the baby to Larsa and watched Elam reaching to stroke the horse's neck. "She likes you," he said admiringly. "You have a gentle and natural hand."

"Nee inz boonifl," he smiled. "Nee mellz guh, nu." He looked from the old mare to the Firstlord and put a self-conscious hand over his mouth.

"I love the smell of horses," Ardenai agreed. "I'm actually going to catch one and ride about for a bit, if Teal will be so kind as to take you back to Belesprit. In the morning, we will begin to repot your plants and pack up your facility."

Teal looked concerned. "You're not going. Do you not feel well? Are you worried about Kee? Marion says he's resting comfortably."

Ardenai held up a placating hand. "Don't fuss. It's been five days since I've slept, and I'm starting to hear voices in my head – everybody's conversations – can't seem to shut them out, especially after hearing Kehailan this morning. I really need some quiet. As a matter of fact, if you'll throw a blanket out as you go, and perhaps a stale flatwrap, I will go sleep under those trees tonight."

"How about a bottle of wine to go with that?" Teal chuckled. "Let me put these good people on Belesprit for the night. I will be back with dinner and gear, and we will both sleep under those trees tonight, pretending that we are home on Viridia, camping in the canyon caves, listening to the river like we did when we were boys, and neither of us will hear voices other than our own."

CHAPTER 5

There were another hundred spots marked on the map. Forty-five uniforms per destination. They would fan out from there and continue taking the first AEW census of Lebonath Jas. It was going to take seasons, Ardenai knew that. This was one city. The planetary capital to be sure, but one city out of five huge cities and dozens of smaller ones on this oddly populated little world. It wasn't that there were too many people for the planet – not the case at all. In fact the planet itself was very sparsely populated. The problem was the distribution of people, and the lack of resources available to them in their present configuration.

The Lebonathis had packed themselves tighter and tighter together, driven by intense heat and who knew what else, until now they occupied only the northern-most of the four huge continents while the others stood empty. Sweltering, denuded deserts full of abandoned cities, towns and what had been farms at one point in time. Huge, dead orchards, scrubby remnants of toppled forests, empty lakes and river beds, empty factories, buckled highways and airfields. It was as if gravity was sucking them closer and closer together – as if they feared any kind of emptiness or privacy. In some ways, that was Ardenai's only hope for anything resembling an accurate census and assessment of the most pressing needs of the Lebonathi people, but it was the "who knew what else," that had him worried. None of this – none of it – felt like something a rational population would do on its own.

Teal had advised him to stop trying to solve the problem and just observe it awhile – narrow the focus – put efforts where they would do the most people the most good. Establish a positive presence. Ardenai was hoping a census would help accomplish that. His biggest worry was that people who had lived in cities all their lives were now scattering into the countryside to loot, pillage, kill and ultimately succumb to the awful heat and lack of water. Much as he hadn't wanted to deploy troops to occupy, he knew he was going to have to, and Teal had agreed. Ardenai had already called up the additional Amberian troops Ulric Hamar had promised, and the SGA was sending another thirty thousand.

He'd told the worlds of the AEW to scout agronomy teams, husbands and wives, families who would be willing to colonize, or at least stay on Lebonath Tras for an extended period of time to plant orchards, vineyards and the vast fields that were going to be needed to feed the people of Lebonath Jas. He also had people out searching for any farmers who might be left. The Lebonathi had food, barely, and of no real quality, but there was food. Somebody had to be raising it. Sensors told them there were huge operations underground – miles of tunnels devoted to mushrooms and long, white tubers, grown in humanure, caronai dung, and dust. On the surface were endless orchards of dates. Not high enough in nutrients to make up for the rest of the miserable food supply, but able to withstand the blistering heat and lack of water, which made them priceless. And then there were the caronai – something Marion Eletsky had described as hornless water buffalo … almost. Cadence's wife Merrilina had described them as giant swine … sort of. Whatever their origins, they were awesome in their ability to live off what turned out to be blocks made of human waste, mushroom spawn, and date palm leaves. One of the teams had brought a block to Ardenai and broken it open for him. "One minute," he'd managed, bolted to the nearest lavage, and lost his breakfast.

The caronai, for all their miraculous properties, had to go. And with their manure, went the mushrooms. Even Equus and the Affined Worlds couldn't feed all these people for very long without them, so six enormous, obsolete continental terraformers were being moved in, courtesy of the

Menorquins, who had converted them to farm ships years ago and now dispatched them as necessary around the AEW. They were a blessing, but a stopgap in the face of the real problems – the population density in a tiny area on Lebonath Jas, the total, discernable lack of any sort of distribution system to serve the population, and the obvious lack of anyone who cared.

As the Amberians and others went out today they would again be asking how many children in the home? Girls, boys? How many parents or grandparents? Did they need anything? Were they safe? Did they have adequate food and water? Each household was handed a sheet of rules that needed to be followed: don't beat your wife, don't keep your children out of school, don't kill anybody – simple, drastic, counter-cultural things – along with information as to where to obtain medical care, food and clean drinking water, which was currently being hauled in part from Lebonath Tras. How long could that go on before it began to affect that planet? Not long.

The priestesses were everywhere, it seemed, working with the anchoresses to form an uneasy but ever-strengthening alliance, trying to make inroads with the male priesthood – the flamen – who had turned out to be their most implacable and vociferous enemy so far. Together priestesses and anchoresses were setting up separate, secure schools for the girls, and big neighborhood kitchens and saneceres to help feed and care for people and keep them from becoming refugees, because on this planet, there was no place for refugees to go. In all those things, they tried to build trust, which was the hardest job of any. "True power rests upon trust," became the mantra of the interposing forces, and Ardenai woke whispering it in the middle of the night.

It was with the Eloi that Io was most involved, and Ardenai saw little of his wife. An occasional kiss in passing, a rare hour to make love. But she wasn't herself these days, and Ardenai was worried. When they had intercourse she got false signals of pregnancy, which ruined the pleasure for both of them, and wearing skins didn't seem to help. He had asked her to go and talk to Pythos and she had brushed him off like a horsefly, so he had gone to Pythos and asked him to make sure she was well. She'd had enough recent pain in the loss of their daughter, pretending that nothing was wrong now could only make matters worse. For once, Pythos had agreed with the Firstlord.

Kehailan was on the mend and back to his duties as Captain of Dragonhorse Equus, though Moonsgold had told him he was doing too much too soon. Pythos had rolled his yellow eyes and hissed something about fathers and sons and to save his breath. Kehailan found time during the day and in the evening to sit beside Eridi and read to her, or speak quietly to her about the day's events, and when he was not with her, Ah'nis usually was.

Io had firmly told the priestess not to feel guilty. Her place was with Eridi, whose place was with her people, not occupying space in the dirt of Lebonath Jas. The girl had not awakened, but her vital signs were steady and growing stronger, and those who cared for her had a rosy image of her opening her eyes one morning and asking for a nice cup of tea.

Those who cared for her did not seem to extend to her father. He had been offered the chance to see her and had turned it down, saying it was all too painful for him. He had refused to tell them where Eridi's mother was, saying it would put her in danger. Konik and company had turned Eridu's apartments inside out and found nothing, and then moved on to the smaller apartments of his wives and concubines. A few of them were loyal, a few were terrified – all were taken into custody and moved to a safer location at the edge of the city with their children. One woman said she had heard Eridi's mother screaming one night, and then nothing. But no one could, or would, corroborate her story. Eridu stuck to his story of Kehailan trying to rape Eridi despite overwhelming physical evidence to the contrary, and he remained in custody, calling himself a poor prisoner of war for whom no one cared.

That part seemed true enough. Though it had been widely publicized that he had been arrested, he'd had no visitors, and no one in the streets seemed to be wailing or gnashing their teeth over it. The High Council members who had occupied the apartments closest to him had, for the most part, left the city for their country estates, and left their people without leadership.

Oddly enough, it was Naram, Nuntius d'affaires, sneering and cynical, who remained available and at least vaguely reasonable. It was he who spoke for justice, and against martial law, and stood up for the Lebonathi and their way of life. It was he who actually had some knowledge of the upper class and some thought for the lower.

What they had discovered to their consternation was that the upper class knew about the upper class. The poor knew about the poor. Religious knew religious. The soldiers knew about the soldiers, males about males, females about females. There seemed to be no middle class at all, very little in the way of a mobile merchant agrarian class upon which Equus was based, along with most of her affined worlds, and again Ardenai wanted to pound his head against the wall for lack of understanding.

Each night now he returned to Lebonath Tras to sleep in a bower under the trees, leaving the clipper half a mile away and walking or catching a horse to ride bareback to his spot beside a deep, waterfall fed pool in a small river of leisurely pace. And he would swim, and sleep in the uncanny silence, and the voices in his head stayed at bay in that manner. Usually Teal went with him, because he, too, heard voices – those of the Lebonathi, which nobody else seemed to be able to hear in their heads, and he needed as much as Ardenai did, to shut those voices off so he could rest. They carved out a little time to laugh and sing, wrestle and run in the meadows, and explore on foot in the evening, or go riding, and speak of simple, familiar things, because they knew that without that time to rest their minds and exercise their bodies, they would quickly become fatigued beyond function. Io did not ask to go, and had actually refused the opportunity, saying she had meetings which ran late into the evening and a warm bath and a bed indoors was more to her liking. Whether it was all the truth or not, Ardenai accepted it, and was relieved, though he missed her company in more ways than one.

He and Teal also found time to swing by almost every evening to check on their original five scientists, who were setting up shop in the sheltered cove they all referred to as Stone Spring. They had stripped their little shed and gladly abandoned it for a canopied outdoor kitchen and a couple of the big airy pavilions like the one Ardenai and Teal had beside the river. Three members of the Horse Guard who had been transporting the horses to Calumet got out the forge used to shape horseshoes, and using metal brought from Lebonath Jas, they built a pony plow, fashioned some harness, and showed Elam how to use it. He had happily hitched up the black and white mare and tilled a garden space on high ground near the spring. Each day they brought a few more plants from their old place to dig into the fertile soil, and they already had seeds, corms and tubers in the ground to see what would grow and what wouldn't.

Timothy McGill had seen to it that they were provided with solid storage for their maps and such equipment as they had, which was precious little. As it turned out, they were all self-taught. None of them had any formal education at all. Ashur and Isin had taught Etana, and together they had taught Larsa and Elam. One evening Ardenai had casually mentioned that perhaps they would enjoy time on Equus at Lycee for some formal education. While the three older people had smiled and said they were happy where they were for the time being, Elam was excited at the prospect, and Larsa was excited for him. Both Teal and Ardenai had long since decided Elam was the smartest of the bunch, so Ardenai suggested to him in private that perhaps the simple surgery that would allow him to speak more normally was now in order, and promised he would be home in time to water his plants the same evening.

Elam had thought about it, nodded, and the next morning just at dawn had joined them in the clipper for the ride to Dragonhorse. Ardenai had handed him over to Pythos before breakfast, checked in on him at noon while he was sleeping off the sedative, and when he had gone to fetch him to go home in the late afternoon, Elam had met him at the sanecere door, flashed him a beautiful and fully toothed smile, and given him a warm hug. "Thank you," he had said in a voice that was a resonant and surprising bass, "You have enriched my life in more ways than I can ever tell you, and for that I will never be able to repay you enough."

They had dropped him into the arms of his ecstatic partner, and Ardenai had said, "There is one more thing you must do," and they had all gone down to the shore as the sun set, and the Firstlord had married them in a traditional Equi ceremony.

"Now if I could just do more of that," he had laughed, and Teal had nodded his agreement, though he seemed a bit sad around the eyes. When pressed he admitted that he missed that woman he occasionally lived with, and her annoying man-child, and Ardenai had laughed and said he was so homesick he even missed Lionel.

One morning as he and Teal arrived on Dragonhorse from Lebonath Tras, Pythos made that undulation of body in Ardenai's direction that meant, "Come here," and Ardenai stepped to one side as the others were going into their usual morning meeting. Pythos motioned again until they were in a space by themselves and said, "Now don't be alarmed ..."

"Which wouldn't be nearly as likely, if you didn't preface it in that manner," Ardenai replied.

"Fine. I am ssending thy ssweet wife home. Thee iss correct in thinking ssomething iss wrong, and sshe admitss it as well. I think a little … check-up iss in order."

"Achernar?" He had asked, trying not to look as alarmed as he felt. Just the thought of what could be wrong made him cold all over.

"Yess," the serpent replied with a hissy chuckle. "Sshe iss fine, Hatchling. Jusst a little more tuning needed, or sso it sseems. We knew thiss healing might well be accomplisshed in sstages. Let her go home. Let her ssee her sson, and Gideon, and have ssome time at Canyon keep for a bit of a resst. Then if sshe dessiress it, sshe can come back to thee ready to be the wife sshe iss meant to be."

"When is she leaving?" Ardenai asked, already feeling her loss and realizing how much just having her there, knowing she was somewhere close, meant to him every day.

"Thiss afternoon," Pythos said, flicking him with his tongue to ease the pain. "Menorquin hass ssent a clipper with sseedstock for the terraformerss. Sshe will go back with them as far as their ssector, and Basshkir will pick her up there. Cheer up, Beloved. All iss going well. We will ssoon be danccing on our own floor in Ccelebration of Sstormss. If thee wisshes, get a messsage ready and sshe can take it to thy golden eyed sson." He laid a frondy hand momentarily on Ardenai's arm, turned, and went back to the Sanecere to check on Eridi.

Ardenai wondered if it would be a good idea to send Eridi to Achernar, as well, but he realized almost in the same second that she would never make the trip alive. He took a deep breath, and went into the meeting.

Another hundred spots marked on the map of the city, forty-five people per destination. Again, and again and again. Twice Ardenai had joined them, looking in the maze of dark streets, homes that were holes in the basements of old buildings, shops in eternal twilight, dungeons like something out of ancient history, looking for Brak. Asking for word of Brak, saying the Equi sought him for questioning, so as not to endanger him. He wondered if going a third time would do any good. Maybe, just for an hour. Then a message to Gideon, then … goodbye to his wife. A thought struck him.

Nik?

The man's eyes flicked his direction for a moment.

Io is going back to Equus, leaving this afternoon. Would you like her to take...

No. When it is time I will take Ah'davan's body home. Thank you.

As you wish.

He did go again into the bowels of the city. It was slightly cooler, but the stench was nearly unbearable to his outdoorsman's nose. This time they passed through an ancient church that was at street level, used mostly as a thoroughfare between tunnels, both ends having been removed and only the sides and roof in place, and as they walked through Ardenai looked up and saw something he'd never seen before – tall metal tubes, different heights, the shortest higher than his six and a half feet. "What is that?" he asked, not expecting an answer.

The young woman walking beside him followed his gaze and narrowed her eyes. "You know … those look like organ pipes," she said, "or what in my culture we would call organ pipes. I'm Demetrian, so I'm not sure how that would translate. I do know that centuries ago this city was called Carillia, and it was known for its beautiful churches and the beautiful organs inside them. And now look at it."

"I've only seen organs in viewseums," Ardenai breathed, totally enthralled by the possibility, "and never one even remotely this big. I'm going to turn aside and take a look."

"Not by yourself!" she said, and caught herself with a wide-eyed look of apology. "What I meant, Firstlord, was ..."

"Not by yourself. I got it," he grinned. "I was going to drag you along, and these two behind us as well. Gentlemen," he said, turning to walk momentarily backwards, "Are you up for a field trip?"

He studied the walls for a minute, then pointed with his chin toward a set of mostly hidden stairs to their left and in front of them. "Maybe up there? It has to be a place big enough to house something that could power those pipes."

Some of the steps were rotten with age, even in this dry climate, and they made their way with caution up fifteen feet or so to a deck with a solid railing that would hide a short adult, or someone who was seated. It was being used as a storage area, and there were dusty boxes, stacks of ancient, yellowed paper, plain heavy quilts folded haphazardly and stacked high. From what appeared to be the center of the dust and disorder, rose the pipes. "I think we found it," he said. "Let's dig it out."

That took nearly half an hour of careful rearranging, given that the clutter took up most of the space. Ardenai stood there, staring at what they'd uncovered. An enormous triple keyboard in a shape reminiscent of a horseshoe, pedals, control buttons on either side, beautiful wood of a kind the Firstlord had never seen before. "This is magnificent" he whispered. "I wonder what powers it."

"Good question," said the older Amberian who had joined them. "I'm Gerritson, by the way. From the way this looks … it's ..."

"Forced air of some kind?" The Firstlord added, half upside down over the back of the instrument. "I'm Ardenai. Pleased to meet you."

"And I am Dresh," said the younger man, who was keeping an eye out over the balcony.

"Um hmmm." Gerritson narrowed his eyes, partially in thought, partially against the dust filtering down. He thought a long while. "A pump? Bellows, like a forge. Something that would force air up?"

The girl was on her back looking up underneath. "This city was famous for these. Surely someone, somewhere, somehow, still has the knowledge to fix it. Maybe even play it. Can you imagine how this would sound?"

Ardenai burst out laughing, and the church rang with it. "That's it!" he exclaimed, "That's it! That's the missing piece of the puzzle! You, child down there, you're a genius!"

"I'm Ellsbeth, and I'm twenty-seven," she said, but his laughter was infectious, and she had to join in. "What puzzle?" she asked, twisting her neck to look up at him.

He put a foot on each side of her, grasped both her hands and slid her out between his legs before standing her up. "Let me give you a roundabout answer," he said. "All Equi have horses in common. No matter what we do from day to day, we share a common heritage of horses. And music. When we sing, we all sing together, no matter our job, or continent, or age. When we sing, we all sing. Again, a common heritage. Now I ask you, what is the common heritage of the Lebonathi people?" There was complete silence as they looked from one to another. "Add that to the list of questions you ask each and every person you meet, and I'll bet you get the same answer. None. Ellsbeth, say what you said in the first place about the city."

She thought back a moment. "This city, centuries ago … that statement?" Ardenai nodded. "This city was called Carillia, and it was famous for its beautiful churches and the organs in them."

"And that, is the answer to the question," Ardenai said, shaking an index finger. "That is the positive cultural bond. This was a city of beautiful places of worship, and of beautiful music. If we can fix this church, and this organ, we can fix this city. If we can fix the city, we can fix the planet. Ellsbeth, Gerritson, Dresh, how would you like to be on special assignment for me?"

"We are yours to command," Gerritson said with a solemn nod. "How may we serve you, Dragonhorse?"

"You have one simple job," he said. "Find the person ..."

"Who knows how to fix the organ," Ellsbeth said with him. "That should be easy."

"Good. You have until tomorrow morning," he said, and laughed at the look on her face. "Let me know when you do find something, or someone, and I will see that you get the help you need. There is one caveat. I don't want you to find an off-worlder to fix this. It has to be a Lebonathi. And see that this organ is well guarded. We don't want the flamen smashing it to spite us and our efforts."

"As you wish," Gerritson said. The three of them nodded and Ardenai gave them a motion and smile of dismissal.

He was walking back by himself, but he really wasn't concerned. There were other Dragonhorse uniforms on the subterranean streets. As he walked he was thinking. Of all the people he had come across who cared about the culture of the Lebonathi, or at least seemed to, Naram was chief among them. He wondered if the man would take him seriously if he asked for help. Even if he didn't, what could it hurt? It made him chuckle. Amir Cohen used that phrase every once in a while. How was Belesprit doing these days without Marion and Kehailan? He realized he hadn't seen Amir, and wondered if he'd transferred off. He also wondered if the kindergarten class was still intact and on board. Maybe children should talk to children, women to women, men to men.

He was just coming around the corner of a huge, ornate column in the middle of what must have been some magnificent structure, when a small child stepped out of one of the endless, darkened archways to his left and beckoned to him. Ardenai turned, paused, thought. Stepping into the darkness could be the biggest mistake of his life.

"For two seconds in two minutes, be ready," the little boy said, and Ardenai immediately went with him. The child was quick and Ardenai had to trot to keep up, hoping he wasn't going to catch the toe of his boot on something and go sprawling. These floors, streets, alleys … whatever they were, did not look to be clean, and if the smell was any indication, they were filthy. The boy stopped, beckoned again and vanished into a doorway.

Ardenai stepped in behind him. "Ahimsa," he said into the darkness, "I wish thee peace."

"Come with me," said a woman's voice, and he followed a feeble light into a small bedchamber. There on the bed, lay Brak, or what was left of him. He'd been beaten within an inch of his life. His legs lay at unnatural angles, and his thumbs were gone.

"Eladeus!" Ardenai groaned, dropping to his knees beside the bed and looking from Brak to the woman. "Who did this?"

"Eridu," she said. "He found out."

Ardenai touched Brak's neck with his fingers and found a pulse. Again he looked up at the woman. "Where are the members of your household? Are there more than you and the boy?"

"Not anymore," she said.

Ardenai bowed his head and closed his eyes, willing his thoughts to get beyond the depths of the city. *Kehailan?* There was nothing. *Kehailan? I need your help.*

Very faintly came, *I am here.*

Quickly! Scramble all the life signs in this room. Can you do that?

I can try, Dad. Hang on.

"Take the boy's hand and give me yours," Ardenai said. "Now. I was followed." He grabbed Brak's arm just as four Lebonathi Royal Guardsmen burst into the room, and as they began firing, the people in the room vanished.

Ardenai found himself on the scrambleshaft pad on his knees with Brak beside him, the woman and child clinging together and smoke from pultronel fire rising off his left shoulder. "Oh..." he breathed, "Very close, very, very close."

Kehailan's disembodied voice, "Are you there?"

"Yes, thank you. We need corpsmen and a stretcher. Brak is badly injured."

Before the corpsmen Kehailan was there, grasping his father's shoulders and asking, "Are you hurt? Why is there a pultronel burn on your shoulder?"

"I think it's just my uniform. Brak on the other hand ..." He gestured. Kehailan looked, groaned and his face hardened. "His wife says it was Eridu. We've had him in custody awhile, so either these wounds are old or he has others doing his dirty work."

"Which is why you need to declare war on these bastards!" Kehailan said angrily. "You treat them kindly and respectfully and this is what happens. There's a reason we put those platforms in place and you need to start using them."

"You need to calm down," Ardenai said quietly.

"No, I don't!" Kehailan retorted. "You need to ramp up! These aren't your precious horses who respond to kind treatment, or your five-year-olds who respond to new ideas, Sire. There are some evil, hidebound people down there, and you need to start killing them. Look what they've done – to you, to me, to Eridi, to Brak, and Eladeus knows who else! Kill the scum!" He pulled his smoldering eyes off Ardenai's face, nodded curtly to the terrified woman, and stalked off past the corpsmen toward the bridge.

Brak's limp body was carefully gathered up and rushed off, and the woman, who had not so much as blinked since their arrival, began to wail softly and pulled the little boy as tightly as she could in front of her, casting fearful glances after Kehailan and equally fearful glances at Ardenai.

"My son will not hurt you. Despite his words, you're in no danger from us," Ardenai said, but she put her forearms in front of her face, grasping her white hair in her hands, and continued to cry softly and rock back and forth, the clinging child rocking with her.

"Let me think, how long ago was it that I was saying I knew the answer to the puzzle?" Ardenai muttered. "I may have to rethink that." He huffed in frustration. "I may also have to consider the possibility that the Captain, for all his abrasiveness, has a valid point."

Sitting, trying to think of what to say to Gideon and having nothing positive coming to him made Ardenai realize how glad he would be when the relay ships were in place so he could speak directly to him, and see home in the background, with Lionel jumping around on the bed or the desk, and see Gideon's golden eyes, alight with intelligence, dancing as he talked about school, and horses, his grandparents and friends, his latest adventures with Criollo, Ah'brianne and Jasreth, how fat Tolbeth was getting and she wasn't even that far along yet. He cut a small crys-tel consisting mostly of I love you, I miss you, things are going well here … take care of Io for me … and put it in with a small packet of things to go home.

It was nearly time for the Menorquin clipper to leave and Ardenai was concerned that he wouldn't see his wife at all before she left, when he turned down a busy corridor aboard Dragonhorse and there she was, walking toward him in a snow white dress with purple sleeves extending across the shoulders to the neck, bearing the seven chevrons of the Firstlord, and caught at the waist with a silver belt that had a running horse for a buckle. He was used to seeing her in riding britches, but these days, she wasn't riding, she was governing. She was stunning. She took his breath away, and he just stopped and smiled as she hurried toward him.

"I was afraid I was going to miss you," they said together, and shared a kiss, oblivious to the stares and smiles. He noticed she was taller. Heels higher than riding boots under those graceful skirts.

"I am so sorry I have to go," she said, dropping her hands from his neck to his chest. "Pythos thinks it's best."

"I do too," Ardenai said gently, tracing her cheekbone with his fingers. "Your health has to come first, Beloved. Besides, Equus and the AEW need at least one of us at the helm. You have done an amazing job here, and this is far from over. There will be more than enough years for you to spend time in this place."

"I know," she said, turning to walk with him toward the scramble-shaft platforms. "At home I want to start getting things organized for surveys and the laying out of keeps ..."

"That's right," the Firstlord said, "I hadn't really thought too much about that, but you are correct. Study the maps with Krush and Timor, and decide how big they should be and how they should be laid out. Can you do that?"

"My math strategy is pretty good," she chuckled.

"I meant," he said quietly, "Are you going to feel good enough?"

"Of course I am," she smiled. "I don't want you to worry about me. Pythos says it's probably nothing major, and I believe him. I will have plenty of time while I'm resting up to go over your maps and lay things out for you. This is going to be a good opportunity for people who don't own land on

Equus, to become keeplords on Lebonath Tras. Calumet with conveniences. I love it."

"And I love you," he said, putting his forehead against hers. "Please take care of yourself."

"I'm not the one getting shot at," she whispered. "Come home to me in one piece, Ah'krill Ardenai Morning Star."

Someone said her name, telling her they were ready to depart, and with a lingering kiss and a quick wave goodbye she was up on the platform and away with a smile.

▲ ▲ ▲ ▲ ▲ ▲ ▲

"I wanted to bring you up here so we could actually have some peace," Ardenai said. "There's something I've been wanting to talk to you about."

Konik nodded, but his eyes were on the scenery. For the first time since Ah'davan's death he looked relaxed, almost mesmerized as he watched the slow undulation of the grass. Ardenai just smiled and parked himself on an outcrop of rock, enjoying the warm breeze on his face and the tapestry of greens and browns spreading below them, stitched with the blue of the river, backed by the sky. Their horses were blowing quietly behind them, adding their good smell to the fragrances on the wind.

"This is stunning," Konik murmured, coming to sit beside him. "I could sit right here and never stir from this spot – just sprout roots and grow old."

"I know exactly what you mean," Ardenai agreed, breathing deep of the fragrant air. "We're on the edge of the first colony grid. The beginning of all things." He let his eyes close momentarily and turned his face up to the sun. "Teal and I have asked for a keep just down the valley there." He opened his eyes and jerked his chin that direction. "Where that small river passes through the meadows to join the big one. You can barely see our pavilions from here. That corner. Rhax vines, for sure. Who knows what else?"

Konik nodded and was silent a bit. "Pomes," he said, and it was almost a sigh. "I've always wanted to raise pomes … make cider and syrup in the crisp days of Oporens." He took a deep breath and banished the dream from his face. "Assuming, however regrettably, that we are not here to sunbathe and discuss future cropping endeavors, what did you want to talk to me about, Dragonhorse?"

"I want you to be Governor of the Lebonathi worlds. Both of them. Military Governor for now. Later, just … Governor."

Konik didn't even turn to look at him. "Mmm." There was no inflection.

"I know you have little reason to love these people or this place, Nik. I know that your home, your family, are on Anguine II."

Knowing Konik was a man of few words and much thought, Ardenai made himself shut up and sit still. He picked a stalk of grain growing at the base of the rock upon which they sat and applied himself to dissecting it – making himself think about what it was, what its parentage probably was, how it could be used in the new agronomy … to keep himself from hearing Konik's thoughts. That had been a problem of late for him. Hearing conversations meant for him was one thing, hearing thoughts that were not, was most disturbing. Pythos had just shrugged in that emerald ripple of snakeskin and hissed, "Thee iss the Dragonhorsse," which explained everything and nothing. He'd take it up next time he was at Mountain hold.

"Not so many seasons ago I was involved in a plot to kill you and overthrow the Government of Equus," Konik said at last. "It was a fantasy to be sure – even funny in a surreal sort of way – but it happened."

Ardenai held his peace, still intent on the grain which he had decided from the shape of the awn was some kind of landrace hulless barley. Hulless meant it could be threshed by farm families rather than having to go to a larger facility. That was good. Long stemmed, which meant long rooted, which meant complex nutrients. That was better yet.

There was another long, quiet spell, woven into the whisper of grass. "From the time I got involved in that, until this day, sitting here with you, I have not been Equi, and Anguine II has not been my home. First it was some fantasy planet that turned out to be the Equi homeworld, and then, after I had been back on Anguine II but a smattering of days, Lebonath Jas became my home. I guess this is by way of saying … I have no home without Addie, and no one to go home to, because my girls are better off without the stench of what I did interfering with them trying to get back to a normal life. So, why not stay here and have purpose?"

"If that purpose is self-flagellation, it does indeed stink," Ardenai said reasonably. "You have served Anguine II admirably as a senator, Equus as a test pilot, the blue team of the Great House as an insuperable polo player. If you want to stay here because you think you can help govern these people fairly, and because it would do your soul and your ego good to do that, then I would be eternally grateful to you. If you only want to stay because you think you have no place else to go … that is not true. The others who were duped into this whole Telenir, Wind Warrior fantasy … myself included … are still on Anguine II and Equus. Sarkhan's parents and his brother are barking mad freaks, but most everybody else seems to be well and trying to get on with their lives."

He took a deep breath and made himself be quiet. He chewed a bit of the grain and found it tasty, chewed the stalk and decided it would make good fodder or bedding. It was sweet, warm from the sun, slightly salty from being in his hand. He wondered how long he'd have to crawl around in these rocks and follow rodents to find enough of this to start a patch for seed.

"Under one condition," Konik said.

"Name it."

"I will work on Lebonath Jas, but I want to live, and farm and garden – maybe even play polo someday, and be part of a community again – here, on Lebonath Tras. I would like a piece of land for that purpose – a keep of whatever size is decided upon. Further," he said, holding up a finger, "Any of those who were involved, any of those who thought they were Telenir, who would like a fresh start, get a piece of land here as well, either within a township as merchants, or a keep to farm. The exceptions being Sardure and Saremanno and their inner circle. Them, I want nothing to do with. I don't imagine any of us do."

Ardenai thought about it. "How many will farm, how many will keep shop?"

"Most would farm," Konik said. "Two families would probably want to run gristmills, as they do now. Some raise horses or sheep. One extended family is full of wainwrights, very good ones – orchardists, dairymen, vintners, smithies, apiarists, masons, coopers ..." he trailed off and shook his head with a glum, self-deprecating chuckle. "What could I possibly have been persuading myself to think … my father and his before him … to be involved in such lunacy? How could loyalty to my parents have made me so blind? There weren't enough of us to do a single thing on our own, and we're farmers, agronomists, one and all. We're just plain Equi, and that should have been more than enough."

"Let's don't talk about who was crazier, you or me. We'll both just get depressed, and we are here now." Ardenai was quiet, figuring in his head and studying the countryside before nodding and speaking. "Nik, if you will take both planets for at least ten years, and one or the other for twenty years or longer, health permitting, of course, I will give you everything you have asked for. I will grant you one quarter of the keeps in each of the first sixteen colony grids that will form the first regional hub. The full keeps look like they'll be over twenty thousand acres down to six hundred and forty acres. Some may be smaller yet. Plus I will give you ten lots in each of the sixty-four townships, ten in the sixteen grid hubs, and ten in the regional hub, with those keeps and lots not claimed going back into the general pool for settlement. Anyone except those you mentioned in the original number I was given of eight hundred and sixty Telenir families, any member of any of those families, may choose to join you in the next three calendar years. Do we have a deal?"

"We do," Konik said, and Ardenai breathed a sigh of relief. There was a pause, and Konik's next words were difficult. "I do need … would like to have … a space now, to be expanded later. I … need to bury my wife."

"Any spot you choose," Ardenai said quietly. "Take the clipper and comb the planet for the place you want to call home. The system of keeps for that grid will be built around your keep."

"Thank you," Konik smiled. He stared at the long lake shimmering below them and to one side, the stands of timber, the verdant meadows sloping gently to the beach. "No place could be more beautiful than right here where I'm sitting. This spot … Addie would love this spot." There was a pause. "Unless this is part of your keep, or previously claimed, I'd like mine to start right here and go north along the lake."

"Then my keep will end right where yours starts. This, my friend, is yours and your family's for all time. Welcome home," Ardenai smiled.

He let a meeting go by that afternoon and sat beside Brak, who was nearly dead from having his legs broken and his thumbs cut off, and wondered about why people did the things they did. Brak had showed not one sign of being interested in anything Equi, and yet he had shut that machine off for an interminable two seconds with thirty, forty, fifty thousand people watching? Why had he taken such a risk? Was it for Ardenai? Was it for Konik? Was it to get back at Eridu for something? Whatever the reason, he'd paid for it. He was set, he was bandaged; he had tubes running in him for blood, nourishment, pain relief. But his thumbs were gone. Ardenai sat studying his own capable hands with their long, blunt fingers and close-clipped nails, little scars here and there, couple of substantial ones, a callus or two from different things, a tiny blue mark still persisting in the palm of the right one – and wondered what he would do without his thumbs. He folded them under as far as he could and contemplated what was left. Cutting the thumbs off a working man was a sentence of slow death. A life of feeling helpless and worthless.

Who had done this monstrous thing? Eridu, or his ilk. No question. Kehailan's words kept ringing in his ears. There were, indeed, some bad people down there. But then there were bad people everywhere. Whose job was it, exactly, to decide who was bad and who was not? Was being bad for one reason acceptable while being bad for another was not? Ardenai knew nothing made people worse than religion, and nothing made them feel more justified in what they were doing. For lack of faith and want of power, men had decided to overwrite the spirit of the Creator with their own rules for society – supposedly so that others could understand and follow the will of the Wisdom Giver – more likely so that influential men could control those rules and mete them out as they fit their own desires.

Eridu, called upon the name of God and did unspeakable things. Not just to Brak, or Kehailan, or Eridi, or Ardenai himself, but to the people he had been ordained to rule over, to care for. Those people in the ruling party bowed and suckled – would have offered him their wives or daughters, or themselves had he wished it. Those in the minority party were terrified of him – would have offered him their wives or daughters, or themselves. Same outcome. The rest of the population with its needs and desires, seemed not to exist at all. In what way was any of this productive? In what way did this man serve anybody but himself? None, that Ardenai could see, and yet even in captivity he was well fed and well cared for – the lights in his cell dim enough to be comfortable. No wonder Kehailan perceived it as a kind of weakness, or at least misguided. When Ardenai thought about it, he agreed. For the lack of something grander to do, Ardenai straightened the blankets covering Brak's comatose form, told him thank you, and went to check on Brak's family.

Ardenai and Teal stayed for dinner with friends and news from home before heading to the surface for the night, and they sat laughing with Marion, Kehailan, Konik, Ulric, Bonfire and Timothy. Oonah, newly arrived from Equus – blushing under her black skin when they teased her about why she'd missed her initial call-up. Her papers had been in order for a vacation incognito, after all. She had brought crys-tels for nearly everyone. Letters from home.

And of course she had news from Equus. Girsu was doing well and beginning to fit in. Seemed to be enjoying Catrio's company. Catrio had said to tell Ardenai, usual equipment, but nice – whatever that meant. Jasreth was doing well in school and had gone home for week's end with Ah'brianne and the boys. Had ridden her little black horse for the first time and promptly fallen in love. She and Gideon were studying extra hard under the tutelage of Master Darley. Criollo and Ah'brianne were helping out where they could.

Gideon had represented his father at the dedication of the next Imperial Clipper to take to the air, and had acquitted himself very well. Ah'krill had gone with him, and spoken of him as her grandson. Jilfan was not currently at the Great House, but visiting with his father's parents on Anguine II. Ah'din had spent a couple of days in the royal apartments, having been summoned by Ah'krill for some reason that was probably in her crys-tel to Teal. The boy … what was his name? Basra, was doing better. Nobody was quite sure what to do with him. For the time being he was staying with two members of the Horse Guard in their quarters and going to school during the day, a guard discreetly standing by. Gideon had thought that was what the Dragonhorse wanted. Cold winter. Snow was deep. There had been polo matches at High Harvest, but no tournament. Parts of two teams were missing.

They were finishing dessert and talking about the need for some kind of a polo team here, and that polo might just be the cure-all for what ailed the planet, wondering if caronai could be saddled, when Teal caught his breath and sat back in his chair, rubbing at his forehead. "What's wrong?" Ardenai asked.

"I … don't know," he said. A second later his elbows came down on the table with a thud and his head dropped into his hands. "Damn!" he said through gritted teeth.

"What …?" Ardenai's arm was quick around Teal as he sat panting and gasping, then his face came up, twisted with pain, blood beginning to run from his nostrils.

"Eridu … is screaming in my head! Oh … Creator, get him out!" Konik, Ardenai, Marion and Kehailan sprinted for the brig. Just on a hunch, Bonfire ran for the sanecere bay, calling for Ulric to come with her. Oonah and Tim caught Teal as he clutched at his ears and collapsed onto the floor of the dining room.

They could hear Eridu long before they got to him, and when they did, he was writhing on the floor, shrieking, urinating, foaming at the mouth, and the sliding door to his cell was somehow blocked from the inside. With him, was Brak's wife, watching. She turned enough at the pounding of their boots, that they could see the knife in her hand.

Kehailan saw the mop handle she'd used to wedge the door and called for help from engineering to reverse the direction of the slide. "Pop it off its mountings, do something! Anything! We have to get in there!"

The woman seemed almost casual in the way she ignored them, fascinated instead by how Eridu was ripping at his skin and clothing, clawing at himself as if trying to remove something from deep inside. He screamed horribly, like he was burning alive, and blood spurted from his throat. She watched him, like she had pulled the wings off a fly. All four of them were begging her to open the door, and she quietly ignored them, as though they were on the periphery of a dream. He began to convulse and gouge at his own eyes and she said, "He laughed when they sawed my husband's thumbs off. He said that would teach him a lesson. Now I think he knows how lessons are taught."

"What in the name of God did you give him?" Marion cried, hands over his ears and horror on his face. "He's going to die!"

"Of course he is," she said. "The person who gave me this said there is no antidote. She said, this is what he uses to execute his political rivals and people who, in general, annoy him. She said he should have the opportunity to try some himself, so I said I would bring him some. He thought it was his favorite after-dinner tidbit. Why was he so foolish as to take it from me, of all people?"

The door slid open in the opposite direction and she came around to face them with the knife. "I was hoping to watch a little longer," she said, and in a swift motion she had slit her own throat and dropped to the floor, with Eridu screaming and wallowing in her blood as he died.

"This is a nightmare," Ardenai groaned, watching with horrified fascination, knowing there was not a single thing any of them could do. "Oh no!" he gasped, "Eladeus! What is happening to Teal?"

Teal? Beloved? Nothing. *Teal!* And by then he was running back toward the dining room. When he got there Teal was unconscious on the floor with his head in Oonah's lap and Tim beside him. "Pythos just touched him and he was out cold," she said.

Ardenai leaned against the table for a few seconds, weak with relief, then turned and started back the way he had come, only to meet Bonfire coming toward him from the direction of the sanecere bay.

"You'd better come and see this," she said soberly.

Brak was dead. His throat had been neatly cut. On the bed beside him, arms around his father, lay the boy, hair matted with his father's blood – eyes staring open in death. He'd been poisoned, or Bonfire missed her guess – something quick, from a mother's love and desperation. He'd been allowed to cuddle with his father until he was dead, then his mother had killed her good husband, to spare him that life of uselessness. Ardenai leaned into Bonfire and they just stood there together, numb, saying nothing. "Come with me," he said finally, and they went back to the brig.

Eridu's body was still twitching, but he, too, was dead. Ardenai walked through the blood as though it wasn't there, picked up Brak's wife, and put her on the bunk. He flipped the covers over her to sop up the gore, picked her up again, and followed by Kehailan, Marion and Bonfire, walked to the sanecere bay, where he laid her on the bed next to Brak and their son. When he turned around, Kehailan had tears streaming down his face and his eyes were full of dismay.

"Is this my fault?" he said in a small voice. "Did I do this with my temper and my sharp tongue? I think I did. I made that woman think she was of no value. As surely as if I'd wielded the knife myself, I did this." He said it again as if he couldn't believe the words. "I did this."

Ardenai's gut reaction was to put his arms around his son and tell him that wasn't true, and it probably wasn't, but just for the moment, just for the lesson, he let him wrestle with the possibility. "I need to check on my kinsman," he said, and walked away from the grief and the guilt and the death.

Teal was groaning his way back to consciousness, pushing the heel of his hand against his temple to ease the pounding. Ardenai helped him up off the floor and into a chair, offering him the glass of wine he hadn't finished earlier. He took a couple of sips and gave his head a good shake, which, from the pain on his face, he immediately regretted. "That was truly awful," he said at last. "What happened to Eridu?"

"Oh, he's dead," Ardenai said lightly, flipping his hands out as though he were telling a funny story. "He's really dead. So is Brak. So is

Brak's wife. So is their little boy. They're all dead."

"And you have blood all over you, or I assume that's Lebonathi blood," Teal observed.

"It is, but I didn't." Ardenai said. "I'm going to go down to the surface, I'll be back."

A few minutes later he was knocking on the door of Naram's apartments, two Amberian troopers watching his back and keeping Naram's personal bodyguards at bay. To Ardenai's surprise, it was a fully clothed Naram who opened the door. "I know it's late," Ardenai said, "But would you please come with me? I need help sorting something out."

"Will I be coming back?" Naram asked quietly.

Ardenai just nodded. There was blood across his mid-section, on his forearms, a little smear high on his chest, just a touch under his chin, and there had been blood on his palms. He'd washed it off in a hurry and missed some. He hadn't killed anyone, but he had carried someone who was bloody and probably dead.

Naram stepped out and closed the door. "Let's go," he said.

He looked first at Eridu, who they had left as he was until the scene could be thoroughly documented and Naram had seen it. He grimaced a little, but said nothing, and Ardenai took him up to the sanecere bay and showed him the three bodies on the bed.

"Eridu had Brak's thumbs cut off," Ardenai said by way of preface. "He cut a working man's thumbs off." Naram could tell that that, for the Dragonhorse, was the worst of it. Fascinating clod that he was. "We think, I think, she poisoned her little boy and let him lie with his father until he passed, then cut Brak's throat, then poisoned Eridu and locked herself in there with him. When we managed to get the door open, she killed herself, but it was too late to help Eridu. Worse, it was too late to help her."

"It was too late to help Eridu the second she gave him that crap," Naram said. He looked at Brak lying there. His legs had been set. His hands carefully bandaged. They had been giving him something in his veins and his face was peaceful. "Her name is Phaedra. The boy's name is Rakba, he was seven years old. Eridu's firstwife, Lulana, was Eridi's mother, and

Phaedra's sister. Eridu had Lulana killed a few days ago, hacked into manageable chunks and dumped in the sewer." He was quiet awhile, looking at the bodies on the bed.

"I'm sorry," Ardenai said into the silence, "I don't know what to do … with them. I don't know what is proper. Do we bury them as a family, are there words to be said? If they were Equi, I would know what to do."

"You forget," Naram said in a hint of his usual voice, "they are Equi, remember? We are all Equi now. And aren't things better? Yes, so much. Thank you."

"I don't know why I thought you'd take pity on these people," Ardenai said, "but I did. In so many ways you are an ass. At times a perceptive one, I grant you, but somehow … I did get the feeling that you care for the Lebonathi people, which I don't think Eridu ever did."

"And now you seek to play on my ego," Naram said.

"I asked for your help!" Ardenai exclaimed angrily. "This family is dead because Brak tried to help me, all right? Why he did it I do not know. I do know this woman did what she thought was best. She did terrible things because she loved her husband and her son. I would have her honored as a Lebonathi, but honoring her as an Equi will do just as well. Thank you for the reminder. What do you want done with The Most Wise Lord Eridu? I can have him sent to your apartments if you'd like. You can have him stuffed and mounted."

"No," Naram said with a slight smile, "Ask your Master Captain Teal where he and Konik went to get the antidote for you, and send his body there – nicely wrapped. I want it to be a surprise."

"And what are you going to do to the anchoresses within?"

"Take them out for a nice dinner," Naram smiled. "With Eridu dead, Addur dead, and Halaf in hiding, nobody will take the job, so you will now be dealing with me as head of the Lebonathi Federation."

"What a delightful prospect," Ardenai said with a glum little chuckle. "Well, since I have you here, Most Wise Lord Naram, and since you've been so helpful this evening, perhaps you can tell me where I can find a Lebonathi craftsman who fixes pipe organs."

Naram took his eyes off the bodies and stared instead at Ardenai. "I think for now, just … Naram. Wisdom does not seem to get us anywhere anymore. And what in Tras is a pipe organ?"

CHAPTER 6

Teal sat straight up, catching his breath as the screams in his head subsided with wakefulness. His pupils adjusted quickly to the dimness in the pavilion and he looked over at Ardenai, sprawled on his back, still sound asleep. That in itself was a blessing. The first two or three nights when Teal had come up off his bed, Ardenai had come up with him, eyes full of concern, all thought of sleep gone as they talked, or walked a little to ease the tension and maybe get themselves another hour or so of rest before their day began.

He made sure the crys-tel he'd gotten from Ah'din was on its chain around his neck, rose as quietly as he could, and slipped out into the cool, starry darkness, taking his robe as he went. Even with as busy as he had been, even as many times as he'd listened to the soothing voice of his wife on the crys-tel he carried, Eridu's screams penetrated his sleep, leaving him more and more exhausted with each passing day.

That first night he hadn't slept at all. Ardenai hadn't, either. They'd helped clean up the horror in the brig, and when morning came, Ardenai and Konik had gone one way to bury the family in the mountains to the east, and Teal had thrown the wrapped body of Eridu over his shoulder and carted it off to the little shop where he and Konik had gotten the antidote. "Special delivery," he'd called, dumping the body on the floor. "Naram says you'll want this." Because he was the kindest of souls he added, "Be warned, there's a body in here."

An anchoress had appeared from the back of the shop, or whatever it was – so many of the dimly lit spaces were deceiving – and looked first at the tarp, then at him. "Thank you, Master Captain," she said, and he recognized her as the woman who had given him the antidote for Ardenai. He had asked her if her name was Ensharra, and she had dropped her eyes and just the slightest hint of a nod as acknowledgement. This was a woman who bore watching. If only Eridi would waken, Ah'nis of the blonde hair and pallid skin would go back to her duties. She, would blend in nicely. Teal had explained who it was wrapped up there on the floor, how he had died, and something in the way he had told it, told her … he'd gotten the screams caught in his head.

"You can hear our voices and our thoughts, can't you?" she had asked, not unkindly, nor with any suspicion, just a simple question, and Teal had said that, yes, he could. More than he wanted to. "Please, stay right there," she had said, disappearing into the darkness, and in a few minutes she had returned to hand him one of those tiny jar, tiny spoon combinations. "I made this for you. This will quiet the noise and help you sleep," she smiled. "I'm not used to prescribing for Equi, so approach with due caution." He had taken it, thanked her, and as he was leaving she had said, "Master Captain, again, thank you." And again she had smiled.

Now as he walked he wondered what they'd done with the corpse. It hadn't appeared in any of the ridiculous number of telegenic tabloids which flashed around the planet several times a day, though Ardenai's somber, 'It is with regret that I must inform you of the death of The Most Wise Lord Eridu, who died by his own hand …." had posted telegenically to immediate wild speculation as to what had actually transpired. Had the Dragonhorse killed him? Had the Dragonhorse eaten him? Had the Dragonhorse … etc. Within an hour of the announcement, Ardenai had acknowledged Naram as Regent and new head of the Lebonathi Federation, which seemed to Teal a little like finding oneself the captain of a ship sinking so fast that the real captain has already drowned. Still, an hour after that, Naram had made a public appearancc to say that hc had seen the body of Eridu, that he had indeed committed suicide, and that Dragonhorse and Company seemed genuinely unhappy to have had such a thing happen in their brig. Speculation then shifted to who was in bed with whom. Was Naram, after his long visit on Equus, a convert? Was the government now secular? Had all hope for the faith been lost? Were the demons even now descending from the fires of Lebonath Tras to sweep up all who had received succor or friendship from the Equi monsters?

It was the statement issued by the anchoresses, saying that Eridu had been executed by Phaedra, the sister of Firstwife Lulana, whom Eridu had murdered and dumped in the sewer, which shut everybody up. How had they known that? That question had taken Teal about one minute to figure out. Ensharra had given Phaedra the fatal dose for Eridu, camouflaged as a sweet. And who knew the whole story to tell Ensharra? Naram. Gruesome as it was, it still made Teal chuckle. Needless to say that, while he hadn't thrown the little jar away, he most certainly hadn't put any of its contents in his mouth – yet. But he just might have to risk it.

He, was not the Dragonhorse. He was big and fast and incredibly strong, but he had not the inner power, the stamina, nor the resilience of his specially bred brother-in-law. Like most Equi males he needed a constant and prodigious number of calories every day, and mostly, he needed sleep in order to properly wield the extra muscle mass he'd been given by genes and the Creator.

He sat beside the deep, quiet pool at the base of the waterfall, took the crys-tel from around his neck, and held it in his hands, expanding it to the size he wanted. There was Ah'din, working at one of the big spinning wheels in what everybody in the family called the Dreamweaver's Corner. A friction fire danced on the hearth and Ah'din's graceful hands seemed to dance as well, moving so fast as she worked that they were almost a blur. She knew he would watch this, over and over, and for a long time she said nothing, as would be the case if he were sitting his chair reading, or carving, or working with leather. Hours they would spend without speaking, warm and comfortable in one another's company.

While Io had grown to be quite lovely in a childlike sort of way, and Ah'ree had been stunning in a fragile-as-glass sort of way, Ah'din, like her mother, was deeply and serenely beautiful, and always had been. From the moment Teal and Ardenai had been seated as a wide-eyed, sober set of eight-year-olds and allowed to hold the new baby, Ah'din had been beautiful. She had gone through stages, of course. Cute, quick, annoying, meddlesome. Too tall, too skinny, too fat, too tall – too few teeth, too much hair, too many questions, too many observations.

And then one day they'd been helping Gidran with the rhax harvest, picking the huge bunches of purple fruit and dumping them into giant buckets to go to the crusher, and she had turned with a full basket and caught her toe somehow on something – something Teal would to this very day build a shrine to if he could figure out what it was – and fallen at his feet, knocking her broad brimmed straw hat off to be whisked away by an errant breeze. He had laughed and held out his hand to her, and she had looked up laughing to take it, and the sunlight had flashed in those huge, green-gold eyes, off those brilliant white teeth, that wealth of shining sable hair … and he had seen the full lips, the high cheekbones … and most of all, he had heard that voice, really heard it, soft and dark as her hair, rich as wine. And he had stood there like an idiot, staring at her, not picking her up, just holding her hand while his heart melted and his jaw sagged, and her smile had changed, grown sweeter and fonder as it filled her eyes, and she'd said, "Well, it's about time."

There it was again, that voice, and he sighed and leaned into it while she told him about what was going on at Canyon keep, and how Ah'rane and Krush were doing; the children, the horses, of course, and the neighbors. Gaknars had moved a little closer to the occupied parts of the keep, and with them, protopeds. Nothing had been harmed so far, but everyone was on heightened alert, as it would be foaling season before they knew it. By now he could almost recite her words. She had been called to the apartments of the Eloi to speak with Ah'krill, who had been most gracious to her, had asked if she and her good husband would be willing to have another son for the Great House in addition to the daughter she knew they wanted. Of course they would raise their own babies. "Did you know, Sir, that you have some of the oldest bloodlines so far traced on planet Equus?" she had smiled, thereby prefacing her statement that Ah'krill and the council of the

Eloi had also decided that Teal was to mate outside marriage, for the good of the Great House. She had practiced saying it, he could tell, because it came out smoothly, matter-of-factly, as though it were nothing unusual. She had told Ah'krill that he was at heart a very shy individual, and that if he were to do this thing he would probably insist that it be in blind matings. Translated, it meant that he'd best ask for just that, because her heart would break if he were to set his head against another woman who was not a hetaera.

She spoke then of the daughter she wanted, and of intimate things that made him ache for want of holding her and making love to her, and that desire, coupled with being so tired, and so traumatized with the screams in his head, made the need for release overwhelming. Quickly, quietly, almost guiltily because of the images of women that streamed through his brain, he pulled up his knees, spread his feet a little more, and pushed down his brief-cloth. For that two minutes, he would have given anything – anything – to be with his wife – to have what came from him be hers, and when he was done and his get was drifting away on the water, there was emptiness along with the relief. Why was this happening to him? He wasn't usually like this. Even when he was in heat it didn't usually bother him much, and he'd been through a heat cycle at Mountain hold. He tucked himself and sat watching the stars dance on the water.

They'd joked of this for about one minute – the men in the family – realizing they were all going to cycle together because of their time at Mountain hold, and who was going to feed the horses? Now, Teal was beginning to wonder, just around the edges of what he allowed himself to think about, if they were going to cycle together at all, or if, like Ardenai, they were going to have an elevated sex drive all the time? And … were they going to be generative all the time? That was difficult to even consider.

It made him realize more fully what Ardenai was going through as familiar thing after familiar thing, function after function changed, went away, became more pronounced, until his whole life seemed to be in flux, like a transmission crys-tel as it came or went. And who had Pythos forced Ardenai into marrying? Ah'riodin, of all people, and Teal admitted he and Ah'din had been all for it. But that was when he was Ah'rane Ardenai Krush, teacher, horse raiser, polo player, grieving widower. An all-around nice fellow who needed a little excitement to bring him back to life. Io certainly brought that in a cleomitite box. From a sexual standpoint he couldn't have married anybody better for him, and she'd probably saved his life on Calumet, but as far as bringing chaos into a life that needed stability, Io won the cup.

She was brilliant, nicely put together, an amazing strategist, a wildly popular Primuxori, and she did truly and deeply adore him. She also had no idea who she really was or who she wanted to be in their relationship. She was a manipulative six-year-old one minute and an indomitable stateswoman the next, went from smiling to petulant and back again in the blink of an eye, constantly in small ways made Ardenai feel guilty for changing, when that was what was expected of him, and had no idea how to change herself to really, deeply, after the fabulous sex was over, meet his needs.

For all those reasons she was absolutely the wrong woman for the Thirteenth Dragonhorse, and he wouldn't trade her for all the cleomitites on Calumet. Wouldn't have another besides her. Privately – very privately – Teal rather thought a lot of that was guilt on Ardenai's part, because he just couldn't let go of her as a daughter and let her be his wife. He hadn't fought for Ah'nora, who would probably have been perfect for him and who was now married to a saddle maker instead of the Firstlord of Equus. He hadn't tried to work his considerable charm and astonishing good looks on Ah'nis, even when he began to realize who she was. His whole focus was on Io, and she knew it all too well. When it came to women Ardenai had two things going, bad luck and bad judgment. It was his only real flaw.

So, who was left to help stabilize Ardenai, to give him something to hang onto that absolutely did not move? Gideon, maybe, though he would change as he grew. Ah'rane and Krush. Ah'din. But who was with him all the time? Who was the calming influence, the soft voice, the one who could punch him in the face and get away with it? He was. *I am,* Teal thought, still watching the water. *And I am so exhausted that I'm sitting here freezing and don't realize it. I've been out for two days with science teams and I don't know what I've seen. I'm starting to miss words and innuendo at meetings.*

Most of all I am making Ardi worry about me, when it is my job to worry about him. I have got to do something.

He went back to the pavilion, made sure he still had a few hours to sleep, and pulled out the tiny jar with the tiny spoon. He thought about it, thought about how brave Ardenai had been and had to continue being, admitted he was probably doing the dumbest thing he'd ever done in his life other than exploding that wine vat when he was ten, scooped his little finger in the potion and quickly stuck it in his mouth before he could change his mind. His tongue tingled a little where he touched it with the concoction. A warm sweetness spread through his mouth, and a fragrance like lavendula or Saint Ann's vine that he could both smell and taste. The image of Ah'din spinning became the dominant thought … the sound of the wheel, the motion of the treadle … the flicker of the fire … he felt the tension go out of his shoulders.

The next thing he smelled was sweet white coffee, and he opened his eyes to see a cup steaming on the woodblock beside his fleecy bed where Ardenai had left it for him. The sides were rolled up on the pavilion, and he could hear Ardenai's clean, minimal splash as he dove into the pool, which meant he'd already been running. He pushed the sleeping robes down off his left shoulder, rolled to his back and sat up, reaching for the coffee and yawning. He had slept, deeply and comfortably. No screams. No voices.

They were so dependent on, and respectful of their own priestesses, and yet they viewed the Lebonathi anchoresses with deepest suspicion, like they were witches, because of Samarra. He wondered if leaving anchoresses just with priestesses was creating a smaller window than need be. They were trying to be all-inclusive, yet the tunnel vision persisted in certain arenas. Maybe this was one of them. All of their Equi priestesses, their precious Eloi, were something else as well: doctors, sociologists, anthropologists, adjudicators, farmers, educators, wives and mothers. Perhaps the anchoresses were, as well. He set the coffee cup aside and stepped out into the morning sunshine, giving himself a good shake and a stretch before setting off at a slow jog upriver.

No need for clothing past a briefcloth. The tempestorians said it was coming summer on this part of Lebonath Tras. The air was cool against his bare skin, but not unpleasantly so, and because the way they'd picked out for their morning ramble was sandy dust, he didn't have to watch his footing overmuch. He ran first beside the river, then moved away more into the valley, picking up speed, looking at the gentle, lightly treed slopes at a distance to his left and wondering again how well rhax vines would grow in the deep, fertile soil. He loved his home on Viridia, but this could be a close second.

He wondered what they'd build their houses and shops out of on this planet. So far as the scientists could tell there was no need to protect themselves from terrible storms such as ravaged their home planet, but there didn't seem to be much volcanic activity, so there would be no way to cluster around hot springs to heat homes and greenhouses and provide power. Would they dig into the sides of the hills for soil-sheltered homes? Use logs or wood, as they did on Calumet? Would they find old quarries and use stone?

It still puzzled him as to how the Lebonathi scientists had removed so much of the evidence of civilization from this planet. Teal was beginning to think that the old tales from the five folk at Stone Spring might be right, if understated. Maybe there never had been much of anything here. Those five scientists were sharp, and they were self-taught – oral tradition – natural classroom thinking, and he wondered if the anchoresses were the same way. Admittedly, his curiosity was piqued by a good night's sleep and the vast relief of having awakened alive, but he wanted to pursue the matter with Ensharra. How were they educated? Had they been getting their potion materials from Ashur and Isin, and if so, where were they going to get them now? They were obviously well informed as to what went on in the larger world, but were they interested in joining it? How many of them were there, and how closely were they intertwined with the flamen, whose seditious, fear-filled rhetoric about the Equi and their sinful ways was making things so much harder?

What kind of mentality did it take to tell hungry people that accepting food from the Equi was a sin for which they would burn for eternity, that the water was poisoning their souls, and that registering their children for school and services would condemn them to the fires of the witch world? It was so hard to know how to deal with things beyond one's experiences and imagination.

When Teal mentioned over first breakfast that he wanted to take time with Ensharra, Ardenai's mouth had turned down in contemplation and after a moment he had nodded and said, "Good idea. Tomorrow we're going to start meeting with – and by that I mean hunting down and dragging in and possibly jettisoning into space – the flamen, and I need to know how closely the anchoresses are associated with them. Good luck, Master Captain, I'll see you at dinner."

He had gone with Konik to 'meet' with four of the provincial governors they'd managed to smoke out of their holes, and excused Teal to spend time with the anchoress, turning back briefly in his walk to the scrambleshafts to tell Teal with worried eyes to watch his back, and his front.

"I shall do both," Teal had smiled, and now he was back in the dim corridors of the old city, which were by this time becoming familiar. The stench was not so overwhelming, the light not so elusive. He was beginning to recognize the faces of the shopkeepers, though they all did look very much alike to him with their shades of pale hair and bluish or pinkish colorless eyes. The Stone Spring scientists, though relatively pale skinned, were not colorless. These people had no pigment. That puzzling attribute could not be accounted for by living underground rather than on the surface, not in the few centuries these buildings had been abandoned.

He arrived at the darkened archway of the anchoresses' shop and went in, hoping he looked more at ease than he felt. "Hello?" he called into the dim interior. "Anchoress?"

He was not about to go around the counter and try to figure out where those doors in the back went. He'd read that particular book of scary stories. He did pay attention to which door she came out of, and when the light hit her face it was, indeed, Ensharra. "Good morning," he said with a gracious nod and a charming smile, "I wanted to thank you for the herbs you gave me for sleep."

She just looked at him, a touch of a smile, but no more. She already knew why he was here, and he could sense it. "And if you have time for me,

I'd like to find out more about you and what you do."

"And what I think," she added.

"That, too," he nodded.

"Please, come with me," she said, gesturing around the end of the counter toward one of the doors. "You are curious about us. Let me begin to satisfy that curiosity of yours. Are you alone?"

"I am, yes," Teal shrugged, and followed her into the blackness behind the door.

"You are on the large side for this place. Put your hand on my shoulder and walk in a straight line directly behind me," she said. "Don't put your hands out to the sides. There are things stored on either side of you, and some of them are sharp."

Teal did as he was told, hoping she realized how tall he was, not just how broad. "Can you not spare yourselves any light?" he asked quietly. This place definitely had fear going for it. There were cold drafts and strange noises. He could smell earth, as though they were in a catacomb, and the slight smell of … "Brimstone? Really? Who are you trying to keep out of here?"

"You have no idea," she said, "And even you do not want to see what you're walking past."

They reached the other end of the seemingly endless hallway, and when she opened another door he felt his pupils contract. It was much lighter, and some of that light was natural. The windows were high and hazy, letting light in from the sides, not the top, though there had been no sense of going up. All of the window sills were filled with plants, tall and spindly but alive, and the walls were lined with books, maps, stacks of paper and claywrite, even something that looked like scrolls. There was a long table with chairs on either side, and something large for scribing on and erasing.

"May I?" Teal asked quietly. "I promise I won't touch."

She gave him that characteristic single nod and that ghost of a smile and he began looking from volume to volume, shelf to shelf, slowly around the room, noticing that as the shelves got lower the books got simpler until the ones at the bottom were clearly for children. He gave her a questioning look.

"This is where our girls learn of things other than religion," she said, and her voice was challenging. "You judge us by Samarra, who was Eridu's creature. If you were not so willing to judge and condemn us ..."

"If I were willing to condemn you, I wouldn't be here," Teal said, and for a moment his face was hard, warning Ensharra. He saw her shoulders shrink the tiniest bit and was immediately contrite. "Sorry. I didn't mean to scare you, at least any more than you scare me. It is our earnest desire to respect you and your work, as we respect our own priestesses. I know that many of your anchoresses are working with our priestesses to feed and tend the people, but that is a time to speak of the immediate, of things and doing. I was hoping we might speak of ideals, and the past, and how you came to be where you are and your institutions came to be in the shape they're in."

"Let us go somewhere more private," she said, gesturing toward another door. "This room will shortly be in use, and your presence would be … intimidating."

Teal nodded, following her without comment down another hallway, this one slightly more inviting and into what appeared to be a tiny living space, with a table and two chairs, and a hammock containing bedding hanging against the wall over the table. Again, there were a few herbs hung to dry, and that unpleasant smell of smoke, cooked flesh, and those who ate flesh, but there was also a high, translucent window where more herbs struggled, and under it there was a small, narrow bench with brightly colored pillows that looked to be hand woven. She gestured him into a chair at the table and as he sat, he reached for one of the pillows. "Did you weave this?" he asked, admiring the fine work and the intricate pattern.

"My grandmother," she said, and as the light caught her eyes, he realized her eyes were brown. Not pink, not blue, but a clear, chestnut brown. "Why are you looking at me like that?"

"I've suddenly realized, being albino isn't natural, is it? It's an affectation, like Taraxian tails."

"It is," she smiled. "Though I have no idea what Taraxian tails are. It does tell you why the people who have subterranean homes are those most able to afford the process."

Teal's brows came slightly toward center. "Doesn't … everybody live underground?"

She shook her shaved head inside the tall stiff collars of her habit, and it reminded Teal of a white allium bulb being screwed into the dark earth of spring. He resisted the image and kept a straight face.

"Most city dwellers these days live in the old tunnels, it's true, but under horrific and sweltering conditions. There is no ventilation, no movement of air, and many die of diseases, or smoke inhalation from cooking fires because of it. Relatively few Lebonathi actually 'live' underground, as in real homes. It is they of whom I speak." Teal nodded and gestured for her to continue. "It is a sign of beauty in our culture to be albinized, though I'm sure it takes years off people's lives. It makes a woman more desirable, and any family that can even remotely afford it, inflicts it to some degree upon their daughters. The lighter, the better. We have seen it throughout history: bound feet, flattened heads, crossed eyes, elongated limbs, removal of ears or eyes or teeth – apparently growing those tails of which you just spoke – and some things that would make us cringe to speak of them, but they all serve a purpose."

"For the women," Teal said, still stroking the pillow and studying the anchoress at the same time, "What about the men?"

"Wealth and power, what else? See what I can afford to have done? Wealth is power. Displaying wealth is also a display of power, and it is granted without question."

Teal nodded. "There's an old joke in our culture that goes, 'That's a beautiful saddle you're carrying. You must be able to ride very well.' I suppose every culture has something like it."

"Would you like some tea?" she asked, and watched his mobile features to gauge his reaction. There was no hesitation and no registering of alarm. Either he was comfortable, or he was playing a different game. Teal, did not strike Ensharra as a player of games.

She gave him a slight smile and added, "I have some tea that Ah'nis gave me the first day she was here. Perhaps you can sniff it for me and tell me what it is, and we can have some of that."

"Brown package with a small orange ribbon?" She nodded. "It is cinnamon orange, the traditional thing one gifts when meeting a person from a different culture. That would be fine, but whatever you have is fine, too."

"And you'll actually drink it?" she asked, again a bit of a challenge in her voice.

"I will. Is today to be about testing one another, or are we going to explore one another's intellect a little bit?" He went on quickly, to give her time to think about a response. "Your grandmother did beautiful work, by the way. My wife would enjoy seeing this piece." He gave the pillow a little fluffing and set it back on the bench. "Ah'din is a master weaver. She is also a medicinal herbalist. You two would get along, I think."

"And you adore her as life itself."

"No, not as life. For me, she is life," he smiled, firmly closing that door.

She turned her back and poked at a tiny grate in the corner. Teal watched the curl of smoke rise and exit through a hole in the ceiling. "We weren't always like this, you know," she said. "When things were good we were just like your priestesses … teachers, doctors, cultural missionaries. Mostly, teachers. When things started getting bad and the flamen and the politicians got together and began the oppression of women, we decided we'd better get up some kind of fortifications, or we were going to be consumed. So we began to weave mystery, to shave our heads, and dress all in black, and mix herbal potions and elixirs, and oils – made a few that would scare people into thinking we were witches, because that was what kept the men at bay. Most especially the flamen."

"That sounds like a terrible risk," Teal said. "Fear and hatred go hand in hand, as do fear and death. They could have killed all of you."

"They killed some of us, corrupted a few more," she agreed, "but they also began to believe their own lies and think we really were witches, and that we might really come back to deal with them. By that time the Samarras amongst us had developed some interesting potions … useful for certain purposes. Most of the rest of us learned how to make them as a kind of self-preservation."

"I've seen some of them at work," Teal said soberly. "Samarra was using one of them on Eridi. How the Dragonhorse stopped himself I will never know, but it took a while to get the catalyst out of his system, or so his wife says." Teal was silent for a bit, wondering if Io had gotten where she was going. He sent up a prayer for her safety and wellbeing.

"And Eridi?" Ensharra asked. There was a concern in her voice bred of familiarity.

"Oh, once Ah'nis got her away from Samarra she improved within hours, literally. In days she was a different girl. Or should I say, she was a girl, not a sex machine. Charming, intelligent, voracious in her quest for knowledge. Those of us who know her love her very much. And then her father broke her neck. She's been in a coma ever since." He looked at Ensharra, who had stopped what she was doing to listen, and there was deep sorrow on her features. "You know her," he said quietly.

"I taught her, as much as I could … as much as Lulana could sneak her away to bring her to me." She thought about what she was going to say and added, "If I had known you could hear us, Master Captain, I would have given you those sleeping herbs before ..."

"... You gave Phaedra the killing herbs for Eridu?" It did make him chuckle. "What exactly would you have said to me to get me to take them without telling me what you were going to do? Which was horrible, by the way. He peeled the skin off his face and gouged his own eyes out before he died." Teal shuddered at the remembered image, the piercing shrieks, and Ensharra watched him with some concern before she spoke again.

"Please remember that he did the same thing, over and over to others, and enjoyed the spectacle. He used to invite people to come and watch. They would have a banquet, and that would be the entertainment. Sometimes he would have it slipped into the food of someone at the table. It served both their bloodlust, and as warning to those who would cross him," she said. "He gave a version of it to the Dragonhorse, and to the man who is now your military governor, and I can't imagine it did them any good."

She took two cups and put them on the table with the teapot, one spoon and a bowl with sugar in the bottom. "I know you like your tea sweeter than this, but sugar is hard to come by. And we will have to share a spoon. I gave my other one away."

Teal sighed and looked across the table at her. "I'm sure just the extra water for two cups of tea is a sacrifice. I do apologize to you, personally, if we have … made things worse for you – for all of you."

"Oh, dear Gods no!" she exclaimed. "Master Captain, people were starving to death every day in the streets. The less fortunate had no access to clean water or any kind of food at all, much less good food such as you provide. At least now those who sleep in doorways have a little food in their bellies. The children are being inoculated and the old cared for. There is hope for medicine, for education. There is hope, despite everything the flamen are doing to quash your efforts."

"Tell me about the flamen," Teal said, sipping at his tea. "Mmmmm, smells like home. Thank you."

"The flamen. Where do I begin? It is my personal opinion that they grew out of the political inclinations of the church. When religion and politics began to intermarry and produce strange, twisted children, there they were, knowing all too well the circle of hate and how to fuel it. Make knowledge sin, make asking questions sinful, and make curiosity the work of the devil. Make people pay for persisting in doing those things – physically, socially, financially – and that, in a ten second encapsulation, is my assessment of the flamen."

"That is an encapsulation of what they do, how they manifest themselves, but who are they? Where do they come from?"

"That's a harder question, because they are shrouded, even more deeply than we are, in secrecy. Again, it is my personal opinion but a well-founded one, that they are the eldest sons of the rich, or maybe the youngest sons? I think, from the depth of their rhetoric and their genuine fear that they are prepared from birth for who they become as adults. I do know they have moved far from the teachings of the Gods and deeply into the teachings of the men who wish to control the people, the institutions and the commodities of this planet, and because they are influenced so young, they will be intractable."

"And who would that be, exactly," Teal asked, "those who wish to control the people, the institutions and the commodities?"

Again Ensharra shook her head. This time she sighed. "The flamen amongst the flamen, the rich amongst the rich. Places where we have absolutely no access and can gain no information."

"And yet for all their influence and all their rhetoric, which flies from lip to lip and over every telegenic device on the planet, we can't find them to talk to them," Teal said, holding his cup in both hands and studying Ensharra. "Talking to them through the general media is useless. If they do not wish to hear us, all they have to do is shut us off and make up their own stories."

"And for that very reason they do not wish to be found," she agreed. "They have to be somewhere with access to telecommunications grids, do they not?"

"Maybe," Teal said, and an idea was forming itself in his brain. "I wonder … if, as they are broadcasting, we could figure out where they are. Not just their equipment. Them. I know that sounds elementary, but it's harder than you might think. Still, it could be done. Their thoughts must be fairly open for them to speak …."

Ensharra watched him as he absorbed the information. It was interesting. He thought with his eyes. They scanned scenarios as though he were reading a book, and his blinking slowed, evident in the movement of his long, dark lashes and the way he gazed at a surface away from the light, allowing his pupils to dilate slightly. He rubbed the base of his bottom lip against the knuckle of his index finger, and not the other way around, which made the muscles in his jaw ripple just a bit. She rose quietly, picked up the teapot and the cups and set them on the little counter beside the basin.

In a few minutes he looked up from his reverie, realized she had cleared the tea, and was waiting patiently for him. "You have been most kind with your time," he said. "Must you care for this place, or is there another? I would like to take you to second breakfast, and to see Eridi, and, if you're brave enough, to visit the witch world that whirls above us in the flames of space."

"I would like that very much," she smiled. "I will simply close the shop for the rest of the day."

"I will wait here, and from here we shall depart," Teal said. "I think it best for your safety that we not be seen walking the streets of the city together."

Ensharra gave him that slight nod, disappeared for a space of five minutes, and returned, carrying a broad-brimmed straw hat. "I rarely venture out, so this is rather an antique," she smiled, indicating the hat, "but if I am actually going to see sunshine, I will need it with my glabrous dome."

"Stand beside me and give me your hand," he smiled. "My signal is stronger than yours."

She caught her breath and would have screamed, but there wasn't time, and for a few moments all she could feel was her hand in his, and they were standing on a platform in a gleaming space on one of the huge white ships which had come calling that day. "Welcome to Dragonhorse Thirteen," he said. "Would you like to see Eridi first, or have breakfast?"

"I would love to see Eridi," she breathed, and he gestured her off the platform and down a hall to her right, then right again, into another gleaming space, this one filled with plants, and light, and comfortable furniture with blue upholstery. In a small, bright room off that space they found Eridi, with Kehailan beside her, reading her a book.

"Macbeth?" Teal grimaced. "You're reading the poor girl Macbeth?"

"Second time through," Kehailan chuckled. "I'm hoping she'll get so sick of it she'll wake up just to make me stop." He nodded pleasantly and set the book aside as he rose. "Anchoress Ensharra, I believe?" At her nod he said, "I am Ah'ree Kehailan Ardenai, Captain of Dragonhorse Thirteen. Welcome aboard. Ahimsa, I wish thee peace."

"Thank you," she smiled, noting the fresh blue scar on his neck. This was the young man Eridu had shot. The son of the Thirteenth Dragonhorse. And he was sitting with Eridi, his concern for her obvious.

"I'm sure you would like some time with the princess," he said. "I will leave you to visit. Ah'nis is having second breakfast and should return shortly if you would like to see her as well." With a gallant nod he was gone and Ensharra turned with a smile to Teal.

"Second breakfast? How many times a day do you Equi eat?"

"Every two and a half hours or so when we can manage it," Teal grinned. "Not big meals, except for breakfast and dinner, but good ones. Please, sit. I will put your hat on that chair yonder and get us both something to drink while you visit with Eridi."

"Please do not leave me alone with her," Ensharra said. "If anything happens to her, I do not want to get the blame."

"Of course," Teal said without hesitation, and sat down on the opposite side of the bed, brushing the girl's forehead with his lips in passing. "Good morning, Eridi."

He tipped his head momentarily toward his dominant hand, then assumed a comfortable position and Ensharra sensed that he, too, sat with the girl. They did love her. In this, as well, they had been truthful. Honest, honorable, straightforward people. Which emotion was it that drove them to take a planet and hold it cupped in the palms of their hands as they blew, however gently, their version of civility into the faces of its population? For some reason it made her want to laugh.

"And what do you read to her?" Ensharra smiled.

"We're reading a fascinating book from Declivis on traditional winemaking, but mostly, I sing to her. I'm more of a singer than a reader, unless it's picture books, or something Ah'din and I are studying together. My wife and I want another baby soon, and I'm looking forward to the picture books."

A young man in a Dragonhorse uniform appeared with two drinks on a tray, greeted both of them pleasantly and handed one glass to Ensharra and one to Teal. She looked at hers with a questioning eye, and Teal reached across the bed, handed her his, and took hers. She looked at the one she had, smiled, and traded back. She sipped the strong sweet drink while she talked to Eridi about small things, mostly asking questions about how she liked her new life and what kinds of things she was doing, and then speaking about how Lebonath Jas was changing at the hands of the Equi, and her hope for schools that were out in the open, and people who could laugh without fear.

While she was talking Teal finished his drink and picked up a book off the windowsill – the one about winemaking, which did make Ensharra laugh.

Ah'nis came back from breakfast and was delighted to see the anchoress, catching her in a quick, heartfelt embrace and immediately settling beside her to visit. At that point Teal pretty much decided second breakfast with Ensharra was out, so he asked her if she wanted anything and excused himself to go and find food.

He found himself sitting with one other person, Cornwallis Mettenger, who informed him that the relay ships were now fully functional and that he could call Equus, or any other planet in the SGA and speak live to anyone he wished. Teal promptly checked the time, leaned forward and tapped the console in the center of the table. He spoke to it, and in a few moments, there was Ah'din, threading one of the big floor looms. "Hello, stranger," he said, and she laughed with delight, turning to flash him a smile that pretty well dazzled Mettenger as well as her doting husband.

They spoke for twenty minutes about a shipment of wine corks, the temperature in the barns, how much Jasreth loved her little horse, kisses to Teal and a thousand thank-yous, the fact that Criollo seemed to be really buckling down in school now that he had what he referred to as, 'purpose in life', which made Teal laugh merrily and together they just shook their heads as parents will do. Teal told her that when they were alone they would discuss what Ah'krill had wanted of them. Gideon was well, but missing his father terribly, and having Io at home was helping. She would be there a couple more days and then she was on to Achernar. Krush and Ah'rane were well. Happy to be at a wider hearth. Perhaps it would work out permanently.

The children were coming home every week's end, which was nice, made the house seem a little less empty, and delighted the grandparents. Lionel had run afoul of Mikilosh, an experience he'd not soon forget, but he had also learned not to jump up on people, which was a minor miracle. Ah'din was now convinced that Gideon could teach anything to do anything and Teal agreed. He told her that he was spending the day with an anchoress of the sort Samarra had definitely not been and that she had a beautiful hand-woven pillow, an ancient straw hat of great character, and a whole shop full of interesting herbs, among other things, and that he hoped Ah'din could meet her someday. He said that, sadly, he had places he had to be, but that he would be in touch very, very soon, and that she was to know he adored her with every fiber of his being.

When he had broken the connection Mettenger said, "You are one lucky sonofabitch, Master Captain. That is a beautiful woman."

"Um hm," Teal said, finishing his last few bites, "She does all things well."

"She looks familiar," Mettenger persisted. "Do I know her? Does she look like somebody I know? What is it?"

Teal looked at him and resisted the urge to ask him if he was joking, though obviously he was not. "She looks like the Firstlord," he said patiently. "Because she's his sister. That's why I refer to Ardenai as my brother-in-law."

Mettenger seemed truly bemused. "I thought … you and Ardenai were brothers," he said.

Konik blew in at that moment, mercifully cutting the conversation short and apologizing for the interruption, but he and Ardenai needed an SGA observer in the conference room where they were talking to the provincial governors, and there did seem to be a certain lack of understanding.

He greeted Teal, noted the long sleeved white shirt and grey trousers of the Expedition, and asked him how his meeting with the anchoress was going. Was he taking her someplace interesting to be dressed as he was? When Teal said she was on board and sitting with Eridi, Konik insisted in walking that far with him, just to say hello. It was at that point Teal realized – actually let it come to the front of his mind – that Ensharra had murdered Eridu, that she could be arrested and imprisoned for the rest of her life, and that Konik had the authority to accomplish it.

He was wondering how to phrase that when Konik gave him a look and said aloud, "Actually I was going to give her a kiss and flowers. The last thing on my mind was arresting her." Teal looked flustered and Konik burst out laughing as they walked into the sanecere bay.

Ensharra was immediately on her feet and Konik gave her a courtly nod to allay her fears, just in case she and Teal were both thinking along the same lines.

"I mean you no harm," he said quickly in his soothing purr of a voice and Ensharra relaxed. He beckoned her away from Eridi's bedside and said, "I just wanted to thank you for the taking of Eridu … In the sense of disposing of his body, of course. What did you do with it, if I may ask?"

"We dissected it to observe the effects of the herbs on various organs, and then incinerated it, lest the rats eat it and get sick," she said soberly.

"Which I will remember, should I ever consider crossing you," Konik murmured, not sure whether she was teasing him or not. Just in case she wasn't, he didn't laugh. "I hope we will see more of you aboard Dragonhorse," he said. "I know Eridi will enjoy knowing that you are here." He nodded to Ah'nis, raised an eyebrow to Teal, and was gone to the conference room.

"We should go as well," Teal said, retrieving Ensharra's hat, and when she and Ah'nis had said their goodbyes he walked her to Dominus and asked for permission to launch. She had nearly screamed when they'd scrambled to the ship, and he wondered how she would do with being shot out into space, but she only stood by the large window and stared as the planet got bigger and bigger in front of them.

"Why can we … scramble … is that the right term?" Teal nodded. "...from Lebonath Jas to Dragonhorse, but not from Dragonhorse to Lebonath Tras?" she asked, coming to sit beside him.

"Dragonhorse is in orbit around Jas, which means it's much closer. This is a bit of a hop. We will be in the air close to an hour, and I have a suggestion, if you will not consider it impertinent. Those robes look hot and heavy, and that collar prevents you from seeing to the sides very well. In the back is a refabricator – a clothing making machine – and if you ask it for something more … comfortable, it will give it to you. Just to walk around the surface." He paused. "I'm not scaring you, am I? It gave me these clothes this morning rather than my Dragonhorse uniform, because I wanted trousers with pockets. One cannot go exploring without pockets for a good cutting tool and some sample bags. This is our AEW Expedition uniform.

It's very comfortable. I said that already, didn't I?" He paused again and realized her eyes were twinkling.

"I think, Master Captain, that I scare you more than you scare me. At least so far," she grinned, "And yes, I think something less constraining in the way of apparel would be advisable."

"Perhaps the day will come when we can stop scaring one another altogether. Come along and I'll show you the refabricator. This uniform is pre-programmed in there with an adjustment for size and height, and it will give you any color you want, in case black is all you are allowed to wear."

When she reappeared it was in a plain black blouse and the same sort of loose fitting gray tweed trousers Teal was wearing. She had tied a gauzy black scarf over her head, and when the hat was in place, the anchoress was gone. In her place was a woman tall for a Lebonathi, squarely built, but thin for lack of nourishment. Broad of shoulder, more straight up and down than curvy. Impressive, and rather pretty.

"May I ask you a personal question?" Teal asked, concentrating on setting the ship down in the lower meadow at Stone Spring.

"Yes," she replied, though her focus was obviously outside.

"What color is your hair?"

"I have no idea. I became an anchoress twenty-five years ago when I was sixteen and haven't seen it since."

"Well, let grow out, will you? You'll need it." The door hissed open, allowing in the breeze and the smell of grass and water. "Anchoress Ensharra, welcome to the witch world, where people go to burn," Teal said with a humorless chuckle, and gestured toward the ramp.

While the five Lebonathi scientists had crept out in fear, Ensharra spread her arms and ran, tumbling in the tall grass like a child making a butterfly in the snow. She rolled over on her face and breathed in the smell of the warm earth and growing things. After a while she got up and walked to the shore of the lake … slowly … feeling the sand, seeing the tiny plants and the huge trees, listening to the lap of the waves as the breeze stirred them. She stood looking at the expanse of clear turquoise water, then bent from the waist and put both hands in it, moved them slowly from side to side, and brought them up full of water, which she splashed on her face, and then she began to cry. She spread her arms again and through her tears she sang a song in a language Teal did not know.

"I sang this place a song, too," he said. "Sing yours again."

She did, and Teal sang his, adjusting the melody just enough to make it harmonize – bright tenor, dark alto, and when they finished they looked at each other and Teal dropped an arm around her shoulders, allowing her to lean into him as they stared out across the lake.

"Can you imagine this place with birds singing?" Teal said finally.

"Give me time," she whispered. "I can't even imagine this place."

There was a soft, blowing snort behind them and Ensharra turned to confront the biggest animal she'd ever seen in her life. At least she assumed it was a real animal. She telegraphed unease and Teal's arm tightened around her shoulders. "It's a horse," he said, holding out his other hand to the black and white mare. "I left your treat in the clipper, old girl." He looked at the anchoress. "I want you to stand right here and just let her smell your breath and nuzzle you a bit. That way she'll know who you are, can you do that?"

Ensharra nodded, and when Teal came back with a handful of dried pomes, she was stroking the mare's silky neck and breathing in the good smell of warm horse. "What is this?" she asked, watching Teal offer the mare tidbits. "I'm assuming that whatever it is, it's real?"

"A horse," Teal said again. "Yes, it is alive, just like you and me."

"No. Not what is it called, Master Captain, what is it?" Teal just looked flummoxed. "And don't tell me again that it is a horse. It has teeth like you do, not as nice, much more pronounced, but the same structure. The eyes are quite the same in many ways. Even, vaguely, you have the same smell to your bodies, and very much the same sweet breath. Now, what is she? Is she getting ready to speak to me and tell me I'm being rude by touching her as I am? She is obviously sentient."

"Finally I understand!" Teal laughed. "She is Equus Legatum, the animal for which our planet is named. We do share characteristics and we are distant cousins, though that was an artificial pairing by the race that created us. She, I don't know whether Elam has given her a name or not, is a mare. She will live about thirty-five or forty years with good care. She can have one foal, one baby, every five and a half seasons – about once in every year's turn. Horses mate sexually, male to female. Ah … she will give birth to a live baby and give it milk from her body. While I can run twenty-five to thirty miles an hour, she can run forty-five or fifty miles an hour for three times as long. If you get on her back she will take you anywhere you want to go, and provide companionship as well … and she's not going to talk to you, though she has many ways of letting you know what she wants." He let out his breath and looked at Ensharra. "Now, have I answered your question?"

"Her name is Sugar," Elam said, coming up behind them and extending his hands to Ensharra. "Anchoress, welcome! Ahimsa, I wish thee peace. It's me. It's Elam."

"Elam?"

He nodded and smiled.

She laughed, taking his hands. "Elam! I wouldn't have known it was you by the voice."

"Nor I you, but by yours," he replied. "You, too, have changed. Do you have time for a bit of a looksee before lunch? Please say you'll stay to eat with us."

Teal nodded, and Elam whisked her away, talking a blue streak and trying to point everywhere at once. Teal leaned into the horse's warm shoulder and watched them go. "There goes the future of the Lebonathi Federation," he said, and Sugar turned her head to look at him. "And you, of course," he chuckled, petting her soft nose. "All of us together, but mostly … them."

When Ensharra arrived back in her room that evening, she found on her table a thank-you note from Teal, a gallon of water, a pound of sugar, and another spoon.

CHAPTER 7

"You're replacing me?" Cornwallis Mettenger bellowed, storming into the dining room, and Ardenai looked up from his dinner. "You're having me sent back to fucking Equus? What in hell for?"

Ardenai put down his eating sticks and turned in his chair. "Apologies," he said to those at the table with him. "Wally, would you like to talk about this outside in private?" He moved his chair back to get up, but Mettenger was on top of him by then.

"No!" he bellowed. "You can explain yourself right now in front of God and his public. I'm an SGA observer ..."

"Who has not been observing," Ardenai said quietly. "Why don't you sit down?"

Mettenger stood there glowering down at him, fists knotting and unknotting at his sides.

"I do my job!" he barked.

Ardenai came out of his chair at that point, and Mettenger found himself entirely too close to a shoulder he could barely see over. He took a half-step back, and landed in the chair Marion had just vacated and shoved behind his knees. Ardenai sat back down.

"You are not doing the job I brought you here to do," he said. "When it comes to the recording and checking end of things you're a genius, and I value you for that, but that you can do from the comfort of your office on

Equus. As far as an actual out in the field doing his job observer, you're not. You're either in the dining room or in somebody's … quarters ..." he thought and was quiet a moment, allowing his temper to cool. "You did not know Teal is married to my sister, something everybody knows. You haven't been paying attention. You sat with me watching Eridu have his tantrum and suggested I kill the little fucker, remember? You have no empathy. Last week Konik sent for you because we had provincial governors to interview, and when you finally showed up and talks got rough you suggested, in their presence, that we give them some of the same herbs Eridu got and let them think about their evil deeds while they died. That tells me you're not using your brain, and you're not properly representing the SGA when you say such things. Today you backed a young officer into a corner and made her feel threatened sexually. That's what tears it."

"That's a crock of crap!" Mettenger snapped. "She's been flirting with me for weeks."

"Smiling and saying good morning does not constitute flirting," Ardenai said patiently. "Something has gone wrong in your head. You're done, Mr. Mettenger. Ambassador Dahman will be here in three days and you will be going back on that ship. Until then ..."

"Dahman?" he spluttered. "The one with the fucking TAIL? You're replacing me with that munching, chittering little shit? Why would you do that? Hell, he eats more than I do! You Equi eat more than anybody!"

"Dahman, does not think with his tail, Mr. Mettenger, he uses his brain and his heart, and food has nothing to do with it. Dahman watches, and he listens, and he assesses what he sees and hears. Your attitude is growing tiresome," Ardenai said in a warning tone. "You may wait in your quarters for the ship, or you may wait in the brig. In either case you will wait quietly, starting now. I am tired, I am hungry, and I am in the middle of a meeting. Please leave. If you want to file a protest by all means do so, but go somewhere else to do it. Now."

There was a slow count of three and Mettenger stood up. "The SGA will hear my side of this."

"Fine," Ardenai said. "Just bear in mind that it hasn't heard anything from me. As far as they know you requested to go home so you could work from there. If they hear anything other than that, it won't be from me unless you push the issue. And of course now you've been the one to broadcast it." When he looked up a few moments later, Mettenger was gone.

Ardenai put his elbows on the table, fingers against his forehead and just sat there, trying to swallow his racing heart. He could feel it pounding in his temples and his ears. Days of no sleep was catching up with him, days of worrying about his wife every minute, even when he was trying to think about other things, including what to do with Mettenger.

"Nobody would blame you if you went home to be with her," Kehailan said gently, reading his sire's body language.

"I can't even begin to get there in time," Ardenai said. "They said that as soon as everything was set up they would start – probably within the next few hours – as soon as she's prepped and stable. Ah'din and Ah'rane are with her. That is as it should be. The doctors will link us up for the actual surgery so I can talk to her and to them." He paused, wanting to add that it would be all right, but he was afraid that would just make it worse. He was afraid, period.

Io had called, all smiles, to say she was on her way to Achernar, and that after her appointment the three of them were going to go to the shore for a couple of days, and swim in the ocean and collect shells and generally be lazy and maybe even rowdy. Eight hours later Ardenai had been called up from a flamen-hunt by Pythos, who took him aside and gave him the bad news. Io's body, her amazingly regenerative Papilli body, had decided to repair itself and had left her with a fallopian tube that had grown around the obstructive surgery. In the process, it had twisted. Where the twisted new tube met the tied-off old tube, there were several masses growing at an alarming rate, and infection was setting in. Everything was convoluted within a tangled coagulum of vessels, some not attached to anything and seeping blood. Her whole reproductive system had to go or she would die of infection. Nothing could be fixed. They were done. No little fruit bat babies to terrorize the Great House. If they waited, no Ah'riodin, either.

"I'm fine," he said, making himself pick up his eating sticks. "Where were we?"

Half an hour later Kehailan excused himself from what had become a general discussion of things which did not particularly apply to him, and headed to the sanecere bay to spend some time with Eridi and let Ah'nis go to dinner before he went back on duty. They were setting a huge Papilli Jocundome into orbit, and he was supervising. He had been with the contingent who wanted people to be able to spend time on Lebonath Tras for recreation, but they'd been outvoted. Too many unknowns down there. Too many things that might be fragile. If people wanted to join research teams, or exploration parties on their days off, they could do so with blessings. That had seemed like a good compromise, and Kehailan had acquiesced.

The Papilli, famous for their beautiful gardens and voluptuous hardscapes, had sent one of their biggest Jocundomes as their contribution to the effort, since soldiering was not in their makeup. It was their planet's only industry, and leasing them out had made them among the richest of the Equi worlds. Towed by deep space tugs and assisted by a huge solar sail, it had arrived in good time for something so large; a sphere just under two hundred miles in diameter. On it were lakes, rivers, bridle paths, polo grounds, villages, gardens, pools, pavilions, fields and forests – even a glowing glass city called Crysalis – all within a protective dome which allowed it to go anywhere and be put to use, either as a recreational facility, or a whole world. It was permanently populated, completely self-sustaining and its huge farms, already in production, would provide much-needed food for the interposing forces, and for Lebonath Jas. It would give them a place to hold meetings in a more natural setting, to cultivate species, to begin wakening the animals. It also had intimate apartments for many different races, and provided well trained hetaera for Equi heat cycles.

Kehailan was beginning to feel like he needed a hetaera. He and Timothy had tried to carve out some time, but they were both so busy, and spaced so far apart, that just slipping away together for a couple of hours when they were off duty was no longer possible. They were both missing the trust, the laughs, the intimacy, and the other friends who sometimes joined them. Things did change, even when it felt like they never would. He thought about Tim – sighed to himself, and went to sit with Eridi.

He nodded to Ah'nis and she rose with a smile, thanking him as she left. "So, Princess, it is our time together. And where were we in Macbeth? It has all the elements of the perfect story, and if my eyes get tired, I can always recite it, which is a plus."

He looked for the book where he'd left it, saw it in the window sill and went to get it. "I can hardly wait for you to see Lebonath Tras," he said. He said it often, and it always made him smile. "You are much too young yet for me to speak to you of marriage, or even a relationship, but if you were old enough, and I were to ask you to marry me and you were to say yes, we could have a home there on the outskirts of some village. Or maybe it would just be a place to take the children for holiday, and we would go swimming and walking and I suppose we'd have to go horseback riding as well, since you seem to have a penchant for the stinky, balky things. Mostly, I think our home would be here on Dragonhorse, in one of the family apartments. When someone told me recently that my children would grow up on huge stellar ships I wanted to laugh, both at the idea of children and of raising a family on a ship. Now I'm glad I didn't."

He had picked up the book by this time, loosened the covers over her toes – Ah'nis always pulled them too tight, like shoes a size too small – and reseated himself facing her where he could touch her hand and watch her face. Except for the apparatus which kept her head immobile on her neck and the machine which beeped softly, hardly more than a heartbeat, she looked like she could be asleep. Peaceful. Pale. Unresponsive.

"I have fallen quite in love with you, and I have no idea why," he said. "If I'd found you this way, perhaps in a crystal coffin or something, I'd think it was because you were unattainable, and therefore without risk on my part. But there you were, daughter of the man who had set my father screaming until his throat bled, trying to help him. And there was such grace in your movements, and such purpose …" he huffed and opened the book. "I just want you to know that I was happy being a self-centered little prince with an easy job and a life back home so placid as to be embarrassing. And then … there was my father, wearing the golden armbands of Equus, and then a ship I'd forgotten I designed, probably the medications Pythos was giving me for pain, and then there was you. And I don't know who in kraa I am, but I know who I can't afford to be anymore. So, where were we?" He flipped the pages and began to read.

"Act Four, Scene One, A dark cavern, full of all things terrifying, and in the middle, a bubbling cauldron. There is a roll of thunder, probably like we have on Equus, the kind that shakes the air, and three hideous old witches enter and stand around the pot, probably wondering what's for dinner. The first witch says, 'Thrice the brindled ped hath mewed.'

"The second one says, 'Thrice and once the hedge-pig whined.' There is no Equi translation for hedge-pig, but I can't imagine it's anything nice. The third witch says, 'Crier calls, it's time, it's time.' Now we get to the good part. The first witch says, 'Round about the cauldron go, in the poisoned entrails throw. Toad that under cold stone days and nights has thirty-one, sweltered venom sleeping got, boil him first in the charmed pot.' Then they all chant, 'Double, double, toil and trouble, fire burn and cauldron bubble.' The second witch says, 'Fillet of a fenny snake, in the cauldron boil and bake. Eye of newt and toe of frog, wool of bat and tongue of dog'..."

"Kehailan?" The voice made him look up and catch his breath. "You may be my husband one day, but you are through as my cook."

By then he had her hand in both of his and he was shaking all over and yelling for Pythos and Ah'nis in his head. "Hi," he said softly. "How long have you been awake?"

"Long enough," she smiled, working to get her eyes open. "I can't move my head. What happened this morning?"

"This morning?" he echoed. "When …?" he prompted. "We ..."

"When we went to see my father. He hit me, didn't he and ..." there was alarm in her eyes, "he shot at you!" She looked at him, saw the mark on his neck, and her features relaxed into bemusement. "He got you, didn't he – but that wound is nearly healed …."

"You have some catching up to do," he said quietly. "A lot has happened, and don't try to move for a bit yet."

"He didn't hurt Ah'nis did he?" she asked, alarmed again.

"Absolutely not. She's … right here," he smiled, "and I think she's going to be very glad to see you, child of her heart. I will go and leave you two. We'll finish Macbeth another time."

He straightened up, and was turning away when she said, "Do not think for one minute you're reading that to our children, Kehailan. It's awful."

"Yes, Princess," he said with a wave over his shoulder, and headed for the bridge, wondering at himself for being a little weak in the knees.

He stopped in the dining room where Teal, Konik and Ardenai were talking and looking at an old map weighted down with wine glasses. They all looked up expectantly. "She's awake," he said. "Sounds like quite her old self. We're going to be doing some bumping and maneuvering here for a while. You may want to launch Dominus before you have to contend with the gravity of that Jocundome." He paused and met Ardenai's gaze. "And too," he added, knowing his father was peering into his soul, "that dome may interfere with communications from the relay ships. We may have to tie up communications on board Dragonhorse to get it in position. You should go, just in case." He gave the three men a dutiful nod, and left the room.

"He's right," Ardenai said. "If you two want to stay here, you are welcome to do so."

"I have things to do toward colonization," the governor said, rising from his chair and rolling up the map. "Please … keep me informed over the next few hours."

"I will leave things in your capable hands," Teal smiled. "My place right now is with my family. I, at least, will plan to see you at first light planet time. We have flamen to filch."

"Pundits to pounce on," Konik added. "Ardenai, my prayers are with you and Io, you know that."

"I do," he nodded, "Thank you."

He was having the oddest feeling of being on the outside looking in, as though this were happening to someone else and he was watching from afar, wrapped up in the story, but not part of it. He went with Teal to Dominus, and as they launched, Kehailan's voice in his head whispered, *I love you, Dad. If you need me, I am thine.*

That night they didn't sleep by the river, but stayed on Dominus, high up, where they could watch the miracle of something the size of a small moon being worked into a stable orbit, and where the signal from a relay ship would be clear of chatter from Dragonhorse and the tugs. Neither of them pretended to sleep to make the other one feel good. They didn't talk much or share what ifs or wine. They drank hot cider so they would both be very, very sharp if they needed to be. If wine was needed later they could always open a bottle or two.

"They're about ready to start," Ah'din said, life-sized on the screen in front of them, and despite her quiet voice, both men jumped. "Sorry. I didn't mean to startle. Where are you?"

"Dominus," Teal said. "It's just the two of us."

Ah'din turned her smile on Ardenai. "Hi, Big Brother. How are you holding up?"

"Not well. You know me. I'm a wreck by now. I'm hoping your husband will help me present a semblance of stability and calm to my wife."

"She's pretty well sedated, so she may not notice all that much," Ah'din said. There was a pause. "I know she says she's come to terms with this, but you have to know she hasn't. She wanted babies with you more than anything else in the world…" she lost control of her bottom lip and two big tears rolled down her face.

Ardenai brought up a warning finger. "I absolutely forbid you to do that, Dini. I'm half off my horse already. Maybe they can save an egg or two, maybe we can do a DNA cultured embryo. Maybe ..."

"We could do one of thosse thingss if thee wass not the Thirteenth Dragonhorsse," one of the physicians said, coming into view. "Thee musst let go. Where is Physsician Pythoss?"

"On Dragonhorse. Princess Eridi woke up, and he felt helping her had more merit than watching helplessly during a surgery where he cannot hope to assist."

The serpent bobbed his head in that undulating nod of agreement common among their kind, and Ardenai realized that, while he had been around Pythos all his life, he hadn't seen much of the other dragon physicians, secretive and solitary creatures that they were.

"He iss wisse. Two of uss will be doing the ssurgery. Two Equi will be asssisssting. We can awaken thy wife if thee wisshes to sspeak to her."

"I … thought she would be awake for this."

"We had hoped," he said, busy with displays on a panel. "Sshe iss having trouble sstaying calm, and that … could be dissasterouss. When all iss in play and sshe iss fully imobilissed, we will waken her consscious mind – in cassse there are decissionss to make."

"What does that mean?' Ardenai grimaced, but the doctor ignored him and Ah'din's face came back.

"Our mother is with your wife," she said, almost formally. "We will sit, one on each side of her, until this is over and she is resting safely. You may watch her face, and ours, or you may watch what the physicians are doing, or we can split the screen – your choice."

"Split the screen," Teal said. He looked at Ardenai, who was starting to tremble. "Split the screen."

"I'm going to vomit," Ardenai managed, starting to get up, and Teal pointed downward and growled,

"Puke on the floor, but you leave your ass in that chair. I mean it, Ardi." He got a defiant glare that would have put a lesser man on his knees, and just shook his head. "Don't even try it. You cannot stand up to an entire planet one minute and turn tail and hide the second you're faced with personal loss. You fell apart when Ah'ree died. You nearly fell apart on Calumet when Io got hurt. You fell apart when Kehailan got shot, and you gave an order that could have cost the Lebonathi scientists their life's work. You've got to get astride this sudden panic that seems to envelop you, Dragonhorse."

Ardenai began to growl deep in his chest and his eyes changed shape, but he stayed in the chair, which pleased his brother-in-law. Hopefully this was not going to come to blows in front of the women.

"This is a perfect time to practice getting a grip, and thinking things through," Teal said quietly.

"What if she dies?" There was that child's voice again. How strange, that a man so strong could have such a weakness.

"You will cry, as Konik did. And then, like Nik, you will get on with your day. If you can't do it, pretend like you can. Watch the screen." Much as Teal wanted to, he didn't put an arm around Ardenai. He folded his arms to stop the motion and sat watching as the screen split.

The instruments went one way up the twisting course of the birth canal, and the other side showed Io, and Ah'rane and Ah'din. That was the side Ardenai watched first. Io's eyes were slightly open, but the fact that they didn't blink said she wasn't really conscious. Her wild array of hair had been collected into a neat braid, probably by Ah'rane, who could braid anything. Her breathing was slow and even. She had a son. He had a son. They had Gideon. They had three fine boys. This was not the end of their world. It was sad, but it was not the end of their world.

He forced himself to take a deep breath. Then another. Teal was right. Better to be fully present than looking over one's shoulder imagining what was happening. Whatever it was, he was here, sending every ounce of his strength and resolve into the body of his wife. More than that, he had to send her hope. He clenched his fists against his chest and sent her his whole heart.

He made himself look at the other monitor and very nearly passed out. An instrument, guided by a physician was going very slowly over a blue mass of slick, undulating tendrils. Snip-hiss. Snip-hiss. Each one being cauterized as it was cut. Dozens, hundreds maybe. Going on, and on, and on for what felt like hours. As those were cleared away by gentle suction into a large jar that was set aside, the tubes themselves and the masses which had formed, became visible. The physicians stopped, made sure nothing was bleeding, and studied the masses closely, assessing and deciding how best to proceed. They spoke so quietly amongst themselves that even Equi ears were not privy to the conversation. Then a needle a hundred times smaller than a hair made its way into one of the masses. Not far, just the tiniest stick. It was removed and the contents studied.

"Time to wake her up," one of the physicians said. Another set about doing that, and the serpent turned to the screen. "Dragonhorsse, iss thee pressent?"

"I am," Ardenai said. He almost asked if something was wrong, but he didn't. He sat and waited patiently, making himself breathe, as Io's mouth, then the movement of her eyes, said she was more awake. Apparently she could see him, because she smiled.

"Hi," he said.

"It iss decission time," the physician said, gesturing to include the family, and his gesture widened the screen so they could see each other. "Ssee here," he said, pointing at one of the masses, "Thiss iss why thee wass getting pregnanccy ssignals, Io. Thesse, are embryoss. Now, before thee getss too exccited, they are not all viable, and perhapss none. Mosst ccertainly they are sstresssed at besst. However, we can try to ssave one if it iss viable, yess?"

He didn't wait for an answer. "Ordinarily we could remove them each very carefully, asssesss their viability and sset them to growing in crèche podss for part or all of their gesstation. In thiss casse, by mosst anccient law, we cannot do that. Not with Dragonhorsse babess. If they leave thy body, they musst, by law, die. What we can do, iss remove them very carefully from their pressent confinement, and if they are viable, implant one of them into thy uteruss, which sshould lasst through a gesstation before it iss removed, IF... IF ... thee iss willing to lie flat on thy back with thy legss up for at leasst two full sseasonss. It may attach, it may not. It may all be for nothing. Choosse, Dragonhorsse. Choosse, Primuxori."

Ardenai smiled at his wife. "Your choice, Beloved. You are the one who will have to go through this."

"I can work with graphs on the ceiling," she said firmly. "Will you be all right without me?"

He knew what she meant. "Absolutely. I choose you. If you choose life, I embrace your decision with all my heart."

"Then we choose the chance for life," she smiled. "Even if these few minutes of hope are all we have, it was more than we thought we'd have going into this."

"Let uss begin," the doctor said. "The first embryo we know iss not viable. It iss dead," Carefully over half an hour or so it was cut away and removed, making sure no blood flowed away from the others to weaken them.

The next one tested was also dead. It was cut away and removed in the same manner. Ardenai stood up and twisted his back a little, but his eyes never left the monitors, either his wife's anxious, hopeful face, or the movement of the tiny instruments. He walked around behind his chair and stood with his hands on the back, rotating his shoulders. He was torn between the want of something to drink and the growing need to relieve himself.

Finally, as they were cutting away the third unviable embryo he said, "I will be right back," and trotted off toward the lavage.

When he returned Teal handed him a cup of hot cider and a round, fruit-studded honeycake and hurried off in the same direction. Ardenai realized they'd been involved with this for hours. Four? Five? He wasn't sure, but parts of him were getting numb, and his churning stomach had gone from nauseated by what they were doing, to churning from hunger. He gratefully bit into the cake.

The fourth embryo, wass viable, "And reassonably sstrong," the physician added. Carefully it was moved into the uterus and encouraged to attach to the wall. Amniotic fluid was added, and a microscopic and temporary tack to keep it in place. "There are two more masses. I would ssuggesst that if there iss one more that iss viable, it be implanted as well. It increassess the chanccess of one of them ssurviving."

And so the process continued by milimikrons. The fifth embryo was viable, but died before they could implant it, and they moved on to the sixth and last.

"Thiss one, iss already riding a horsse and wanting to ssuck," the physician said. "I think he, or sshe, is the oldesst. Good, nourisshing blood flow, as well. Thiss one may actually have a chancce." It was lifted while everyone held their breath, and implanted as carefully as the first. "We have done what we can," the physician said, and turned to Io. "Ssay goodnight to thy good hussband for a bit."

She smiled at him and the stress of the last many hours stood hard on her features. "Not very romantic, was it? I'd tell you what they are ...

if I knew."

"There will be time enough for all of that, Beloved. You and those babies sleep tight. I'll be home to see you as soon as I can."

"No hurry," she said. "No point in both of us being bored."

"Enjoy your boredom while you can," Ardenai said, and they spirited her away without the chance for either of them to say goodbye.

It took Ardenai a moment to recover from the abruptness of the departure, then he said, "Thank you," and the serpent nodded. For a surreal moment Ardenai knew it was Pythos.

"Thou art welcome, Dragonhorsse."

"When will I be able to speak to her again?"

"Thee may sspeak to her any time, but there iss ccertainly no need to hurry home," he said with that hissy, bobbing smile Pythos exhibited when he was amused. "Sshe will not hear thee, for about two sseassons. We told thee that."

Ardenai's eyes got wide and his head cocked slowly to one side. "Two seasons? One hundred and twenty-eight days? When, exactly, did you say that?"

"We asssumed thee would know what we meant when we told thy busy, hyperactive wife sshe would have to hold sstill for that long." He began to hiss in earnest, writhing at his own humor. "I sshall let thee sspeak to the resst of thy womenfolk," he managed, and went off after the others, leaving Ah'din and Ah'rane alone.

"I wish I could hug you, Ardi," Ah'rane said, holding a hand out as though to touch him, and he very much wished that she could. "Things will be fine, Sweetheart. Just think, there might be twins in the house by this time next year."

"And another babe on the way," Teal said quietly. "I promise, Din. We need to go. We've had this channel open for almost … eight hours? Is that possible? I will be in touch soon. Are you two heading for home, or are you going to go to the beach first like Io wanted to do?"

"Beach," Ah'din said firmly. "We need some sea shells for the baby's room."

The connection was severed and they stood for a minute or two, still staring at the screen. Then Ardenai sighed and Teal's arm came around him. "You're cold, and so am I," Teal said. "Come on, I'll give you a bath before breakfast."

Ardenai managed to look Teal in the eye without letting his expression change and said, "Why do I feel like … this is not going to go well?"

"Because you have no control over the situation, and you're tired, and you're hungry, and you're more sectors away than either of us would care to be at this point. In any case, the decision was hers, and you did absolutely the right thing by letting her make it. Let's do something about the things we can. We can bathe, we can eat, and if you'll uproot yourself, we might even find time for a nap on the way back to Dragonhorse."

Ardenai nodded, and with a last glance at the blank screen, allowed Teal to steer him toward the warmth and comfort of the bathing pool.

CHAPTER 8

Eladeus," Ardenai murmured, "I thought we had found the darkest places on this dark planet. Now I see that we did not."

"Not even close," Konik responded. "It does explain why we couldn't find any farmers."

They were standing in one of the subterranean tunnels they'd seen early on, but hadn't really gotten around to exploring past an initial cursory examination to determine what they were. They'd known that was where they grew mushrooms. Period. Now, in the stifling heat and the awful stench, they were discovering who tended the mushrooms.

Naked, cadaverously thin men chained to carts which ran on tracks, just enough chain length to reach the spawn beds. Prisoners, maybe criminal, maybe political, it was hard to tell. Many of them had been tortured and some had their tongues cut out. Some had no genitals. Some who had tried to escape had all their toes cut off.

The tunnels closest to the surface hadn't been too bad. That's where the inspectors came, when they came. That's where the buyers came. That's where the AEW troopers had come. But past the first two hundred yards, around the corner where the lights got dim and the smell of human and animal excrement got worse, that's where the tracks picked up the bigger carts and the human racks of bones who pushed them.

Teal and Konik were watching Ardenai. He'd been chained to an ore cart in the cleomitite mines on Calumet – beaten, starved, deprived of water and sleep. The physical scars he still bore were obvious. They were both wondering if some of the unseen scars would manifest themselves at this point.

"It was you, wasn't it?" he said finally, addressing Konik but not looking at him. "It was you who got word to Io and Teal to watch the mines for Gideon and me."

Konik grunted and the corners of his mouth twitched momentarily. "Ummm. Word moves so kraaling slow on that planet I'm surprised they found you at all. What are we going to do here?"

"Talk to them," Ardenai said. "Find out who they are and how they ended up in here. We can't just let them go, because some of them may be very dangerous men."

Even as he was speaking he was looking at them, lined up where they'd been herded on either side of the tracks; pale bodies vanishing into the dimness as far as the light would let them see. None of them weighed a hundred pounds or even close to it. How could they possibly be dangerous?

"All told, these tunnels run for hundreds of miles. Let's get a count of about how many men there are per mile and figure out how many we're dealing with. If there are thirty men per mile ... fifty … a hundred …." he stopped speaking and left the others to figure it out. It was mind boggling. It was overwhelming, and then they were left with the task of figuring out who was going to grow the mushrooms.

"What we could do," Konik said, blue eyes blinking hard as he tried to wipe the sweat off his face with the back of his hand. "Damn, that burns. We could go down the lines, figure out who is so badly hurt or so sick they can't stay, and who is actually dangerous – get the others food, water, decent ventilation and a decent place to sleep for a reasonable amount of time every night … and leave them to do what they're doing, just for now, until we figure out whether we need the mushrooming operations to feed the population. I know that's not a very good solution …."

"But it's not a bad one, either," Ardenai said. "Have we figured out where they warehouse these men?"

"Not so far," Teal shrugged, trying without success to get the sweat off his own face. His clothes were soaked and there was no place to wipe his hands. He ended up shaking the moisture off his fingertips onto the ground. "They won't talk to us. Won't say a word, even with the guards out of ear-shot and out of commission."

"Notice," Ardenai said, "They're not sweating. They're too dehydrated. From the way this place smells they're not unchained to defecate. There's not much ammonia smell, so they're drinking their own urine at least part of the time."

Konik nodded in agreement. "I'm going to walk this line a distance and look into some eyes. I will bet I can find someone aware enough, and verbal enough, to talk to us." He walked slowly down one side for a hundred feet or so, turned and walked back up the other side. He repeated the process and this time he pulled a man out of the line on the left hand side halfway down. He took him by the arm, walked him slowly back to the others, and presented him to Ardenai.

The Firstlord motioned toward the upper end of the tunnel and they took the man, who hobbled along in his leg chains on his mutilated feet. Near the top where the air was moving a little more, Ardenai gestured for the man to sit in the dirt against the wall, swished the water in the flask at his waist and offered it to him. He wouldn't take it. Ardenai uncapped it, drank some, and offered it to him again. The man just looked at him.

"So, Nik. Why did you choose this one?"

"Look at his feet – no toes. He's a runner. He's tried to get away and more than once, or I miss my guess. He won't drink because he's afraid the water has something in it."

"Ardenai drank it," Teal said.

"Just because we're all hominoidea, doesn't mean we're all the same," Ardenai reasoned. We're aliens. It could be something we drink every day that would kill him."

"They must get water," Teal said. "The electrolytes and acids from urine would get more and more concentrated with each pass until their bodies just shut down. They have to be getting water or something like it as their primary source of liquid."

"Do they water mushrooms?" Konik asked, squatting on his heels to look at the seated prisoner. "Do you water the mushrooms, my friend?"

Teal jerked his chin at the man and asked quietly, "Does he have a tongue?"

"That's a very good question, and I am being exceptionally rude," Ardenai said, squatting beside Konik. "Forgive me. I speak as though you have no understanding simply because you have been stripped of your status. I am Ardenai, Firstlord of Equus. The taller of my companions is Teal, Master Captain. The better looking one is Konik, Military Governor of the Lebonathi worlds. Ahimsa, we wish thee peace. Can you speak?" To their surprise the man nodded. "Would you tell us your name?" He just looked at them.

"He has absolutely no reason to trust us," Teal sighed. "But I know someone he might trust. I will be back in a few minutes."

He strode toward daylight and Konik straightened up, pushing at his sternum with a gasp of pain and a short bark of laughter. "The joys of getting shot in the chest," he said, and grinned at Ardenai. "I'm fine. How is Ah'riodin?"

"In a crèche pod in a medically induced coma," Ardenai said. "I try to visit with her every day. She's been in there six days and we haven't had an argument for nearly a week. The doctors say both babies are still alive, so that's a hopeful sign."

"It is indeed. Io was going to lay out the keeps, wasn't she?"

Ardenai nodded. "I'm wondering if I could get my father to do it. Maybe my parents together. I'm sure they have nothing better to do." He snorted without humor. "I'm joking … I think. I need to find someone who is up for the task, and soon, or it's going to be riding double on your horse, Governor."

"Have you met a woman named Ah'cora?" Konik asked. "She is a topnotch cartographer."

"Sarkhan's sister? I met her very briefly at Mountain hold."

"Step. His father married her mother late in the chukka and proceeded to drive her barking mad, though she was never far from it. Saw her husband and son get squashed when a grist wheel flew off its plate, and never got over it." He paused, glanced sideways at Ardenai, then nodded. "Yes, that one. Huge piece of equipment at an Agricultural Exposition. My grandfather and my sister died in that same accident, along with a couple dozen other onlookers. Anyway, Ah'cora's a fine young woman. She'd probably be pathetically grateful for a break from the old folks, and she might be a real addition to the mapping teams on Lebonath Tras."

The man looked up suddenly and his eyes got big. He muttered something they couldn't make out, and dropped his eyes again.

"You said something that woke him up."

"And now the poor man is even more terrified. The farm ships are here and in stable orbit. Maybe we should take all these fellows up there and put them to work, let some of those Menorquin crews go home," Konik said, and got a thumbs up from Ardenai.

"Very good idea, Governor. Ah, here comes the Master Captain with ..." he looked closer. The light was bright at the mouth of the tunnel and all he could see was a black outline. "Someone."

It turned out to be Ensharra. She had modified her long black robes and high, restrictive collar to a pair of loose black trousers and a black tunic with a simple banded collar. She had a diaphanous black scarf tied around her head, and she was wearing her old straw hat. She gave Ardenai and Konik a cool nod.

"Dragonhorse. Governor," she said, and sat down without hesitation in front of the prisoner, who immediately put his knees together to hide his nakedness. "I am Ensharra, Anchoress of the Ancient City. Are these men treating you well?" He nodded. "What is your name?"

"Bona," he murmured, hanging onto his knees.

"Who imprisoned you here?"

"The flamen," he said. His voice was scarcely a whisper, and his eyes darted from side to side in fear. "They said they watch all the time, Anchoress. You should be careful."

"They are not watching today," she said. "I am thirsty. Will one of you share your water with me?" Konik handed her his hip canteen, and she shook it and then drank. "That is very good, thank you," she said, and offered the canteen to Bona, who took it eagerly and began to drink. "Not too much at once or you'll get sick, Bona. What did you do to make them imprison you here?"

His eyes, already lowered with the canteen, dropped to the ground and his shoulders hunched. "I would not give them my daughter." He whispered. He looked up and his eyes were pleading for understanding. "They offered me money for her – my little girl. My Uzalla. They said they would make her a queen. A goddess, like the others, but I said no. But they took her, and I fought. My wife fought, and now she is dead, and my daughter is gone somewhere. I meant no disrespect, Anchoress. I only wanted them to wait a little. To let her choose. I meant no disrespect." He dropped his head to his knees and rocked back and forth to comfort himself.

"How long have you been here?" she asked.

"I do not know, a long time," he responded, not looking up. "My son is all alone."

"These big men are Equi," she said, gesturing toward where they sat a respectful way down the wall. "They are good people. They have food and water. They will help you get home. They will help all of you get home who deserve to go. But you need to answer their questions so they can help you find your way. Can you do that?" He nodded. "Can they come and talk to you?" He nodded again.

She moved to get up and his eyes registered panic. "Don't leave!" he pleaded. "Don't leave. I will talk to the soft one if you will stay."

"The soft one?" she asked. "Which one is the soft one?"

"That one," he said, pointing a filthy finger at Konik. "The soft one."

Konik rose without hesitation and came to sit beside Ensharra facing Bona. "I am Konik," he said. He glanced at Ensharra and mouthed, "Any idea why I'm the soft one?"

"I think it's your voice," she whispered. "What do you need to know first?"

"Bona, is there a central area, a place where you go at night to sleep, or eat, or get water? A place where they hold you sometimes?"

He nodded, pointing down the tunnel. "Far," he said, "Where there is no light and light again that way. Where the guards come in from the side."

"I am of no help here," Teal said, turning to Ardenai as the others went on speaking. "This has put me off your mother's Mushroom Javari for probably the rest of my life, so I think I'll go see if I can figure out where he's talking about. Perhaps I can encourage one of the Lebonathi guards to enlighten me. Field trip, Ardenai Teacher?" He offered the Firstlord a hand up from the dirt floor.

A few minutes later, having persuaded a guard by size if not reason, Teal and Ardenai started off down a paved path on the side of an expansive date orchard. They could feel the heat of the sidewalk through their field boots, and a fitful wind kicked dust from the overworked ground into their eyes and hair. They ducked their heads and trudged a quarter mile or so until they came to a small sign on a round white post, with an arrow pointing left and down. They went down a ramp and through double doors into a huge space clearly used for loading. Only the presence of their military contingent had stopped the movement of half a dozen freight cars, sitting on a side rail, already loaded. Not only mushrooms down here, but narrow gauge trains, as well. They stood where the guard had told them to, and got their bearings.

"Through there," Ardenai said, pointing eighty or so feet ahead and slightly to their right. It was a wide steel door with a bar across it. No padlock. "This is where he said we would find the staging area for the prisoners." He lifted up on the heavy metal bar. "Seems an odd place for it," he said. He opened the door, and staggered back against Teal, gagging at the sight and the smell. It was stacked with corpses in various stages of decay. "Creator Spirit have mercy!" Ardenai exclaimed, retching as he slammed the door. "What … who are these people that they can do such things?"

There was a pounding from an identical door to their right, and they gave each other a long, searching look before raising the bar and opening it

… just a crack, then wider. In this dark, stinking hole, were living beings, crowding together, pointing and gibbering in slow motion, some hiding, some rocking back and forth. All walling their eyes and making exaggerated faces which said they could not comprehend what they were seeing.

"They've lost their minds," Teal said quietly, taking one step in. "They've either been driven mad by being here, or the mad are warehoused as criminals on this planet. I think this one is just a child." Teal crouched on his heels, extending his hand to calm the boy, and found his arm grabbed and thoroughly bitten by the person in question.

"Ow!" he exclaimed, thumping the boy hard with thumb and fore-finger to make him let go. It took two tries, and he finally had to pull his arm away, boy and all, tearing the flesh. "Ow. Damn!" He backed up, clutching at the wound and watching the child lick the blood off his lips and smile. The others began sniffing the air and looking at the blood dripping onto the floor.

"We're in trouble," Ardenai said quietly, and Teal just nodded.

"We need to get out of here, now …." They stepped back slowly, then grabbed the door and slammed it, dropping the bar a split second before the first prisoner hit it.

"This is going nowhere," the Firstlord snapped, looking around with thinly veiled anger. "I think this is where we should start using the pulse cannons." He looked at Teal, who was still clutching his forearm. "How badly are you hurt?"

Teal moved his hand, and the blood welled up and began running down his arm, pale blue mixing with the dust and dirt. "I'm not," he shrugged, wiping his bloody left hand on his sweat-soaked pants. "It'll clean itself out. There's only one more door. That has to be it."

But it wasn't. It was a shipping office, abandoned in haste, artificially lighted, and artificially cooled. There was a jug of water, but they didn't touch it. Instead they went back across the narrow gauge tracks and through the double doors into the open air before stopping for a drink from their hip canteens. Teal poured some water on the stinging wound, rubbed it with his opposing forearm and dismissed it.

When Ardenai got back to the squat white building which housed the guards and the records for the mushrooming operation, he stalked past the two Amberian troopers and grabbed the guard who had directed them. "Where did you send us?" he snarled, and the man nearly passed out.

"You … Firstlord, I thought … you asked where we warehoused our … workers. Is that not what you asked? I thought I told you what you wanted to know. The bodies we grind up for fertilizer, the others ..."

"You thought would kill us when we opened the door to your little asylum." The man's face hardened with the truth, and Ardenai dropped him on the floor. "Chain him to a cart," Ardenai said, and went on to leave instructions for dealing with the prisoners they'd found locked away as well as the corpses.

They went back to the tunnel where they'd started, and found Konik and Ensharra walking among the prisoners, calming them, encouraging them with a smile or a touch.

"I think," Ardenai said quietly, "that we should try persuading the anchoress to join us as an observer. She gives us credibility with the common folk. She speaks their language, knows their hearts."

Teal nodded thoughtfully. "If she will spare us her time," he said, watching her and the effect she was having on the men she spoke to. "I think we must recognize that there are two distinct wellsprings feeding the river of religion that flows across this planet. Ensharra, and those like her, who tend the soup kitchens and the makeshift saneceres with our priestesses, who teach in secret the women and children. They of great faith, who speak to and for the majority of the people. And the flamen, who seem to speak for those of wealth and who fan the flames of hatred among the rich and fear among the poor. It is the flamen who are getting all the air time. I know we said we weren't going to get involved in a war of words, but perhaps … we should. We should begin to show the people what we're actually doing. And we could begin to give the anchoresses some air time as well. We are documenting everything we are doing. If Ensharra would use our historia to speak to some of the things she personally has seen, perhaps we could begin to alter the course of that river."

The Firstlord looked from Teal to the anchoress, who was slowly walking their way, and back to Teal. "If we make her a threat, or an enemy of the flamen, they may do to her what they did to Brak. They may break into her shop, find her educational materials, and start killing every woman and child who can count past ten."

"It is a risk," Teal muttered. "One she would have to agree to."

"No, Ardenai said. "She's too valuable as she is."

"I've got it," Teal said, obviously frustrated, "Let's get the Achernareans to make an android of her for us. We know they have the technology. Ardi, every step takes us deeper into the quicksand! We are either going to have to do what Kehailan suggests and start killing people, and I have troops and weaponry in place to do just that either directly or indirectly, or we can start taking risks of a more social nature, but we can't keep going as we are – we don't have enough of an information system in place yet even to reach everyone, much less convince anybody. We have got to have help to do that." He paused, tipped his head slightly to one side, stood for a moment. "I must go. My reinforcements are here. I will see you at dinner." He slapped his kinsman on the shoulder, asked him to see to Ensharra's safe return, and trotted off up the tunnel toward daylight.

"Get that wound looked at," Ardenai called after him, and he waved without turning around.

It took Teal most of the afternoon to get back to Dragonhorse, but when he did, he untied the bandage he'd found for his bite, waterfalled to rinse off the sweat-crusted filth, then went to the bathing pools and scrubbed himself again before heading off to the sanecere bay. A corpsman cleaned and disinfected the wound, used kedges to close the worst of the tearing, and wrapped it in gauze.

Teal thanked him, wishing Pythos were here to take a look at the thing, but he was worlds away. Now that Eridi could make the trip in relative safety, Pythos had bundled her into Dominus's sister ship, the IEC Regence, and taken her to Achernar for treatment. Everyone knew that wasn't his only reason for going; he wanted to check on Io, as well, and Ardenai had not objected. Knowing Pythos, he'd probably spend a few days at Canyon keep before coming back. Teal took a deep, envious breath and presented a much improved version of himself to his dinner companions.

Konik was slightly ahead of him, Ardenai close behind. Kehailan and Captain Gallios joined them and they spent two hours discussing what they'd found at the mushrooming operation and how to proceed to best advantage. Having done the math and concluding that the huge, ancient terraformers were bigger by nearly half than all the discovered tunnels combined, it was decided that those men who were sane and healthy, those being relative terms, would be transferred to the Menorquin farm ships to continue their tending of plants, and the mushrooming operation would be shut down until the tunnels could be refurbished for legitimate growing operations.

Kehailan had good news – wonderful news, as a matter of fact. The Potami had stepped forward and asked if they could negotiate for the caronai. They were recolonizing an abandoned planet near their homeworld, and, like Calumet, it wouldn't support technology of any kind. It was fertile, but it was hot. It was primitive. They wanted to train the big, rugged animals to pull plows. Since the Potami were big and rugged themselves, Ardenai thought it a good match and gave his blessing. He wondered if that was all the Potami had been after when they'd considered invasion. It would have been enough. Without the caronai the Lebonathi would have starved in short order. In any case, Ardenai gave them the caronai, barter for benefit of the Lebonathi to be negotiated at some future time. For now, just come and take them away, the quicker the better.

He and Teal were still chuckling about it as they headed for Lebonath Tras. Neither of them had eaten much at dinner, the heat, the stress and the smell having taken their toll, and they had a small meal and a glass of wine while they discussed, under better conditions, how best to utilize Ensharra should she choose to allow them that privilege. They set Dominus a little closer than usual to their pavilion and walked there in the fading twilight.

"I do love the planetary time difference," Teal smiled, gesturing toward the remnants of sunset. "This is just about my favorite time of day here. Everything smells extra good."

"Our home away from home," Ardenai said, stripping and tossing his clothes on his sleeping platform. "Our first encampment on the new world, and I am retaining it for our family. Not a big keep, mind you – compared to Equus none of them are, really – but a place to come and relax. You can plant rhax vines to see how they will do, and I will plant fruit trees. Dini can plant a big garden if she chooses. We can have our own experimental station, and we'll have a place for us and the children to swim and ride."

"I'd like that," Teal said, and his eyes were far away in a warm room with a fire on the hearth and a loom clicking quietly while he read. "I think I'll skip a swim tonight. I'm really tired." He stripped to his briefcloth, stretched out on his fleecy bed, and in moments he was asleep. He didn't waken when Ardenai came in from his swim, and the Firstlord put a cover over him, pleased that he was sleeping well.

Ardenai was used to being the first one up. He was one of those annoying people who awoke all at once and sprang out of bed and into his day. Teal, woke more slowly and was not particularly fond of initial bustle if he could avoid it. Ardenai put a cup of sweet white coffee on the block beside him and headed out for his morning run.

When he returned an hour later he dropped his running shoes at the water's edge and dove into the pool, wondering why he hadn't passed Teal coming back. He swam a couple of laps and then began to realize … there was no sense of his kinsman at all. Not awake. Not asleep. Nothing. He waded into the shallows and looked. Dominus was where they had left it the night before. Ardenai got out of the water, grabbed the towel he'd dropped before his run, and dried himself off as he walked to the pavilion. Teal was still in bed. He hadn't moved from his right side, and his coffee was untouched.

"Time to greet the morning," Ardenai said in a voice tinged with worry. There was no response.

Ardenai dropped to his knees beside the low sleeping platform. "Teal? Beloved?" He put the back of his hand to Teal's cheek, and it was like touching a stove. "Teal?" he said, and gave his shoulder a gentle shake.

Then, he looked at the arm. The veins were standing up slightly and the skin had taken on an almost transparent, jelly-like quality. He pushed Teal onto his back, unwrapped the gauze, and realized the wound itself was moving, pulsing maybe, but moving. Now he was truly scared.

Think! He told himself firmly. His first thought, of course, was to put him on Dominus and take him to Dragonhorse to the sanecere bay, but he'd already been there, and look where it had landed him. Pythos wasn't even remotely available. The ship's corpsmen knew nothing of Lebonathi potions. They might not know what to do about Lebonathi germs, either. But Ensharra did. Ensharra. Teal to Ensharra, Ensharra to Teal? Even as frightened as he was, Ardenai felt a certain sense of pride in his ability to think this through. Teal would be proud. Ardenai sighed. Everything these days was a test.

Even in the few seconds he debated his options and applauded his clarity, another thought entered his head. When Ardenai had been drugged by Eridu, Pythos hadn't been able to sense his thoughts. Now Ardenai couldn't sense Teal's. Even when Equi were sick, delirious, dying, another Equi could sense their thoughts. The Lebonathi had something that blocked that. Whether it was good or bad the Firstlord wasn't prepared to say, but he decided that taking Teal to the planet's surface where others might discover and broadcast what he already knew, was not a good idea. He didn't need publicity. What he did need was help, and fast. Here, in a clean environment. He squeezed one of the crys-tels on the chain around his neck and sent his thoughts to Dragonhorse Thirteen.

Nik? Can you hear me without me speaking?

Certainly. Good morning, Dragonhorse.

Where are you?

On board. Ardi, what's wrong? Has something happened to Io?

I can't waken Teal, and he's really feverish. He got bit by one of the prisoners yesterday. Can you tell Ensharra what happened and get her here as quickly as possible?

You don't want to bring him up here?

No. Please, just do as I ask. I'll explain when you get here. Please don't tell anyone. I'll explain that, as well.

Of course. I'm on my way.

Konik took a chance and scrambled directly to the spot where the sensors said Ensharra would be, hoping she wasn't bathing or sleeping or … something. He appeared in the schoolroom, to the consternation of several mothers and children.

"Forgive me," he said with a gracious nod and a smile to the children. "Ahimsa, I wish thee peace." Ensharra was looking at him expectantly and not particularly invitingly and he quickly steered her aside and whispered, "Teal is very sick. The Dragonhorse wants you to come."

Ensharra nodded, beckoned immediately to another anchoress who stepped into her place, and took Konik by the elbow, guiding him down one of the long halls that would take them back to the pharma. "What do you mean he's very sick?" she asked, concern standing in her eyes.

Smart looking woman, Konik thought, surprising himself. "According to the Dragonhorse, Teal got bit by one of the prisoners yesterday, and …"

Ensharra slammed to a halt and spun Konik to face her. "He what?" she exclaimed.

"He got bit," Konik said, realizing from the fear in her eyes that they were in trouble.

"By whom? Which prisoner?"

"I … don't know. I'm guessing ..."

"You may not guess!" she said sharply. "Which prisoner?"

Konik leaned against the wall and pinched the bridge of his nose, remembering with a shudder what it had been like to try to get thoughts out of this rat maze. Could he hope to get a telepathic communication all the way to Lebonath Tras? They were close to the surface, which would help. There were thousands more Equi minds on the planet at this point. Hopefully that would help as well. He squeezed one of the crys-tels around his own neck to boost the signal and concentrated.

Ardi? Can you hear me?

Yes. What?

Ensharra needs to know exactly which prisoner.

Ardenai chose not to argue about why she would need to know such a seemingly insignificant detail, though it struck him as odd. *It was a young boy ... in ... amongst the unreasoned.*

Thanks. How is the Master Captain?

Burning up. Just get her here, please!

Konik straightened up and took a quick breath. "He says it was a young boy amongst the unreasoned. I'm assuming he meant that roomful of men they found. The ones you said were ..."

"Drugged. Yes. They're drugged to control them, and if they die from the drugs – the potency, the combination, the quality – nobody cares. Stand right here, Governor. Do not move."

It gave him time to figure out how to get them there in the quickest way possible. When she arrived with her bag and her hat he said, "Take my hand, Anchoress. We are going to make a series of jumps."

In the next second they had scrambled and found themselves on Dragonhorse XIII. Once they had paused for a few seconds, Konik nodded to the technician and they found themselves on Belesprit, which was moving with the survey parties into orbit around Lebonath Tras. "We will be in range in three minutes," the technician said, and Konik realized he was still holding Ensharra's hand.

"We're good," he said, smiling and letting go. "Are you doing all right so far?"

"I am," she replied, studying his face.

"What?"

"You have blue eyes. I noticed them, of course, because they're ..." she caught herself. "... kind. But I thought all High Equi had some shade of green eyes. Does that mean you're not a full-blooded Equi?"

"No," he grinned. "It means these aren't my original eyes." He laughed at her expression and added, "I lost my vision in a training accident. It was a field hospital far from home and these were the only ones they had that matched my orbital sockets and nerve specs, so …" and they were standing next to Dominus in the meadow near the shining white pavilion which flew the banners of the Firstlord of Equus. "... I have had blue eyes instead of green for the last eighty years. My wife likes … liked them, so I never bothered to have them dyed. How are you feeling after those jumps? Little weak in the knees? Dizzy in the head?"

"Until you said eighty years, I was fine," she said in a half-muttered chuckle, picked up her long skirts and handed Konik the bag so she could take his arm to walk through the grass. "Hopefully I'll get a chance to use the magic refabricator. These skirts are an annoyance on anything but pavement."

Another few steps and they were inside with Ardenai scooting aside to let her kneel beside the sleeping platform. "He hasn't twitched," he said quietly. "The cool towels aren't helping much."

She put her hand on his forehead, then his cheeks, then looked at the wound, grimaced and shook her head. "You are so careful to assess the big things that will get you killed, and spend too little time considering all the insignificant things that will kill you just as fast."

"He's really sick, isn't he?" Ardenai asked.

"The only reason he's alive is because of his body mass."

She began going through her bag and setting things out. "I need Elam," she said, and Konik was gone. Before she was through preparing things he was back. She felt the rush of air which Dominus pushed as it landed and Elam was beside her.

"I am going to need much more Telarepere than I have," she said. "Have you brought some down?"

Elam looked stricken. "I have only a tiny bit and it struggles. Telarepere grows where it grows and hates to be moved. I can check the dry stores; there may be a little."

Ardenai's ears pricked up. His sister used that phrase. It grows where it grows and nowhere else. Could it be? "Tell me what this plant looks like that you seek," he said. "Has it tiny leaves and pink and white flowers that form a hairy green web on the ground or over rocks?"

"Maybe," Elam nodded. "I have only had bits of it in a pot."

Ardenai turned to Ensharra. "Do you have any at all? Can I smell it?" She crushed a single smidgen of leaf between thumb and index finger and waved it under his nose. "Evangeline's Carpet!" he exclaimed. "Teal brought some of this back his very first day on Tras. Two plancts … no, three

… with exactly the same herb? How is that possible?"

"I don't know, but it's growing all around where I buried my wife," Konik said. "We will be right back. Do you need anything else from Stone Spring?"

The anchoress shook her head. "Hurry."

Elam, using the tiny, rudimentary kitchen, boiled water and herbs, and Ensharra began making a series of small cuts in the standing vessels within the wound itself. When Elam returned she took the boiling water a bit at a time and began injecting it into the vessels to spurt out the holes she'd made, taking the impurities with it as it cooked the flesh. "I am so glad you're not awake for this," she whispered, watching his face from time to time as she worked.

The morning sun slanted through the trees and into the pavilion where the sides were rolled up, and she remarked to herself what a pristine and pleasant atmosphere it created in which to practice; the sounds of the waterfall, the dance of dust particles in the rays of sunshine, the occasional patter of a leaf on the canopy above. If it weren't for her gentle friend lying sick in front of her, it would be perfect.

She couldn't help wondering what it would be like to take all of her clothes off and get in that clear, cool pool. She had never done that. She had never had a real bath. She wondered if they would laugh at her if she mentioned her desire. If they would think she was dirty if she said she'd occasionally rinsed her underthings or brushed her teeth in tea too stale to drink – never had more than a bowl bath her whole life.

She processed the Telarepere they brought back, and when she wasn't instructing Elam as to what she was doing to cleanse the wound and stop the spread of the organisms, she was lecturing Ardenai and Konik about the stupidity of assuming that because one was all-powerful and all-knowing on one world, one could take that same stance on another. She also informed them that the men they had found in the small room the day before were drugged, heavily sedated to keep them in check until they could be dealt with. Teal, by being bitten, had been injected as well. Gods only knew what else had been in that boy's system. She could only guess and hope for the best.

She set Elam to brewing the prepared plants, which she had crushed up and mixed with other herbs. “I wish I had time to sneak up on this a little more slowly,” she sighed. “Unfortunately, I don’t. Teal doesn’t. The fact that his wife uses the same herb does make me a little more comfortable.”

Elam brought her what he had brewed and she tasted it, nodding and telling him he had done a good job. When it had cooled a little, she injected it into the vessels around the wound and into the wound itself, then into the veins in his neck, his abdomen and the tops of his thighs.

Over the next few hours she treated him at given intervals, sometimes adding ingredients, sometimes using more or less of the infusion, sometimes injecting liquid into his veins, sometimes injecting or pouring smaller amounts into the wound itself. In between times, when she wasn’t watching him, she went to Dominus and refabricated something cooler and more comfortable to wear, had a bite to eat, and sat with Konik and Ardenai while Elam prepared the Telarepere for drying.

“This is a blessing for us, you know,” she said, watching Elam. “There is more of that herb in what you gathered today than we have had my whole lifetime and before. If not for the scientists on the mountain, we would have been out long ago. They are the ones who went without water to bathe, to drink, to cook with, so we could have that herb. It is a very powerful antibiotic and cleansing agent, but you knew that.”

Ardenai nodded. He was quiet for a minute or two and despite his best efforts worry flooded his eyes. “He is going to be all right, isn’t he? Because if anything happens to him, I’ve not only lost my best friend, but my sister has lost her husband.”

Konik spared Ensharra an answer. “You won’t suffer long,” he said comfortingly. “If Ah’din thinks you had anything to do with this, she’ll put you out of your misery in a big hurry.” He laughed, and Ardenai had to smile with him.

Their talk drifted to Dragonhorse Thirteen, and Kehailan’s design, and the small hiccups that were being worked out, and then to Dominus, and Konik asked if Ardenai had pretty much gotten the bucks out of that, as well.

He nodded, saying, "The only real trouble I had with her was when she quit on Gideon and me and we ended up on Hector in the middle of a white shale wasteland being sold to slavers. Thanks for rescuing her, by the way. Again, I know it was you."

Konik just smiled. "She's a beauty. You did an amazing job of designing her. You did a good part of the design of the Dragonhorse cruisers, as well, didn't you?"

"Not really. The programming, yes, but imagining the capabilities, that was Kee. He earned the helm of that ship."

"All of you do so many different things," Ensharra said to Ardenai. "You design space ships and head the biggest government in the Seventh Galactic Alliance. Anything else?"

"I dabble in computer technology," he said modestly, though Konik snorted with amusement at the understatement. "My father and I raise horses together. Very often on Equus we do one thing that is linear, and one thing that is uniquely ours. Mainly, until I rose to be Firstlord, I was a creppia nonage teacher." He sighed. "Five and six-year-olds. I do miss short people with high voices."

"You may come and visit my classroom anytime," she smiled. "As a matter of fact, I think you should." She turned to Konik, who was sitting where the light was slanting across the pavilion to touch his close-cropped mane of silver hair. "And what do you do, Sir? Or did you do until you became Military Governor of our worlds?"

"I have always been a military man and a politician," he said, and it came out as an apology. "Two of my degrees are in history of governance, and mechanical engineering. I was a test pilot for many years, and a senator, and my father and I raised horses too, which is how I came to know Ardenai when he was just a colt himself." He smiled, started to add to his comment, then fell silent. The Firstlord wondered if he'd been going to mention his love of music.

Ensharra made a mollifying gesture in Konik's direction and said, "I know this is a rude question, or at least it sounds rude in my head, but … since I'm still working on how long you've had your blue eyes, indulge me.

How old are you?"

"I look older than I am," Konik said. Again that apologetic tone that made her wonder. "I'm a hundred and eighteen." He laughed at her expression. "Usually a hundred and eighteen looks better than this. I have a condition that they tried to … shock out of me … literally, and all they managed to do was wreck the pigment in my hair follicles. I've been grey since I was forty."

"Relax," Ardenai said, "You'll be around another hundred and thirty years or so."

She just shook her head and made a little wondering sound in her throat. "What about this fellow?" she said, gesturing toward Teal. The sun was just touching his shoulder and the side of his face and he looked more asleep than unconscious. She willed that to be the case. "What does he do when he's not getting bitten by strange boys or tricking Eridu into leading him to an antidote for his best friend?"

"Amazing man," Ardenai said admiringly. "He has a Secundoctora in Equine medicine and behavior. Until very recently his primary career as Master of Horse was pairing the perfect horse with the perfect rider, as well as deciding what kind of work each horse is best suited for. He also has two advanced degrees in military strategies, one in weapons telemetry and one in direct combat strategy, which has always seemed strange to me. They must belong to the darker side of him that I don't recognize."

"You really don't see it?" Konik asked, pouring another round of cider and handing a glass to Elam. "As you say, his primary career is right horse, right condition. There are, what, a hundred and fifty thousand horses, maybe more, just in the cavalry? How can you send an animal into battle without understanding what battle is all about?"

"You know, that makes perfect sense," Ardenai nodded. "You could well be right. He may never have expected to find himself being utilized in the position. It's a shame he's so good at it." The Firstlord chuckled, but his eyes were not amused. "When he has the time and his father is home, his linear family business is winemaking. Excellent wines, by the way. He is a good husband and father, and my parents adore him every bit as much as they do me."

Ensharra knelt beside Teal again and tapped at the wound with a fingernail. "I think this is as hard as it's going to get," she said. "What hasn't lost its color will need to be cut away, along with the whole top, so it is going to bleed. I will need towels, and hot water, and if you have it, gauze and packing. If you don't, I can make do with what I have."

"Let me get you what you need," Ardenai said.

He made himself sit and watch as she cut a careful perimeter around the wound and lifted the top two layers off, as well as part of the third, cutting just above the muscle and removing the welted vessels in the process, leaving long, open trenches that made Ardenai wince. She did no stitching or kedging, but cleaned and packed the wound with a poultice of honey and Evangeline's Carpet, put a thick pad over it, and wrapped it tight with gauze.

"I have done what I can do," she said simply. "Now we wait."

The afternoon sun was hot, and Ardenai offered her a hand up off the floor, saying, "Would you like to take time for a bit of a swim? I'm sure Elam and Governor Konik can watch Teal and let you know if anything changes."

"You think I can swim?" she scoffed. "In which cup of water would I have learned to do that?"

"It's an expression, Anchoress. Would you like a sit in the water, or a wade in the water, or a splash ...?"

"I got it," she laughed, and her eyes sparkled with excitement. "I have never been in the water! What does one wear for this sort of activity, besides one's hat, of course?"

"Well, I know what we Equi wear, but I doubt you would be comfortable. I can ask the refabricator for the appropriate garb if you would like to enjoy the water for a bit." She nodded with just a hint of shyness, and he took her with him to Dominus, asked for modest swimming attire, showed her how to put it on, and left her to change.

When she appeared it was in a long robe and sandals, which she wore until she reached the edge of the water. "Don't look at me," she said.

Ardenai nodded and went back into the pavilion, but knowing how quickly that pool got deep, he did strip to a briefcloth and kept an eye on her, just in case. She put the robe aside and waded in, very slowly, savoring every inch and marveling at the buoyancy which increased with every step.

When she got up to her waist she bounced up and down a little. "This is amazing!" she laughed. She was still laughing when her bounces carried her just a little too far forward. She went off the sand ledge and the water closed over her head.

Two seconds later he had her under the arms and was laughing in her face. "It never ceases to amaze me how people who can do big things like saving someone's life, can turn around and do something as silly as getting in water over their heads and drowning, just because they don't understand the real nature of water. Don't you agree, Anchoress?"

"I told you not to look," she said, coughing and laughing as she clung to his arm. She wiped the water from her eyes and pushed her now soggy old hat back down on her head. "Fortunately you didn't listen."

"Never forget, I used to teach five-year-olds," he said, tucking her under his arm and carting her back to where the water was shallow enough for her to stand comfortably. "No matter what else I may become, I will always be that." He backed a little further into the shallows and sat down up to his chest in the water, leaving her with the feel of his bare skin against hers. That, too, was a first for her, and very pleasant.

"It is traditional for us Equi to bathe each other, which I'm sure is far from your desire. However, if you would like to bathe yourself before you get out, there is a smaller, warmer pool behind those rocks, which will offer you all the privacy you need. There you will find a basket of scrubbing sand and foaming rosemary, as well as some towels. I will be inside with Teal, so try not to drown yourself for however long you're in here, hm?" He stood up and waded out, and when he had gone, she found the basket, removed her swim garb, and took the first real bath of her life.

She admitted later that it might well have been the unspeakable luxury of a bath which made her so amenable, but in the meeting they held during the hours of the warm, quiet afternoon, she did agree to become an SGA observer on behalf of her homeworld, and she also agreed to try her hand at exposing the lies of the flamen, starting with the one about the witch world. Ardenai and Konik both told her it might be dangerous for her and those of her ilk, and she said she would speak individually with the few she had contact with. They were solitary by choice after their schooling ended, simply because if the flamen decided to start killing them, they couldn't get all of them at once.

When Ensharra had settled for a bit of a nap, Elam took over watching Teal, and Konik and Ardenai went for a swim of their own. They sat in the sandy shallows under the shade of an overhanging tree and discussed again the idea that they had to control the flamen and their rhetoric if they were going to control the planet with a minimum of bloodshed. And how were they going to catch the flamen, and how were they going to figure out who was in control of that particular faction? What kind of trap could they set, and with what bait, to catch flamen? So far, nothing had worked.

It was nearly dark when Teal's breathing changed and his fingers moved slightly on the sheet. His brows came together and he made a sound more puzzlement than pain. When he managed to get his eyes open, Ardenai was sitting on his heels looking at him. "You're awake," he smiled, and heaved a sigh of relief. "How do you feel?"

"Sleepy," he managed. "You're … wearing that look, Ardi."

By then Ensharra had sat up from her nap on Ardenai's bed and was beside him as well. She put her hand first on his forehead, then the back of her hand to his cheek and smiled as she looked at him. "Still feverish, but no longer hot enough to cook on. Good evening, Master Captain. You gave us quite a scare."

"Mmmmm," he responded. How had he scared them? Why was he so dizzy, and why were his friends looking at him like he was back from the dead? What had happened? He squeezed his eyes shut and slid around in the muck, feeling for something that would make sense of this. He could tell from the way his back felt that he'd been lying down longer than he was used to. What had happened to people lately? Nik and Ardi had been tortured, Kee had been shot … neither of those things had happened to him. He was pretty sure he wasn't pregnant in a crèche pod. His head moved, so his neck wasn't broken.

"What?" he groused. He went to rub his forehead and a pain shot up his right arm that left him gasping. He focused on the arm, heavily bandaged from his wrist to his elbow. "Oh," he said. "That."

Ensharra gave him an utterly disgusted look. "And how did you clean the wound, Master Captain? Did you spit on it? Piss on it? Pour water on it and then rub it with your dirty hand, or did you just assume that because it bled it would clean itself out?"

"Mostly, the last two," he muttered. "I've been too dry to spit since the day I got here. In all fairness I did … go to the sanecere bay and …" he stopped and swallowed hard. Things were beginning to swim in the room and it was making him sick to his stomach. "Sorry," he managed. "Dizzy."

"You need water," she said, and they sat him up enough to get a few ounces in him. They left him sitting partway up, padded with pillows, and his color said the rest of him was not feeling as cocky as his mouth would have them believe.

Ensharra carefully went over with a very attentive Elam how to tend the wound, what to feed him, what to offer him to drink, what to expect over the next few days. He was not to be up until the drugs had run their course and there was no sign of infection in the wound. A sudden dizzy spell followed by a quick concussion was not going to help things any. She drew some blood for Moonsgold to test. When there was nothing foreign in it, he could be up and back to work. No sooner.

She apologized for the need to go, but she was concerned that she would be missed by the flamen before she could see to her own safety, and that the Dragonhorse would be receiving her head, ceremoniously wrapped in a box. That comment startled Konik and he stated quietly but with that undeniable firmness which men who are good fathers and grandfathers develop over time, that he was going with her, and that he was staying with her, or she with him, until they could find a safe place for her to be. She was still arguing with him and he was still wearing that implacable look of his when they left the scrambleshaft platform on Dominus, headed for Belesprit.

Realizing he wasn't going anywhere, and knowing that they needed this information to keep others safe, Teal allowed himself to become an object of study. Both Ensharra and Moonsgold checked blood, urine and saliva, and watched how the drugs and the infection progressed in his system. For two days he barely spoke, couldn't move at all, and the nausea and vertigo were intensely unpleasant if he tried. By the end of the second day there was also a headache which pounded hard at his eyes and temples for twenty-four hours or so. All that time Elam was there, saying little, keeping the wound open and clean and repacking it several times a day, offering his comforting presence and cups of peppermint tea to ease the nausea.

They drew extra blood, and by giving him a little more of the suspect herb, they established by his reaction which herb was causing the headache, as well as which one would assuage it. Ensharra knew which herb it was that caused head pain in Lebonathi. Now they knew which one caused it in Equi. Same one. Oddly enough, it affected the Equi, who were bigger people, much more than it affected the Lebonathi. Over time they would figure out in what ways their anatomical profiles were alike and where they differed, and medical treatment between Equi and Lebonathi would be more effective as they formed closer ties and needed medical exchanges.

Winslow Moonsgold worked especially hard at trying to establish which herb it was that caused that disturbing lack of mental communication. Ensharra helped the effort by showing him which herbs the torturing compound had in common with the concoction the young boy had been given before he bit Teal. In all of this Teal remained his usual calm, good-humored self, saying only once that he felt like one of his wife's pincushions.

With Belesprit close to Tras, and in synchronous orbit with Dragonhorse Thirteen, it became effortless to hop from planet to ship, to ship, to planet or Jocundome in either direction, cutting the entire commute to a span of minutes and making Dominus redundant. Ardenai took his ship back to Dragonhorse for restocking, then stored it in the shunt bay, leaving their landscape largely untrammeled.

The third day a mid-range horse transport arrived, sent by Master of Cavalry Abeyan. This one bore three hundred and twenty-five members of the cavalry's crack science unit – sixty-five each of geologists, botanists, archaeologists, microcartographers and tempestorians, as well as their personal mounts, all highly trained expedition horses. Only hours behind that transport came another, loaded with more saddle stock, draft horses, and packhorses, and this small corner of Lebonath Tras began to look, sound, and smell like Equus.

With horses and riders came farriers, saddlesmiths, harness makers, equine doctors like Teal, and, happily, Tarpan and his wife Ah'keena to help supervise. They set up their main encampment two miles north, where the meadows bowed out into a lush, lightly treed valley before narrowing into a gorge filled mostly with the rush of the river. Just beyond that it widened again to form the long, sinuous lake at the edge of which sat Stone Spring.

From the main camp they would disperse small parties to begin an intimate evaluation of the land designated as the first colony grid. Each expedition would take with it a team of five expert cavalry scientists, three SGA technicians including a recording historian, plus a stockman and a minimum of pack animals, sixty-five parties in all. It was an insignificant number given the vastness of just the first grid, much less the rest of the continents, but it was a place to start, and one that would leave very little footprint should they discover that they were disturbing things best left alone. Over the next couple of days the SGA scientists would be paired with a horse, packs would be readied, and the teams would head out, dropped in various locations by transport and kept track of by communications networks aboard Belesprit.

Within the larger shipment, and personally selected by Keeplord Krush, came a dozen horses, all beautiful animals, for the personal use of the Firstlord, Master Captain, and Governor, and Teal said that hearing horses blowing and moving about near the pavilion helped him feel better instantly, though he felt his recovery was ridiculously slow given the things he had to do.

Among the dozen was a quick, short-coupled little palomino mare that Ah'din had sent along for Ensharra, saying the horse had herb-sense, and that if the anchoress were to ride out looking for such things she would need a helper. Edlyn would be the perfect companion. Ardenai noticed to his amusement that Pavil was also amongst the dozen. Apparently Krush shared his son-in-law's opinion that he was a lost cause as a polo pony. "Exiled you did they?" he said, patting the sleek black neck. "Never you mind. There will be plenty for you to do here." He proved it the next afternoon by saddling the horse and taking him for a brisk canter to explore one of the canyons before dinner.

It turned out to be an unremarkable blind box, with layered stone well coated with decent soil in most places. The trees and shrubs all looked the same as what he'd seen in other explorations. He sat by a small spring which bubbled up to form a bright green keyhole in the darker green and brown corner of the canyon floor, and stared at the tiny plants. Why did he keep expecting to find signs of recent life? Why did he keep expecting to hear birdsong, or to flush a covey of greybonnets? And now, and more remarkably, how did they find exactly the same herb on Lebonath Tras that grew on Equus? There just had to be more to this. He talked it over with Pavil, who said nothing about the Firstlord's expectations, but approved of the quality of the grasses on the canyon floor. Beautiful horse. Not particularly smart.

When he returned two hours before sunset he found Konik doing ground work with Ensharra and Edlyn, and Teal sitting outside under a spreading, broad-leafed tree, watching.

"Sweet woman," Teal observed quietly, "but neither a natural rider, nor a natural swimmer. Luckily she is intrepid, which makes up for a good many shortcomings."

Ardenai sat beside him under the trees and watched the two in the meadow. "Does she know you're out here?" he asked cautiously. Teal was chafing under her firm hand, and his temper was growing increasingly quick.

"Yes, Mother. She knows I'm out here and she knows I'm going back to work tomorrow."

"Did she say you could?"

"We're still negotiating, but I'm bigger and so far, I'm winning."

"Don't be too sure," Ardenai said, working canyon dirt out from under his fingernails with the tip of a twig and avoiding eye contact. "She lost to Konik when it came to sleeping somewhere safe. She's now being scrambled up to Dragonhorse when her colleagues think she's asleep in her chambers, and when she's awake and back in her chambers, he's got a couple of big Amberians close by every minute. She doesn't like it, and I guarantee she doesn't like being dictated to. Best step carefully."

"I have done my part," Teal replied. "I have no drugs in my system that the boy had in his. I have no signs of infection in the wound which, by the way, looks like … I don't know … like I tried to grab a protoped's kitten." He looked at the swath of bandages and just shook his head. "I'm going to be wearing long sleeves awhile to hide this, I can tell you. And again, do not tell your sister what happened. I told her I'd been in the field and out of contact for a few days; that's all she needs to know. I have done my part. Ensharra needs to turn me loose, or I will do it myself."

He went back to watching the little palomino mare, and Ardenai could tell that he was resisting the urge to jump up off the ground and trot out there. Active man. Healthy man. It made Ardenai smile and send up a prayer of thanks. They'd both come so close to death on this campaign with never a shot being fired at them. With one exception, Ardenai corrected the thought. Still, it did give one pause. And yet, here they were, shoulders just brushing one another as they leaned against the tree trunk. Both alive and, for the moment, well. That seemed almost enough. "Teal," Ardenai said abruptly, prefacing it with his questioning whuffle, "Why are there no birds here? How could they possibly have caught all the birds?"

"Good question," Teal replied leaning over his knees and adjusting his back a little. Too many days in bed. He needed a swim to loosen up. Definitely needed a bath, as well. "Maybe they just took a sampling and killed the rest."

"Why would they do that?"

"So the planet didn't get overrun with birds? We own a sailboat; you know how caustic bird guano can be. With no predators they could be the size of Dominus by now."

"Why aren't there any bird skeletons if they killed them all? Why aren't there any animal skeletons at all? Why aren't there any graves, any human bones? Where did everything go?"

Teal had by this time begun to chuckle. "You know you're being five?"

"Yes, I do. If being five means asking questions because I'm curious, then yes, I'm being five. Why do all the signs of life on this world seem to be … planted? If you go to that Jocundome up there, you will find themed venues. Why does this feel like one of them?"

"We have all effect and no cause yet. It's bound to feel unbalanced. To be honest I'm more concerned that we're going to find something that will stop us colonizing, and this is a rich and beautiful world. I spent some time after lunch looking at some of the cold climate explorations, and I think we should go check them out as part of our review week coming up. So far the weather here seems exceptionally good. Rain, some wind, snow. Almost no volcanic activity, so no ash in the air. I'll be anxious to see what the tempestorians bring back in terms of the weather history. Until then," he said pointedly, "we should probably apply ourselves to the problem of the flamen."

"I think we've left off trying to catch or reason with them for now," Ardenai said, still watching Ensharra and Konik. He'd helped her into the saddle and was letting her out a bit at a time on a long line. She was nervous and the mare sensed it, moving slowly and carefully so as not to startle her rider. Smart animal. Good choice for a rookie rider. "I think we can be more effective using the anchoresses, most especially Ensharra, to get accurate information out to the masses. I'm not sure grabbing these men and forcing them to go where we want them to, is going to help matters."

"I'm not sure it would hurt," Teal muttered.

He maintained that position the next day back on Dragonhorse. Kehailan, Konik and Ulric came down firmly on his side, and Ardenai grudgingly agreed to try both at the same time. "But you, Master Captain, get to see to their capture," he added. "So far the only ones we've been able to catch are those in the far provinces. They influence relatively few people, and seem quite unsophisticated compared to the rhetoric we hear. If you're going to set a snare, at least catch something big."

CHAPTER 9

You are not listening to me!" Naram said, beginning to lose patience. "If you do not tone back your rhetoric they are going to come for you, and your fate at that point will be very uncertain." He glared at the council members and the flamen from their districts, and resisted the urge to look over his shoulder at the same time. "The Dragonhorse has caught you in lie after lie. He has Anchoress Ensharra speaking to the people, showing them historia ..."

"They are the ones who lie!" said a thin, pallid man with the eyes of a zealot. "They show historia of a world we know does not exist! We are told of the flames in the ancient writings, and those who doubt the writings are doomed to the fire of the witch world!" There was a murmur of assent, which encouraged him to raise his voice even higher. "They show us the horrors of where our food comes from? We know this is not true. We know those who tend the food mines do so happily and under perfectly acceptable conditions, or did so until they were kidnapped by the Equi. They turn the people against us with their brown, unclean food and their water, probably filled with mind-altering drugs. They show us the sky above us, filled with huge ships, six of them strapped together to form something they say stretches for miles in every direction? We know this is not possible! Something that heavy would plummet from the skies. To say that on those ships they are growing food for us, having freed those who tended the food mines? That is insanity! People who allow themselves to believe that, are insane! They place a light in the sky and tell us it is a world in a bubble? A world that will feed us, and teach us how to feed ourselves? These are all lies, Naram! That many ships would bump into each other. We would not be able to see the stars for the ships. Surely you are not being seduced by these evil, godless people!"

"Nagar, WAKE UP!" Naram shouted. "There's a difference between being seduced, and being convinced! It's over! Evil and godless or not, they have us!" He paced the length of the chamber to cool himself, and turned back to Nagar.

"You have no idea how much I hate these people. They are cloddish peasants whose lack of sophistication defies description. That being said, they are also people who speak the truth. I lived among them, and that much I do know. They do speak the truth, and they are powerful beyond anything we can even imagine. Much as I hate to admit it even to myself, the Dragonhorse is brilliant, and he surrounds himself with brilliance, beyond anything we can hope to combat. They say they do not want to kill us, and I believe them. They say they will kill us if we do not follow instructions, and I believe them."

"Then we will die for our cause, as did the ancient lapidae!" Nagar intoned, raising one hand above his head and beginning to rock back and forth, singing under his breath.

"Fine," Naram snapped, "die if you must, but don't take the rest of us with you. The more we fight them, the more we call attention to ourselves and what we have, the more they will come, and look, and take. For the sake of the Gods and all we hold dear, just shut up! The sooner we do that the sooner they will leave us in peace. We will be changed, to be sure, but we will be alive, which I, for one, consider a positive circumstance."

"You don't care that they are trying to destroy our faith?" asked Lagash. As he said it he reached for a piece of black-market fruit, and it made Naram laugh in spite of himself.

"Eating their food while you plot their demise doesn't seem to faze you," he said. "Many religions have survived in the darkness for a very long time. Ours will survive as well."

"Not if the demons continue turning our wives and children against us!" Nagar shouted, and Naram wondered if the man ever said anything in a normal tone of voice.

"I will admit …" Naram sighed, "that part is going to be gone soon, the part where we rule our households. But then, we don't rule our planet anymore, either, do we, so what's the point? If they decide to kill all of us then it is they who our women will straddle, not us, it is they who will teach our children right from wrong, not us. It is fine in books to resist overwhelming odds. It is fine in the stories of the Lapidae, who died for their faith and ultimately won the war for the hearts of men. In reality, it will end in death, and any vestige of our way of life will be gone."

"They are blinding the people," Nagar persisted. "Soon there will be none with vision. We must encourage the people to rise up and fight them, to put aside their filthy food and their tainted water, and fight them!"

"Since when have you cared about the people? You know nothing about them and you are an idiot if you think they're going to do that," said Naram. "The Dragonhorse told Eridu that first day that we were on the brink of civil war because of lack of food and ..."

"Our beloved and Most Wise Lord Eridu, eldest son of an eldest son," Aruda intoned, interrupting Naram. "If only he were here to lead us now."

"And didn't he do a great job?" Naram sneered. "Did he put ships in the air when Konik and Ardenai disappeared? No. He was feeding his face and fucking your fourteen-year-old daughter the morning they came back and said, 'Welcome to Equus'."

"He honored her with his attention and his seed. Even now she bears his child. The last scion of the Great Lord Eridu. As a man he will rule the Lebonathi Federation."

"Don't bet on it," Naram muttered, mostly to himself.

"Bless the Great Lord Eridu. He was one of us!" said Nagar, again waving his hand in praise.

"If you mean by that statement he was flamen, yes. We put up with an egocentric, charismatic dolt for thirty years! At least his father used his brain on rare occasions. Not Eridu. Instead of making alliances through the usual channels he decides to try a fleshgift to the Dragonhorse, despite how that turned out seven hundred years ago! He also decides to make an alliance with the Telenir without first establishing who, exactly, they are, and by kidnapping someone the entire AEW will invade us to rescue! That was brilliant. He was lazy, self-indulgent, bloodthirsty, and ignorant of what went on outside his sphere ..."

"And the Dragonhorse killed him," Aruda said sadly, as if that forgave everything.

"No, the Dragonhorse did not kill him. Phaedra killed him for what he did to her husband and her sister. The anchoresses told the truth. I was taken to the scene. I saw the bodies. All of them."

"And how do we know you didn't have something to do with it?" Nagar challenged. "You had much to gain both in vengeance and in office, Naram. When Eridu killed Phaedra's sister, he killed your sister as well, don't forget."

"I'm not likely to," Naram muttered. "One does not easily forget losing both one's sisters and a favorite nephew in a single week."

"And where did Phaedra get the drugs that killed our beloved Eridu?" Nagar went on. "From Ensharra, who now speaks for the invaders? I think so. She who probably straddles the Dragonhorse at night. She who should have died for what she did to Eridu, and what have you done about that, Naram?"

"What would you have me do, given that I can prove exactly nothing? The drugs he took are very much like the ones he gave Governor Konik, and the Dragonhorse. You have been to his dinner parties where he used them on political prisoners, so have I. Who had those drugs? Eridu did. If I try to prove it was Ensharra, I will turn the poisonous eyes of the Dragonhorse on us, here in this room. I can accomplish far more if I keep his eyes off us, and so can you. Which brings me back to my original statement. TONE DOWN YOUR RHETORIC! You're putting all of us in danger."

There was a faint mechanical noise; the kind made when several scrambleshafts were employed at once, and a room which had held twenty-six people, now held forty, fourteen in Dragonhorse uniforms, and well-armed.

"Shit," Naram said under his breath.

"Ahimsa, we wish thee peace. I am Teal, Master Captain. The man beside me is Kehailan, Captain of Dragonhorse Equus. He has graciously consented to take us on some short field trips to different venues which you may or may not be familiar with. From the information you are putting out to the people, we have concluded that you have some misconceptions about us. We are going to fix that over the course of the next day or so. Consider yourselves our guests. Please stand in four groups of five and one group of six."

"No!" Nagar screamed. "No, No, No!" Despite several colleagues trying to grab and silence him, he pulled out a knife, raised it over his head and made a fruitless and rather comic run at Teal, shrieking, "We would rather die, you godless filth!"

The Master Captain pointed casually with the index finger on his left hand, there was a soft whump, the air moved slightly, and Nagar dropped like a stone.

"He would rather die," Naram amended.

"Would anyone else like a demonstration of the accuracy of an astricting pulse fired from a platform in orbit? No? Are you sure? Twenty-four would be an ideal number for our excursions. Well then, please stand in five groups of five," Teal said calmly, and the others complied without further comment.

"Is he … dead?" Aruda asked, hastily stepping around the body to get into one of the groups.

"For all intents and purposes, yes," Teal said quietly, "He is. But don't worry about the body; we won't leave it here in this heat." He made a gesture to activate the scrambleshafts, and when everyone was gone he opened a crys-tel and a delicate man with eyes and ears much like Io's appeared. "We have one already," Teal said, and there was a hint of sadness in his voice.

When he arrived on Dragonhorse the Lebonathis were bunched together surrounded by SGA troopers. Kehailan, Konik, Ah'nis and Ensharra were standing nearby, and Ardenai was just coming around a corner. Teal made a slight gesture toward their guests. "Big enough?" he smiled.

"I am truly impressed," Ardenai laughed. "Gentlemen, we have something special planned for you today. I understand that there has already been an unfortunate loss in the person of Nagar, purveyor of some truly inflammatory elocution. Be aware that he did not die because of his words, but because of his actions. We trust the rest of you will be more cautious, thereby returning to your homes unscathed at the end of this."

"It seems many of you did not believe the pictures of the mushrooming operations … what you call food mining … that we had Anchoress Ensharra discuss publicly, so that is where we will begin," Teal said. "I am not able to join you for this activity, but the Dragonhorse will see that you are properly instructed."

The men were herded onto the scrambleshaft, and when they materialized it was in the stinking tunnels where Teal had been bitten a fortnight before. Over Ensharra's protestations and despite the fact that many of them were already moaning and vomiting they were ordered to strip naked, and when that was accomplished they were chained by SGA troopers to mushroom carts facing the blackness of the tunnels.

"These carts need to be full," Ardenai said sharply. "When they are full you will push them to the loading docks. Then, and only then, will you be unchained. Do not ask for water, do not ask to be unchained to use the lavage, do not ask what you are stepping in. You are going to walk in the footsteps of those who slaved in here for seasons and years, and who died in here and were ground up for fertilizer and spread on what you eat every night!" By now his ears were pinned tight, he was snarling, and the Lebonathi cowered away from the flash of his teeth and his eyes. "Get to work!" he ordered, expertly cracking one of the tunnel whips, and they did.

He turned and walked back up the tunnel toward the light, and when Ensharra caught up with him to give him a piece of her mind, she realized it was not sweat running down his face, but tears.

"These are living, breathing beings who I am treating in such a manner," he said quietly. "I have no words to tell you how that makes me feel." She turned and went back into the tunnels.

For the time they worked they were informed of how many thousands of men had slaved here without adequate food or water, defecating in their tracks, wetting their lips with their own urine to stay alive, sleeping on the dirt beside their cart with no hope of ever seeing the sun, or feeling a breeze on their face, or seeing their loved ones. They were told how many of the ones they had rescued had been maimed by having their toes cut off, their genitals cut off, their tongues cut out, how many of them had been driven mad, driven to commit suicide, or murder, turned to cannibalism in the desperation of needing something, anything to eat.

At the end of an hour the carts were not nearly full, the men were staggering and crying, some were still vomiting, some just starting, some had passed out at least once. At the end of two hours they were drenched in sweat, their hair, hands and faces filthy. None were crying. None were vomiting. They were too exhausted, and too aware that they needed their strength. Ardenai unchained them one at a time and said, "Stand over there." They did so, terrified not to – terrified even to look at him – terrified of what was coming next. They were pushed into a cowering knot, clinging to each other past all vanity ... and suddenly found themselves in an incredibly long room with waterfall heads coming out of the wall on both sides.

Ardenai handed each of them a towel and said, "Bathe, then stand over there."

He tossed the grimy troopers each a towel, then one to Konik, one to Kehailan, took one for himself, and with a sigh of relief, joined them in the cool water. It was at that point that several of the Lebonathi noticed the terrible whip scar that sliced across the Firstlord's back and curled over his shoulder. Noted that Konik had had something go in at his back and explode out through his breast bone, leaving another terrible scar. They saw the healing pultronel burns on Kehailan's chest and neck – the ones Eridu had given him. They also noticed that the Equi scrubbed each other in the spots they couldn't reach. Given the circumstances, it looked like a very good idea to many of the Lebonathi who ordinarily wouldn't give each other a second thought. Today, they bathed each other.

Teal and another trooper brought uniforms for the Equi, and a gangly, pleasantly odd looking fellow with elongated eye sockets, bright lavender eyes, and almost no nose or ears, gave each of the Lebonathi a dark blue jumpsuit and sandals.

"They will stretch to fit," he said in a voice that gurgled slightly, like he was under water. "I am Gallios. I am Menorquin, and I am the general manager of this operation. Welcome aboard the combined terraformers. Ordinarily terraformers are used to shape continents to make them more livable or to create soil where there is only rock, beds for lakes, rivers, even seas – perhaps a pad for a beautiful new city. These are old now. Their mechanisms no longer worked, so they were gutted and refurbished as farming ships. It is our pleasure to loan them to you as one of our sister worlds, and through you, to our beloved Ardenai Firstlord. Please come with me."

They looked at each other, got a smiling nod from Ensharra, who had joined them in her own blue jumpsuit, and walked out into a space so vast they couldn't comprehend what they were looking at; a ship so huge it created its own horizons. It felt like they were in the sunshine, and when they looked up that is what it seemed they saw. There was a slight breeze and the sound of what Gallios said were birds, strange but not unpleasant. In front of them stretched rows four or five feet wide, row upon row as far as the eye could see. Along those rows, many people were working.

"You must be thirsty after your time in the tunnels," Gallios said. "Please, have something to drink." Ensharra drank first, dippering water from the bowl of a fountain into a cup, and the others gratefully followed suit. Gallios showed them where to put the cups to be washed, then beckoned them into one of the pathways and said, "Despite the fact that you think these ships cannot exist because of their size, they do. They are each eight miles wide and ten miles long, which sounds impossible until you think about the task of reforming a whole continent, or a whole planet – then they seem very small. On each of the six ships, which are linked together by short, jointed overpasses, there are one hundred levels one hundred feet high – which is about two AEW statute miles. Each level, if it is configured as this one is, will accommodate four thousand rows of vegetables five feet wide and ten miles long, minus a few places to cut across," he chuckled. "Two of the ships are configured as this one is. One of them contains annual vegetables, one perennial. They are intercropped.

"Fields containing crops which come back year after year, like alcibus, various greens, nuts, fruits and berries, are solid for ninety-nine levels, with one level being devoted to water storage, housing, and processing. Seven thousand nine hundred and twenty statute-square miles under intense cultivation on each of those ships. Again, there are two. As you probably know, not a single civilization has survived which depended upon annual crops for their food supply. We take that very seriously." He graciously ignored the communal blank look he received and gestured outward as he spoke, laughter gurgling quietly in his chest.

"The remainder of the space on this ship and her sister, is for the people who work here. There are dormitories, family apartments, saneceres, schools, shops, theaters, gymnasiums, places for concerts, ball games, parks, pools and gardens. There are huge kitchens, dining rooms, and places to process the millions of tons of seeds, fruits, nuts, grains and greens we will produce for your people to eat, as well as for us. As you undoubtedly already know, in order to be an Affined Equi World, you must be primarily vegetarian, and we will get you there in fine style."

He laughed again, and Kehailan laughed with him, reminding the Lebonathi that they were not alone. "Captain Kehailan and I were boys together," Gallios said, putting a large, partially webbed hand on Kehailan's shoulder. "When Ardenai Firstlord was serving his second appointment as Ambassador to Terren and my father was the Ambassador from Menorquin, it was. We had many fine adventures in that time." He gestured outward with his other hand and resumed his lecture.

"It is here on these ships that you will find most of the men who so recently worked the tunnels you just experienced. Like you, they were brought up here, allowed to bathe, issued clothing. Unlike you, they were given a medical examination. All were, and still are, severely malnourished.

Some are maimed, as you know. Some we could not keep because they were too ill or too dangerous. Those we could keep, and there are tens of thousands, are being slowly reunited with their families, who are coming up here to live with them. Their children are being enrolled in the schools, and anchoresses are providing religious instruction if the families or individuals so choose. When these ships are no longer needed and the men return to the surface of Jas or Tras, they will be first class agrarians, versed in a variety of disciplines."

He pushed a button on his belt and a chain of open cars came scooting into view. "We are at the side nearest the living spaces for this community, and I have been asked to take you on a tour. Everyone hop in, and we shall see the sights."

To their credit, the Lebonathi did as they were told with a minimum of muttering. Most of them seemed at least slightly interested in what they were seeing, and a few, including Ensharra, were genuinely delighted. Row after row of purple and green rosettes zipped past, then something that looked like big family gardens and a sprinkling of mature shade trees in a long, rather narrow park, and then a long town with tall buildings and paved streets, even sidewalks on which people strolled from shop to shop and into the various restaurants and dining establishments. "We tend to go up rather than out with housing on this ship, as only two thousand two hundred feet of width five miles long on each of twenty levels was allowed for living space. That isn't much, given the number of people it takes to run one of these growing operations. That space, and doubling up a little, is how we could so easily accommodate the unfortunate souls from the … food mines." He shuddered a little with disgust.

"Is the rest of the space that would be for housing given to plants?" Ensharra asked.

"Water generation and storage," Gallios replied. "This particular ship grows many rotations of crops in a single year, mostly greens. Greens take water. After we eat I will show you one of the ships that does not change. Right now I know that the Equi amongst us are famished, as they usually are, so we will stop right … here …" He pulled the cars over along the sidewalk next to the park. "… and walk across the street to have something for lunch. Like Equus, Menorquin is not a moneyed culture. Please take what you want to eat. Small samples of many things is acceptable."

"Also be aware," Ardenai added with a smile, "that the dishes labeled as seafood, are made with Menorquin sea grass or blue kelp, and they are spicier and saltier than anything you can imagine. Enjoy your lunch, feel free to ask questions while you eat. If you need the lavage, please ask an SGA trooper to accompany you."

That subtle reminder that they were not free agents actually startled Naram for a moment, and he realized he'd let his guard down. It would be interesting to see if any of the flamen had done the same by now. Naram just shook his head. How had that damned Master Captain found out about the meeting? He had captured about eighty percent of the most powerful flamen in the city, and he'd already killed one of them. Ah, poor, stupid Nagar. Losing his voice in the council of flamen was like lancing an abscess on the ass of reason. The flamen were so hidebound Naram was surprised Teal had only had to kill one of them. Idiots. Useless idiots. He wondered if they actually believed they were on a ship. He was having trouble with the idea, and he had been exposed to technology over the years. He watched as Gallios modeled how to get food from the long line of dishes, taking what he wanted and choosing a place to sit at the large round tables. The Lebonathi and the Equi joined the lines of workers and families and visited as they went through. It felt almost … normal, whatever that had come to mean.

A very thin man who looked Surface Lebonathi shuffled out of the kitchen bringing drinks on a tray, and when he realized he was serving Konik, he nearly dropped the tray as he went down on his knees. "Soft One," he said, bowing his head to the floor, and Konik was on his knees beside him in an instant, lifting him up to look him in the eye, and grasping his forearms in friendship.

"Do not bow to me. We are equals." he said quietly. "You have spent enough time bent under the weight of another."

"You saved us," the man said simply.

"And you are saving your world by what you are doing here," Konik smiled. "Come, on your feet, my friend. You have meaningful work to do and I am keeping you from it." He got the man to his feet, helped him pick up the tray, and sat himself back down with a rather embarrassed whuffle to stare at his plate. "Sorry about that," he said to no one in particular, and picked up his soup spoon.

"You are the oddest man I've ever met," Ensharra said from across the table where she was sitting between Naram and Aruda. "You spent days, not just supervising the removal of men from those tunnels, but personally freeing as many of them as you could, unchaining them, picking them up off the ground, washing their hands and faces, giving them food and water. Once you took your shirt off, I couldn't tell you from them when I went in there. What they ate, you ate and nothing more as far as I could see. You were in the tunnels all day and you were spending all night trying to figure out who they were, where their families were – I don't think you slept anywhere but at your desk."

"Your point being?"

"You did an amazing thing for those men, but when one of them tries to thank you ..."

He held up a silencing hand. "It is my job to take care of these people," he said. "I was doing what I see as my job. No man should be bowed to for doing his job. No man should be knelt before, or asked to kneel before another for any reason. Besides which, Anchoress, how do you know so much about what I was doing if you weren't right in there with me? You didn't smell any sweeter than I did for a few days, and he didn't bow to you."

Now he had her on the defensive. "That's different," she sniffed. "I'm Lebonathi, and I'm a woman."

"Oh, so now anytime you want to be invisible, or make excuses for yourself you can just say, 'I'm a woman', and that will explain it. Addie does that." He was suddenly quiet, pushing at the noodles in his bowl. "Excuse me," he said, got up from the table and went outside. He walked across the street into the park, sat down with his back against a tree to the outside of the space, and sobbed.

Ardenai shook his head slightly when the anchoress even thought to go after him. "He needs time alone," he said. "He'll join us when he regains his composure."

"Did I … cause that?" Ensharra asked, wincing with the possibility.

"No," Ardenai said with a comforting smile. "He just startled himself into the reality of losing Ah'davan. I did that for a long time after I lost Kehailan's mother. I'd be having a perfectly normal, even humorous conversation, and … wham. That pit opens up and you just … fall." His shoulders jerked slightly. "It's physically stunning, like being hit with something heavy and blunt. He'll reel under it and then get a cinch on it again. In time the memories don't hurt so much, or so they tell me."

"Your beautiful Ah'ree was such a kind woman," said Gallios. "She and my mother used to take us to the shore, and we would have cider and honey-cakes and build sand castles at low tide."

"And you always swam too far out," Kehailan grinned, "Your mother called you her little fish."

"Good memories," Gallios agreed, setting aside his napkin. "We should be on our way. I know there is much more you wish our guests to see."

"We are not guests," Aruda said. "We are … prisoners. I thought you knew that."

"You may be his prisoners, but you are my guests," Gallios laughed. "Please come with me."

"Don't think of it as being prisoners," Teal advised, giving Aruda a slightly dangerous smile. "After all, you're not in prison. You're detainees, at best. Think of it more as one of those trips you go on because you promised you would, even after you've decided it's not where you want to be."

"I've never been on one of those," Aruda said.

"See, now you can say you have been," Teal replied, and motioned the man forward with his hand.

"The next ship over is one we would like you to see," said Gallios. "Is Governor Konik coming with us?"

Ardenai shook his head. "He'll catch up with us at the next stop. Lead on."

They got back in the open cars and Gallios continued talking to them about the things they grew, and how they controlled the rain and the weather, how they could suspend and add partial levels hydroponically if the need was great enough, what part of each ship was a processing plant, and as he was talking they went shooting off into one of the domed overpasses. He slowed down and let them feel the motion and look at the outsides of the ships with the little repair tenders zipping around like miniature models – the unmistakable spin of stars and ships above and below them in space.

"I agree," he said without anyone having actually said anything, "It's an amazing sight, and I see it all the time. And yes, it does make me giddy."

He sped up again, and they found themselves among endless rows of trees. "The clusters of boxes you see are bee hives," he said. "They are spaced all around when anything is flowering. This is an orchard ship. These trees will last for a hundred years or more with care. While trellis-trees produce more fruit per acre, we have chosen on these ships to plant full sized, old-fashioned trees because of their biomass, which is critical to the life-support and water production systems. These are nut trees that the Equi call ammons. This particular ship is devoted to them, since they are a staple of the AEW diet. On this ship there are one hundred and twenty million trees, each producing about fifty net pounds of drupes per tree. That is three million statute tons of ammons per year. The next ship over is a mixed orchard ship. We can do that because each level is controlled separately. We can have, for instance, twenty levels of five different things and they will all thrive in their own micro-climate. Each level can also be controlled as a different season, so there is a constant harvest. That particular ship is actually thirty-three levels of two things, roughly one hundred and fourteen thousand trees each of oranges and verdanbutters, and thirty-four levels of a third, pomes. All highly nutritious, and heavily produced in relatively tight spaces. Again, millions of tons of food.

"We are very grateful to the Papilli for loaning your world that huge Jocundome, which is a priceless gift – probably in no small part due to the fact that the Dragonhorse married well – a beautiful Papilli cross. On their farms will grow much of the grain you will need for the next few years until Lebonath Jas starts diversifying and Lebonath Tras comes into full production. For now we can devote more ground here to various kinds of phaselus and the leafy green varieties of annual alcibus which will fully nourish your population, especially your children."

He swung the cars around and headed down a long, narrow series of switchbacks that he said made wonderful race ramps for the youngsters, and took them to the bottom of the ship. "This is a processing facility," he said. "Each ship has its own, as the ships do get put into use as single units. For instance, if the kartfels fail on Amberia, we might move in just a single ship devoted to that crop. Because all of us within the AEW are strong trading partners, and because the movement of food is based on need not on price, we can usually make up for each other's shortages. At least we try. Now, this machine removes the outer husks from the ammons before the shell itself is removed ..."

Ensharra was nodding and still vaguely interested, but part of her was feeling sad that Konik had been wounded by something she might have said. She was looking a little more into space than at the processing machinery when Teal's hand closed over hers where it rested on a safety rail.

"It wasn't you," he said quietly. "He needed to hear what you had to say, regardless. He's both hard-ridden and intensely private, and as a result it's difficult for him to hear nice things about himself. When one of those nice things reminds him of why Ah'davan married him – it's a shock."

"You know," she said, looking up at Teal, "It's ..." she gave it a little more thought, "... it's almost like he's doing penance for something. Like he's driving himself as punishment. I can't really put my finger on why I feel that way."

Teal just nodded. She was sharp indeed. But if that story were ever to be told it was going to come from Konik, not him. "He's an enigma, that one," he said at last. "Incredibly brave in the face of great personal risk. Honorable when honor could spell death. I know women find him handsome and desirable, and despite some very attractive temptation he never turned his head, never wavered in his character, even when he was nursing a very sick wife. That says a lot about a man."

"Does it ever tempt you to waver when women tell you you're handsome, Master Captain? You must hear it a lot."

Teal laughed at that point, and took his hand off hers, which made her giggle to herself. He was fun to tease, and she knew exactly how to do it. "Women don't tell me I'm handsome. They do tell me I'm tall. Here we go, back in the carts."

At the end of the circuit Gallios thanked them deeply and sincerely for coming, invited their return with wives and children or school groups for a tour, to spend time enjoying the parks and pools, to help with the harvest should they be so inclined, and dropped them at the main scrambleshaft for that level.

Again they were asked to stand together, again they were made aware of the presence of armed SGA personnel, and again they felt that eerie rush and tingle which moved them from one venue to the next. They had a moment to wonder if they were going back to the tunnels before they found themselves standing in the central receiving area of a beautiful crystalline dome.

"Welcome to Jocundome number three, built and administered by the government of Papillia under the auspices of the Affined Equi Worlds," said a pleasant female voice. "All weapons are to be checked before you arrive unless you are authorized to carry. If you engage in any sort of personal violence, or if you abuse alcohol, you will be removed or prosecuted. Please be careful with fire, and do not molest or intimidate the animals. Leave things as you find them, and if you find something out of order, please report it at once. You are required to register in the main service area before leaving the building, and to check out before leaving the dome. Thank you for visiting with us, and enjoy your stay."

"I hope by personal violence they're not including polo," Teal said. "I understand they have some absolutely pristine fields here. I wonder if they have any ponies or if we have to bring our own?"

"And … how, exactly would we play polo?" Konik asked, popping up fresh-faced from somewhere in the crowd to join them. "Not that I don't think it's a splendid idea, I do."

"Nik, hello!" Teal said, "There's you, and Ardi, Tarpan and me. Two on two – fast and rough, just the way I like it."

"We're talking about polo and not sex, aren't we?" Konik smiled. "Which, by the way ..."

"Boys," Ardenai said, and nodded to the man at the main desk. "I am ..."

"Of course you are!" the man exclaimed. "Of course you are! Oh, this is such an honor, Dragonhorse. My name is gate … no, my name is Pyron, and I am the gatemaster. How may we serve you and your guests?"

"For the moment, I would like to show these people one of the grain growing operations, if you will accommodate us," Ardenai replied, pinching his cheeks between thumb and fingers to control a spreading grin.

"Of course," Pyron said again, still nodding, "One has been selected for you. Please step onto the platform … all of you at once is fine. When you are ready to come back stand in a group and use this programmable pass that I'm going to give you to put around your neck. Pinch the yellow tab. It will always bring you right back here to this very spot. You're off!" And they were once again in a strange place, in front of a series of huge, colorful barns with white trim, tall brown and red alcibus waving in a gentle breeze as far as the eye could see.

"Again we are going to talk about food?" Naram asked, nearly yawning with boredom. "How can we convince you that we get it? You're going to feed us so we can all go to school."

"This is not going to be a handout, Regent. You're going to learn to feed yourselves so you can all go to school, and I'll be convinced that you get it when your flamen stop telling the people we're poisoning them!" Ardenai snapped. "When your flamen stop telling them that having enough to eat is a sin. Who in the name of Eladeus is twisted enough to tell people that having enough for their children to eat is going to land them in the flames of the witch world? Every step of this day, every minute of this day is going on crys-tel, and it is going to be broadcast, and I don't think anything is going to be more telling than watching all of your flamen filling their plates and their stomachs with the same food they're telling the people is tainted. If that food is going to send anybody to burn, your flamen are at the head of the line."

"Let's get something straight," Naram said, impatiently gesturing the Firstlord aside and dropping his voice. "They are not 'my flamen'. They are more or less Eridu's flamen. Mostly they are an entity unto themselves with their own codes and their own hierarchy. Eridu was flamen himself before he became the Gods' scion of whatever-the-Tras he thought he was. He started out well, just like his father before him. That lasted about ten minutes. Do I recognize the flamen? Yes. Do I approve of what they do? No. Do I approve of them more than I approve of you? Not sure yet, but when I decide I will let you know. In the meantime, the only thing that is mine, is me, so knock off the, 'your flamen' shit. After this they're probably going to kill me anyway, and I don't want to die with those idiots on my shoulders."

"I stand corrected," Ardenai said with a curt nod. He turned back to where a Papilli farmer was speaking to the others, just inviting them into one of the big barns to see how the grain was recorded and stored.

The Lebonathi were once again taking on a bit of a swagger, that faint aroma of a trip to the viewseum to see the peasantry, when the man who was changing information on one of the big reader boards turned around and smiled at them. "Welcome," he said in a pleasant tone of voice. "We are pleased that you have come to visit us today." It was Nagar.

The whole group just stopped and gawped. He was darker of skin and hair, but it was definitely him. "Nagar?" one of the men ventured, "It's me, Dagan. What are you doing here?"

Nagar looked puzzled. "I work here. I live here, but I am pleased to meet you ... Dagan, did you say?"

"You are Lebonathi!" Dagan exclaimed. "You are flamen!"

"You are mistaken," Nagar said gently. "I am Lebonathi, yes, but for as long as I can remember my life has been interwoven with crops and the seasons."

Dagan spun on Teal. "What did you do to him, you piece of Equi shit?"

"Over there," Teal said through his teeth, flipping an index finger away from Nagar. When they had walked a distance away, trailed by most of the others, Teal said, "I told you this morning what I did to him, did you not believe me?"

"He is not who he was! Neither is he dead! What did you do to him?"

"Dagan," Teal said, pointing with his chin toward Nagar, "What you are seeing is the Equi version of ultimate punishment. His mind was wiped clean and a new person created in his place. When I told you this morning that I had killed him, I was not lying. Flamen Nagar is no more. The same fate, or full-body death, awaits any of you who try what he did, or anything like it, for that matter. Remember that very first day we came? Naram told you that we could do this to all of you, and that your culture would be dead in an instant. I confirmed it, and you heard me. Now do you understand what we meant?"

"You brought us to this place on purpose," Karun breathed, "Just so we could see this."

"And so you could see how grain-alcibus is grown and processed," Teal amended, "But, this too. I wanted each and every one of you to understand just how quickly and how thoroughly this can be done. When we say we will do something, we mean it. We do not, we will not lie to you, nor will we spare you if you leave us no choice."

"He had a wife, and children ..." Dagan said, and there was actual sadness mixed with the anger.

"Oh, so he did," Teal said, seeming surprised. "I heard that somewhere." He turned to Nagar, who was being occupied by Konik and Ensharra and called, "Excuse me, Nagar?"

He looked over and smiled. "Yes, Master Captain?"

"Are you married?"

"I am," he said, and his smile widened. "I have a wife and two very small boys."

"And where are they?"

He thought a moment. "Visiting … someone … my wife's mother, I think. Isn't that odd, I can't remember. I must be tired. They should be home in a day or so."

"Thank you," Teal smiled, and turned back to Dagan and the others. "This is where we find out if you care at all for each other. Do you understand?"

"I understand very well," Naram said, surprising himself with the urge to smile, and Dagan nodded.

"They are out of the city, but I will go get them, and I will bring them to the chambers of the anchoress at mid-day tomorrow," Dagan said. "You're not going to ..." he made a subtle wiping motion with one hand.

"She will be given some choices," Teal said. "And make it day after tomorrow."

They made a cursory tour of the facilities, then Ardenai gathered them and said, "We are all tired and you had an especially busy morning. You have another busy day tomorrow. We will go back to Dragonhorse, where you will have a brief medical exam and be our guests for the night. Tomorrow, we will see the witch world, where the wicked go to burn."

If they were still afraid the Lebonathi hid it well. They scrambled back to the entresol dome, where Ardenai was told by the gatemaster that he was to keep the pass. It had been designed for him. He could use it to go wherever he wanted without going through the entresol. "You can go directly to your apartments, which have been prepared for you here within the crystal, or anywhere on the surface."

"It is very kind of you to think of my comfort in the city," Ardenai smiled. "What if I get lost in the woods?"

Pyron reminded that it would take him anywhere on the surface that he wanted, "Just tell it where you want to go or what you want to see," but it would always bring him back to the entresol. He could come incognito, but leaving that way would be a different matter. "We are just finishing up security measures for that part of the program," he said apologetically, and with a nod and a smile that reminded Ardenai of Io to the point where he ached inside, Pyron sent them back to Dragonhorse.

The Lebonathi were assigned quarters two to a room – not the brig – and in their rooms they found the clothing they had left in the tunnels, cleaned and waiting for them. They were asked to report to the sanecere bay for a physical before dinner, and when they arrived as a group they found Teal, Ardenai and Konik waiting for them. "You three are the stuff of nightmares, you know," Naram said, but there was no sneer in his voice, just a certain resignation that made Ardenai wonder if he was getting ready to pull something. Naram was not one to give up easily.

"Aruda mentioned earlier in the day that you were prisoners," the Firstlord said, parking one muscular hip on a windowsill and giving Ensharra a brief wave as she walked in. "While you are not prisoners, you are no longer free men, either. Physician Pythos and Doctor Moonsgold are going to give each of you a cursory examination to make sure you didn't pick up anything nasty from those tunnels. The Master Captain nearly died of an infection, and that's where he got it." All eyes went to the wrist to elbow bandage, and back to Ardenai's face.

"You are also going to be given an injection which is completely painless and has no side effects whatsoever. It carries a blood and tissue marker that allows us to find you, no matter where you are. It is not something we are going to monitor, but if you get out of line and we hear about it, we are going to know exactly where to come and get you and haul you in here. Please do not think it is something that one of your so-called doctors can dig out of you, bleed out of you, or bleach out of you. They cannot, so don't let them try it. The Master Captain, the governor and I have already had the injection, and the anchoress has volunteered to go first so you can see that is safe for the Lebonathi physiology.

"When you are finished, Anchoress Ensharra and Governor Konik will bring you to dinner. The rest of the evening is yours to explore the ship or rest in your quarters. Please ask one of the SGA personnel to accompany you should you choose to explore." He gave everyone a gracious nod and tipped his head for Teal to follow him toward the smaller dining room they had reserved for the evening's guests.

"All right," he said, seating himself and putting his elbows on the table to stare with amusement at his kinsman, "I've been dying to know all day. How did you do it?"

"It was so ridiculously simple that if I tell you, you'll lose all respect for me," Teal grinned.

"Try me," Ardenai responded, and gestured to one of the wait staff to bring a bottle of wine and two glasses. "Did Kee and Ulric help you, or did you figure this out all on your own?"

"We discussed it," Teal shrugged, uncorking the bottle and pouring the wine as he spoke. "Ensharra got me to thinking we were over-complicating it. They're not telepathic. They had to be meeting in person together to discuss policy and strategy. If they'd been doing it telegenically we'd have heard them. We used the ground sensors to locate every reasonably luxurious chamber in the old city big enough to hold the council members and the flamen together, and put a monitored crys-tel in each of them. We were prepared to keep spreading out from the center of our grid until we hit the right place. Fortunately, we caught them early." He set the bottle down and gestured outward in conclusion. "Simple."

Ardenai just shook his head. "What told you to look for the flamen and the council members together?"

"Ensharra mentioned in the course of conversation one day while I was her prisoner that the flamen represented districts, just like the council members. It seemed logical they would meet together."

"Well, you were right, my friend. We got more flamen than council members, but a goodly catch of both." Ardenai sipped his wine and leaned back for a minute to close his eyes. "I assume you noticed that Halaf is still conspicuously absent?"

"I think Halaf has found himself a dark and permanent hole in which to hide," Teal murmured. "If we have to deal with someone, I think Naram may be the best of a dubious lot. At least he's not a coward. Cowards can be so dangerous. And he's not flamen. That, too, is in our favor."

Ardenai nodded, rubbing at his neck in that manner which indicated he was both tired and dealing with more than one thought. "I … am going to stay on Dragonhorse in my quarters tonight. I think I should, being that we have so many guests."

"Then I will meet you on Tras tomorrow. We are drawing blood from the new horses as they arrive, then from a sampling every few days to see how their bodies are processing the various grasses and grains, and reacting to the water on Tras. If I get up and get busy I will have time to do that before you arrive with the Lebonathi. Did you get a chance to tell Isin and the others that we're coming?"

"No," Ardenai said, and drew a deep breath, fighting the agitation which had started on the Jocundome earlier. "I … forgot."

"Don't be concerned. I'll do it as I head down tonight," he said, smiling at his brother-in-law. He picked up the bottle of wine, knowing what the matter was, wondering what to say next. "Pyron certainly reminded me of Io, how about you?"

"He's Papilli. Despite lots of different coloring, they do have some striking characteristics in common."

"That they do," Teal smiled, and got up from his chair. "If I'm going to stop at Stone Spring I'd better get moving. I will take Dominus, and if we need her tomorrow to squire people around a little, we'll have her. If that's all right."

"Of course it is," Ardenai smiled. "Have a good evening."

"You too," Teal said, knowing as he left that Ardenai would have nothing of the kind. He would go to his quarters, which smelled like his wife, and reminded him of his wife, and he would talk to his wife, who was not going to respond, and he'd spend a miserable, sexually frustrated and unfulfilled night. He'd had a few of those already on Tras, and he would be horrified if he knew that Teal was aware of it. Again, there was that puzzle of Ardenai and his need to test himself sexually, to see how frustrated he could get before he lost his focus during the day and started screaming in his sleep.

"Well, it is absolutely, positively none of my business," Teal said aloud, dropping Dominus out of the shunt bay and meandering toward Lebonath Tras. Of course it was, and he knew it. He was married to a woman with Dragonhorse blood, and when she was in heat, she was absolutely everything he could deal with and stay in one piece. Ardenai dealt with those feelings every day. Superlative being that he was, he was not perfect. Teal felt a little … embarrassed … he wasn't sure that was the right word, exactly, but he touched the console and brought up Mountain hold and Kestrel's sharp-featured, slightly haughty face. Of all people, it would have to be him.

"Master Captain," he said. No smile, no inflection.

"He's about at the end of his tether," Teal responded without preamble. There was something about Kestrel that annoyed him, like an insect bite he couldn't quite reach. "Io's in a coma and he's in a war zone. If Wren is the only one he can be with, then she needs to be here."

Kestrel just looked at him for a moment. "She is there."

"What? So are a hundred thousand other people!" Teal exclaimed. "If she's here, why hasn't she said something? Isn't that her job?"

"Like any other Equi she has more than one job, and the Great Himself hasn't asked for her."

"Who is he supposed to ask, you?"

"If I am the one who is here at the time, why not me?"

Teal resisted the urge to whip out a list. "Because he probably figures you'll give him a lecture about something."

"Nevertheless, if he wants her, he needs to let somebody here know that he has need of her, so he can be told where she is."

"And he's probably not going to do that, Kestrel. You know how he is."

"Then let him suffer," Kestrel shrugged. "Stiff neck, stiff phallus. Serves him right. There's a reason he's supposed to have three wives, but no, not him, and now he doesn't even have one, which we're going to have to fix. He was given specific instructions when he was here and he persists in ignoring that one particular aspect out of everything he was told to do. He figured out the Telenir, and would have even without Harrier's big mouth. He's well on the way to getting the first stage of the incursion onto the Lebonathi worlds under control. He found Konik, which was absolutely essential. He's doing everything he's supposed to do, except learning how to keep himself sexually cool. He cannot pre-sex babies if he's so sexually overwrought that he can't control his ejaculations. That's part of his job no less than anything else, and he's not doing it. He deserves every bit of that pain, because that pain is what's going to teach him a lesson, and don't you dare go looking for Wren. Do you hear me? You stick to your expeditionary forces and your livestock and your own business. Go suck blood out of some horses. You'll feel better."

"I hear you," Teal muttered. "Have I told you I think you're a piece of… really flawed technology?" He slapped off the connection and slumped back in the captain's chair. "Shit, is what I meant to say. You are a miserable piece of shit."

He fought his temper and thanked the Creator Spirit that he didn't have to fight his sex drive as well. He swung low over Stone Spring with daylight to spare and laughed quietly to see Sugar trotting to meet the clipper. He grabbed a handful of dried pomes along with a hypodermic needle and a syringe as he opened the door. Sugar was always willing to trade blood for treats. He set the blood-filled syringe back in the clipper in the cold box and walked toward the pavilions with Sugar ambling alongside, munching what Teal was handing her. Isin and Etana were learning to swim in the shallows of the lake, Elam and Ashur fixing dinner in the outdoor kitchen, and Larsa walked to meet him, carrying Umma, who immediately waved her arms and reached for Teal.

"Uff, you weigh a ton!" he said, holding her up to kiss her bare belly. "When you are all together I would speak with thee for a bit. But in the meantime, I would like to sit right here in the sand and flirt with this lovely young lady … and just watch the sun set."

"And you will stay for supper," Larsa said firmly, sensing his weariness and need for normalcy. "Where is the Dragonhorse?"

"He's staying aloft tonight. We have guests on board."

Over a simple dinner eaten out of doors, he explained who those guests were, and that Ardenai wanted to bring them there the next day. Not for long, just to show them a little of the research and let them know that there were those who had kept the faith, not just the religion.

They certainly weren't excited at the prospect, not even particularly pleased, but they nodded graciously and agreed. They spoke for a bit about what they would show these people who had made their lives so miserable for so long – what they would say, and in what tone of voice. Teal let them get it out of their systems, knowing that tomorrow, they would reflect who they were at heart.

Talk turned to the fact that, while it was warming now, it wasn't going to be warm forever, and the tempestorians weren't sure just how uncomfortable it would get here during the cold months. They should be making some decisions about what they wanted to live in if they wanted to stay on Tras year round. The pavilions were good for three seasons, but might be uncomfortable if it got cold enough. Did they want Equi yurts for the first season of storms? Did they want to start building, and if so, with what and where? Would they rather have whole buildings delivered and set on the old stone foundations?

Teal realized he was starting to yawn and excused himself to head upriver, saying he would see them tomorrow, and that they were to display their work with great pride. He kissed the sleepy baby, gave the old mare a pat, and skimmed up river, through the gorge, past the spreading encampment of Equi cavalry, and landed with a soft hiss near his own version of home. How perfect it would be, he thought, to walk in and find Ah'din waiting. How much they enjoyed evenings like this at Canyon keep, listening to the river talk to the rocks, and the calls of night birds and insects. On impulse he opened the data banks and made a crys-tel of Equi night sounds. He took it with him to the pavilion, and played it as he drifted off to sleep, wondering why he hadn't done it sooner.

He was up and running in the predawn, allowing his ophidian pupils to expand until his eyes were nearly black and the path was plain by the light of the last few stars. He was swimming with the first pinks and corals of the day, eating a hasty breakfast, drinking sweet white coffee, putting a thick, three-strand overbraid in his hair. Ardenai usually did that for him, and he for Ardenai. He wondered how the Dragonhorse had passed the night. He tucked the braid up under itself, fastened it with a standard cavalry clip, and wondered momentarily how he would look with hair as short as Konik's. Ten swipes with a towel, ten seconds with a comb, and he was done. Very tempting at times. He snickered. His wife would kill him. She kept his hair trimmed perfectly straight across exactly six inches up from his waistline –

had for nearly sixty years. Not something that was likely to change. It was going to be hot today and he was going to be on Tras. He opted for the lightweight summer uniform of the Expedition and stomped into his riding boots.

He wished there was time to ride down river to the encampment, but there wasn't. He made sure the supplies he would need were in the clipper and slowly hopped the two miles just above the top of the grass, gliding in next to one of the horse transports. Horses, cinnamon orange tea, good leather. The perfect smells of a sunny Segens morning. He breathed them in as he walked with data crys-tels and syringes toward one of the huge pavilions where most everyone was finishing breakfast. He was hailed from several quarters and slid in across from Tarpan, stealing a quick kiss from his bride and giving her a wink.

"Careful, Master Captain. My husband is a jealous man," Ah'keena laughed, returning the kiss.

"I can't help myself," Teal responded. "It's a beautiful morning. A kiss from a beautiful girl makes it all the better."

"And no one can resist the charms of the Master Captain of the Great House of Equus," Tarpan grinned, stirring his tea. "I have a horse I'd like you to look at this morning if you would be so kind. He's a big horse meant for a heavier rider than I, and ..." he thought a moment, adjusting himself in an imaginary saddle, "... three inches above my knee on the offside … I can feel a tad more movement than I think should be there. Maybe the horse himself, maybe the saddle, maybe his reaction to the saddle. It's so subtle I can't figure it out, and I don't want to issue him to somebody and then have problems."

"I'd be happy to do that," Teal smiled, refusing with a hand the tea that Ah'keena was offering him. "Thank you, I don't have time to relax and chat, but I will, and soon. Today the Lebonathi High Council and some of the Flamen are coming for a looksee. When we have turned them loose again I plan to spend at least a couple of days here. Where can I find the horse?"

"I'll show you," Tarpan said, draining his cup and crimping a grin. He owed this man so much, and had so few occasions to pay him back. He carried his dishes to a collection station and gestured back through the front of the pavilion and then right, through the grass to the smaller holding pens. "We've been pitched here for two days, so we'll have to move pavilions tomorrow," he said, noticing the trampled grass in spots. "This is beautiful country, Teal. I've gone out with the transport to drop off teams, just so I could see some of it. Ah'keena and I are both thinking we would like to put our names in for a small keep."

"We would miss you at the Great House," Teal smiled, "but I wouldn't blame you a bit."

"Perhaps we should stop pretending that this is ever going to belong to Lebonath Jas, and build a Great House right here," Tarpan said, glancing at Teal out of the corner of his eye. He wasn't the first one who'd thought it or said it, but he was the first one with the temerity to broach it with an authority figure. Teal just nodded and smiled.

"When the surveys are done we'll have a clearer idea what's best," he said. "But, just between you and me and that absolutely beautiful silver dapple we're coming up on, I agree with you. I can see this as an entity all its own, populated with AEW farm folk."

As a matter of fact, Teal was beginning to think that if he was going to be here for an extended period of time, he, too, would like to build a home and have his wife come and live with him and be farm folk with the rest of them. Not that separating his wife from her parents was something he would ever do. He sighed to himself. Suddenly, it made sense that Ardenai should have three wives, and Teal slowed momentarily, wondering why it had come so strongly into his mind at that moment. He looked at Tarpan and grinned, banishing the thought.

"And here he is," Tarpan said. "This is Poseidon. Abeyan must have sent him for you. He's too big for anybody but you or the Firstlord, and you are Abeyan's commanding officer."

Teal had seen thousands of horses, worked with thousands, and every once in a while one, like this one, took his breath away. He was a tall, broad chested horse with lavish white feathered fetlocks, carrying a silver dapple gene, and he shaded from grey that was almost black in the front, to huge, light grey dapples in the back. He shook a brilliant white mane and switched an equally snowy tail, snorting softly with curiosity as he watched the men approach. "Good morning, Poseidon. Oh, Precious Equus, you're a beauty," Teal said, blowing gently into the horse's nostrils. He patted him and began running his hands over the spot in question. "I don't feel anything on the ground. I'll need to see his saddle, and ride him out a bit."

A very tall, raven haired woman came out of the tack pavilion carrying a saddle and bridle. "I have that right here," she said. "Good morning, Master Captain Teal." He looked over the horse's back. It was Wren.

Not a word, she cautioned. *We need to talk.*

▲ ▲ ▲ ▲ ▲ ▲ ▲

The flamen were literally being held by force on the scrambleshaft platform, and Ardenai was losing patience. He'd had very little sleep and his ability to sympathize with these people was frayed at best. "I'm tired of trying to reason with you," he snapped, and made a circling motion with an index finger to the technician. "Just send them. If they end up in a lake of fire, so be it."

The moans and screams were lost in a swirl of maroon and blue, and the Lebonathi found themselves collapsing in a field of green grass, dotted with small blue and yellow flowers. "Now don't you feel silly?" Ensharra demanded, standing over them. "Did you really think Governor Konik and I would have gotten on that platform with you if we'd been scrambling into a fire? It is hard enough to make these people think we're worth anything, and then you act like cowards. He said he wasn't going to hurt us. He hasn't hurt us yet."

The men looked rather shamefaced and the anchoress took a moment to note who was still standing: Naram, herself, Konik, Aruda, Dagan. That was it. "You would shame us, you whore!" Hamazi snarled as he got up. "Look at you in your shameful, revealing garb! You have no fear of fire because you already burn. You already straddle the Equi dirt eaters, pleasuring them instead of the Gods." He had taken a single step in her direction when Konik's hand came up.

"Careful," he said, not threateningly, but firmly. "Anchoress Ensharra has begged for your lives on more than one occasion, and so far as I know it never involved having sex with any of us. I don't really think she's that sort of woman, and it would behoove you to think likewise, at least around me." His blue eyes bored into Hamazi until the man looked down and away. "Apologies, Anchoress," Konik said.

"Thank you," she said quietly, and looked up at him to touch his arm before looking away. He wasn't tall for an Equi, but tall nonetheless. It made her look into the sun. "Oh look, here comes Sugar," she said, and her swinging stride took her quickly away from the men as she fished in her trouser pocket for the treats she had brought, calling in a high, sweet voice for the old mare.

Ardenai arrived at that moment, along with most of the SGA personnel. "I see nobody made a run for it except Ensharra," he chuckled. "Gentlemen, that is a horse, a living animal, and this is Stone Spring. It is in this spot that the five scientists we have found so far have chosen to begin to rebuild the flora and fauna of Jas and Tras."

He began walking with them, explaining the surroundings, how the place had been found on a scouting mission, how the scientists had been found clinging to life on the side of a mountain, pouring what little water they had onto their precious plants instead of into themselves. Isin and Elam came to meet them and took over the conversation, and Ensharra walked up beside Konik, who was slouched effortlessly against a boulder at the back of the assembly.

"It was kind of you to speak for me," she said. "And you're right. I haven't used my vast sexual prowess to woo any Equi so far. As a matter of fact, I've never used any sex at all – ever, on anybody." She shrugged, "Take that warning for what it's worth." She moved on with the group toward the edge of the lake, leaving Konik rubbing his forehead as he did when he was trying to make sense of something.

Teal appeared at that moment, skimming inches above the meadow on silent wings to settle Dominus in her usual spot in the sand further along the shoreline. "Sorry I'm late," he said quietly, walking up beside Ardenai. "I've been riding an absolutely phenomenal horse that Abeyan sent. Tarpan thinks he has a twitch, but I can't find it. I'll try again this evening when I can go out bareback and without boots. Oh, and we've been invited to dinner at headquarters. I accepted for both of us."

"Good," Ardenai said absently, and for a few moments his thoughts were obviously elsewhere. "Notice," he said in a half whisper, "They're not nearly as fascinated by the water as the others were. If one is rich, one has access to water. I wonder where."

"There are oceans on Lebonath Jas."

"That may be it, though the shorelines are clogged with industry and desalinization plants and power generating stations and garbage in general until the water is hardly inviting. I think we're still missing information."

"And we will for a long time yet," Teal said comfortingly. "Things are settling down here, Ardi. Hopefully you will be able to go home soon and make sure things are running smoothly. Hug your boy, look in on your wife."

"That should be you," Ardenai said, moving at the back of the group toward the pavilions and the demonstrations which the scientists had laid out. "All I can do is look at my wife through a glass bubble and hope she's actually alive. Your wife wants to be settled with a child."

Teal just looked at him. "That is not a very good reason, I'm afraid. I am a military man. My wife knows what I am. You, are the head of the AEW, the Thirteenth Dragonhorse. You have eleven other planets to govern. You cannot study the details and ignore the big picture for too much longer."

"I conference every day. I make rulings every day. I look into the faces of the council on our world and nearly a dozen others, every day, just as I would if I were at the Great House," Ardenai said.

Had they really been here that long? It felt like yesterday and forever. How good it would feel to hug Gideon and his parents and Ah'din. So many of his friends were here, Teal was here, Marion, Tim, Oonah, Moonsgold and ... Kehailan. His oldest son was here. Why did he ache with emptiness? Why did he feel like Io was never going to wake up, like Io and the babies had become a fantasy created to keep him sane? His expression soured.

"Besides, I am where I was told to go by Mountain hold. I am where I'm supposed to be in the wondrous order of things. You know that as well as I do."

Teal disappeared, and when he reappeared, he was carrying Umma – plumping up and gurgling happily, her golden brown fuzz shining in a wild little aura. Teal whispered something to her and she did a rather accomplished job of blowing Ardenai a kiss before waving herself into his arms.

"Look at you with a tooth coming in," the Firstlord chuckled, "Mother's going to be teaching you some suckling manners soon." He held her close and rocked her a bit and she pulled herself up on his shoulder and busied herself trying to get the clip out of his hair while he patted her butt and listened to what Ashur was saying about the plants they'd found.

He realized that Naram was not listening to Ashur, so much as watching him with the baby, and he comforted himself with the fact that there was no way anybody could get off Lebonath Jas without hijacking a scrambleshaft, and one had to know several codes to be able to do that. Still, Naram didn't look hostile. When Ardenai thought about it, it wasn't a look he could put his finger on.

"I guess I should tell you I got some news this morning," Ardenai said, turning to face away from the Lebonathi and walking a short distance to look out at the water.

Something in his voice told Teal it hadn't been good. "Personal, or professional?"

"Both," Ardenai sighed. "And it affects you as much or more than it does me, Brother Mine. Abeyan has given notice that he is resigning as head of the Equi Cavalry."

"What?" Teal grimaced. "He's devoted his life to the cavalry."

"He does not want to have to deal with or be subservient to me. He believes Io lost his granddaughter because of me, is in a coma because of me, because I seduced her, because she feels she has to do whatever it takes to please me. He thinks she is going to die, and he says he doesn't want to be close enough to kill me when she does. He says every time he sees me, he sees me having sex with his daughter … he didn't put it that politely ..."

"As I remember that day, he was the one who stood on tradition,"

Teal said with some heat, “and Io said she loved having him there, that it let him relive being with Luna.”

“Well, he has changed his tune. He does not want his only grandson from his union with Luna to be influenced by me, or by Ah’krill, or by the woman I have turned his daughter into, so he and his wife are moving to Anguine II in order to be close to Salerno’s parents, and taking Jilfan with them. He says that since his daughter is as good as dead to him, even when she’s up and around, he and Ah’kra have decided to have a daughter of their own and forget as much as they can about us and Equus.”

“That hurts,” Teal said quietly. “Would you like me to try to talk to him?”

Ardenai shook his head. “He doesn’t want to deal with you, either. The limb has snapped from the tree. There is no propping up or mending.”

“And you’re not going to say anything about him taking Jilfan so far away?”

Ardenai sighed and puffed out his cheeks. “I know for sure the boy doesn’t want to be with me. He’s spent most of his life with Salerno’s parents, and they’ll be close by to keep an eye on him. If Io wants that arrangement to change, it needs to be her choice, not mine. I don’t want to start throwing my weight around and rile Abeyan up any more than he is already. It just might reflect on his treatment of Jilfan… or Io.”

“You do know this is not your fault, Dragonhorse. Abeyan has had his nose out of joint since the second you rose to be Firstlord. I think he believed it would be him, I really do. He’s not upset that you got Io hurt or put her in a coma, he’s jealous that she chose you over him. I will also bet you a new saddle that he thought you would make him Military Governor of Lebonath Jas, and instead you turn to someone he considers a traitor. Ardenai, I know you love the man, but at least recognize that in this case he does not have a valid point, and then, keep a bit of an eye on him. If you don’t, I will.”

“I am reminded of that speech in Macbeth,” Ardenai said, “That one about not looking to have troops of friends, but instead curses, not loud, but deep.”

“That, is out of context,” Teal replied, side-arming a stone into the lake. "Why you and Kee love that play so much is beyond me. You have done none of the things Macbeth did to get where he was, but how about this one from the lady of the castle. 'You lack the season of all natures, sleep.' We are both but young in deed, as Macbeth would say, and if we are to be a team, you must be able to lean into the harness with all your mind and not be split in your thinking. It saps your strength. You have got to be sexually cool and mentally reasoned if you are going to keep up this pace."

"Precious Equus! You're starting to sound like Kestrel!"

"And why would I do that?" Teal snapped sarcastically. "What could someone ten thousand years old who has been through twelve Dragonhorses possibly know about what it takes to be Dragonhorse?"

"If you two are going to get into a fistfight, which I would enjoy more than you can possibly imagine, you'd better give me the baby." Ardenai looked away from the smoke in Teals' eyes and saw Naram standing there, holding out his hands palms up. "I know perfectly well how to hold a baby. I have never been a father, but I was a doting uncle."

Umma was mostly asleep, and Ardenai peeled her gently off his shoulder and handed her over. He had a momentarily horrifying image of Naram grabbing her by the ankles and bashing her head against a rock, but he made himself let go. He could tell by the look on Teal's face that he'd had pretty much the same thought, and they gave each other a look askance that lasted half a second on their faces and half a minute in their eyes.

"Idiots," Naram muttered, walking away with the child, "I'd kill either of you if I thought I could get away with it, or that it would do my people any good, but not her."

If Larsa sees who we handed her off to, Naram isn't going to have to kill us, Teal observed, brushing drool off Ardenai's shoulder.

"New beginnings," the Firstlord whispered, pointing with his chin to where Konik and Ensharra had joined Naram to entertain Umma.

What good it did they could not ascertain, but they spent the day introducing the Lebonathi to the planet: the water, the trees, the grass, the horses. They took them to Expedition Headquarters for lunch, and had some of the scientists there explain to them how the planet was being evaluated.

Those same scientists also explained that when this planet was off to a good start, they would begin to renew the resources of Lebonath Jas. Most of the way through the afternoon, when every Lebonathi had been invited at least half a dozen times to join a research team, learn to ride a horse, come back with their families and spend time, Teal and Ardenai took them back to Belesprit, showed them the animals in stasis, then on to Dragonhorse, where they were thanked for their kind attention over the last two days and Dagan was reminded of his promise to bring Nagar's wife and sons on the morrow.

"I hope this has given you a little better idea of who we are and what we hope to accomplish with your help," Ardenai said, nodding to the technician, and the Lebonathis found themselves back in the room where they had started.

They all looked at each other in silence for a long minute before Naram said, "Well, gentlemen, I think that illustrates all too graphically the point I was trying to make. Let me say again, tone down your rhetoric. We can be part of building our future and retaining our faith and our culture, or as quickly and efficiently as they killed Nagar, they will kill the rest of us."

He made his glum, solitary way back toward his apartments, then turned aside up a seldom used stone staircase to the surface, through a narrow alley and down again into a sprawl of shops, service entrances and storage rooms. He leaned casually against a wall for a few minutes to make sure no one had followed him, and ducked into a doorway.

"Naram?" said a soft voice.

"Shhhhh," he hissed, and pointed toward the back of the place, to a wilderness of stacked boxes, fabrics, rolled carpets and dry goods.

When they slipped behind a large wooden case the woman turned and put her arms around his neck. "I was so worried when you didn't come home yesterday," she said, resting her head on his shoulder. "I stalled with the house cleaning as long as I could."

"It probably needed it," he smiled, "given that your housecleaning duties don't usually involve cleaning house." He kissed her, sat on the cool stone floor and patted a spot beside him.

"What's wrong?" She asked.

"We can't keep doing this, Akadia. When we were on Equus you played the poor servant girl who had to do my bidding, but now …"

"Telloh won't find out."

"Yes, he will," Naram said, touching her face. "He beat you badly for suspected transgressions while you were on Equus, and he was right. He suspects you again, he'll kill you."

"I don't care," she whispered. "Living with him is like death anyway. There has to be something we can do."

Naram just shook his head, staring at the floor. "Right now, all I want to do is keep you safe. I've lost Lulana, Phaedra, Rakba … I don't want to lose you as well."

"Think of something, please," she whispered. "Where can we run? Where can we hide? There has to be someplace."

Naram was still shaking his head. "No," he said. "As long as I'm representing Lebonath Jas, there isn't."

He sighed, which was unlike him. There was one person he could ask to give Akadia sanctuary. He could ask the Dragonhorse.

"What are you thinking?" she asked, and he dropped his head over against hers.

"Nothing."

CHAPTER 10

Late that afternoon, just as the dust coming up from the horse's hooves turned gold in the slanting sunlight, Ardenai and Teal appeared together on horseback at Expedition Headquarters. They reined up next to where Teal had left Dominus earlier in the day and dismounted, though Ardenai would have ridden on into camp. "We need to tarry here just a bit," Teal said apologetically, and Ah'keena appeared as if by some pre-arranged signal to take the horses.

"Oh, I'm not going to like this, am I?" Ardenai muttered, realizing something was afoot.

"Yes and no," Teal responded. He put an arm around the Firstlord's shoulder and steered him up the ramp into the dim interior of the clipper. "Just please remember that none of us planned for things to happen as they did."

"But they must happen as they ought," said a growly alto, and Wren appeared, freshly dressed, just toweling her hair after a bath. "Ahimsa, I wish thee peace. Please, both of you sit and be comfortable." Ardenai was too stunned not to comply, and Teal already knew what was coming, so they both landed without ceremony in the chairs next to the dining table. She sat across from them and gave Ardenai a genuinely delightful smile. "It's so good to see you again, Dragonhorse."

He cleared his throat to force blood to his brain and responded, "And you, Wren. Have you been here long?"

"I arrived with the expeditionary teams."

For thirty protracted seconds that felt like a lifetime there was a deep and awkward silence while Ardenai rummaged around in his head. "I … did not send for you," Ardenai said at last. "Did I?"

"No. I was sent to you so you have some help. I do have other talents, you know. Primarily, I am an adjudicator with six thousand eight hundred years of Equi Statute Law in my repertoire. I am also quite a good cartographer, amongst other things. As a bonus, I play an ass-kicking game of polo, and I am no shucks at volleys over. Your Firstwife was to begin mapping the keeps, but she is not able to do that, nor is she able to be the kind of companion you need, so I have been sent by command of Mountain hold and by the Great House, to help fill that void."

Teal's body language told Ardenai that this was not the whole story. "You knew about this?" he growled.

Despite the tone, Teal didn't flinch. "Not until this morning. I came to work with the stock, and more or less bumped into Ah'ren. We spoke at some length, which is why I was late to Stone Spring."

"I see. You are Ah'ren, so your relative position has changed. Both of you are twitching like creppias, so I'm assuming that we've not gotten to the core of this yet?"

"No," Ah'ren sighed, "and Teal is kindly but unwillingly here because I don't want you storming out of here before you hear me out … husband."

Ardenai's hands and aquiline profile went skyward. "Ohhhh … PRECIOUS EQUUS!" he exclaimed. "How did I know those were going to be the next words out of your mouth?"

His fists hit the table, but not very hard. Annoyed as he was on some levels, parts of him were sincerely happy to see her beautiful face. That voice was like massage oil. And she played polo. He winced physically as his guilt began to change shape.

"Surely this cannot be of your own accord," Ardenai said in a much quieter tone, "I … to my lasting shame … I picked you up and threw you across the room. I spoke to you as though you were less than I. Surely you cannot want to be with me after that."

"You apologized at length for that, Dragonhorse. I accepted your apology, and I was happy when I found out I was being sent to you as a companion wife. We are over that chevron and on to what is best for Equus, her people, and her beloved Firstlord. That, apparently, is us in tandem."

"Are we already married," he growled, "or is there a ceremony yet to be accomplished?"

"Your choice," she said. "But the contract is in force. Ardenai, listen to me. Ah'nis told you that Ah'krill and Mountain hold might have plans for you that you wouldn't like. This is it. Not necessarily permanently. But for a while. You are far past the need of a hetaera. You need a wife beside you. I have talents to offer as well as pleasure and companionship, and you need help with the myriad aspects of governance. Ah'riodin is in a medically induced coma and will be there for seasons ..."

"And the one thing she didn't want, was for me to be with you."

"I know that, and I'm not any happier than you are about that part, which is only one part of many, and, you must admit, more her problem than ours. When she is up and around and back to her duties you can arrange for me to be killed in some kind of bizarre accident, and I will go back to Mountain hold and to being what I was, your hetaera … if that is what you want when the time comes.

"I do want you to know that this is not a precedent. I was wife to the Fourth Dragonhorse, the Eighth Dragonhorse, and to your great grandfather, who was also named Ardenai, and who was the Tenth Dragonhorse. I loved it, and I loved him with all my heart!" She sat back and laughed softly. "I love being out in the world as a wife, learning and practicing various crafts, helping the other wives tend their children, being thought of as a person rather than as a repository of intellect. If you are not willing to grant me anything else, please grant me that. Grant me anonymity. And let me stay awhile and explore this place."

Ardenai took a deep breath and smiled at her. "My whole family knows who you are, Wren … Ah'ren. Anonymity might be a hard thing to maintain."

"Your family will probably find me vaguely familiar and take assurance from that, but they will not know me," she responded. "Tarpan will not remember me at all. Even Ah'krill knows only that someone from Mountain hold has been sent to care for you. Teal alone will know who and what I was originally. Gideon will have a vague memory of me, Criollo none at all, just as he has no real memory of Lark anymore. You noticed none of the children recognized Chirion when he became Darley. Almost any conscious memory can be adjusted as you well know, having done it yourself on occasion. Their memories have been blurred, nothing more, I promise. Mountain hold and the Great House mean you no harm, Dragonhorse, but they insist that you comply."

Ardenai held up a hand. "Enough said. I see that no matter what I do or say, I cannot win on the larger battlefield. It is the will of the wisest and eldest, and I must bow to it." He sat back in his chair, huffed with annoyance, and looked a little sulkier than he actually felt.

"So," Teal said, sliding his chair to look at both of them, "What is your pleasure in this? Should I ask our friends to prepare to celebrate your wedding this evening? Do you want to formalize the marriage? Do you want to say nothing at all beyond the announcement of the Great House itself? Speak, before I leave you alone a while."

"If we are married by documentation, we will be married by tradition as well," Ardenai said quietly. "I do not want anyone questioning either of us about the propriety of this. Please ask Governor Konik to be here in an hour or so to marry us. That way we can celebrate with dinner afterward. Ask our friends from Dragonhorse, Belesprit and Stone Spring, Ensharra … whomever you think appropriate. I seem to have an odd habit of marrying on far-off worlds." He turned to Ah'ren. "I hope a cavalry dining pavilion and the presence of future friends will do. I cannot offer you more than that."

"On a beautiful starlit night, who needs more?" she smiled. "I promise, I will try to make this a happy time for you, Dragonhorse."

"Thank you," Ardenai said quietly. "I hope you will be happy as well. Oh, Teal, as a courtesy, invite Naram, will you?"

"I will. I am going to leave you two alone to decide the story, and to get more comfortable with one another while I make arrangements and change clothes," Teal said. With a courtly nod and a heart that ached for Ardenai, he was gone.

The Firstlord got up, walked to the console and closed the door, then sat back down, squeezed his eyes shut, and took a couple of long, steadying breaths. "I cannot believe I am letting this happen," he said. "Why am I letting this happen?"

"Because the arguments for it are to the benefit of your people and your worlds, and the arguments against it benefit only your private sense of morality." Ah'ren said quietly. "Always, there is the sense that I am being forced on you. That is not a good feeling. I should go and at least brush my hair before I marry the thirteenth Dragonhorse."

She walked toward the stateroom, turning at the door to look at him. "I was on Achernar for some minor procedures, and I did go check in on Io while I was there. She seems very comfortable, and very … aware. I truly think 'medically induced coma' is too strong and too frightening a term. One member or another of your family is almost always there. They are playing music for her, and she hears your voice, and what is going on in the world, and Grandsire Krush has put some storybooks on crys-tel, and the babes hear those. They, too, seem strong so far. I know that it is natural to be concerned, Ardenai, but I wouldn't worry."

"Thank you," Ardenai said. "What procedures? Should I worry about you, too?"

"No," she grinned. "Strictly cosmetic protocols. Nothing will begin to squeak or fall off, I promise."

"So I can take you out in public?"

"Yes," she laughed. "Though I've never been out in public with you, either. You don't know what you've gotten into, but then, neither do I. Try to remember that."

He nodded and rose from where he was sitting to follow her into the stateroom. "You need to get your hair done, and I suppose I should look in the reflector as well, having not done that all day. Do you have a sense of smell?"

"Of course I do," she laughed, looking at his reflection as she tipped her head to one side and began to comb her long black hair. "I am much more human than machine in every way."

"Then I'd better take a bath."

It was quick, but it made him feel better. He came back with a towel around his waist, shaking his damp hair through his fingers as he walked, and found her in briefcloth and underbodice, holding a tunic in each hand and looking in the mirror. This meant something to her, he realized. She was not just pretending to be human to make him less aware that she was not. He paused behind her to look, then kissed the top of her bare shoulder and said, "The pale green one is traditional. The emerald green one is dazzling." She smelled incredibly good. Tasted incredibly good.

She looked at him in the reflector, feeling his lips start again where neck met shoulder, and meeting his eyes as well. "We have forty minutes, Dragonhorse, and I can dress in six if I let my hair flow from a clip."

"What could be more beautiful than your hair flowing from a clip?" he asked gently, and turned her to face him.

She draped her arms around Ardenai's neck and let him kiss her, long and deep. He put his hands under her bodice beside her breasts, his thumbs caressing her nipples, as he kissed her throat and the side of her neck. She hooked her fingers into the wrap on the towel, gave it a casual toss to one side, and ran both hands up the extended shaft of his phallus. "How long does it take you to do your hair?" she murmured.

"Depends on how I do it," he answered, still kissing her neck.

"A braid is traditional. Flowing from a clip, is dazzling," she said, and moaned softly, pushing down her briefcloth and stepping out of it.

"Not even close to six minutes," he responded, and tipped onto his back on the bed. "Come to me. Please," he whispered.

It was half an hour later when he sighed with contentment and said, "You know what we're going to smell like. And it's not what we should smell like before we get married, or in public even after we're married."

"Mmmmm," she responded, lying back across his chest to kiss his mouth and suck momentarily and gently on his bottom lip. "Just once more for now," she said, pushing her hands against his chest and arching her back, doing the work as he groaned deep with animal pleasure and released himself to her.

They had both returned from a lightning fast neck down mutual scrubbing, and he was laughing about how glad he was that Equi didn't have facial hair, when Ah'ren said, "If you can't dance as well as you can make love, I'm going to be terribly disappointed."

"Funny," Ardenai said around the clip in his teeth, "I was about to say the same thing." He took the clip, fastened it in the part of his hair he had pulled back, and reached for the plain summer tunic of the Thirteenth Dragonhorse.

"Really?" she said, raising one eyebrow and giving the garment a sidelong look which hinted at disappointment.

He let the tunic drop to his side and whuffled a little with frustration. "I … Ah'ren, I'm sorry, I just can't do the pale blue groom's robe, tunic, whatever. That part of my life belonged to Ah'ree and to her only. I did it with Io, for Io, I guess. I hated it, and I can't do it again. Please forgive me."

"I have an idea," she said. "Give me five minutes with the refabricator while you put your britches and boots on and pour us each a glass of wine. If you don't like what I come back with, I will help you with that tunic and no more said, I promise."

He had poured the wine and was walking toward the bed chamber with it when she met him. "What do you think?" she asked, and held up two close fitting, sleeveless tunics, one shimmering in royal purple, one in emerald green, each with the seven chevrons of the Firstlord sloping on the shoulders and a python on the banded collar. "Since I am a gift to you from the old dragons of Achernar."

"I am pleased," he said quietly, and she gave him a deep, respectful nod.

"I am going to tell them the truth, you know," Ardenai said as they left the clipper. "It will be a carefully selected truth, but with the truth comes ease of retelling."

"I will trust your judgment," she said softly, and he took her hand as they walked through the twilight.

When they entered the big pavilion which had been re-arranged for the occasion, people literally caught their breath. They were a stunning couple – lithe, raven haired and regal.

When everyone had gathered in the traditional, wide semi-circle, Ardenai turned to them saying, "Thank you for being here. Because Ah'riodin is trying to keep herself and our babes alive right now and can take no part in governance or intimacy, Mountain hold and the Great House of Equus have summoned Ah'ren to be joined with me as my wife. As you know, I did not want more than one wife, but I, too, must bend to the wishes of the Great House when I am summoned to do so. In that I have no choice, just as this lovely creature had none … until now. This evening, Ah'ren and I come together as strangers for the good of the Equi worlds. If she chooses of her own free will to marry me, I will gratefully join with her, as I joined with all of you when I rose to be Firstlord."

"You know I do," she said, just above a whisper.

They turned to Konik, who grinned and said, "I'm six feet tall and I feel like I should be standing on a box for you two."

"Would you like one?" Tarpan laughed.

"No. Nobody needs to see me. Are you ready?" They nodded. "Then let us begin. Ah'ren, come thee here of thine own free will to be joined with Ardenai as his wife?"

"I come of mine own free will to be joined with Ardenai as his companion wife," she said, smiling at the Firstlord, and Ardenai noticed that she had added the word, 'companion'. He wondered if it was to make him feel less guilty about what he was doing, or make it easier for her to leave.

"Ardenai, come thee here of thine own free will to be joined with Ah'ren as her husband?"

Ardenai felt his stomach drop, but his voice didn't waver. "I come of mine own free will to be joined with Ah'ren as her husband."

As he had done so recently with Io, Ardenai took both Ah'ren's hands in his, turned them palms up, and kissed each one. "I vow to thee gentleness always, my wife. For as long as I live, I am thine."

She took his hands, kissed the back of each one and said, "I vow to thee companionship always, my husband. For as long as I live, I am thine."

Together they brushed the palms of their right hands across the backs of their left in ancient gesture. "Ahimsa, I vow to thee peace," they said together.

"Take one another's hands. Thou art become Galician Ah'ren Ardenai Morning Star, companion-wife of Ardenai, Firstlord of Equus. And thee, Ah'krill Ardenai Morning Star, have become husband to Ah'ren. Be kind and considerate in these first days, and in all the days which follow, and may the blessings of peace, joy and companionship fill your home and your lives. You are wed. Wife, kiss your husband. Husband, kiss your wife." Konik then kissed them both on the forehead as was traditional, and released them to their friends.

"When you have kissed the lovely bride and handsome groom least once, dinner is served," Tarpan called over the laughing chatter, and the Firstlord realized he was starved.

As much as Ardenai hated to admit it, mostly because of what Io would say or do if he did, he found himself enjoying this wedding considerably more than he had theirs. He was surrounded by friends, food, music and dancing with no need to rush off, no huge, thinly veiled and humiliating agenda in his immediate future. While there was the personal disappointment of having done something he'd vowed to himself and anyone else who would listen he wouldn't do, they had been kind enough to structure the summons so there was no shame in it, and none of the stunning shock and sickening guilt there had been in knowing he was about to have sex with someone he had thought of as a daughter. It made him shudder just thinking about it, and Ah'ren's hand touched his, asking him if he was chilly.

As a matter of fact, the sex part of this had already been delightful, and he was relaxed and laughing, knowing that Ah'ren would apply her expertise and her stability to the work needing to be done, and that she would come to his bed with no long, personal history between them, just present, and maybe future. He didn't let himself think too far ahead. That would come soon enough. Right now, right here, he was happy.

He noticed that Naram had come, and that he was speaking with the scientists from Stone Spring. That was interesting. Was he changing, or was he just changing his game? Teal joined the conversation, and something he said caused Naram to nod. Tomorrow would be soon enough to ask questions. Tonight, was about music, and laughter and the incredibly beautiful woman leaning comfortably against him as she spoke to Ensharra.

The music drove them out onto the floor of the pavilion, and she could, indeed, dance. She was light and graceful on her feet, and her sense of rhythm was perfect. Wherever he led, she followed effortlessly, and when she laughed, it lifted his heart. He rather wished he didn't know she was a machine, and chalked it up to wine and nerves.

Teal took her for a spin around the floor and Ardenai sat with a whoosh to catch his breath. "Be careful," Kehailan said, laughter in his voice, "Too much sudden exercise can kill a man."

"But what a way to go," Marion sighed, watching Teal dance with Ah'ren. "Look at that, will you? My God, if I could dance like that man, I could take over the galaxy." He looked over at Ardenai and burst out laughing. "But I can't, so don't consider me a threat. Did you see that dance … thing he was doing with Bonfire earlier? The one everybody was chanting for? How can he even undulate like that?"

"Beats me," Ardenai snorted. "That's the Phyllan Wolf Dance. According to legend it's supposed to culminate in sex, but she hasn't been able to get him to do that."

"Where did he …?"

Ardenai laughed and held up a hand. "I have no idea. He was rather an unbridled youth." He took his eyes off the dancers and looked instead at Eletsky. "How are you liking the ship so far? Remember, there are no wrong answers."

"I … honestly don't know. She's a fabulous piece of technology, but I love the science, Ardi. Maybe when I have a full crew and we're doing more science-type things instead of watching my … Belesprit have all the fun …."

"Would you like to see if Bonfire wants to trade places awhile?"

"Really?" Marion asked, and his eyes said he was ecstatic at the possibility.

"I don't think it would be such a bad idea, especially since you're both fully briefed on what the other is doing. She has already said she wants the Dragonhorse that just came off the line. She could train first on the one you have. Or … she could just have yours and you could take back your beloved Belesprit. We'll talk to her. Ah, Teal is bringing Ah'ren back, and the music is slowing down. I should attend to my groomly duties."

Kehailan's arm came around his father's shoulder, and he laid his head casually against Ardenai's. *Dad, I love you, and I want you to listen to me for about ten seconds. Io has been playing mind games with you since she was two years old. She separated us with her jealousy, and she will separate you from Ah'ren if you let her. I'm begging you, don't let her make you feel guilty about this, or drive a wedge between you two.*

Ardenai nodded, gave Kehailan a lingering kiss on the temple, and spun his bride expertly out onto the floor.

Things were winding down a little when Teal came to sit beside Ardenai, who was with Tarpan, talking cavalry matters, drinking tea and watching some of the dancers – Elam, bouncing around with Umma while Ashur danced with Larsa. Kehailan dancing with Ah'ren, Konik teaching Ensharra off to one side. "Doing all right so far?" Teal asked quietly, and Tarpan excused himself to go dance with his wife.

"I'm fine," Ardenai nodded. "I must believe that things done in good faith work for the best. She's smart, she's funny … she plays polo. Do you believe that? I wonder if she's bluffing."

Teal snorted and shook his head. "I'm betting she's not. You did a good job of explaining things tonight. The simple truth is always better than a lie, even an artful one." He heaved a sigh and leaned into Ardenai's shoulder. "I am so sorry that, again, you've been thrust within hours into a marriage that should have taken years of courtship, and for any part I had in it I beg your forgiveness."

"No apologies necessary, Beloved. I admit, it would be nice to be in love before I got married. I would have liked time for that. Time to plan and anticipate and dream a little. But I had that with Ah'ree, and it was joy enough, and dream enough for a lifetime. I am happy with my pouncing little fledermaus, despite her fluttery ways, and … I watched Nik with Ah'da-van and wondered what it would be like to be married to a wise older woman. Now I have the best of both worlds. Two incredibly beautiful women, different as night and day, and I didn't have to put forth an ounce of effort or a single bouquet to get either one of them. I think I'm pretty lucky. And I will be until Io wakes up. Then, I'll most likely be dead."

"Do not underestimate the character of Abeyan Ah'riodin Ardenai Morning Star," Teal chuckled. "You said it yourself, Ardi. She never ceases to amaze you. Meantime, we have a more immediate logistical problem." Ardenai cocked an eyebrow. "Where are you taking your bride for the night? Because I don't want to end up in the same place."

"Good question," Ardenai said, nibbling at the corner of his mouth. "I was thinking I would take her to the Jocundome as kind of an overnight wedding trip. But … I'm pretty sure Gallios was right when he said we have that dome because I'm married to a Papilli cross. Might not be smart to take my new Equi bride to the chambers I know they prepared for Io and me. My quarters on board Dragonhorse are as much Io's as mine right now, so that won't do. That leaves the pavilion under the trees, or … Dominus, I guess. Unless you've run into someplace especially romantic under the old city."

"Ordinarily, I wouldn't even dignify that with a response," Teal said. "Take my advice, go for the pavilion. The wind whispering in the grasses, the sound of horses, the rush of the water in the river. Oh, and beside my bed there's a crys-tel of Viridian night sounds. I will offer you my horse so you can ride back by starlight, or you may want to get home a little faster, so I will leave you the clipper and sleep in my quarters on Dragonhorse tonight. That way you have the choice."

"You're very kind," Ardenai grinned. "Will you be able to sleep with the background noise?"

"After dancing most of the evening, I think I could sleep anywhere," Teal chuckled. "I'll pitch another pavilion somewhere in the trees in a day or so. Right now I'm going to borrow the clipper for about an hour, and I'll be back so you two can get on about your acquaintanceship."

He was as good as his word, and with a kiss for the bride, a warm hug for the groom, he left with the rest of the off-world guests, saying with a wink, "I am meeting with Nagar's wife and children at high sun in the Anchoress's shop should you be available by then."

"We should be going as well," Ardenai said, holding out a hand to Ah'ren. "Would you like to ride back, or take the clipper?"

"I would love the ride," she said, taking his hand, "but I have things that need to go with me from my quarters. So, the clipper, please."

Ardenai nodded his approval. "Tarpan, may we leave our horses overnight?"

"You may leave them as long as you like," the man smiled. "When you have time we will continue our conversation about cavalry matters. Right now, you two would probably like some rest. Or at least some alone time."

Ardenai, Tarpan and Ah'keena helped Ah'ren gather her things from her quarters, and the Firstlord was surprised by the amount she had. "Most of this is judge stuff and mapping stuff, not girl stuff," she said, reading his body language. "I need to get busy laying out the keeps, which means I need lists of who wants one. Do we have any of those yet?" She winked at Ah'keena, who was attempting to wave a heavily laden hand from behind Ardenai's back.

"Some," Ardenai said, swinging an armload of map cases up the ramp into the clipper. It struck him at that point that people were with them and the entire clipper was a wide open pouncing shambles complete with thrown clothes and who knew what kinds of fluids in various places. Ardenai reminded himself that he was Firstlord of the Equi Worlds, which made him feel worse by example, steeled himself and walked in with his load of materials to dump them on the nearest surface. The clipper was spotless. The bed was made – no signs of hurried dressing, hurried sex – nothing to embarrass the Firstlord or his bride. Ardenai breathed a small sigh of relief. *Thank you, Teal! I'm such a prude.* To his surprise, there was a chuckling response.

I know this. You're welcome, Ardi. Try to get some sleep.

Two hours before dawn, Ardenai was finally ready to do just that and nothing more. He was lying with Ah'ren tucked in the crook of his arm, enjoying the cool breeze coming from the rolled up sides of the pavilion when a thought struck him. "Wren, do you sleep?"

"Mmmmm? Sorry, I dozed off. What did you say?"

"Funny. Seriously, do you need to sleep?"

"Yes. I need sleep. I need to eat. I need to expel waste. I laugh. I cry. I hurt both physically and emotionally. I bleed. I get too cold, I get too hot, I get too tired. Occasionally, I get really pissed off. Why is it so easy for you to say and so hard for you to believe that I am, for all intents and purposes a being just like you? The only thing I cannot do is reproduce, hence the title, companion-wife. Meaning, we are not expected to produce children together."

Ardenai chose his words. "Have you ever wished … you could have babies?"

"In many ways yes, in many ways, no. I can't imagine anything more horrible than outliving ..." she caught herself, and the Firstlord let it go by, though she felt him wince.

"So … physically, you're real. Mostly. I'm not going to be making love to you and accidentally hit an off-switch or something, am I?"

She sighed quietly in the darkness. "No, Dear. I do not have a screw for a belly button, or cosmoscopic relays in my eyes. I do not have an off-switch. Just an on-switch, and we've pretty well pounced on it enough for the moment."

"Your programming. Are you … how do I phrase this without getting myself in trouble …when we were at Mountain hold together you said that you could not tell anybody but Pythos what we were doing. I do not have any such parameters. There is no firewall in my brain except my common sense that tells me what to share and what not to share." She was silent, waiting for him to think, and he appreciated it. "Kestrel said that Mountain hold knows everything about me. I guess I'm trying to ask if you're programmed to report to anybody. If you have … programmable protocols beyond which you cannot go, or must go, in making judgments, decisions … Am I making any sense?"

"For someone who's been awake for two or three days, in shock from being married off without warning, and in a deep post-coital stupor, not bad. Under more favorable circumstances, we might be having a discussion about feelings, because until you fully comprehend and accept the fact that I have just as many as you have, you're not going to understand me, or relax with me."

She rolled more onto her side and propped herself up on one elbow, tracing his profile with her index finger as she spoke. "Ah'krill Ardenai Morning Star, I am your wife. There is no program for that. What I said at Mountain hold, I said to reassure you and help you get over your guilt at having sex with someone other than Ah'riodin. If you took it as programming, that was your misconception. I am not programmed. Like you, I am guided only by my common sense. There's no programming to tell me not to jump off a cliff or throw myself under one of those awful atomic buses on Declivis, and there never has been. I have my training intact, my schooling, and my experiences, just like you. I don't remember everything, just like you don't. I have a superior, highly telepathic brain, just like you do, and I am responsible for using it wisely. The part of me that is machine is so deeply hidden, even from me, that I rarely even know it's there. There is nothing whatsoever in my brain that tells my conscious being I am a machine. I know it only because I have the memory of it. The only thing you will notice, is that I will not age naturally. If we stay together, I will age cosmetically."

"Thank you for the insight," Ardenai said quietly. "It must be very sad to watch the ones you love die, while you go on and on forever."

"I have my companions at Mountain hold, and with their help I have gotten … used to it. In most cases there is more joy in the living than there is sadness in the death. And, I am low maintenance," she said brightly, changing the subject. "Rarely need to be tinkered with, don't often catch cold or get myself a poisoned palm prick, or nearly lose my arm to infection, that kind of thing. My bones will break, because that's what they are. Bones.

But I mend like anybody else. Because I am your wife, Pythos will be my physician, no questions asked. Does that help?"

"Mmmmm," he breathed, and was asleep before the sound died.

He awoke with the sun in his face, sweet white coffee beside the bed, and a very nice view of Ah'ren toweling off after a swim. "You found the pool by the waterfall."

"I did," she smiled. "And I found the path you and Teal run every morning. It's beautiful."

Ardenai sat up and reached for the coffee. "Thank you," he said, gesturing with the mug. "Did you not sleep that you've been running and swimming already?"

"I did not, but I have slept well the last few nights, so I am still relatively refreshed." She sat on the low platform beside him and stroked the sleep-dampened tendrils of hair back from his face. "Have you had enough sleep, is the question."

"Whatever I've had, it will have to do," he said. He set the coffee down, yawned, stretched and flipped the covers aside. "I will swim a few laps to see if I can wake up ..." he yawned again, "and then we should get going. I'm pretty sure I've already missed my breakfast meeting."

"Summer Dragonhorse uniforms all around?" she asked, walking toward Dominus. He nodded and returned from his swim to fresh clothes, a fully dressed wife, and breakfast, which he ate while she braided his hair. "I brought you something," she said, almost shyly, and handed him a small box. "It belonged to your great-grandfather. I thought you might like to wear it today."

Setting his plate aside he opened the box and took out an intricate hair clasp fashioned as a running horse inlaid in pressed Menorquin sea crystal and outlined in cleomitite. "It's beautiful," he said softly, admiring the work. "And very old."

"Yes. Ancient. Thank you for pointing that out," she drawled, and it made Ardenai laugh. "It was his favorite. He wore it the day he rose to be Firstlord. It was a wedding gift from your great grandmother. I thought you might find meaning in that."

"You know I do. Thank you, Ah'ren. I will cherish this, and I would be honored to wear it." He handed it over his shoulder to her, and she tucked his braid up under itself and fastened it with the clasp.

"It suits you," she smiled, kissing the top of his head. "Do you have an office on Dragonhorse? I need a space for my maps and materials if you can spare a corner."

"You shall have an office of your own," he replied. "We will take some things today and some tomorrow, since most of today will be getting you acquainted with your new surroundings. We do need to hurry. Teal has a meeting at high sun, Jas time, and I don't want him going alone."

From the clipper Ah'ren grabbed the first armload of maps, Ardenai the second, wondering if the woman knew how to use a computator and dimensional projections. She snorted under her breath but said nothing, and they scrambled from Dominus to Belesprit, and thence to Dragonhorse, where they were met by Konik and a smiling Kehailan, who reached for some of Ah'ren's maps and said, "Right this way, Mistress. I have a space for you that I hope will suit your needs. If it does not, by all means say so." As they walked he added, "It is rather at the hub of activity, so if the noise bothers you let me know. It is close to the main dining rooms, so you can spread out maps if need be. If you need to meet with a lot of colonists or other people at once you have a choice of rooms close by, and it has plenty of wall space for projecting things or pinning them up, as the mood and the need takes you."

The door slid open and they stepped into a good sized room, long and slightly narrow, with a curving wall that gave it the shape of a bow. In the bowed wall were three windows with wide, plant-filled window sills and programmable panes in case the whirl of space grew tiresome. There was a long, lighted map table with a desk butted up at each end, a seating area, a smallish conference table, and storage and book shelves. "What do you think?" Kehailan asked.

"Perfect," she said. "Absolutely perfect. Does your father have an office close by?"

Kehailan began pointing from the right as he recited. "In order of their appearance. Bridge in the nose on this level, navigation technologies, my office, First Officer's, so it's empty, two together fitted as Governance chambers, Konik's, Ah'nis's, empty, Teal's, yours, empty, Ardenai's, empty, Io's. Beyond that is medical, quarters for officers and guests, family apartments, conference rooms and so on. Dining in the middle, kitchens and various technologies on the far side. When you're settled I'll show you around." He paused and laughed self-consciously. "Did I even answer your question?"

"You did," she replied, looking around and smiling. "Close enough for ease of access, far enough away to miss each other's heated discussions. I will be working closely with the governor, and he's right there. It's really perfect, Captain, thank you."

"Nik and I have that meeting," Ardenai said. "Did you want to come, or would you rather get settled?"

"Coming with you," Ah'ren said. "Kee, thank you." She turned quickly and took Ardenai's outstretched hand, leaving with Konik beside them. Kehailan just shook his head and laughed quietly to himself as he went back to the bridge. The things his father told himself that just were not true.

They scrambled to the surface and passed through the Port of Entry which occupied a relatively modest space to one side of the main city square. "In case we have to set a ship down in here again," Ardenai said, and rolled an eye upward toward the relentless inferno of brownish orange sky. "Another balmy day."

"I was on Andal in snow up to my waist a week ago," Ah'ren groaned. "I'm trying to remember what I thought was wrong with that."

"We'll just lean into you and you can think shivering, tooth-chattering thoughts," Konik grinned. "It gets better when we're out of the sun."

While it was better, better was a relative term, and Ah'ren arrived at the door to the Anchoress's chambers soaked with sweat from the roots of her waist-length hair to the squish in her boots, and wishing desperately that she'd had more to drink before she left either camp or Dragonhorse. To make matters worse, the door was padlocked, meaning Ensharra had gone outside to lock it. Ah'ren leaned against the wall beside the door and Ardenai put the back of his hand to her cheek. "You're too warm," he observed.

"Yes," she smiled. "I am that."

"And I forgot to get you a hip canteen or a water pack before we left the ship."

"If I'd paid more attention to where I was going I'd have thought to ask for at least a water flask," she said, wiping her forehead with the back of her arm, and Ardenai handed her his.

He twisted her hair up in his hand and blew on the back of her neck. "Think cool evening breeze," he chuckled, "Where is Ensharra, where is Teal? Do we need to be worried?" Ardenai looked around and shifted restlessly from one foot to the other. "Drink that. You'll need it until you get used to the heat. Where are they?"

"We're waiting on Dagan, Nagar's wife, and two little bitty boys being brought from who knows where. Could be halfway across the city … or the country," Konik said soothingly. "Just the boys could be holding this up, if they're anything like my grandchildren."

"How many do you have?" Ah'ren smiled, lowering the half-empty canteen.

"Two. Rowdy boy, frilly girl." He made a slight, nearly silent laugh in his throat and looked at the wall instead of at Ah'ren.

They spoke politely to the groups of people walking by in the corridors and chuckled at the stares and whispers that seeing the Dragonhorse and the governor with a beautiful girl brought. The announcement would be made today, along with historia from last night. By tomorrow they'd all be talking about seeing the Dragonhorse with his new wife. Ardenai stole a look at her as she talked to Konik, and his heart fluttered a little in his throat, which made him cough to hide his laughter. He was so kraaling fickle these days. He wondered if that had surfaced with the rest of the Dragonhorse proclivities.

After a few more minutes Konik said, "All right, I admit it. I'm worried. I can explain why Dagan and Nagar's wife might not be here yet, but Teal and Ensharra? That worries me. We should have checked Dragonhorse for them before we came down."

Ardenai dropped his head a little to the left, squeezed the crys-tel around his neck and closed his eyes in concentration. *Teal, where are you?*

There was a pause. *Bit of a dust-up ... we're all right. We're just now back ... on Dragonhorse.*

Ardenai's face registered concern, and his eyes came open, staring at the filthy floor. *You don't sound good, and what do you mean, back? They were supposed to meet us here. Do you have Dagan, and Nagar's wife?*

Yes, kind of. Would it be possible to meet here? Ensharra's got a nasty bump on the head ... I scraped my arm ... It's a long story.

We'll be there in a few minutes. "We're going back up," Ardenai said abruptly, and took off at a fast trot. "Sounds like they went looking for trouble and found it. Ah'ren, I'm sorry to drag you around in this heat. We try not to use the scrambleshafts where people can see us coming and going. Are you all right?"

"I'm fine," she sighed, easily keeping pace with her long legged husband. "Thinking shivering, tooth-chattering thoughts."

They arrived to find three bodies, one of them Dagan's, yet another terrified Lebonathi woman clinging to her children while Ah'nis tried to calm her, and a disturbing quantity of pale blue high Equi blood underfoot on the scrambleshaft platform. Kehailan looked up grim-faced and jerked his chin toward the sanecere bay.

Ensharra was lying down with ice on the left side of her face, trying to tell Winslow Moonsgold not to close Teal's wound with anything that would seal in infection, Teal was telling her that she should be resting rather than worrying about him despite the fact that he was bleeding profusely, and Moonsgold was trying to tell Ensharra that he couldn't do what she wanted him to do without the herbs she kept saying he needed to do it. Konik went to Ensharra's side, Ardenai to Teal, and Ah'ren said, "I'll be right back," and trotted off down the hall.

"What happened?" Konik asked quietly, moving the ice pack just enough to look at the long, welted scrape on the side of Ensharra's face, and sucking air through his teeth as he carefully put it back.

"We were ambushed," she said with such a sense of annoyance that it made Konik want to chuckle. "Dagan said Nagar's wife wouldn't come alone with him for fear of what he was going to do to her, or so the story went, so Teal and I decided we would go and serve as escort, and when we got there … they ambushed us."

"Who is 'they'?" Ardenai asked, watching his brother-in-law trying to squeeze his arm tightly enough to stop the bleeding and fend off the doctor, who was growing increasingly alarmed by Teal's blood loss.

"It just took the scab off, Winnie. It's not going to hurt it to bleed. I'll head down to the surface here in a bit and get what Ensharra needs to doctor it." He let his head rest against the pillows for a moment and closed his eyes. "They … must have been flamen. Dagan had given Nika and the boys plenty of time to be ready to go, so either she contacted some of Nagar's friends and told them when and where to be, or some of the flamen or council members did and she didn't know about it. I've seen what they do to their women, so I can't blame her for not wanting to be alone with him." He paused again, elevating his arm a little higher on his chest. "Or, Dagan sacrificed himself to the cause for some reason."

Moonsgold tried again. "There is a difference between scraping off a scab and laying yourself wide open, Master Captain, and you are going to pass out in about one minute. At least let this poor old inferior specimen of a doctor clamp the wound for a few minutes. Just until you spring off that bed and prance off to the surface for the yarbs you need, hm?"

"Oh … fine," Teal groused. He was beginning to get clammy, and Ardenai quickly lowered the head of the bed and laid him flat while Moonsgold put a couple of large, painful looking clamps on his arm.

"They came in shooting, Dagan pushed Ensharra out of the way and she hit the rounded edge of a big stone table. They shot Dagan, I shot them, told Nika if she ran I'd shoot her too, called Kehailan for a scramble, and here we are. I was stupid to let us go down there without harness on."

"And how did you skin the top off that arm?" Konik asked.

"I have no idea," Teal sighed. "Not a clue. I just looked down, the bandage was peeled back, and it was bleeding. I must have scraped it on something."

"Really?" Moonsgold chuckled. "What a remarkably astute assumption. By the way, you have no blood pressure at all."

Teal looked exasperated. "I'm fine, Mother. It's not as deep as it was, so I know it's pretty well healed."

At that juncture Ah'ren trotted back into the room with Evangeline's carpet in one hand and a pot of raw honey in the other. "Well, the kitchen officially thinks you married a mad woman," she said, going to the sink to scrub her hands and wash the plants. "Anchoress, if you feel well enough, tell me what to do here and I will prepare these herbs for Doctor Moonsgold."

Smart way to handle it! The Firstlord thought, and even though it elicited a twinge of guilt, he sent up a quiet prayer of thanks for the arrival of Ah'ren in his life.

As Moonsgold was applying a loose bandage over the poultice, Ardenai thought to ask Ah'ren where she'd found the Evangeline's carpet. She smiled and said, "It's a gift from Ah'davan. The Governor mentioned in passing last evening that it perfumed her resting place. Kehailan knew where that was, and we dropped down and got some. I hope you don't mind. I will plant something as a thank-you. Maybe a rohanth bush."

Konik looked at the girl and smiled his slow, sweet smile. "We don't mind in the least," he said, and adjusted the ice pack on Ensharra's face.

"In the one minute I was on Tras I couldn't help noticing it's about thirty-five degrees cooler there than it is on Jas," Ah'ren observed, "Oh, and Captain Kehailan wants to know what to do with the Lebonathi woman and the little boys."

"Make sure she's not carrying any poison, for one thing," Ensharra muttered, trying gingerly to feel her face. Konik pulled her hand away and put it back at her side, where he kept it with his own. "If she's the one who wanted us punished by the Gods in the form of the flamen, she won't hesitate to kill herself or her children in the name of the cause."

"Why don't you let me go and take care of that," Ah'ren said. "I am an SGA Adjudicator. I am also female, so she can't raise that as an issue. I will have her and the boys strip and bathe while I watch. We can put them in jumpsuits and tuck them away someplace safe until we're all ready to decide the case. If nobody objects."

"Nobody objects," Ardenai chuckled. "As a matter of fact, I know at least one lucky man who approves wholeheartedly."

"And I'm sure Ardenai does, as well," Konik mugged, and Ah'ren waved them off as she turned to go.

"Slow down long enough to get something to drink," Ardenai called after her.

"I should go tend to those bodies," Konik said, looking first at En-sharra, then at Ardenai. "After lunch we'll get Naram up here to identify them for us."

"Naram … was supposed to come to the meeting this morning," Teal said, ratcheting himself into a sitting position and pressing his fingers into his temples. He swung his legs over the edge of the bed and sat there, watching the floor pass in waves like the sea beneath his feet. "I asked him last night to come and he said he would be there. You don't think the flamen got him as well, do you?"

"We wouldn't get that lucky," Ardenai muttered, hanging onto Teal without making it obvious. "You know, I shouldn't say that. Compared to the complete ass he was when he was on Equus, he hasn't put in too bad a showing here. Where do you think you're going, exactly?"

"Check on Naram," Teal said. "He is, after all an Equi citizen."

"That he is," Konik agreed. "Why don't you stay here and make sure the anchoress doesn't do anything stupid. For instance, like what you're doing right now. And I will go and check on Naram."

"Not alone," Ardenai said. "Teal, lie down. Drink a few glasses of something sweet and try this again. We'll meet for a late lunch and share experiences, how's that?"

"Oh sure," Teal groused. "Pretending like I have bones will only make me seem all the more foolish as you're suctioning me up off the floor."

"I have an old Declivian blood building tea," Moonsgold said. "I'll brew him some."

It made Teal laugh, then clutch at his head, and slouch back against the pillows. "I've been warned about you cesspit Declivians, you know," he muttered.

"I was being serious!" Moonsgold exclaimed.

"Which makes it funnier yet," Teal laughed, and Ardenai left him with a gentle slap on the shoulder to follow Konik back to the surface.

"Please tell me you're carrying a weapon slightly more modern than a slingshot," Konik said, eyeing the utility belt at Ardenai's waist.

"Pultronel," the Firstlord answered as they stepped through the main Port of Entry doors. "I hope it works better than the one I had on Hector, which is how we came to be taken by those absolutely gigantic sand savages. Those were three of the most miserable days of my life."

"Followed by a few more in rapid succession," Konik added.

"Nik," Ardenai prefaced and gave the man a peripheral glance. "I saw you that day the slavers unloaded us on Calumet. You knew where we were going, which meant you'd already found Dominus. Why did you tractor it all the way to Corvus?"

"Why do you think I did?"

"I don't know. That's why I asked."

"When you have a theory let me know, because to this day I'm not really sure." They nodded to a pair of white clad Lebonathi Royal Guardsmen who nodded respectfully in return as they walked past. "If only that were a genuine gesture," Konik said. "Unfortunately fear is not respect, but it will have to do for now. I don't trust the LRG one little bit, and since they took a shot at you a few weeks back, I'm wondering if they shouldn't be disbanded altogether."

"And then what would we do with them?" Ardenai muttered. "At least in white they're easier to spot. Speaking of which, it doesn't seem like we made much of an impression on the flamen, does it?"

"I'm not sure," Konik said thoughtfully, turning left down the corridor which led to Naram's apartments. "Dagan was doing what he was asked to do, or so we assume. The other bodies I don't recognize, so they weren't with us."

"Maybe they all need the same outing. We'll put the Master Captain back on the case. Here we are." Ardenai stopped and looked up at the double metal doors before applying the heavy knocker. "Have you made note of the fact that he has not moved into the chambers of the Late Great Lord Eridu?" Konik asked as the door swung open.

"And he's not going to," Naram said. "What do you want?"

"He's not dead or in trouble, let's go," Konik snapped. "I want to make sure that woman isn't doing anything bullheaded about now, like trying to get up before we figure out whether or not her head is cracked open."

"Pray, come in, Conquering Heroes," Naram sneered, complete with gallant bow and expansive gesture. When they were inside he closed the door and gestured toward the furniture. "To what do I owe this honor?"

Ardenai perched on the arm of a chair and said, "Teal told us he invited you last night to come to the meeting with Nagar's wife and sons. It went sideways, the Master Captain and the Anchoress both got themselves hurt, and it occurred to Teal that the same … whomever, probably flamen, who jumped them, might have done you harm as well. We said we'd come and check."

"I'm touched. Who were these people?"

"That is something you'll have to tell us, if you will be so kind," said Konik. "They're both dead. Unfortunately, so is Dagan, who was trying to get the anchoress out of the line of fire. Nagar's wife and sons seem to have made the trip unscathed and uncooperative. Ah'ren is currently making sure mother and sons are all three around and poison free for the discussion this afternoon."

"Ah'ren is a lovely woman," Naram said. "I'm sorry she's stuck with you."

"She probably is, too," Ardenai chuckled, hoping she was nothing of the kind. "Thanks for coming last night. Seriously. Umma thinks you're the best thing ever." Ardenai stood up and headed toward the door before turning in mid-step to say, "If you have a chance this afternoon would you come and see if you can tell us who these two men are? Ensharra doesn't know, and Dagan, unfortunately, cannot help. We're going to have that hearing for Nagar's family mid-afternoon. Again, it would be good if you could attend, and maybe bring a council member. I think you need Paracletes even more than I do. You are all by yourself."

"I'll do both in one trip," Naram growled. "Don't worry your pretty head about my status, but if you're going to go on killing people at least figure out how to access the citizenship records so you don't keep bothering me." He opened the door for them and as they were exiting he said, "I was there, by the way. The door was padlocked."

When they returned to the ship they checked first on Teal and Ensharra, then Konik excused himself to go to his office for a brief period before lunch, and Ardenai went to find Ah'ren, only to be intercepted by Kehailan and turned back down the corridor past the sanecere bay to the officers' quarters and the family apartments.

"It has occurred to me," Kehailan said, "That you have no really private space on Dragonhorse to call your own, so I have taken the liberty of creating one for you as a kind of wedding-wedding present, so to speak."

"You've been reading my mind," Ardenai agreed. "The quarters I have with Io ..."

"Are no longer yours. I had everything moved. What I have for you is an apartment with three sleeping chambers. Two of them are exactly the same size, one is larger. That one is yours. Io and Ah'ren each get a room of their own. Everybody has their own lavage, minimal as they must be on a ship this size. There is a comfortable family space with lounges, a basic kitchen and a table that will seat six."

Ardenai looked at Kehailan and the depth of his dimples said he was trying hard not to laugh. "There are times," he said shaking his head, "when you remind me so much of both your mother and your grandmother. Practical down to the size of the table. It sounds perfect. Thank you."

"It's a temporary fix, but it will do until the baby or the babies get big enough to need a room of their own."

"That's sad," Ardenai said quietly. "I hadn't even thought about them. I guess I'm not letting myself get my hopes up. In any case, I am grateful for the space, Kee. I don't want to exclude Io in any way, but I don't want Ah'ren to have to put up with all of Io's belongings, either. A personal space for each of them will solve that, and a room of my own may just solve a lot of things. This is very kind of you."

"Here we are at what would be the captain's quarters if the captain had a wife and family, which he won't for a while yet," Kehailan said, and Ardenai found himself toward the back of the ship in a bright, pleasant space that was again in the shape of a bow as it followed the contour of the hull. None of the sleeping chambers were huge, but adequate enough for each to hold a big, fleecy Equi bed, storage space and closet space enough for laundered rather than refabricated clothing, a small personal desk and a comfortable chair, and in the largest room, a priapic bench in a plant filled space between bedroom and lavage.

Kehailan gestured toward the space closest to the door. "In this room I put all of Io's things – well, I didn't, but Oonah came and did it for me because I wasn't … I didn't want to handle some of that... those items. Anyway, I put your things in the biggest room, and when Ah'ren has a chance she says she will put a few of her things in the last, which is the one she chose, by the way." He looked momentarily defensive. "She is the one who's here, after all. As you can see, the common area is limited in size, but comfortable enough to relax in for the three minutes a week you will actually be in here and relaxing. When things slow down a bit and we have a full complement I will carve out a more sumptuous space for you and your wives."

"You amaze me," Ardenai said, really studying Kehailan. How much he looked like his beautiful mother. How tall he was. Nearly as tall as the Firstlord himself. Slender, straight, strikingly handsome. "I am amazed by your brains in the design of this ship, in your ability to command it as you do, in your ability be graceful about the things that are happening to me, and in your capacity to accept everything that is happening to you because of me. I honestly don't know what I would do without you, Kehailan."

He walked over and activated one of the viewing windows, calling up winter on Viridia, and stood watching it as he spoke. "You were right, of course, about Io. She was a marauding, manipulative, horrid brat. She was so jealous of you and me and our time together. And by the time she was gone, you were gone, and then your mother started getting sick, and until now there has been no time for us – for you and me. And I'm just wondering if there is any way I can make all those years up to you?"

"Yes," Kehailan said, "There is. Be happy. I can't even fathom the responsibility you have as you administer the affairs of the AEW, but that, I know you can do. What I have seen clawing at you, is guilt, and every bit of it swirls around your relationship with Io. Even in your happier moments there has been this sense of remorse … until last night. Last night, in your eyes, in your face, in your laugh, there was pure joy, like there used to be when Mother was well and you were a teacher. That's how you can make those years up to me, by letting me see that profound joy you're capable of, and this time, I want to share it."

"I promise," Ardenai said quietly.

Kehailan took his father in his arms for a long minute. "I'm going to hold you to it," he said. "Come on, Dragonhorse, it's time for lunch. Stunning hairclip by the way. Wedding gift from Ah'ren?"

▲ ▲ ▲ ▲ ▲ ▲ ▲

"I had a very interesting if not particularly pleasant conversation with Nika and her boys while we were bathing," Ah'ren said. "I have a lot more insight than I did about their religion, which is at the root of so many of the problems here."

Ardenai cocked his head, wondering if he'd heard her right. "You bathed with them?"

"I did," she grinned. "My husband dragged me around in the heat this morning until I felt like the sweat pad off a hard-ridden horse. Nika had never seen an Equi bathing facility before, or an Equi before, much less a mostly naked one. Plus the boys were going every which way. It was practical, and it was more comfortable for her, since we were both embarrassed."

"There's a strange, but obvious logic there," Konik chuckled. "And it seemed to work. Where are they at this point?"

Kehailan paused with food partway to his mouth. "I put them in an apartment in the officer's quarters and asked Ah'nis and company if they would watch them for a bit," he said. "Ah'ren thought that was the best way to do it and I agreed. Did you find Naram in one piece?"

"We did," Ardenai nodded, "Though I'm not sure how long he's going to stay that way. He's not flamen. Once they figure out that we're not going to hunt them down and kill them, they may decide to assert themselves again politically, and the first person to go, will be Naram."

"I have to agree," Teal said. He was up straight and eating, though his eyes looked tired, and he was pale under his tanned skin. Both Moonsgold and Ensharra had tried to get him to stay a bit longer and rest, have some more Declivian Blood Building tea, but he'd waved them off laughing and said he had things to do. "Of course I haven't completely given up the notion of hunting them down and killing them. I rather like the idea, myself."

"We think alike in that aspect," Konik nodded. "So, Master Captain, what did you find this morning that nearly got you killed?"

"I don't know yet," Teal said. "I need to go back to those coordinates with some support and see what else is there besides that one room. I got the sense that it was very plush, wherever we were. Aside from the apartments in the old city, we haven't been able to find many of the compounds of the privileged. That may have been one of them."

"Please don't go today ..." Ardenai began.

"We need you at Nika's hearing," Ah'ren interjected.

"Especially since Ensharra's down with a concussion," Konik added, and he looked worried.

"I hadn't planned to go today," Teal said, resisting the urge to chortle at seeing his brother-in-law's fussing headed off so adroitly, and at the same time responding to the worry on Konik's face. The governor was fond of Ensharra in some form or another, and she of him. His first instinct was to say something comforting to Konik, but that would point up the relationship, and that would not sit well. "Ah'ren, you said you got some insight during your time with Nika. Have you processed it enough to share it with us?"

"Ah … maybe," she scowled, and worked her mouth a little to one side. "I think we have a barrier that we are not recognizing – maybe language, maybe relevance. For instance," she picked up a piece of sweet-root with her eating sticks, "what to us is sweet-root, is carottia to Declivians, yamayama to Amberians, and so on. But we have, in this case, something to point at, or to describe by taste or texture, so we can communicate the idea and obtain the object." She popped the food into her mouth and thought a minute while she chewed. "What if … we had only the words to describe the thing we wanted, and because we knew exactly what it was, ate it every day for every meal, we impatiently described it to perfect strangers from another culture as, 'that food that tastes sweet'? How open would that be for interpretation?"

"Very," Kehailan said, looking puzzled. "What have sweet-roots to do with religion?"

"Everything," Ah'ren said. "If we loved sweet-root enough to eat it every day for every meal, are we not going to be equally careful about knowing how to describe it accurately to whomever needs to know? If we can't be precise about sweet-root it would take us a long time to get anybody to understand what we were talking about, and in the meantime we'd be hungry and they'd be confused.

"I don't think we're recognizing that even though we think we're talking about the same 'God,'" she made the appropriate gesture with her fingers, "we're not, and the fact that we have no structured religion, is not helping."

"Now I'm intrigued," Ardenai said. "Eladeus, is not Eladeus?"

"No, of course not, at least not insofar as hominoid understanding goes, and nearly all of us in the fifth, sixth and seventh galactic alliances, having been seeded by the same progenitors are, basically hominoidea. We have the same type of brain function, which means we all arrive at understanding through basically the same set of processes which involve somewhere between three and seven senses, depending on which race we're talking about. If I understand our faith, and I hope I do, Eladeus is not an entity, but rather a transformation. Eladeus is the best that is within each of us and the life force which swirls around us. The Wisdom Giver. The Creator Spirit. To put it in elementary terms, God, to us, is a word that describes action, not necessarily an immutable being, but a spirit in motion."

"I would agree," Teal nodded, easing himself back in his chair.

"And we think we understand the Lebonathi version of religion, which is structured, manmade, simple, if not downright simple-minded, and we've pretty much dismissed it as backward and oppressive, am I right?"

Ardenai nodded, feeling the sting of the truth.

"So, what are we offering them that's better? Are we just assuming they'll change their religious beliefs because we're giving them food and medicine? These people actually, deep in their guts, believe they will go to kraa, or the witch world, or tras, or hell, if they step out of line. They're terrified, and we're dismissing it. How much time are we really spending trying to help them understand our faith and make it relevant for them? I ask you, since we have been here, has there been one, single recognizable demonstration of our faith in terms the Lebonathi could understand and relate to? Because it is always in motion and manifests itself in actions which speak to the needs of others and not in outward expressions of worship, it doesn't appear to them to be faith at all, which is why they keep saying we're godless. I know that it's been almost a thousand years since we took anybody over, but surely there must be a precedent somewhere for introducing our faith to other cultures and we'd better be finding it if we hope to make any real progress here." She gave her companions a look half question, half challenge, and went back to her lunch.

"And that's it?" Kehailan said. "That's where you leave us?"

"No," she said around a mouthful of salad greens, "that's where you pick up the slack and start helping me figure it out. Because until we can speak of and appropriately demonstrate Eladeus and our beautiful and ingrained faith with these people the same way we can speak of sweet-root with the SGA, we're going to have a huge hole in our politics."

"I don't get the feeling Ensharra looks at God in the same simple-minded way the flamen do," Konik mused. "I think she sees God in things, and actions."

"Do you get the feeling she and the flamen agree on anything?" Teal asked.

Konik shook his head. "No. You're right." He took a sharp breath and pushed his plate away. "Can we get started with this hearing? I have a busy afternoon."

The Firstlord admitted freely that he'd had a stereotypical image of what flamen women would be like. They would be cowering and afraid – pathetically grateful to be freed from the tyranny of their husbands. Or they would look like Brak's wife had looked – strong and desperate. They would look like Nika had looked on the scrambleshaft platform, clinging to her children. What they would not look like was the haughty woman who curled her lip and sneered as she was brought in by Ah'nis and offered a seat at the round table in the governance offices.

"Priestess Ah'nis," Ardenai said, "Can you stay, since Anchoress Ensharra is indisposed?"

Ah'nis said, "I can," just as Nika said,

"I hope the whore dies."

"Best not wish that," Ardenai said. "My name is ..."

"Yes, whatever, Shit Eater. I know who you are. Get on with it."

Ardenai was not deterred. "You need to know who is in the room, Mistress Nika. You have met SGA Adjudicator Ah'ren, and Governing Priestess Ah'nis. This is Military Governor Konik, Master Captain Teal, Captain Kehailan, Lebonathi Federation Regent Naram, and High Council Member Aruda. This was to be a simple hearing to determine if you wanted to join your husband at his new place of residence, and if you were willing to undergo the adjustments to your memory that would be necessary to do that. But now we have an attack on SGA personnel and dead bodies to talk about."

"They were martyrs!" she exclaimed, and dropped immediately into that odd singsong that Ardenai remembered so well from Samarra. "Blessed be the martyrs who died trying to save flamen children from the snake-eyed savages, the godless ones …"

"Enough," Ardenai said.

"... The Evil One incarnate, with living snakes embracing him upon his arms ..."

"I thought that too," Naram interjected. "They're just very realistic permanent drawings."

"They're Achernarean chain tattoos," Ardenai amended. "I wear them to honor someone. Snakes do not mean to us what they mean to you."

"How do you know what anything means to us?" she cried. "You come as conquerors to crush our way of life, to kill us, as you did my good husband."

That rocked Ardenai back a little and Teal said, "Your good husband was running at me with a knife. Nika, listen to me. The part of him that was flamen is no more, but part of him that loves you and your boys is yet living, and if you want ..."

"The part of him that was flamen was all of him that mattered!" she exclaimed. Like Nagar she seemed incapable of saying anything in a conversational tone. "The practice of his religion was his life. If that is gone, then he is gone and what is left is an abomination."

Konik leaned forward and purred, "I understand that you're upset, but we're not going to hurt you. Tell us about the men that got killed this morning. Who were they and why were they there?"

"They came to save me from him!" Nika said, and spit across the table at Teal.

Konik ignored it. "Did Dagan know they were coming? Was he there to help you as well?"

"Dagan wanted me to hear your words. Dagan said you would give me some choices," she said mockingly. "This is what you call choices? To starve with no husband and two little mouths to feed, or become wife to an abomination? I wanted him to die, just like I wanted that snake-eyed savage across the table, and that whore of an anchoress to die! Two good men are dead, but part of the Evil One died as well. He lost an arm in the form of Dagan. And you," she said, glaring at Teal, "your time will come as well. Today it is our time to die, my sons and me. But you will die soon, big man. Already those wheels are turning."

"You want to throw yourself down a flight of stairs be my guest," Ardenai said, "but you will not threaten SGA personnel, and you will not kill your children."

"I will!" she shrieked, and grabbed for the toddler closest to her. Ah'nis snatched the child away and he began to cry with fright.

"Nika," Ardenai said quietly, and she froze. Her head turned slowly to look at him. "You do not want to kill that little boy. That little boy needs his father and his mother. You do want him to grow up with a father and a mother, don't you?"

"Yes," she said.

"You do realize that I'm controlling your actions and emotions now, don't you?"

"Yes."

"Are you still capable of making choices?"

"Yes."

"Are you sure?"

"I still hate you," she said, and there was the barest hint of a sneer.

"I'll take that as an affirmative. Do you want to go and live out your life with Nagar and your boys in pleasant surroundings, do you want to go back to your home without the boys, or do you want to die here and now and have the boys go home to their father, who remembers and loves them? The choice is yours."

She thought about it, looking at her fingernails, looking at the little boys. "I want to go see my husband." There was a pause and she began to smile just a bit. "I … have been away visiting my mother for a few days, but I am ready to go home now. The boys miss their father, and I … I … have chores to do as well. I think we should go now."

"I think so too," Ardenai said. He closed his eyes, pinched one of the crys-tels around his neck, and in a few moments Nika and the boys vanished. When Ardenai looked up, it was with sadness. "I don't know why I thought she would listen to us."

"The poor people listen to you," Naram said. "Nika is from a rich family. The men you killed are flamen, and it doesn't matter what they were trying to do to you, they're still going to be viewed as martyrs. She and Nagar will have been 'murdered by the Equi' no matter what you say or show to that segment of the population. Do you understand?"

"Oh, I do understand!" Ardenai snapped. "What the flamen will understand one way or another is that the common people have a heritage more than just dust and hunger. We have places – small moons, big old ships, which will easily hold every last flamen, every last person of privilege on this hot, miserable rock, if that is the way it needs to be done! If that won't work, so help me, I'll give them to the Potami to help them settle their new planet!"

"Controlling the mind of another is exhausting work when you are exhausted yourself," Teal observed quietly, and Ardenai realized he'd spoken more harshly than he ought. "The boys will grow up with their parents and be none the wiser. Given the circumstances, that's the best we can do."

"I consider Nika fairly judged," Ah'nis said, and Kehailan nodded.

"Agreed," Konik and Ah'ren said together.

"I suppose," Naram said. "I don't know what else you could have done, except let her and the boys go home, of course, which I thought was part of the deal."

"I did too," the Firstlord said, "right up until she decided to murder her children in front of us. It was pretty clear what she'd do to them if we let her out of our sight."

Ah'ren put down her water glass and asked, "What did she mean about starving with two little mouths to feed? I thought they were rich."

"When are you people going to wake up?" Naram exclaimed, and Ah'ren stopped him with a look and a quick, palms-up gesture.

"I just got here. Indulge me."

"Sorry," Naram said, which surprised everyone at the table. "The men have the money. The men have the power. Nika came from a rich family. Came. As fresh goods she's priceless, but she's used goods, and has no value. If she'd been willing to spare the boys, they might have been raised by Nagar's family as flamen. Then again, maybe not. The palest Lebonathi don't have a lot of tolerance for one another's children, especially not boys."

"Why?" Ah'ren asked, and her eyes were troubled.

Naram looked at Aruda, who said, "Competition is fierce in the hierarchy of flamen. The more entrants, the fiercer the competition for coveted spots. Naram is correct in thinking Nika had become a discard. I'm a little surprised she was still alive."

"This much I can tell you; Nika wanted to do exactly what she did,"

Ardenai said. "Naram, Aruda, thank you for coming. Again I must ask, what should we do with the bodies?"

"I will get Dagan's body to his family," Aruda said, "if I can have help carrying it."

"We will set you and Dagan down by scrambleshaft wherever you need to be," Kehailan said, and rose to go with him.

"Put the other two bodies in cold storage and I'll try to find someone to claim them," Naram said. "Thank you for a swell afternoon, full of surprises as usual. I know my own way out by now."

Teal had just leaned back with a sigh of relief when the telecommunications pad in front of him on the table lit up. He pressed it and Ah'keena appeared. "Ahimsa, Master Captain. We have a serious situation with a horse, and everyone is in the field just now. Could you possibly ..."

"Of course. I'll be right there."

"I'll come with you," Ardenai said, rising from his chair. "I need to consult with you and Tarpan about this cavalry situation, and I might as well do it while we work." He kissed his wife on the top of her head, said that with any luck he'd see her for dinner, thanked the others for attending, and left.

Ah'ren gave him an absent wave over her shoulder. "Governor, do you need help with the historia of today's proceedings?" she asked. He shook his head. "Then I need to get myself organized and start parceling out a planet, if you'll excuse me." She gave Konik a pleasant nod and departed as quickly as her husband.

It was an hour before dinner when Ah'ren looked through Konik's open door and found him slouched in an easy chair, staring at the projection of an ancient map and rubbing absently at the place where Sarkhan's arrow had shattered his breastbone.

Ah'ren," he smiled, starting to rise in welcome. He winced, caught his breath and, momentarily, the arms of his chair to steady himself. "Sorry," he muttered, and looked embarrassed as she gestured him back into his seat.

"Please, don't get up," she said, pretending not to notice his discomfort. She closed the door behind her and turned to the projection as she sat.

"This is stunning. Is this the old city?"

"It is," he said, forcing a smile and gesturing at the projection. "Carillia. Like some mythical ruin from a storybook, rising out of the desert sand. I'm excited to see it restored." He studied her face for a moment. "But you are not here to speak of cities."

"No," she smiled, letting her eyes go back to the projection as she chose her words. "I do not mean to intrude in any way, Governor, but I was wondering if there was something I could learn to do that would help you stay up with things while you're … away."

"That obvious, hm?" he said, and looked disgusted. "It was the plate pushing, wasn't it?"

"No, and it's not at all obvious. But I am trained to be companion to the Dragonhorse."

"And you can see one coming." He shifted restlessly, dragging one hand through his hair as he stared at the map. "I guess I thought the shock of losing my wife would circumvent the thing, just once, but no such luck. I don't …. Anyway, forgive me, I'm rambling."

Ah'ren opened her mouth, closed it while she thought, and opened it again with a tenuous smile at the governor. "You … Eridu, had you locked up for a long time … more than one hundred and twenty-eight days from … anyway, I'm trying to ask … you must have gone through a heat cycle. How did you …you know."

Konik gave her an evil smirk and shook his head. "I don't know. Please be very specific." Her eyes got wider and he gave a short laugh and turned back to stare at the map. "As luck would have it, I was just going into a heat cycle when Eridu and company decided I needed a full dose of whatever in kraa that potion is … was. Suffice it to say it was an exceptionally unpleasant experience. Which pain was which, I couldn't really say, but there was plenty of it. So," he took his eyes off the projection and smiled at Ah'ren, "there is something you can do for me. Keep an eye on the anchoress. She's intrepid, and being caught up in such sweeping changes as we've initialized here has made her a little heedless."

"Donc. It will give me a chance to get to know her better. Maybe we can go riding together."

"I … may have a day or two yet before I have to leave," Konik said, "But I do have to be extra careful, because I am …" he trailed off.

"Hyperphilic?"

"Shit!" he snarled, springing out of the chair and spinning directly toward her. For a split second she saw what was underneath – why Mountain hold had told her to take very close care of this one for a bit yet. She flinched, not because he had frightened her, but because she hated testing him in so indiscreet a manner. Again, Kestrel's instructions. She was going to have to make some decisions about when and how to use his ideas if she wanted to have any friends.

"Sorry," she whispered, rising to stand beside him. "I'm so sorry."

He caught himself, took two quick breaths, and his face settled back into its usual gentle expression. "How do you know that?" he asked with some annoyance. "Seeing a Dragonhorse cycle coming on, maybe, but being hypersexual? It disturbs me deeply to think that I might be that transparent, that I am going to be working with someone that perspicacious. I'm not sure I can take that kind of scrutiny."

"Let me assure you, Governor Konik, you are not in the least transparent." She paused, wondering how much she should tell him, and how much she had already ruined by listening to Kestrel, who made it a point never to leave Andal when there was a dragonhorse in power. "I … had prior knowledge of you from Mountain hold. They are aware that when a dragonhorse rises, many very powerful males of all different ages and all different abilities rise with him, and each of them, directly or indirectly, now or in the future, has a purpose. You happen to be one of the six in my circle of friends and family, and I am to care for you as best I can. They told me you were brilliant and essential to what is happening here, and that I should help you in any way I could. They saw fit to tell me some things about you, so I'd be better prepared to fully support you should the need arise."

"They also told you to shock me, to see how deeply the monster sleeps." It wasn't a question, nor stated with any hostility, just a rather resigned observation by someone used to being observed.

Ah'ren noted with concern that his voice had become tired, his face momentarily grey, and he winced as he took a breath. "Yes," she nodded, knowing better than to ask if he was alright.

He smiled, and she was struck by his artless good looks – the young face and the silvering hair – how he exuded charisma, even as he dropped his eyes in that slightly shy manner that reminded her of Ardenai. "I didn't think you would say such a thing of your own accord, Ah'ren. Not that you should have said it at all."

"I wouldn't say it, but … a couple of things do give you away to the observant. Some rather charming tells."

"Name one," he drawled, but he was obviously intrigued. He eased back into his chair and the pain went out of his eyes.

"Biggest giveaway is your voice. Classic hyperphilic timbre. Absolutely hypnotic. I'll bet you sing with incredible talent."

He just shrugged without denying it. "And the other?"

"Animal magnetism," she grinned. "You'll probably start noticing the looks you get from women when … Ah'davan's loss is not so fresh." She put a momentary hand on his shoulder. "You naturally attract people of both sexes, Nik. It's a gift, not a curse."

"Definitely feels like a curse," he sighed. "Of all the things I don't want and can't afford to be, sex magnet is at the top of the list. It's pretty much interchangeable with complete, raging maniac every hundred and twenty-eight days. Swift, who has been my hetaera for ninety years and knows how to handle me, is …" he shrugged with annoyance, "I don't know. Somewhere. Not here. My wife's body isn't even cold, and yet I find myself harboring some deep, completely unrealistic feelings for someone who…" again there was something between a shrug and a shudder as he stopped the thought. "And what I was going to say earlier, Mistress, was not hyperphilic, but Military Governor. I have to be careful because I am Military Governor of Lebonath Jas. And don't tell the anchoress, please. Not what I am, what I'm really like, not where I've gone. She wouldn't understand, and I need her … as an ally." He looked past the map, out the window to the eternal whirl of space, and sighed. "Because that is all she can be. Ever."

Ah'ren looked momentarily enlightened, then uncomfortable, then determined. "You are in a strange place at a very vulnerable time, Governor Konik, and your health has been compromised by your imprisonment and treatment at the hands of Eridu and his ilk. Have you actually made sure …"

"I have a safe place to go and be a raging maniac?" he finished. "I did have a chance to check out the facilities on the Jocundome when we were taking the flamen around. They're set up for those of us who go through troublesome heat cycles. Apparently they have a cage just for me, so Mountain hold whispered in their ear, as well. Embarrassing, but reassuring at the same time."

"Good," she responded, smiling to herself. "I feel better now. We have a little time before dinner. Show me some of what you do as governor of Lebonath Jas. Tell me what you know of these people's needs, wants and desires. What do they value? What do they love?"

He smiled at her and crossed one leg over the other in an easy motion. "In a moment we will do that. You do owe me for the shock, Mistress. So tell me something by way of repayment. You said there were six in your circle."

"Um hm. I probably shouldn't have told you, but I did."

"I will not speak of it, you have my word."

"Thank you," she smiled, hoping she hadn't made her second major blunder.

So, there's Ardenai, of course, and Kehailan. Myself, by your admission. The insuperable Master Captain being number four?"

"Obviously."

"Criollo, as he has Dragonhorse blood?" She nodded. "And the sixth would be …?"

Her smile widened a little, and her eyes challenged him to figure it out. "Remember, I know only who you are, not what your purpose may be."

He sat quietly thinking, and then nodded. "Gideon?" he said, mostly to himself. "It has to be Gideon."

"And so it is," she smiled. "Tell me about the Lebonathi."

CHAPTER 11

"You're sure you don't mind?" Teal asked again, and Ardenai laughed at him. "You're sure your new bride won't mind then?"

"Teal, I'm sure," Ardenai smiled. "You're fifty yards down river with a second waterfall pounding away. You're not going to disturb us, hopefully we're not going to disturb you. I think that's a very good spot for another pavilion. There are trees, there's even another pool." He waved to the four people who had come to set up the big tent. "Right there is fine," he called, and they began staking out the corners for the raised floor. "I have also asked for a central kitchen and a heated bath like they have at Stone Spring," Ardenai said. "We're going to wake up some chilly, rainy morning and wish we had one."

"Since we have a woman in our midst, I would agree," Teal said. He put his hands against the small of his back and leaned into them before swinging first to one side, then the other. He'd slept hard the night before, and little movement during sleep meant a stiff body the next morning, even after a run and a swim. "Did you enjoy the new quarters on Dragonhorse last night?"

"Very comfortable," Ardenai said. "Moonsgold was worried about you down here by yourself, though. Are you sure you're up for horses this morning?"

"I'm fine, but we do need to get going. I have a dozen horses to monitor, one to check on, and I want to check out the spot where Ensharra and I got jumped yesterday." As he was speaking they were walking out into the meadow, enjoying the fragrance of trees, grass and the river, and the warmth of the early morning sun.

"My quarters aboard Dragonhorse are very nice," Ardenai said, pausing to whistle for Pavil, "but this is the spot that breathes new life into me. I'm so glad that Ah'ren likes it as well."

"Where is your bride this morning?" Teal asked, slipping a halter onto Poseidon, who shook his head and blew his nose on the front of Teal's clean tunic. "Why, thank you," he chuckled. He turned and began leading the horse back toward the saddles, which were sitting on racks under a huge tree with big, sweet smelling leaves and a spreading habit much like a Viridian Sycamore. Teal and Ardenai had both pictured it with a baby swing in one of the lower branches, and Teal found himself doing it again this morning.

Ardenai began applying a soft brush to Pavil, and smiled at the grunt of contentment it brought. "She was up before dawn and off somewhere with Nik. I think she said they were going to check out the polo grounds on the Jocundome."

"And you believed her?" Teal grinned, tossing a light, flat saddle up on Poseidon's back and tightening both cinches before slapping the horse gently on the shoulder and reaching for his bridle.

"No," Ardenai replied, saddling his own horse, "but she didn't expect me to. When Nik asks her what she told me, that's what she'll say. I think she'll make sure our governor is where he needs to be, check out the chambers that Pyron said had been prepared for me in Chrysalis, and then, if she has time before she needs to start on other things, she will check out the polo grounds."

"Is she going to be acting governor while he's out of commission?"

"No," Ardenai said, swinging up onto Pavil's back. "That duty will fall to Ah'nis, though I'm sure Ah'ren will have her fingers in it. She's also stuck with guarding the anchoress while Konik is away, and that in itself could be a full time job if he's gone long enough."

"Why don't you send her to Stone Spring to recuperate?" Teal suggested. "There's plenty to keep her as busy as she should be until her head heals up, and she can't get away if you don't want her to." He swung effortlessly the seventeen hands onto Poseidon's back, shut off the mane-tag which kept each animal within the wireless fence, and pointed the horse's nose toward Expedition Headquarters.

They set off at an easy jog, and Ardenai watched Teal and the big gelding with open admiration. "You've had horses that suited you, but that one takes the prize," the Firstlord said. "I can't help wondering … with what was going through Abeyan's head at the time he was sending horses and equipment to us … as angry as he was, why did he send this magnificent animal to you?"

"Maybe he wasn't supposed to be for me," Teal said solemnly. "Maybe he was supposed to be for you, and that little tick Tarpan felt was a tiny bomb, working its way deep into the flesh where it will go off when you least expect it."

"There's a flaw in your thinking," Ardenai laughed. "I'm not going to be the one that's on him."

"Very true," Teal nodded. "Oh well, better me than you, Firstlord. What a beautiful morning! I think we should sing something. I think you should write a song about this place."

"I agree. I'll do that in all my spare time. Meanwhile ..." and he began to sing 'Summer Meadows', with Teal joining him on harmony, and their voices rang across the valley as they urged the horses into a ground eating canter.

With Ah'keena's help they drew blood from and examined six horses before second breakfast, did another six after, and went on to examine the horse they'd treated the day before. His eyes were wary, but his head and his ears were up.

"His gut sounds better today," Teal said, giving him a gentle pat. "We should see the oil we gave him yesterday start moving through him by this afternoon or tomorrow morning. After that we'll give him something to clear the sand out of his system." Teal put a hand under the horse's throat latch and scratched him for a minute or so. "Sorry to torment you," he said. He made sure that his notes were in order, the blood was in the cold box for the lab techs, and then turned to Ardenai. "You ready to go up?"

"My heart says no, but my lips say yes," Ardenai chuckled. "As our governor often says, 'I am a creature of duty.' Mecklin and company grabbed a half-dozen regional governors-slash-warlords, and since Konik is suddenly gone for a bit, I'd like you there as well as Ah'nis and Dahman when we talk to them. Naram wants to meet briefly, and I'd like to go with you when you go back to where you got jumped yesterday. This could be our first glimpse of how the wealthiest faction of Lebonathi live outside the capitol apartments."

"Could be our last, too," Teal muttered, and finished his sentence on the scramble pad of Dragonhorse Thirteen. "I'm taking SGA troops, and I'm redirecting an AP Platform so all we have to do is point. I need fifteen minutes to wash up and find a tunic that isn't embroidered with horse snot."

"A good idea for us both," the Firstlord nodded, and they trotted off in the direction of the officers' quarters.

It occurred to Ardenai that it was some distance back to his apartments, and that perhaps keeping a clean tunic in his office would be smart. He threw his clothes on the bed in his room and himself into the waterfall for a once-over with foaming rosemary while he wondered what Naram wanted. For him to ask for a meeting was unheard of, and there was no telling by his tone of voice what was on his mind. He was a master of sneering indifference and whether it was a smokescreen or not, it was effective in repelling insight.

He had time to wonder briefly if this meeting with regional governors would go any better than those of the past. Dahman was here, and if nothing else he was a good conversation starter. Ardenai had to laugh. What two animals did the Lebonathi hate? Snakes and rats. Probably because they, were real. He was still chuckling when he got to the meeting, nodding to the participants as he took his seat. The six men facing them all had alabaster white skin, stark white hair and absolutely colorless eyes. Obviously wealthy, but were they Flamen?

"Ahimsa, I wish thee peace," Ardenai said. "We may begin."

"I am Shabra. We demand to know why we were forced to have an injection," said the older man nearest the middle.

"Shabra, you honor Equus by your presence," Ardenai smiled. "We are injecting everyone, just as a precaution against the spread of anything. There are so many alien species mingling these days. All of us in this room have had the injection. So has Regent Naram. So have most of the local flamen. You will not notice any side effects."

The man farthest to the left curled his lip at Ah'nis and said, "I am Akkad, son of Shabra. We will not speak with Equi whores in the room."

"Not a problem," Ardenai said, "There aren't any. I am Ardenai Firstlord, the Thirteenth Dragonhorse. Next to me is Teal, Master Captain. Beside him is Dahman, Seventh Galactic Alliance Observer from Taraxia. The lady is Priestess Ah'nis, Acting Military Governor. And … just coming in, Ah'ren, SGA Adjudicator. This is a pleasant surprise."

"I will be your recording historian," she said, sitting next to Teal. "What have I missed?"

"Ah, ah, this gentleman, who said his name is Akkad," Dahman said, in his quick little voice, "has said he will not speak with whores in the room. He said that just now."

"I hope he will be pleased with those the Firstlord has chosen to serve his needs today," Ah'ren smiled. "Priestess Ah'nis is a virgin in service to God, and I am the dutiful wife of the Thirteenth Dragonhorse. Is it acceptable for us to be here?"

The man looked surprised. "Why … yes," he said, obviously taken back.

"May we speak if we are not disrespectful?"

"Yes," he said, and she smiled and dropped her eyes.

"Thank you." *Go Ardi. Dahman, can you hear me?*

He looked at her and smiled. "A good wife is a treasure," he said, and winked his black button eyes, first one, then the other.

"I agree," Ardenai nodded. One wife a tactician, one a diplomat. How lucky could a former creppia nonage teacher get? "Gentlemen, we are here to discuss what we will need from you, and what you may request of us," he said, which prefaced an hour of pleasantly reasoned discourse. Most of Ah'ren's questions were directed through Ardenai or Teal. Ah'nis, seeing the effectiveness of the approach, did likewise, though Ardenai could tell by her mental tone that it galled her to do so.

At the end of the hour the six men thanked Ardenai and Teal for their time, complimented Ardenai on his wife, and nodded to the women and Dahman before departing.

"Excuse me for a minute," Ardenai said, "There is something I must do." He took Ah'ren in his arms and kissed her thoroughly. "That was absolutely magnificent. High theater! Ah'nis, I know that irked you no end, and I'm grateful for the part you played. Dahman, you as well."

"They wondered if you'd found me in a trap somewhere and changed me into a man," Dahman laughed, and they realized that someone besides Teal now heard the Lebonathi.

"Ambassador, you honor us with your presence," Ardenai said with a bow. "How are you enjoying your assignment so far?"

"Oh, very nice, very nice. Much better than the first time when everything was so orchestrated and we really couldn't learn anything. It's very much better, yes."

"And you brought your wife and children?"

"I did. Yes. I did. The little ones grow up so fast it's hard to be away. My good and dear wife just follows along so nicely with the kittens in tow. She is my very special blessing. She and the kits. We must get together soon."

"Yes, I agree," Ardenai smiled. "I have asked the kitchen to make some of those little vegetable stuffed pastries that you like so well. I think they should be ready by now."

"You are most kind," Dahman smiled, bobbing both hands in front of him in the manner of Taraxian thanks. "I will go, yes I will. I am just famished and some of those little stuffed pastries sound just wonderful, yes, they do. Thank you so much Ardenai Teacher."

Excited as he was about the pastries he didn't catch his misspeak, and Ardenai didn't correct him. It felt so good, just for that moment, to be Ardenai Teacher again. He could hear Mahruss saying it, see his fresh-scrubbed little face and round, intelligent eyes.

Ah'ren took his hand and laid the side of her head against his. *Once a week, just for an hour, teach a class of little ones. Make it your sacred time to feed your soul.*

What? What would I teach?

What you are learning. Ardenai, allow yourself to do what you do best, what anchors you most firmly to the deepest parts of yourself. Teach. For the sake of your sanity, surround yourself with children, and teach.

Ardenai closed his eyes and took a long, deep breath, visualizing thoughts, ideas, emotions, plans, beginning to shape themselves into an ever closing circle. It struck him funny and made him feel like a child, probably a girl child at that, but at the same time it felt … settling. One last tiny bit of Ah'leah, making a little halo of the chaos of seasons? Maybe.

Ah'ren kissed his temple and let go of his hand. "I'm going to go and ask the kitchen for something to eat and some drinks, if that's all right," she said, and left without waiting for an answer.

"Just my lowly female impression, but I think those are the most dangerous men we've run into so far," Ah'nis said. "I must attend to my duties as Governor," She nodded curtly to Teal, gave Ardenai a penetrating look, and swept out, straight backed and sober as ever.

Teal gave the Firstlord a searching look as well. "Ah'ren said something to you that made you look ten years younger. May I ask, or will it shock me?"

"Shock you? The man who does the Phyllan Wolf Dance?" Ardenai chuckled. "She told me I should teach a class of little ones once a week for an hour."

Teal thought a moment, then nodded and smiled, more to himself than to Ardenai. "A good balance," he said.

"Any thoughts on what Naram wants?" Ardenai asked, parking a hip on the table. "Besides wanting us gone?"

"He knows that's not going to happen," Teal said. "I give him that much reasoning power. He's highly educated for a Lebonathi who isn't flamen, and whatever else he may be, he is smart, and he is capable of seeing more than one aspect of what's going on."

Ah'ren returned with a tray of kurbis bread, seed cakes and a pitcher of icy spiced tea, which she placed on the table beside her husband. "Do you need me to stay for your interview with Naram?" she asked, beginning to pour the drinks.

Ardenai thought about that. "Yes, please. He said he thought you were a lovely woman, and that he was sorry you were stuck with me, so he is capable of sympathy. Sit, listen, and tell us what you hear that is not spoken. Of course, if you have nothing more pressing."

"Nothing that can't wait," she smiled.

"The men who were just here, Shabra, Akkad and the others. Ah'nis said they struck her as very dangerous men," Teal said. "Did you get that impression?"

"Absolutely. They reeked of wealth and power. The fact that they'd allowed themselves to be detained was oozing out of every pore. They were not here to find out what we want from them, they were here to assess us, our technology and find out more about our strategies. My opinion, of course, but I think we've gotten our first glimpse of the true power behind the flamen."

"I agree," Teal said, accepting the drink she handed him. "A subject worthy of further and more leisurely discussion, preferably when Governor Konik gets back."

"Speaking of our good governor, how was your pre-dawn jaunt to the polo grounds?" Ardenai smiled.

"Somewhat stressful," she shrugged. "Thinking we have a plan for playing polo and actually having a plan for playing polo are quite different things. Busy, hard-ridden people tend that direction, and, luckily, others prepare for us. Anyway, while I was in Crysalis I looked at the space they prepared for you, and I must say, it is incredible, even by Papilli standards. Very private, but all clear and prismed glass," she sighed. "It has a beautiful, fragrant garden, a fantasy bathing pool ... Ardi, it's gorgeous. It really is."

Ardenai pulled a disgusted face and shook his head. "You are such a girl, Ah'ren." He quickly tempered the joke with a kiss and said, "I have a pass pad that will let us go straight there. Maybe this evening?"

"So, enough about the lovemaking," Teal grumped. "Did you or did you not get a chance to actually check out the polo grounds?"

"I did," she grinned. "Absolutely pristine. They have a huge stable of ponies, they're setting up leagues, and I declared for one. You two, Nik, and Tarpan, even if we change players later. The quicker we're in, the quicker we'll get to pick our mounts and the sooner we'll get to play."

"I didn't hear your name in there," Teal said. "Aren't you going to compete?"

"They're setting up a woman's league," she said with shining eyes. "I've never gotten to play with other girls before. And ..." she gave Ardenai a half-comic look of apology, "I signed us up to try out ponies this evening. Maybe we could go to Crysalis another day?"

Ardenai just laughed, and that was when Naram appeared. He moved like he was tired, and his eyes were shadowed. He took the chair Ardenai offered him without comment, and released the set of his jaw just long enough to give Ah'ren a half-smile of thanks for the tea.

"I come bearing gifts," he said bluntly, "but they're going to cost you a favor in return."

"You look worried," Ardenai said, hooking a chair with one foot and settling himself.

"I'm always worried," Naram growled. "My planet has been invaded by dirt-eating dolts who want to talk about feelings and make everybody happy about dining and dressing like peasants, while the class that has supported the peasantry for centuries is being systematically dismantled."

Ah'ren's bright laughter filled the room. "You have a wonderful sense of situational irony," she said, "But even you must admit our means are not so ridiculously disproportionate to our expressed desire for an outcome as what could have befallen you at the hands of others."

"Oh," he said, "You mean the star creatures to whom we would have been microscopic and summarily squashed, or the cannibals who would have eaten the fattest of us first and kept the rest in pens like caronai?"

"You really are unhappy," Ardenai said. "You would not have asked for a meeting if you didn't think we could help you. Tell us what you need."

Naram studied his fingernails for a bit, choosing his words despite having practiced them at some length. "I need a woman given sanctuary and her brain expunged, as you did Nika and Nagar, or a man killed, and I don't care how. Whichever one is easier and faster."

Teal just dropped his forehead to the fingertips of one hand and shook his head, Ardenai looked bemused, and Ah'ren said, "We would do this legally, how?"

"I don't give a shit about your legal system," Naram sneered. "I've seen you," he said with a glare in Teal's direction, "point your finger at some-one and have him drop dead. And you, Dragonhorse, I watched you turn Nika from one person to another in a matter of seconds. You made it look so simple."

"Actually all I did was prepare her for transformation," he said, "but … yes, it is simple. Frighteningly so. That's not the point here. Tell us what the situation is and maybe we can figure something out."

"Fine," he growled. "Remember Akadia?" Both men nodded. "She and I have been in love for years. She was promised to someone else, and he got her, which has not stopped us from, shall we say, staying in touch. With my profile as high as it is these days it's just a matter of time until we get caught and her husband kills her for it." He pointed a finger at Teal, who had a question formed in his brain and partway to his opening mouth.

"Don't bother saying something like, 'Why doesn't she divorce him?' She can't. He can divorce her, but not the other way around. She's miserable. She says she'd rather be dead, blah, blah, which is just nonsense. If you tweaked her brain a little and made her happy on one of those big farms in the sky, she'd be safe from Telloh and she wouldn't remember me and we'd all be better off. Or, you could kill her husband in some devious and preferably horrible manner."

"Why don't you kill him?" Teal suggested.

"And then marry his wife? Don't think it hasn't crossed my mind, especially when I see her with bruises all over her. Bastard. He's as bad as that fucking Eridu. Sorry, Ah'ren. It's too transparent. Telloh's family would kill her and me, probably in the same aforementioned horrible manner." He sighed and looked genuinely distressed.

Someone actually loved Naram? Why did that seem almost impossible, almost laughable? Ardenai really looked at the man. He wasn't bad looking in a semi-bleached sort of way. His eyes were a nice shade of blue. Broad shoulders, square jaw, pretty much square all over. Solid, but not corpulent like many of the paler Lebonathi. Aside from the pervasive sneer in his voice it wasn't unpleasant. He didn't dress like a fop. He'd put his back into those mushroom carts, and had seemed to accept Ardenai's whispered apology for subjecting him to that lest he look like a turncoat. Perhaps. Just perhaps.

"You know, and you said it yourself, Naram, you're all Equi citizens now. Under Equi law she can divorce him, and he can be detained for beating her."

"Won't do any good," Ah'ren interjected, "unless you want to detain his whole family for the rest of their lives." Naram shrugged agreement.

"Then how about this?" Ardenai said. "Akadia goes to the Jocundome, sets up a job and a residence, divorces Telloh by Equi law without telling him where she is, which is perfectly legal. Once she is divorced, you can marry her under Equi law and be like the rest of us, who see our wives and families when the opportunity arises. You could go home to her every night, for that matter. Nobody knows where you go, or who you see. Not perfect, but perfectly legal."

Naram gave it some thought. "What if Telloh decides to explore the dome?"

"Put him on a no-go list," Teal said, "Or give Akadia some warning to be discreet. That's a big dome up there, Naram."

"What do we do when the Papilli take it back?"

Ardenai's dimples asserted themselves, though he didn't laugh. "It's on a fifty year lease, remember? You'll be what, ninety? That's ten years past your projected lifespan. That's a pretty long temporary situation. If things settle down and you feel safe having Akadia and your children on the surface, that's always a possibility."

The thought of a family hadn't occurred to Naram. Ardenai could see it in the lightening of his features. Legitimacy had been dismissed as impossible. "You could go from doting uncle to doting father."

For the first time that Ardenai could remember, Naram looked deeply, genuinely startled. "How did you know about Rakba?" he demanded, and when Ardenai looked startled in return, Naram realized, he hadn't known. Naram's face went from angry to perplexed.

"When you asked to hold Umma," Ardenai said quietly. "You said you had never been a father, but you had been a ..."

"Doting uncle," Naram finished. "Well now you know. It won't gain you any leverage over me. What's done is done."

"Just one point of clarification," Ardenai said apologetically, "since our records are incomplete. Brak was your ....?"

"Brother-in-law. Phaedra and Lulana were my sisters, and Eridi is my niece. Not something I cared to have known then, and not something I care to have known now."

There was a pause before the question in Teal's eyes presented itself. "But … Eridi does know you're her uncle?"

Naram just shook his head and sighed. "Yes, you moron. Of course she knows. I do not want anybody else to know. Is that clear enough?"

"Absolutely," Ardenai said. "Do you want to proceed with this other matter?"

"Of course I do," he said, some of the old scorn back in his voice. "Tell me what to do."

"Nothing," Teal said. "Does she have family who will worry, other than Telloh?"

"Two brothers and two sisters and their families, but I can take care of that later."

"Is there someplace she legitimately goes where no one sees her for a while?"

"She cleans my apartments every day," Naram said, "has for years. I pay her well and her husband spends the money."

"What time does she clean?"

Naram told him and Teal nodded. "Do not say a single word to her. I've met her. She has a very expressive face. She won't be able to hide this from her husband. After we have her in protective custody we will let you know. Do not try to contact her in the meantime."

"I get it," Naram muttered. "Thank you."

"You're welcome," Ardenai grinned. "Hopefully this will make up just a little for being invaded by dirt-eating dolts and having to deal with morons. You said you came bearing gifts?"

Naram reached into his pocket and pulled out a slip of paper which had been scribed on in black ink. He held it up between his first two fingers, then handed it to Ardenai. There was a name and an address. Ardenai cocked an eyebrow.

"Kish, Street of the Bells, Ancient Sector, basement. I'm intrigued. How is this gentleman of import?"

"He is not. What he may be able to do, is."

"Go on," Ardenai said impatiently.

"He shrinks heads," Naram snapped. "I thought perhaps it would help you keep a more permanent record of your conquests. You could just write on our foreheads and stack us in neat rows by season and date." He stopped himself with a humorless grunt and forced a more civil tone. "Word has it he was ancient a long time ago. But if you should find him alive and right in the head, I am told that his grandfather and before, fixed carillia – what you called pipe organs."

"You went to this trouble for me?" Ardenai said, genuine pleasure lighting his face.

"Make no mistake, I do nothing for you," Naram sneered. "Some things I do for the Lebonathi people, most things I do toward my own ends. In this case I needed a bargaining chip, nothing more. If you will excuse me. I have another meeting and I have to let my housekeeper in before I go."

Ardenai held up the little slip of paper. "Thank you," he said.

"Your priorities stink," Naram said over his shoulder, and was gone.

"How could we have doubted that someone would be in love with that man?" Ardenai drawled.

"I think he's adorable," Ah'ren said. "I just want to pinch those little cheeks." She did it to herself and burst out laughing. "This housekeeper he's letting in now is the one he wants … elevated is she not?"

Teal nodded. "I assume so. We'll have to hope she actually shows up again tomorrow. Naram does not strike me as one to worry needlessly, or at all, for that matter. If he's worried, it may already be too late for Akadia, and she is a nice young woman. I'd like to see her have a chance to be happy."

"She's the one who warned Ah'nis that Samarra was going to try to poison Eridi," Ardenai said. "I'd especially hate to see anything happen to her." He swung a leg over the back of his chair like he was getting off a horse, and stood up. "I feel terrible about showing him his sister and his nephew all bloody and dead. His brother-in-law ….ugh … Oh, Precious Equus, Eridu was his brother-in-law as well! Two … no, four in one night. Now I really feel rotten."

"I don't think he felt much of a twinge for Eridu," Teal said. "May actually have made up for Brak … and the others. That man has lost a great deal very quickly."

Ah'ren stared out the window in thought, then said, "If you're so worried about Akadia's safety, why are you taking her tomorrow and not today?"

Teal and Ardenai looked at each other. "Naram thinks she's being taken tomorrow. That's when he wanted it done," Ardenai said.

"Exactly," she smiled. "It does seem to me that we'd be better off grabbing her today, and before she gets to his apartments, so blame doesn't fall hard on Naram. Disappearing out of his apartment seems a little suspicious to me. If we grab her early and don't tell him, his dismay will be genuine indeed when he's questioned by the husband, yes?"

"Good point," Ardenai said. "I like it. Teal, get your troopers ready to go, and I'll go get Akadia, since I know what she looks like."

"You should eat," Ah'ren said. "You're going to be away from food awhile. Set your head against mine and give me an image of the woman. I can find her."

Ten minutes later, when the sensors showed that it was just Naram in his apartments, Ah'ren scrambled into a momentarily unoccupied corridor on the route Akadia would follow, and backed into the deep shadows. After a few minutes of waiting she heard a man cursing, and someone she assumed was Telloh appeared, yanking a bloodied Akadia along by her hair.

"I'm going to kill you in front of him, you whore!" he snarled, jerking her from side to side in the corridor before slapping her again until blood spurted from her nose and lips and she stumbled under the blows.

Ah'ren waited until they had just passed her hiding spot before she stepped out, gave Telloh a quick jab on the temples to drop him, and put a hand over Akadia's mouth all in one motion. "Shhhhh," she whispered. "I'm a friend of Naram's." *Kehailan, now please.* They were gone before the next people came into sight to remark at the derelict lying in a public thoroughfare.

"Don't be afraid," Ah'ren said, giving Akadia a one-armed hug. "You're on board Dragonhorse Equus. You're safe."

She explained to Akadia what Naram had asked, then told her it was her choice to do whatever she wanted. She took her to the sanecere bay for some comfort from the familiar face of Ensharra and some tending by a corpsman, and went back to her maps and a working lunch.

Half an hour later Naram's somewhat battered face appeared on her viewing screen. "My housekeeper never showed up," he grated, "but her husband did. Accused me of copulating with his wife. Accused me of abducting her, which I can honestly say I did not do. Any of your men know anything about this?"

"I can absolutely assure you that none of the men on this ship accosted your housekeeper's husband, or kidnapped your housekeeper," Ah'ren said. "From the looks of your face, her husband did more than just ask. Would you like him detained, Regent Naram?"

"No," he said. "We Lebonathi have our own rules, and it was a relatively fair fight. Besides, everyone knows your communications are monitored by every telegenic service on the planet. He'd find a hole to hide in before you could ever catch him."

"You are the head of the Lebonathi Federation, Regent Naram. You should not have to put up with an assault in any form. If you want him found, he will be. Did he perhaps kill his own wife and then accuse you to discredit you amongst your constituents?"

"I do not know," Naram said. "All I know is that I have to find a new housekeeper."

"I am sorry you will have to do that," Ah'ren said. "I apologize to you for the assault on your person. The SGA will put your housekeeper's husband on a closely monitored list. What is his name?

"Telloh," Naram said. "Telloh from the Old Capital Sector."

"Thank you," Ah'ren said. "As a reminder, you are expected at a dinner meeting on board Dragonhorse Thirteen this evening." She smiled, severed the connection and once again went back to her maps, laughing quietly to herself.

Ah'ren had images of the planet from space, and Teal had taken some wonderful images from Dominus. Information from the science teams was already pouring in, but Ah'ren knew that all the photos, maps, elevations and distance calculations put together were not going to be as good as getting out on horseback or with a flyer and seeing the country firsthand. It was First Segens on that part of the planet where they had their encampment – where Konik had buried Ah'davan. Now was the time to evaluate it. She wished Io had actually gotten started in the process so she could be sure she was going in the same direction with things. At all costs, she wanted to avoid crossing Ah'riodin.

She flopped into an overstuffed chair, wrapped her arms around her legs, put her chin on her knees and stared out the window. At what percentage of the planet should they freeze the agricultural footprint? How big should the keeps be? For what general purpose should they be recommended? What shape should the settlement grids take? Were there going to be issues with water rights? Were the same keep rules going to apply here as applied on Equus, that they could not be bought or sold, only traded, given away or passed down? What about the people like Ardi and Teal, who said they just wanted 'a little place to relax'? Should there be recreational properties? Ah'ren had never known an Equi to be satisfied for long with 'a little place'. Equi were, by nature, sprawlers – busy sprawlers. But were they considering only AEW folk and those Lebonathi who wanted to farm? Lebonathis were merchants. Should there be more towns than there were on Equus? If only there wasn't so much pressure to start producing food for Lebonath Jas.

She twisted restlessly in the chair. She wanted to be out doing something. Rescuing Akadia had been a momentary and rewarding diversion, though Ah'ren wished she'd had time to plant a hard right to Telloh's face. Hopefully Naram had landed a few. She'd wanted to go with Ardenai and Teal, but she couldn't be in two places at once. She wanted to be out surveying the planet, pouncing with her husband in the apartments on Crysalis, choosing a polo pony. Out. Doing.

She made herself settle down mentally and review the list of those who wanted keeps. Konik was at the top of the list, and he wasn't here to talk to. She wondered if all those hundreds of keeps he'd asked for had to be contiguous, because that could be difficult if not impossible. It was going to be tricky to give him even a moderately sized personal keep covering the land he wanted – the land which included Ah'davan's gravesite – and still give Ardenai and Teal the land they had designs on; they weren't that far apart. She'd already decided that Teal and Ardenai were going to receive a full keep apiece, regardless – no matter what size the biggest ones turned out to be. While they were incredibly close – more than most brothers – they would have children and grandchildren for generations yet to come who might not love each other quite so much. Better have something big that could be dealt with legally. And that raised another question. What percentage of the land should be set aside for future claims and keeps, planetary parks and public spaces? She sighed, got up, and went back one more time to the maps, wondering enviously if the boys were having more fun than she was.

"This is the spot," Teal said, looking around the room, "I remember that." He nodded toward a white stone table with an intricately carved edge which sat in front of one of the lounges. "We weren't here more than a few seconds before they jumped us. They came from ..." he turned and scanned the room, "... over that way. I know they were behind me as I was talking to Nika. Luckily Dagan saw them come in or the anchoress and I would both be dead."

As he was remembering, he was walking in the direction he'd pointed, taking in the dimly lit, artificially cooled room as he went – big caronai leather lounges, beautifully made throw pillows, sumptuous draperies and hand hooked carpets – things that spoke of wealth and the desire to display it.

"There's Lebonathi blood on the edge of this table," said an SGA trooper, "and there's also the Master Captain's blood and tissue. You hit it somehow, Teal. Are you sure Dagan didn't push both you and Ensharra?"

Teal just shook his head. "No idea. So … if the blood is still here, does that mean no one has come back into this room?"

"I wouldn't count on it," Ardenai said. He walked over and, being careful not to stand in front of the window, pulled back a curtain. He looked out and his jaw dropped. "You have got to see this!"

He was looking into a slightly dim but verdant garden, complete with lawns, flowering plants, and a central fountain sending gallon after gallon of water into the air every minute. Beyond the garden was a pool for swimming, and beyond that a wide cart path leading into an expanse that appeared to be meadows and woods. "Can we go out there?" Ardenai asked, and Teal nodded.

"I'm not picking up any hominoid life signs nearby," he said, "but our readings are obviously being blocked or distorted somehow or we'd have seen this from space." He turned to the troopers and gestured. "Four of you, check out the house, but please be careful. See if you can figure out to whom it belongs. Could it possibly be Nagar's? Is that why no one is here?" He just shook his head. "The other four of you, please come with us. Be sure your scrambling harnesses are on high alert and the sensors are working, so they can jerk you out of here if you need it."

They opened the double glass doors leading out to the gardens, and with weapons drawn, proceeded into a pleasantly-scented space full of flowers and birdsong. "What's above us?" the Firstlord asked, squinting upward. It appeared to be sky, but dimmer and lower with a definite green tinge.

"A variation of that gaming cage we pulled you and Nik out of," Teal replied, checking his instruments. "Some kind of wirelight infused glastaline, which explains why this whole area reads as solid. So did that. T'was telepathy saved you from that dome, not technology, Brother Mine. This one is different, though. A scrambleshaft wouldn't penetrate the one you were in. We've obviously scrambled through this one, and more than once. Why can't we see it from the surface? Are we underground?"

"Good questions both. So … what have we found?" Ardenai breathed, pricking up his ears and turning slowly to discern any sounds beyond the obvious. "That's odd … all the birds are over there in one spot," he said, pointing with his chin to a corner of the gardens.

"Probably robotic," Teal said, turning aside to examine a cage with two long-limbed primates in it. They swung languidly back and forth, chittering quietly and watching the visitors with their black button eyes. "Like these. Expensively made, no doubt, but not real."

A rambling walk of another hundred feet or so took them to an aviary where a dozen birds were fluttering around, obviously in distress. Three already lay in the bottom of the cage. There was no food. There was no water. "I think these are very real, and no one has been here to care for them," Ardenai said sadly, and immediately began looking around for food. They found it in a small space behind an area used for storing vehicles. There was room for three, two in evidence.

"Maybe we should go for a little spin," Teal suggested, eyeing wheeled contraptions much like the ones they saw daily on the surface. "How … did they get these down here? How do they get down here, for that matter?"

"More questions," Ardenai said, filling the feeder and finding running water. He put food and water in the cage, removed the dead birds and put them in a collecting bag. "I wonder why no onc fcd these poor birds."

"Maybe they're not used to having real pets," Teal replied, "or maybe our arrival disrupted their routine."

"I wonder if these birds were once a wild species. We certainly haven't seen their like on the surface."

"We haven't seen many animals on the surface except caronai. Of course we haven't really gotten out into the wilds a lot yet."

One of the troopers appeared beside the aviary and said, "That pool has over sixty thousand statute gallons of water in it, but apparently it's not a swimming pool. As far as we can tell nobody has ever been in the water. It has been dyed blue and treated to keep it from growing, but it hasn't been tended for a few days. The fountain is recirculating from a different source."

"A display of wealth only," Teal muttered, "while people on the surface are dying of thirst."

"This is craziness," Ardenai said, brows pulled together as he looked around again.

"It's a puzzle for sure," Teal amended. He turned to the troopers, and pointed to the left of where he was standing. "Fan out a little and go that way for fifteen minutes. See what you can find, and come back. If you feel threatened, activate your harness. Don't wait to see how much trouble you're in, please."

They smiled, nodded and took off at a jogtrot down the cart path and off in different directions into the trees. Teal gestured to the right and grinned, "Shall we?"

Ardenai nodded, and they struck off in that direction, following the path through an impossibly green landscape bordered by trees and shrubs. They saw gazebos for picnicking, a small lake with little boats tied up along a dock and ducks sitting near the water. Past the lake was another opulent residence, and on the opposite side, a third. A fish jumped. Ardenai and Teal dropped back into the cover of trees and looked at each other.

"This is a whole different world," Teal said, wonder in his voice. "If this is an imitation of what the planet was like …."

Ardenai was just shaking his head. "Can you imagine the technology it took to create this space?" he said. "Can you imagine the resources it takes to maintain it? And this may not be the only one. How strange … that they can do something like this, and yet they're dependent on the Nargas for such space flight as they have. It makes me want to pound my head against … something. Speaking of which …." He reached up for a tree branch, snapped off a twig, looked at it, and crushed a leaf. "Seems to be real, not hardscaping. Grass is real. The shrubs at the house are real. Birds are real."

"I think this is very old," Teal said. "Back when they were making progress and things were good and technology was advancing. This is not the product of their more modern and much more rudimentary education. Whomever has this inherited it, they didn't create it."

"And it is totally unsustainable," Ardenai added. "No wonder the flamen are worried about their future. They have a little more to lose than the average Lebonathi, I would say. But, shock and disgust aside, what a treasure trove! Look at all the varieties of trees and shrubs. We saw ducks and a fish which we hope are real. What else is down here that can help us restore the surface? Assuming we are beneath the surface of the planet."

"Water," Teal said, and his voice was resigned. "Herein lies another dilemma. Do we allow this to continue for the good it contains, or do we shut it down because it is literally raping the surface for precious resources? Eladeus, no wonder the city's a wreck. Nobody with power has to care; they have this."

"Do you suppose Naram knows about this?" Ardenai asked.

"Knows, maybe. Has, I don't think so. He said most emphatically that he was not flamen, and from his attitude and his vocabulary – the way he accesses things in general – I don't think he's from the very richest of the rich. What we see before us, most definitely is."

"So, Master Captain, how do you want to proceed?" Ardenai asked, standing from his crouch and turning to go back in the direction they had come.

"Let's see what everybody else found out and then have that discussion," Teal suggested, and Ardenai nodded in agreement as they set a good pace back down the cart path.

"Here's another question," Ardenai said. "Who maintains this? Who does all the work? Why haven't we heard a single rumor, folktale or legend about this place?"

"Maybe the servants that are here don't know how to get out," Teal said. "Maybe they're better off, but no less prisoners than the men we found chained to the ore carts. Maybe … this is where those young girls go that the flamen take from the outside."

"Maybe we'll find Bona's daughter in here," Ardenai said.

"I think we're going to find a lot of things in here," Teal muttered. "Now that we've found the place."

"And how did we do that?" the Firstlord asked. "Really? This is the best kept secret on Lebonath Jas, and yet here we are, because someone who is supposedly flamen, brought us here. Why would he do that?"

Teal thought about that for a bit. "Couple of possibilities. Number one, Ensharra and I were never supposed to leave. We were supposed to die here. If Lebonathi technology is as lacking as we think it is, then perhaps Dagan had no real concept of how easy it would be to find us, whether we actually came back or not."

"Neh ..." Ardenai responded. "Well, maybe. It still seems an incredible risk, unless ..."

"Hm?"

"Patience, Kinsman. We know there are political rivalries over which people are killed on a regular basis around here. What if … showing us this is revenge? What if this isn't where Dagan's faction lives, but someone else's? What if these homes don't belong to the flamen at all?"

"Considering it exposes the technology, it's pretty expensive revenge."

"I didn't say it was smart, but revenge seldom is. Maybe those who were shooting weren't just shooting at you, but at Dagan, as well. What if Dagan asked you to meet him here, not expecting them to come home and find you?"

"Anything is possible," Teal said, turning off the cart path and back into the gardens. "I will be anxious to see what the others found."

When the ten of them had gathered in the room where Teal and Ensharra had been attacked, Teal asked, "Did any of you see any Lebonathis?"

"I did," said a young man with paralleled Declivian chins. "I saw someone working on the grounds of a house like this one, but I don't think he saw me."

"Anybody else?" There was a mutual shaking of heads. "Then I think we should go before we are discovered. Did you leave this house exactly as you found it?"

"Yes," said an older Amberian woman.

"But we're not leaving everything exactly as we found it," the Declivian said. "We have left footprints. Dragonhorse, you fed the birds, and you took the ones that were dead. The feed might have stretched, but the numbers would not have diminished. With food in the cage the birds would not have died in any case."

"Good point," Teal said, and Ardenai looked slightly abashed if unrepentant. "Let us … take the all the birds with us. We can swing the door open and perhaps the owners will think it was an accident."

"Or they'll kill the servant who was careless," Ardenai muttered. He still had nightmares about what they'd done to Brak.

"Take the birds," Teal said. "They are undoubtedly of value. The rest is speculation." He looked apologetically at his brother-in-law. "No offense."

"None taken," Ardenai sighed. "Let's go."

They regrouped in one of the private conference rooms, and over lunch they discussed what they had uncovered. They had found a total of six houses in the time they'd had for discovery, though there could be more in either direction. Only one person had seen another living soul, at a distance and most likely a gardener. Ardenai and Teal had seen ducks and a fish jump. Someone else had seen what she thought might be a fox – couldn't tell whether or not it was robotic. One of the Demetrians described something that looked like a shooting range, with big wire cages behind and beside to keep game cornered. No telling whether it was still in use or not. Maybe nowadays they hunted robotic animals; that would fit with what the Stone Spring scientists had said.

Of the house, they could say little. Parts were not accessible without breaking down doors, and there was no way to scramble inside. Only the one room had allowed them entry or egress – like a portal of some kind. There were no personal items of any kind in evidence. The pantries were well stocked with items not available to the average Lebonathi, and not a single person had seen anything being grown that they recognized as food – not in the gardens, not in the meadows nor among the trees. Again, that could be further along than they had gotten.

Teal swore them all to absolute secrecy until they knew more about what they had seen. They would assess as quickly and thoroughly as they could what was there, most especially plants and animals. For that they would utilize their five Stone Spring scientists, hopefully some old scholars that Konik had turned up in the dusty library of what had once been a thriving university, and science teams from Belesprit, led by Timothy McGill. As soon as they possibly could they would begin tapping into the water supply to take some of the pressure off Lebonath Tras and the Menorquin farm ships.

The Firstlord said he would take the sensor information they had gathered and see if he could create a recognition code for the wirelight infused glastaline ceilings. If he could do that, they could find all the compounds worldwide, and with them, much of the thirsty planet's water supply. Could they farm in there? Could they build housing in there? All questions that would take time to answer.

"I just had an awful thought," Teal said as they were wrapping up. "What if we think Lebonath Tras is abandoned because our sensors won't read wirelight infused glastaline?"

"What if we think they have no advanced ships or technology because they're all hidden under this stuff?" someone else said.

"What if glastaline itself is a weapon that can be triggered?" said the Declivian. "We saw it blow up once when they were rescuing you and the governor, and that dome we were in today is big enough to take the whole city with it."

Ardenai was alarmed by the comments, and it registered on his face.

As far as he was concerned, one or all of them could be true to one extent or another. When the meeting broke up he sat for a few minutes, rubbing morosely at the persistent blue mark on the palm of his right hand and thinking through his options. If he was going to create a recognition code in the least amount of time, he needed a sample of wirelight infused glastaline. He was pretty sure he knew where to find some, but willing himself to go back to that place was almost more than he could manage. He thought about sending a couple of big Amberians instead, and realized this was yet another test. Could he make himself go? Second question. Where, exactly had he been? He could remember part of the walk, part of the way. He remembered Brak ducking under his arm and lending him support as the pain built in his head, his legs, and his back. Just the remembrance made the small of his back ache, and he could feel the mine boss kicking him over and over. He heard himself gasp with that pain, and took a deep, steadying breath.

They had gone in, and down the widest of the corridors. He knew where that started. Had they turned anywhere? Had the corridor narrowed? Were there other exits? There had been a huge crowd. How had they gotten in and out? Kehailan, Ah'davan and Teal had been with him mentally. Maybe the ship's sensors had been there as well. Maybe troops had been there by now. There were so many people going in so many directions it was impossible to keep track in any detail. He stood up abruptly, jerked his tunic into place and walked himself to the bridge and the sensor historia.

Kehailan looked up and smiled, asking if he needed something, and Ardenai nodded. "That first day," he said. "When you pulled Nik and me out of that dome. Do you have those coordinates? I need to go back there."

Kehailan thought a moment, more about why than where, and produced the information on a crys-tel, which he handed to his father. "Is this something I can do for you?" he asked, careful to leave inflection out of his voice. Ardenai shook his head. "May I at least come along? I don't get down to the surface much."

If Ardenai suspected Kehailan's motives he hid it, thanked him for the offer of company, and the two of them walked to the scrambleshaft. "Pultronel," Ardenai said, and they turned aside momentarily to pick up weapons. Ardenai also tucked a slingshot into his equipment belt, and it made Kehailan chuckle.

"Going to slay giants are we?" he asked.

"I've had these things quit on me," Ardenai replied, tapping the pultronel. "I've never had a slingshot do that."

Kehailan was aware, as he always was when he walked with his father, of the admiring glances they received as a pair. At first it had made him feel as though he was leading a parade, but, like a lot of other things, he'd gotten more used to it. He was maybe even a little pleased by it. That thought, he was careful to hide. His father might consider it ego; Kehailan, considered it growth. "Are you going to tell me why we're going down there?"

"I need some fragments of glastaline," Ardenai said, nodding to the trooper on duty, and they found themselves in the Port of Entry.

He retraced his steps from that first day for as far as he could, until the pain in his head had begun to blind him and the movement of his legs had become motor memory only. He took out the crys-tel, checked the coordinates and they went on, down and down until the set of doors appeared in front of them. He took a deep breath, shot a glance at Kehailan, and shoved them open.

There was the field, as huge as he remembered it. Dim and dusty. A group of boys was playing a rough game midway down the space, and the two men stopped short, not wanting to disturb them.

"How can they do that in this heat?" Ardenai groaned.

"No idea. What makes you think any part of that dome is still here?" Kehailan queried, looking around at the scattered bits of trash. "I would have guessed they'd cleaned it up and hauled it away by now."

"If they had nothing better to do," Ardenai shrugged, beginning to kick carefully through the dust so as not to raise the filthy powder. "They probably got the big pieces, but all I need is a little one."

"What the clean-up crews didn't get, the trophy hunters most likely did," Kehailan said, but he was working the trash with his feet as he said it. "Which came first, do you suppose, moving underground or bleaching their skins as they do?"

Ardenai was sitting on his boot heels, examining a small patch of dirt, and he looked up at Kehailan, squinting as the sweat escaped his eyebrows to sting his eyes. "If galactic history serves, the bleaching came first, and started with the women. A man proved his wealth and position by having a wife who couldn't do anything physical, and taking all the color out of a body would certainly render them ineffective in a climate like this..." He swiped the back of his arm across his forehead, "... or even vaguely like this."

"So times got good and everybody started doing it?" Kehailan asked, moving an errant scrap of blood stiffened shirt aside with the tips of a gloved thumb and forefinger. "Because nobody was interested in working outdoors nobody realized the damage they were doing to themselves?"

"I have no idea. The more I know, the less I understand. We have issued an interposition saying the practice is no longer acceptable. We do have doctors and herbalists working on a way to reverse the condition so we can get these people back on the surface..."

"Got one!" Kehailan exclaimed, holding up a shard half the length of his little finger and about as wide. "Is this big enough?"

"Good job!" Ardenai replied, then laughed softly and looked repentant. "Sorry. I didn't mean to treat you like a five-year-old. My … Ah'ren suggested I start teaching again on a regular basis, once a week for an hour, and I guess that vocabulary is filling my head."

Kehailan was about to say that it was all right to refer to the woman as his wife, and that she'd had a very good idea, when there was a scream from the game players. One was down, some scattered, and two came running their way, yelling for help.

Even as Ardenai was running toward them he was pleased. These children had realized the men in the Dragonhorse uniforms would help them. He was also wondering if it was a trap.

If the scene was an indicator, it was not. The boy's femur was protruding through his skin and blood was pumping out. Kehailan grabbed for the primedica bag on his equipment belt to make a tourniquet, but Ardenai shook his head and stood up with the screaming boy flat along his arms. "No good," he said. "He'll be dead in a matter of minutes. Get us out of here."

"Medical emergency. Scramble all life signs!" Kehailan exclaimed, and in a second they were gone – the two men, the injured boy, and the two boys who had run to them for help.

Ardenai ran for the sanecere bay and Kehailan put a hand on the shoulder of each of the boys they'd brought up with them. "Sorry," he smiled. "I didn't mean to grab you up without your permission. Would you like to go back where you were?"

They were looking around rather than looking at him, and an answer was slow in coming. "It's really cold in here," one of them said. "And really bright."

"It's comfortable for us," Kehailan smiled. "We come from a cool climate. It's snowing there right now."

"What's snow?" the second boy asked. Kehailan looked at them. Both were fair, but neither had been albinized.

"My name is Kehailan," he said. "I would be happy to tell you about snow, but I am concerned that nobody knows where you are. I do not want your mothers to worry, and the boy who is injured ..."

"Anshra," the taller boy said. "He's my older brother."

"We should let your parents know where he is," Kehailan said. "If you will go back with me now so we can tell them, you can come back up when they do, and I will tell you about snow, how's that?"

"I guess that's best." The boy sighed with obvious reticence. A nod to the technician found the three of them back in the spot they'd just left. "The quickest way out of here is through the schoolroom. We use this as our playground."

They had gone no more than a few steps when the door they were heading toward flew open and several boys and four men came bursting through at a run. "Where is he?" one of the men demanded. "Where is Anshra?"

"Ahimsa, I wish thee peace," Kehailan said quickly. "His leg was badly broken ..."

"Where is he?" the man said again, and the taller boy stepped forward. His father seized him by the shoulders and gave him a quick shake. "Anmar, where is your brother? What have they done with him?"

"Kehailan was trying to tell you," the boy began, and his father slapped him, which made Kehailan wince, though he didn't step in.

"He's on the big white ship," Kehailan said, trying not to sound as angry as he felt. "Anmar was kind enough to help me find you so I could let you know. If you will get your wife I will take all of you back up there so you can be with him."

"You will bring him back here, right now," the man said.

"I can't do that," Kehailan replied. "He was bleeding badly. My sire has taken him to our sanecere, what you call a lazarette? I will take you to him, but not the other way around. I'm sorry."

"Then you will be our prisoner as he is yours," the man growled.

"If you think that's best," Kehailan replied. "Anmar, and …?" he looked at the smaller boy.

"Rupak," he said shyly.

"Rupak," Kehailan smiled. "I will show you some snow another time, and in return you can teach me that game you were playing. Now, Gentlemen, let me tell you what the flaw is in your plan. If anybody thinks I am in trouble, even for an instant, we will have SGA troops all over this place, and you will probably not be going home for a while. More importantly, if Anshra is in need of your help, you will not be there to help him, as a father should be, and my father will not be able to contact me to let you know this."

Rupak hung his head and went sadly to a slightly younger and darker man who had come through the door with the others. "I wanted to learn about snow," he said, putting his arms around his father's waist. He looked up and smiled. "I got to feel all tingly, and then we were on the big, white ship. Kehailan said he would tell us about snow."

"You were on the ship?" Anshra's father asked, peeling his lips back slightly, and for the first time Kehailan began to feel danger in the situation.

"I apologize for that," he said. "I wasn't specific enough when I said … scramble all life-signs."

▲▲▲▲▲▲▲

"Devious," Teal smiled, stretching his legs out in front of him and swirling the wine in his glass before holding it up to the light. "Smart though. Your father and I have both discovered that these people can move pretty quickly when they've a mind to."

"When it was all over they did seem to enjoy themselves," Kehailan replied. "And the boy is still here. That's a good sign."

"Maybe we should do that more often," Ardenai said. "Just grab people at random and take them to the school science lab to make snow. By the way, do you still have my shard of glastaline?"

Kehailan fished it out of his equipment belt and tossed it across the table to his father. "Thanks," Ardenai grinned. "I'm going to be meeting with Ellsbeth and Company to give them this name from Naram, and then I'll be in my office, writing a code for this material." He held up the piece of green glass.

"Aren't you at least going to sit a spell first," Kehailan scowled, "have something to drink and a bite to eat? Where's your wife?"

"No idea," Ardenai said with a dismissive wave over his shoulder. "I'll eat later."

The young Captain sat back with a gesture of annoyance. "Didn't he just marry the most beautiful woman in the galaxy? Why did I think that would provide him with some distraction? Why did I think he'd get some exercise of a more pleasant sort and then get some sleep? He's so kraaling tired, Teal. He can't keep going like this."

"You sound a little tired yourself," his uncle smiled, concern standing in his eyes. "Have you had any time to get away by yourself, or with Timothy?"

"I spent four days flat on my back," he responded. "Most of that time I'm sure I was asleep."

"Not quite the time in bed I had in mind," Teal chuckled. "That was many weeks ago, and besides, recuperating from pultronel burns doesn't exactly constitute recreation. At least come tonight and sleep by the river.

Get some fresh air, take an early morning swim, and enjoy the sunshine for a bit. You were the one who pushed for taking leave on Tras rather than on the Jocundome, and you haven't been down on the surface except to your father's wedding."

Kehailan gave it some thought. "I will come with you and enjoy it," he grinned, "if you don't ask me to ride a horse, or play polo ..."

"Polo!" Teal exclaimed. "We're picking out polo ponies tonight! Would you like ..."

"No, I would not," Kehailan laughed. "Try not to get a mallet to the head, and I will meet you on Tras whenever you're through. I may go down a little early and stretch my legs."

Teal, too, chose to leave a little early. With a gentle knock on Ah'ren's office door, he informed her that he'd meet them at the polo fields, traded field boots for riding boots, and went to the Jocundome. He was met by Pyron, who gave him a passkey of his own. Like Ardenai's, it gave Teal access to anywhere on the small world.

"I am most grateful," Teal said. "I will make sure not to abuse my privileges."

"I'm sure you will not," the man smiled. "In what other way may I serve you, Master Captain? Something is surely on your mind."

"Yes, several things," Teal nodded, "if you have an hour to spare me."

Pyron showed him into a sunlit space full of birdsong and flowers, offered him refreshments, and settled himself in a listening pose. "I am thine," he said.

"I need to spend most of this time speaking with you about security, and how you want us to deal with Lebonathi access to the dome. But first I have a more personal matter I promised I would discuss on behalf of the Dragonhorse." He paused to choose his words. "Ardenai Firstlord is concerned that he and Ah'ren might not be fully welcomed in the chambers you prepared so beautifully for Io and him, and I want to be sure the collective you are not vexed in that area."

Pyron's expressive Papilli face filled with circumspection. "Have we given him any reason to think that?"

"I doubt it very much," Teal soothed. "Ardenai has, his whole life, been one who is hypersensitive to giving offense. He is very keenly attuned to the nuances of any creature that draws breath, and because of that he occasionally expresses concern when there is no need."

"And in this case there is certainly no need," Pyron smiled. He held out a tiny piece of nectar bread on the tip of a finger and a large, electric blue butterfly with black velvet markings came to settle, working the tidbit with tongue and forelegs, its wings fanning slowly as it balanced itself. It was almost hypnotic, and Teal could feel his breathing slow and deepen as he relaxed. "We heard his explanation," Pyron continued quietly. "We know that Io made some very difficult choices that Ardenai agreed to, and however willingly and lovingly it was done, it still left him alone." The butterfly flew away and Pyron brought his hand down and raised his voice a little. "Sometimes even the breath of speaking disturbs them," he smiled, watching its flight. "We understand nuance better than most, Master Captain. Always, at his very heart, the Firstlord has you. He has Kehailan, but he is Dragonhorse, and as such he needs a mate. Ah'ren is a lovely woman. She seems kind in the actions which have reached us. We felt his joy in having her, even as they were wed."

Teal nodded. "I think she's a good balance for him, but I know that she, too, is concerned that she is invading space meant for Io."

"Then we shall create a space for her that is her own," Pyron said, "just as we created one for Io. The Firstlord may visit with whichever one he wishes." He smiled, "We have one for you and your beloved wife, as well, Master Captain. When we are through here I will show you."

"You didn't have to do that," Teal replied. "I would not presume to take space from ..."

"Whom?" Pyron laughed. It made his beautiful, butterfly wing ears flutter just a little, and it made Teal ache for assurance that Io was really going to be all right and back among them. "You are a most worthy recipient, Master Captain, and no less in need of a place to relax where you have instant access to all manner of services and entertainments. A more … urbane setting, if you will, than your bower amongst the trees. Captain Kehailan has a suite, though he has not yet seen it, and Governor Konik has his own space as well." There was a moment's pause. "It seems to suit his needs," Pyron added, which answered a question Teal wasn't sure how to ask, and at the same time assured him that Konik was all right. Perceptive man, Pyron.

Teal had to admit heat cycles had been on his mind of late, not so much because he was due for another fairly soon, but because Ah'din was, as well. Her cycle at Mountain hold had been just about all he could gracefully, safely and lovingly handle, and he wondered if things were going to keep escalating. Krush had come out of his time with Ah'rane looking for the first time more like he'd been playing polo than making love. Kehailan was certainly more … masculine … not the right term, exactly, but it would have to do. He had thickened in the arms and legs a little, his muscles had become more defined, his handsome young face slightly more angular. Where he had always been biphilic, he was now leaning more toward females, less toward males, so his hormones were changing. Maybe it was maturity. He was close to fifty. It was time. How nice it would be, how comforting, to believe that. And who was the last of the Dragonhorse blood? Criollo, and how was this going to affect him, and how soon? He was still a child with two years to go before he was considered a young adult. Where would his sexual cycles be in two years? Teal made up his mind to have this discussion with Ah'ren. He didn't have any answers, and it was causing him to be distracted on behalf of his family.

He spent another hour with Pyron discussing security, and in the course of it decided that Akadia would be better off on one of the Menorquin farm ships than on the dome. There would be more of her own kind, and fewer rules to learn. She would not stand out so much, and therefore had a better chance for a normal existence. Teal had felt odd as it was, taking a man's wife because another man had asked them to. He consoled himself that the man was a wife-beater, but it still felt a little like cheating, and that was one thing Teal tried never to do.

When they had exhausted the subjects Teal had come to discuss, Pyron took him back to the main scrambleshaft platforms in the entresol, and, standing with him, told him to activate the small orange tab on his passkey. "It represents the home fire," Pyron smiled.

"Very nice ..." Teal sighed, looking around in wonder, "I like it, and my wife will, too." It was sunlit and intimate, with a beautiful garden containing all manner of flowers, herbs and vegetables. There was a bathing pool nestled in a small grotto to one side, and a living space for all the world like the Dreamweaver's corner at Canyon keep, complete with a magnificent floor loom, baskets of exotic fleeces and simple, comfortable furniture. There was a large kitchen, which Pyron said was unusual for a crystal suite, but they had thought Ah'din might appreciate it. The bedroom was also large, with access to the grotto and an ithyphallic chamber, as well as a luxurious lavage.

"If you should desire the services of a hetaera," Pyron said, "or if your wife should, you have only to activate this pad. They have already been selected for you by Mountain hold and your personal physician. I have been instructed to introduce you to yours when you take your initial tour, so if you will indulge me for one moment ..." he touched a pad on the wall of the ithyphallic chamber.

Teal tensed up. He'd had need of a hetaera only infrequently, and this was momentarily disconcerting. It did make him snicker silently inside, wondering if some of his brother-in-law was rubbing off. A minute or two later a door opened at the back of the chamber and a young woman appeared. She smiled as she came toward them and nodded deeply to Teal.

"Ahimsa, Master Captain, I wish thee peace," she said. "I am Robin."

She was sweet, with a soft, laughing voice and a slightly round face more cherubic than classically beautiful. Almond eyes, high cheekbones. She had long, dark blonde hair which hung in a thick braid over one breast, and she was typically tall, leggy and, in her case, a little coltish.

"I have other jobs to keep me busy here, but my main function is to serve you as companion and friend should you desire it. Someone to talk to. Even if you just want a hiking or dancing partner, I am thine."

"Thank you," Teal smiled. "I will not hesitate to call."

She nodded, returned the smile, and exited the way she had come. He wondered if she was Androtech, like Ah'ren. If Pyron knew, he did not mention it and Teal didn't ask. Perhaps all the hetaeras for the Dragonhorse family were Androtech. That might not be such a bad idea, Teal thought, though why he would need one was a bit of a mystery. He and Krush were just related to that hot blood through marriage. Maybe Robin was more for respite than recreation. Maybe when Ah'din had used him up and cast him aside he could crawl to Robin for comfort while Ah'din and her hetaera continued the sexual odyssey upon which Teal had not the stamina to go. Teal closed his eyes for a minute and felt the foundations of his most private and precious world shaking … crumbling … and he was helpless.

"Are you all right?" Pyron asked, touching his arm. "Is this room disquieting you?"

"I'm fine," Teal said, dragging out his usual rag of an excuse, "I'm just tired. This is more than I could ever have asked for, Pyron. Do you think I could have a few moments to explore by myself?"

"Certainly," Pyron replied. He walked from the ithyphallic chamber back into the living space with Teal, showed him which button to activate to get back to the main entresol and thence to the stables, and vanished.

Teal flopped onto the lounge and told himself firmly not to blubber. Ardenai was one of those men who cried easily and gracefully without diminishing himself in the least. Teal, was not. He never felt better after he cried, only more foolish. He stared out into the garden, hearing the birdsong, watching the butterflies that filled all such spaces in the Papilli world. He wondered if butterflies ever ate each other.

"What I need is more substance and less speculation," he said aloud to the pillow he was holding. He wondered if Robin really would be someone to talk to. She had said that was her function. It would be nice to talk to someone without feeling like he was adding to their burden. Why in the name of Equus had they given him an Androtech companion, as she almost certainly was? He would never rough up a hetaera. He took a deep breath, focused on the birdsong, and the butterflies, and emptied his mind.

Because she was discreet? Because there was no guilt associated with her? Again, he was Teal, not Ardenai. Like Ardenai, he'd had sex with very few women other than his trainers – never needed or wanted to. Ah'din was his whole world. He let himself hear her voice, feel her hands on his shoulders, hear her words … and then, he had a possible answer. Oldest bloodlines on Equus. He was to mate outside marriage. Ardenai, who mated outside marriage, was allowed to spill his seed only into those chosen by the Great House and Mountain hold. Had Teal now been added to that column? Interesting. Maybe in fifty or a hundred years one of his daughters with some unknown woman would be presented to Ardenai to produce the Fourteenth Dragonhorse. The thought made Teal laugh out loud. The weightlessness of change dissipated and with a last approving look around he touched his passkey and found himself back in the entresol.

The next jump took him to the stables at the polo fields where he found Ardenai, Ah'ren, Tarpan and Ah'keena listening to stable master Liadin. He cruised up beside them in time to hear the man say, "You may choose three for each of you, plus four extra for the team, a total of sixteen horses. Ah'ren, you will be able to choose two horses for yourself. Ah'keena, are you competing?"

Ah'keena shook her head. "I am groom, leg-wrapper, and general go-to person," she said.

"You could play," Ah'ren said. "There are women's teams forming."

"It would not be wise," Ah'keena said, giving her belly a little pat, just as Tarpan said,

"My wife is … settled with a child."

His reticence of speech and judiciousness in not meeting Ardenai's eyes told the Firstlord that the child had been unexpected, and that it had happened on Calumet, thanks to him. He felt a little sick, and had no idea what to say. Tarpan and Ah'keena were young, and they were newlyweds. Having a child so soon deprived them of years they needed to get to know one another.

"Felicitations!" Ah'ren said. "Much joy! Now I know why you are anxious for a keep of your own. Let's you and I go and scout for just the place you want."

"I'd like that," Ah'keena grinned.

"Quite a crop of colts coming on next year," Teal said to no one in particular. "If my wife settles as she should, we're all going to be pacing the floor. Well, except for Nik."

"I may be able to loan him one," Ardenai said, rolling his eyes.

Everyone laughed, and for the moment the awkwardness passed. Tarpan put an arm around his wife, knowing their babe was growing safe and strong in her womb. How hard it must be for Ardenai not knowing – having three lives hanging in the balance day after day.

Tarpan, guard your thoughts!

The young man jerked, glanced at his commanding officer, and looked uncomfortable.

Liadin, patient with Equi ways, said, "Horses. Polo ponies. Some were sent from the Great House with the last shipment of expedition stock. Landais chose them, saying he thought the three of you and Governor Konik would want to play polo while you were here. Ah'ren, your father-in-law says he will send additional ponies for you. In the meantime, find what you can to get you started."

What they supposed would take hours, took Teal, Tarpan and Ardenai but a few delightful minutes. Landais had sent each of them two of their best-seasoned mares, and one in which they had seen future promise. Then, with Teal's expert help, Ah'ren picked out two nice mares for herself, and Tarpan, who was closest in height and weight to Konik, helped Teal choose two for the governor. They picked two extra, and with that done they saddled up, grabbed their helmets and rode out to play a little two on two – "A's against the T's," Ah'keena laughed, throwing out the willow bark ball.

That short workout told the men that Ah'ren was in no way a braggart. She was a formidable opponent, even on a strange horse. Knocking the ball around while the sun set and the lights came on made all of them feel grounded and content, the joy of the game pushing the homesickness to the backs of their minds. They groomed their animals and scrambled from dome to Dragonhorse to planet, pausing to watch the Jocundome rise as a small, shining moon amongst the stars of Lebonath Tras.

CHAPTER 12

A shirtless, unshod Kehailan flipped his hands palms up in the family gesture of bemusement and reiterated his statement. “They just said the scrambleshafts were having problems because of some spatial disturbance. Nobody is scrambling and they’re not willing to launch any vessels for the moment. We are stranded in this awful place.”

“Oh no,” Ardenai yawned, stretching out in the warm sand beside the pool and raking a bit of gravel from the waistband of his briefcloth. He had dallied with his wife in the first light of morning, and now he was wishing he’d gotten a bit more sleep. Apparently, wishes sometimes came true. Blessed with the knowledge that there wasn’t a single thing he could accomplish at this juncture without his computator, he locked his hands behind his head, closed his eyes, and was promptly asleep in the sunshine.

“So much for two on two team sports,” Ah’ren groused, sliding off her running shoes and wading up to her ankles in the pool. The ripples from the waterfall created a thousand sparkling tips, and she put up a hand to shield her eyes. “What a beautiful morning to be doing something besides working in an office.”

“Horseback ride?” Teal suggested. “My father-in-law sent us some very nice mounts, and I haven’t had much chance to put Poseidon through his paces.”

Ah’ren smiled up at him and nodded enthusiastically. “After breakfast?"

Teal returned the smile. "After breakfast."

The full outdoor kitchen was already in place, and Teal was glad they hadn't put off asking for it. If they had, they'd have nothing but the basics until they could ride to Expedition Headquarters. As it was, they put Ardenai's breakfast aside for him to find when he awoke, saddled their horses, and discussed whether they wanted to go exploring, or hunt up friends at ECHQ.

"They might find something productive for us to do if we go there," Ah'ren warned, and they decided to ford the river and explore on the other side. Kehailan said he would stay close to camp and protect his frail old father from the dangers of the place, chief among them probably sunburn, and as they rode away he was already in the water.

They found a spot up river to cross where the horses could wade most of the way, and rode easily side by side along the beach and up the gently sloping side of the bank to the sun-dappled forest beyond. "No cutaway in the bank," Teal observed, "Probably doesn't do a lot of flooding, at least in the tributaries. Mother River could be a different story."

"I doubt it," Ah'ren replied. "This place is incredibly beautiful, and seemingly placid, as well."

"And there's no record of it in the annals of Mountain hold?"

"Not as far as I know, but I do not have the totality of that library in my head, either, unbelievable as that may seem. If there is information, we'll have to find it next time we're there."

Teal chuckled. "Thanks for the splendid segue. Can I talk to you about Mountain hold?"

"Certainly," she said. They came out of the widely spaced trees and into a huge meadow like the one on the other side of the river, only this one was more heavily treed on both sides. There was no gentle rising of foothills to stop this one so far as they could see, and they jogged along a seemingly endless green corridor in companionable silence while Teal organized his thoughts.

"What has your experience been with Dragonhorse women? By that

I mean those who have Dragonhorse blood in their veins."

"Mixed," Ah'ren replied. "Ask me specific questions if you want specific answers."

"Very well, let me try again. My mother-in-law, who is Ardenai's half-sister, and the gentlest of creatures next to my wife, beat the snot out of my father-in-law during her heat cycle at Mountain hold. She's never done that before, I know it. My sweet wife … was all I could handle. She's usually a little rough, but this was violently out of character. I was literally bruised and bleeding. I know, so far this is not a question," Teal smiled. "Have you noticed that there is no storied structure to this forest? It's canopy only. That seems odd."

"Its growth habit is more like a planted windbreak, isn't it? Low shrubs, then deciduous trees, then tall evergreens. The wind could be howling from either of two directions and we wouldn't feel it much at all in here."

"Maybe it's an old runway," Teal said. "This would be ideal for winged, heavier-than-air craft." They looked at each other and grinned. "Maybe we'll find ruins."

"Maybe we're riding on top of wirelight infused glastaline," Ah'ren said.

"Oh, don't say that," Teal sighed. "That stuff, knowing what it can hide, is enough to give a body nightmares."

"Make a nice racetrack," Ah'ren said, giving him a sidelong glance. "Once we've ridden it to know what the footing is ..."

"Pavil's fast, and he did choose you right away this morning, so he'll do his best for you. But can he outrun Poseidon? Not a chance."

"And if he does?" Ah'ren challenged.

"Your wish is my command."

"Teach me the Phyllan Wolf Dance?"

"Done. Now, back to the question part of my question, which is what I win, and since I'm going to win, you might as well answer me now."

"Of course you are," she snickered. "Actually, I know this is bothering you, so I'll answer for free, how's that?"

"A blessing," Teal said quietly. A slight breeze stirred and he held his face up to it, enjoying the cool fragrance. “Ardenai’s heat cycles would have kept accelerating until they killed him. The Twelfth Dragonhorse told me that. Is Ah’din going to do the same thing? Is Ah’rane? Is Kehailan?” He felt his eyes sting a little and made himself take a breath. “Ah’ren, I’m scared. I’m afraid I’m going to lose my family.”

“Don’t be,” she said. “We got Ardi under control and we know … they know … where everybody else is now. The next time we all sequester together, it will be to get the rest of the family leveled off. And to answer your very first, very general question, this is what usually happens when a Dragonhorse rises. It’s usually most pronounced in males, but we do see it in females, and we certainly do this time around.”

“Dini wants to be settled with a daughter. I managed to keep that from happening this last time, but I’m not sure I can do it again. I’m not sure I want to, but I’d like to know I’m capable.”

“Which is why, when the two of you come into heat this time, you’ll be taking a few days off to join her at Mountain hold, period. She will go through basically what Ardenai did, though on a much smaller scale, and as she comes out of her heat and they put her back to bed, they’re going to put you in there on top of her, and you’ll put a baby in her like she wants you to.”

Teal winced, and it showed on his face. “And who is going to be on top of her in the meantime?”

“Someone trained for that specific job,” Ah’ren said, and gave him a sympathetic smile.

“Please, not Kestrel. Don’t tell me it’s him. The thought of him with my wife ...”

“No, not Kestrel. Kestrel is homophilic. There are many more of us than the ones you’ve seen so far, Beloved. She won’t be hurt. Ah’rane is going to have to go through the same thing. You and Krush can catch up on your reading and your sleep, and both Robin and Lark will be there in case either of you need company.”

Teal rode for a while without speaking, listening to the jingle as the horses worked their bits, the slight squeak of leather on leather where boot met saddle flap, the occasional ping as shrubs brushed stirrup irons. “Thank you. I know what you told me should make me feel better," he said at last.

"I didn't expect it to," she said. "Not right now, at least. Your life is changing, just like Ardi's. Things will calm down for the Rumpus Brothers, but it's going to be bumpy for a bit yet. We'll see if Kehailan has enough of his father in him that he needs gentling, and sooner or later we'll have to do the same thing for Criollo, which I know is your next question. Lark says he's fine for now, and she's good with the young ones, Teal. He won't be going back to Mountain hold for a couple of years, and that should keep him stable. Next question?"

Teal laughed in spite of himself. "I didn't bring you riding just to pick your brain, Ah'ren. You're my sister-in-law. I wanted your company. Ardi is so happy, so really joyful for the first time since Ah'ree got sick. I wanted to thank you for that, and to let you know that, because he loves you, I do too, and to let you know that I am thine, just as he is. You have but to ask."

"Thank you. His joy is mine, as well. It has been a long time since I've been in love with someone, and Ardenai is such a kind and gentle soul." She laughed and patted Pavil's neck as he tripped on a root. "Oops, careful there, handsome. I hope things work out for Ardenai and me."

"Me too," Teal said. "Very much."

He looked skyward and cocked his head slightly. "Did you hear that?" A few minutes later they could see the belly of an Imperial Time Whip Clipper as it slowed and settled below the tree line in the direction from which they'd come. "Looks like things are back to normal. We should probably head back."

They turned, and as they struck an easy canter Ah'ren pointed and said, "See that shrub way down there? The one that looks like a bent fishing pole on the right side of the runway?"

"I do," Teal sneered. "Surely you can't be serious about this. Pavil is all leg and no brain. He couldn't possibly run that far without forgetting what he's doing and veering off into the trees with you on board."

Ah'ren returned the sneer accompanied by a dismissive gesture. "Surely you don't think that draft horse you're riding can outrun a horse that's all leg, Master Captain. He's pretty, but he's a clopper. He has feet like dinner plates. He'll get tangled up in them and you'll be plowing the ground with your chin long before I'm being scraped off by a tree branch. I guarantee it."

"Have it your way," Teal said. "On three?"

"Absolutely." They counted together, laughing. "One. Two. Three!"

▲ ▲ ▲ ▲ ▲ ▲ ▲

Ardenai opened one eye and realized they were about to have company. He'd heard it enter the atmosphere, and now the white dot was growing larger. He got up grudgingly, dipped himself to wash off the sand, and went into the pavilion to brush his hair and put on something more than a briefcloth. He groused aloud as he tossed things onto the sleeping platform. "Trousers, socks, shirt, boots …" he'd really hoped to lie beside that pool with barely a stitch on for the entire day … a quick brush through the hair and a simple clip at the crown. He looked in the reflector. Acceptable. Little bleary in the eyes from sleeping with his face to the sun. He was wondering where everybody else was when he heard Kehailan's voice saying, "We put our clothes on for nothing. It's not Dominus, it's Regence. Pythos is back!"

That was different. Ardenai was out of the pavilion and halfway to the clipper with Kehailan when Pythos emerged and toddled toward them through the grass, arms extended for a hug. "Hatchlingss!" he hissed, flicking them both with his tongue and hugging them thoroughly. "My Babiess!"

"We've missed you!" Ardenai exclaimed. "Come, sit. Tell us news of home. How are Io and the twins? How is Eridi?"

They sat in the comfortable chairs in front of the kitchen pavilion and Kehailan excused himself to get them all something to drink. "Thee iss happy with thy new wife?" Pythos asked while Kehailan was gone.

"Very. Yes."

"Thee could learn to love her? To overlook her … mechanical inclinations?"

"I think so," Ardenai smiled, and dropped his eyes, telling the old doctor that it was progressing nicely. Good. If the Firstlord didn't look more rested he at least looked less wild in the eyes. His smile was quicker, his respiration slower. The correct choice had been made.

Kehailan returned and handed each of them a drink. "No sugar melon, I'm afraid," he smiled. "Right season, wrong planet. We'll have to ask them to plant a test patch at Stone Spring. Please, how are Io and Eridi?"

Pythos hissed with pleasure. Kehailan was finally a grown man. He looked like one and he acted like one. What a joy that was. He told them that Io was doing well. Her weight had gone up a little, and she was not going to be at all happy about the muscle tone she was losing, but both babies had attached themselves to the uterine wall and were growing until there was hardly any difference in size. "Boys, girls one of each?" Ardenai prompted, and Pythos just laughed his hissy laughter.

"Thee musst be patient."

"And Eridi?" Kehailan asked. "Will she recover?"

"Niccely, yess," Pythos replied, and described to them the procedure which had repaired the damage to her spinal column. She would be there a few more weeks for observation, and then she would be coming back here. Not in time for the Celebration of Storms, but shortly thereafter. Kehailan nodded and smiled, but both his father and Pythos sensed his disappointment.

"And thee, will not be home, young Captain. Thy sship keepss thee here."

"We will celebrate on board Dragonhorse," Kehailan smiled. "I won't be the only soul who is away from home for the Celebration. Who knows, we may all scramble down to one of the snow fields here on Tras and romp around for a day." He lost his smile and became more serious. "I do think Teal and the Firstlord should go home, at least for a bit...." he trailed off and shrugged slightly, moving his eyes from Pythos to the waterfall. "I worry about Gideon being separated from our father for so long. Ardenai is his whole world."

"Thee iss kind to think of thy family," Pythos responded. "Where iss thy uncle thiss fine morning?"

"Out riding with Ah'ren," Kehailan grinned. "I've told them it's you, so they're coming back a little more willingly."

"Sso," the old serpent hissed, casting his robes aside and toddling off to test the water, "hass everyone kept their ssecret?"

Kehailan and Ardenai looked at one another and grinned. Pythos was positively fierce about the 'who-got-who' of the gift giving. They knew if they so much as hinted in jest that the secret was out, he'd have a fit. It was tempting.

Having determined that the water was warm enough, Pythos toppled over, and a body that was awkward on land was suddenly sinuous and graceful, weaving in and out of the big pool, under the waterfall and back, humming with pleasure. *No one has answered me. Thee will not get the treats I brought if I am not pleased with the answers, hatchlings.*

I can only speak for myself, Ardenai responded, heading for the kitchen, *but I have not told anyone who I got, nor has anyone told me who they got. I hope by treats you don't mean a cage of tree toads, Pythos, hungry though I am. Ah, this looks promising.*

I am not likely to waste good tree toads on such as thyself, Firstlord. Make no mistake.

I've neither revealed, nor heard, Kehailan added. *I swear.*

"Then thee will get thy treat," Pythos said aloud, sliding out onto the sand to bake himself in the sun. "As ssoon as thy uncle and thy sstepmother return."

Kehailan burst out laughing at the image of Ah'ren as stepmother, and he was still chortling quietly from time to time when they heard voices and the slow canter of horses coming back to camp.

"Pythos!" Ah'ren exclaimed, and slid off Pavil's back to give the doctor a hug.

"You know Pythos?" Kehailan asked, catching Pavil's reins, and the two of them nodded together from their embrace.

"Many years," Ah'ren said. "Everybody knows Pythos."

"I … delivered Ah'ren," Pythos said, "In a manner of speaking."

The girl laughed. "By that he means he had me delivered here to be a wife for your father."

"Becausse I got hiss name for Ccelebration of Sstormss, and I wanted to give him ssomething extra nicce," Pythos hissed.

"Precious Equus," Teal laughed, coming to collect his own hug, "You, of all people, are the first to spill the secret? I'm glad you're back, my friend. How was your trip?"

"It wass wonderful, though I am feeling quite tired at this juncture," the doctor said, flicking Teal with his long tongue. "Pleasse, ssit. I would sspeak with the four of thee."

They sat obediently in the chairs and Pythos stood in front of them, teacher-like, and examined each of them. His babies. His precious hatchlings. He took Ardenai's right hand and turned it palm up. Still that mark persisted. Kehailan's pultronel burns were fading but apparent on his neck. Teal's arm was bandaged from wrist to elbow, but it didn't seem to be paining him, so there was a story that was probably going to end well. Ah'ren – beautiful Ah'ren – face alight with the joy of having a husband and family. What a blessing she was going to be.

"It iss very nearly time for the Ccelebration of Sstormss, and many of our own sstormss have we had thiss year, even ssince we drew namess. Io and Jilfan will not be particcipating, I am ssorry to ssay, but we have added Ardenai's lovely wife, who, as I sstated, iss my gift to him. And, from her ssmile, I would like to think sshe hass been gifted as well." He paused for dramatic emphasis, and pointed with a frondy finger toward Regence. "Io, drew Kehailan'ss name. Sshe ssusspected sshe might not be … available to ccelebrate with uss thiss year, and sshe alsso knew Kee would probably not get to come home. It wass therefore her hope that her gift to Kehailan would sserve as her love-gift to all of thee. Sso, with love from Io … a blesssed ccelebration!"

The door on the clipper opened, and out streaked Lionel, barking and running in circles to be followed by Gideon, Ah'rane, Krush, Criollo, and Ah'din. There was a moment of breathless, overjoyed shock, followed by laughing chaos as everyone tried to hug everyone else all at once. In the midst of it Gideon found Ardenai and buried his face against his father's neck, sobbing with joy and holding him as tight as he could for a long minute. Nearer the clipper Teal walked into Ah'din's outstretched arms with a sigh of relief which ended in laughter as he swung her around and kissed her thoroughly before hugging his son. Kehailan wrapped himself in the embrace of his grandparents and brother, allowing himself to be smothered in kisses and reveling in the exuberance around him. He always remembered that point in that day – where he was standing, even what people were wearing – because any lingering resentment he harbored toward Io slipped into memory and he, too, allowed Io to grow up.

Pythos stood with an arm around Ah'ren, watching the celebration. "Our very own herd of dragonhorssess," he chuckled. "I hope thee won't regret throwing in thy lot with them."

"Never," she replied. "My only worry is that Ardenai will choose to send me back when Io is well again."

"A choicce only he can make," the old physician hissed. The thought made him a little sad, because, knowing Io's grip on Ardenai, it was a real possibility.

As if to contradict Pythos' gloomy thoughts, Ardenai walked to where they were standing, gave him a long hug and asked if he could borrow his bride for a few minutes. Pythos nodded, and Ardenai turned to his family with his arm around Ah'ren. "I have someone I'd like all of you to meet," he said, and they gave him their attention. "This is Ah'ren. As you have probably seen via cosmoscope, we are married by order of the Great House and Mountain hold, and I can only hope she is as happy as I am about that."

"I am," she laughed. "Hello again, family!"

"And this time we know it's true!" Ah'rane said, extending her arms to the girl.

They swept her into a communal hug and Ardenai found himself once again bemused. It was Krush who extricated himself from the happy tangle and came to embrace his son a second time, kissing his temple and standing beside him. "We met her when she was on Achernar," he explained. "She was tempted to ask you to postpone the wedding a few days so we could be here, but, firstly, she wasn't sure you were going to want to marry her, and, secondly, she didn't want to maybe give away Io's surprise. Nice lady. Very thoughtful. And you do seem happy with her."

"I am thrice blessed a lucky husband," Ardenai said, scooping up Lionel with one hand and putting the other arm back around his father. "I'm so glad you're here. I've missed all of you very much." He held Lionel up beyond range of the frantic little tongue and gave him a cursory examination. "Gideon has grown over the last seasons. I see Lionel has not."

"Actually, he has. He's now a full six inches tall at the shoulder, four pounds one ounce of solid muscle and undiluted energy," Krush drawled. "Kraaling good mouser. I find him slightly more personable than your sister's ped, but don't tell her I said so."

There was a soft boom, and a cargo tender appeared, landing close to Regence in the meadow. A crew alighted and, with some suggestions, set up three more pavilions spaced amongst the trees along the river. Comfortable chairs, fleecy beds and furnishings went in with amazing speed, and Teal's two beds were traded for one bigger one. More chairs and fresh supplies were added to the kitchen, towels to the hot water lavage, and with friendly waves and wishes for an enjoyable holiday, the crew was gone, back to Dragonhorse.

"I assume the whole thing with the scrambleshafts was a ruse," Ardenai smiled, leaning into Gideon as they sat beside Pythos in the warm sand.

"Yess," Pythos chuckled. "It wass. I didn't want thee to sscatter. Sstill," he said, rolling over to toast the other side, "The sshaftss will not work for thee, nor will any of the craft leave the atmossphere for thee, until thee hass sspent three full dayss with thy family."

"You're going back so soon?" Ardenai asked, his face registering disappointment.

"No," Gideon said, hugging him close for the hundredth time and kissing his temple. "I think Pythos is saying you can go back to work in three days and not before. We'll be here awhile yet."

"How long?"

Ever close-mouthed, Gideon just smiled. "I think we're going to talk about that this evening over dinner," he said. He took off his boots and socks, tossed his shirt and trousers to one side and stretched out beside the old doctor. "I must say, this is a welcome change from the Great House of Equus and environs. I have leg muscles like a workhorse from pulling my feet through the snow." He wiggled his fingers in the warm sand, and the tiny dog scooched a little closer without getting up. "Naptime," he managed, and in the next breath he was asleep.

"It wass a long trip, and a little crowded," Pythos said by way of explanation, and his eyes, too, snicked shut and stayed that way.

Ardenai looked around. Criollo was sprawled on a huge boulder watching the waterfall, Ah'rane and Krush were lounging in the shade, sipping drinks and visiting quietly with Kehailan and Ah'ren, and Teal and Ah'din were walking slowly hand in hand on the path he and Teal usually ran in the morning. There was a good hour left before lunch. The temptation was just too much. He threw his clothes into the pile with Gideon's, and went back to sleep.

▲ ▲ ▲ ▲ ▲ ▲ ▲

"It's pretty well healed," Teal was saying. "Please don't worry. It's fine."

"I'll feel better if you let me look at it," Ah'din replied, and in her quiet voice was the end of a discussion Teal was not wanting to have at that point. He just wanted to hold her, and look at her, and hold her some more. He didn't want to talk, necessarily, and he certainly didn't want to have to explain that wretched bite.

"Right now? Can't we just visit awhile first? I can't believe you're here, Ah'din. I keep expecting to wake up."

"Ah'clare Teal Gidran. Sit, and quit trying to distract me. I won't be able to think about another thing until I know you're not fibbing about that … expanse of bandage."

He looked at the set of her mouth and parked obediently on a boulder, extending his arm. "All right, but you'll have to re-bandage it if you unwrap it, which means we'll have to go back to camp. There's probably material to do that in Regence. Maybe not though. I knocked the scab off two or three days ago and Ensharra says the chance of reinfection is pretty high if I'm not careful with it."

No luck. She was going to unwrap the thing, take one look at it, and start screaming. He just knew it. Their quiet morning ramble to some remote and romantic location was going to turn into a visit to the sanecere bay on Dragonhorse, or he missed his guess.

She took off the tape, carefully unwrapped the gauze, and groaned at the circular wound and long radiating scars where the anchoress had cut away flesh. "Oh, Sweetheart," she breathed, and looked at him with pity in her eyes. "This must have hurt terribly."

"Not so much," he smiled, tracing the side of her face with his finger. "What the boy had in his system made me a little sick for a few days, but I'm good now."

To his surprise she nodded. "I can see that. This is beautiful work, given the circumstances." She discarded the packing, replaced the gauze without further comment and gave the arm a tiny pat.

"Really? That's it?"

"Really," she smiled, putting her arms around his neck. "I'm looking forward to meeting Anchoress Ensharra."

Teal slid his arms around her waist and kissed her, laving himself in the taste and fragrance of her – the way her skin felt against his. "You'll like her," he murmured, lips against her neck. "Probably won't have to knock her out or anything."

"Good," Ah'din laughed. "Say, Master Captain, I don't suppose there's another place along this river where we could go for a private little swim, is there? I am not used to this heat."

"If you're up for walking another couple furlongs, I know a quiet pool where the trees hang over the river and the rocks are big and smooth," Teal replied, moving the collar of her blouse with one finger and teething gently where her neck met her shoulder.

"Mmmmm," she responded. "Are we going to be late for lunch?"

"Depends on what you think is on the menu," her husband laughed.

They did talk after a while, resting in the shallows with their backs against an ancient boulder, facing away from the sun, looking at the tall trees and verdant hills – speaking of small things – the beautiful surroundings and whether rhax vines might grow here, the Evangeline's Carpet which grew in profusion, the romantic suite in the crystal city.

At that point Teal hesitated, just momentarily, but for Ah'din, it was enough. "What's wrong?" she asked gently, turning to catch his face in her hands.

"Nothing," he smiled, putting his hand over hers to kiss her palm. "How could anything be wrong with you here?"

"Nothing usually means something," she replied, gliding over into his lap. His response was quick, and he pulled her tight against him to gain entry again.

"Nothing means something if you're a woman," he grinned, and cocked his head to nibble along her neck. "If you're a man, nothing usually means nothing."

He caught her hips as he pushed up and she put her hands on the rock behind him – watching his wonderfully expressive face, loving the pleasure she brought him.

▲ ▲ ▲ ▲ ▲ ▲ ▲

"I'd ask what you two have been up to," Krush grinned, "but I think your general state speaks to that." Ah'rane poked him in the thigh and he subsided with a snort and a snicker to continue his lunch.

"We forgot to take towels," Teal said. "Air drying tends to rumple one."

"Which explains everything," Krush replied, eyes fixed on his plate so as not to get another poke. That woman knew exactly where to jab her finger, and exactly how hard, to cause damage. He controlled his smile and looked up at his son-in-law. "Has your wife had a chance to look at your arm?"

"I have," Ah'din smiled. Her nose had gotten a little sun, and the water and perspiration had curled the tendrils of hair escaping her thick braid.

She already looks so much better, Krush thought. *It was the right choice to come, just to get her into the arms of her good husband. They truly do adore one another.*

"I think it might be ready for a little air, but I'll want to talk to Ensharra first."

"Would you like to meet her this afternoon?" Teal asked. "She got a concussion a couple of days ago, so we have her recuperating at Stone Spring. I'm sure she's more than ready for company."

"Tomorrow," Ah'din smiled. "Today I just want to be with my family."

"And by that she means her husband, her brother and her eldest nephew," Criollo said, reaching for the juice pitcher. "After five days in a fifty foot clipper, she's seen more than enough of the rest of us."

"It was a little smaller than I remembered it," Gideon admitted, not wanting to sound whiny. "Of course Regence is set up differently than Dominus. There's no master suite for the Dragonhorse. That freed up some room in the front. Those four foot wide bunks were nice. A little tight after my six footer at home." He took a bite of food. "Criollo snores."

"Criollo does not snore," that one replied, "your dog snores like a rooting cerastaper."

"Perhaps having the two of you sharing a pavilion for however long isn't such a good idea," Ah'rane said. "Which one of you would like to sleep with your grandsire and me?" She fixed the two of them in that gaze grandmothers get the instant the first grandchild is born, and then cocked her head to one side and smiled. "Are you going to be comfortable together then?" They both nodded.

"Well that's a load off my mind," Krush said. "I don't care for a crowded bed, myself. Which reminds me, which of these inviting spaces belongs to whom?"

"This closest one is Ah'ren's and mine," Ardenai said. "It's the original. The one farthest downriver by the other pool was set up for Teal. I honestly haven't looked and didn't pay attention. Are they all the same?"

"Field trip," Kehailan laughed, mimicking his father. They all got up and walked a hundred feet or so through the dappled sunlight toward the pavilion closest to the waterfall and slightly upriver from Ardenai's space.

"This is wonderful," Ah'rane sighed. "I love winter, I do, but to be able to smell the grass and the leaves and the water … feel the sun on my skin …." she sighed again with contentment and put her head on Krush's shoulder as they walked.

They reached the pavilion, rolled up the front and looked inside. Thick rugs, comfortable chairs, low table with cushioned seating, a large fleecy bed on a platform, small storage chest on each side, grooming table and reflector fitting in one of the solid corners, a scattering of luxurious pillows. Gideon stood to one side and leaned into his father.

I hope they're not all like this. Criollo's already miffed because he had to come, and if he has to sleep with Lionel and me another night there will be open warfare.

I'll make sure you have separate beds. Or do you need separate tents as well?

We'll be fine, I hope. We're both tired of being cooped up, and Criollo didn't want to leave Jasreth. Once he gets interested in other things he'll come around.

"Moving on," Krush said, smiling at the two of them, and they walked back further into the trees and again slightly upriver another long hundred feet to where a fourth large, square pavilion had been pitched. "All the same size outside," he observed.

"All standard Horse Guard issue," Teal smiled. He took the cord for the front section and rolled it up as he spoke. "And so far, all the same on the inside, as well."

"I know they can change the interiors in these very fast," Ardenai said. "Teal had that one changed for Ah'ren and me."

"From the time I called them until the job was done and I'd inspected it was just about an hour and a half, so they're quick," Teal affirmed, sensing tension. "You and Gideon don't have to worry about sharing a bed. As a matter of fact, would you like separate quarters? I think we have some smaller pavilions."

"We're good," Criollo grinned. "How can we plot mischief if we're separated?"

"Good point," his sire nodded and shot a glance at Ardenai, who smothered a snort of amusement as he winked at his brother-in-law.

The last pavilion was furthest back in the trees and downriver between Ardenai and Teal. In that one they found two beds set up as Ardenai's had been originally. "This one is definitely ours," Criollo said. "Which bed?"

Gideon shook his head. "You've had to listen to Lionel snore for five days. You choose."

Criollo pointed to the one with the head downriver, and without a word between them the boys walked to the clipper to begin collecting their things.

"Pythos?" Kehailan asked. "Have you chosen a spot? You are welcome to share my pavilion to whatever extent you desire."

"Then I sshall keep my thingss in thy pavilion and ssleep in yonder tree," he hissed, gesturing toward the big tree at the edge of the meadow. "Thy thoughtfulness in assking iss much apprecciated, Captain."

"So, are we now sorted out?" Ardenai asked. "Mother, which space would please you most?"

"If it pleases my husband, the one by the waterfall," she smiled. "Kehailan, do you mind?"

"Not at all," he said. "I'm sure your vacation will last longer than mine, and I will probably be sleeping onboard most of the time, so you sleep wherever your heart desires."

"Well now that we've figured out for sleeping, how about doing something with our awake time?" Ah'ren said. "Teal and I had our ride cut short this morning. Would anyone fancy an afternoon canter?"

"Wonderful idea!" Krush laughed. "Wife?"

Ah'rane immediately agreed, the two boys willingly put their housekeeping duties aside, Kehailan said he'd enjoy it, which surprised everyone – even him – and Ardenai was excited. His whole family was going riding. Pythos said he would guard the camp, and everyone else went to the meadow to select a mount. "I think I should tell you," Teal said, leaning into Ardenai, "Pavil has fallen in love with someone else and wants a divorce."

"I'm devastated," Ardenai chuckled. "He's fallen for my wife, hasn't he, the fickle creature."

"Absolutely adores her."

"Fine," Ardenai laughed. "Ah'ren," he called, "As my traditional wedding gift, groom to bride – consider Pavil your own."

"Really?" she laughed, and he could see that she was truly excited. She could love a horse that Ardenai had never been able to. That made it a double gift. Ah'ren got Pavil, Pavil got Ah'ren.

"Really."

"Now you need a horse," Teal chuckled. He raised his voice and made a gesture to include all of them. "If one of these animals is already yours, take it." Ah'ren immediately called Pavil, and Teal gestured for her to remove Poseidon, as well.

Krush caught a big bay with one white stocking, saying, "We get along well."

So, Krush had sent himself a horse, Ardenai thought. How long had he known they were coming? Many things to be explored in conversation while they were here.

"Everyone else, stand at a distance from one another, extend your arms wide, low and in front of you, palms up. Good. Close your eyes, and exhale slowly and fully. Empty your minds – just keep breathing." He extended his arms in the same gesture, watching his family, then the horses. At first they didn't move at all, then slowly and curiously they began to move from one person to another, muzzles extended, ears forward, nostrils flared.

Ah'ren was spellbound. She stole a look at Krush, who put a finger to his lips.

The Master of Horse at work, he smiled. *Can you hear me, Ah'ren?*

Thank you, yes. What is he doing?

Inviting the horses to find common ground with the riders. Opening the receptors and finding like markers within the chemistry of their breath. People aren't very good at that, but horses do it very well.

So the rider is not choosing the horse, the horse is choosing a rider?

For the moment. Teal hasn't had much time with these individual horses, so this isn't as thorough as it would ordinarily be. Since we're just going for an afternoon canter and not off to war or into competition, it isn't nearly as important – more a courtesy to the horses.

How much of this is Teal controlling?

I can marvel, but I cannot explain.

Ah'ren's mouth formed an admiring Ohh, and she leaned against Pavil, watching the horses mosey around slower and slower until they finally stopped. Like the spinners in a child's game, each animal came to stand in front a rider, necks outstretched to smell their breath, before dropping their heads and relaxing their ears.

"Your horses stand before you," Teal said quietly. "Open your eyes and acquaint yourselves."

Ardenai found himself facing a big, bright chestnut mare with a flaxen mane and tail, Ah'din's mare was pure white and dainty despite her formidable sixteen hands. Criollo was looking at a paint like his own Bimini, and later discovered they were brothers. Ah'rane extended her hand to a sweet-faced palomino, and Kehailan returned the gentle gaze of a blaze-faced bay. Gideon opened just one eye, assuming that since he was not Equi he had not attracted a mount, but a sassy buckskin gelding with mischievous eyes shook his black mane as if to ask what he was waiting for.

They rode companionably in groups, the three women laughing, talking about herbs and gardens and how lovely it would be to have a cold weather keep here and live in endless flowers and growth. Criollo and Gideon rode off to one side, pointing at different landmarks and getting their bearings while Lionel lolled out of his special backpack and looked curiously around. The four men jogged slowly abreast, and even as they were talking Ardenai was keenly aware that his father was studying them one at a time, first himself, then Teal, then Kehailan. It was his right and duty as patriarch, and at some point his evaluation would be forthcoming. In the meantime all of them enjoyed his company, eager to share their adventures and observations.

They all stopped at one point and listened. Apart from the breathing of the horses and the movement of tack, the river in the distance and the slight soughing of wind in the grass, there was not a sound – not the whine of an insect, the song of a bird. Nothing.

"Part of the mystery of the planet," Ardenai said, and between Teal and himself they explained as best they could what legend and science thought may have happened.

No, there was no evidence that it had been terraformed, or re-terraformed. Deep scans had not produced roads, buildings, bunkers or power stations. No construction debris such as gravel pits or quarries. No cemeteries, no skeletons. No animals bigger than burrowing bats or miniature rock pykies – nothing that burrowed deep – so far nothing that swam, swarmed or left a footprint big enough to see unless one laid on the ground and stared awhile.

"It took thought," Ah'din said. "The insects would have taken over the planet if they hadn't left the bats."

"Or planted the bats," Gideon added.

"Fascinating," Ah'rane said. "Maybe what you think are ruins, were props. They would register as habitation from space, and anyone cruising by would think the place was populated."

Ardenai chewed on that for a minute or so. "Maybe," he said. "It just seems to me that if you wanted a place to seem populated you'd go to a little more work than that."

"Maybe they burned the bodies to ash, and that's why there's no trace," Criollo suggested.

"Maybe the mother ship picked them up and said they'd found someplace more hospitable to colonize," Ah'ren added. "They took everything with them so as not to leave a footprint."

"There's always the Glastaline Theory," Teal muttered.

Just saying the word gave him the shivers. He could still hear Ardenai screaming, blood forming at the corners of his mouth as his throat tore. How close they had come to not getting him out of there. Teal shook his head to make the screams subside. Time for a little more of Ensharra's quieting concoction. How grateful he was that Ardenai had been too traumatized to remember much about it. If he did remember, it never surfaced in thought or sleep.

"What's the Glastaline Theory?" Ah'din asked, sensing her husband's discomfort, and Teal explained as best he could about the original fighting dome from which they'd extricated Ardenai and Konik, and the subterranean one they'd found only recently – much larger and more sophisticated – and the secrets it so capably held.

"And you're thinking we're riding on top of one like it?" Krush asked. The thought struck him funny, but obviously it was in no way amusing to his son-in-law.

"I'm not completely convinced we're not," Teal said, adding an apologetic eyebrow. "Ardi's working on a recognition code, and I should just let it go until then."

"You don't think the horses would recognize it?" Criollo asked. "Don't they know when they're on top of anything hollow, no matter how deep it is?"

"So history tells us," Krush smiled.

"Aren't we supposed to be on holiday?" Gideon said in a quavering voice, and when they looked at him he burst out laughing. "Well, aren't we? We've been apart for such a miserably long time, can't the planet take care of itself awhile – three days? Then we'll all go to work on this problem. At least I will. I promise."

"The family oracle has spoken," Ardenai grinned, and the subject was changed.

They reined east and rode higher into the foothills as the shadows grew longer and the grass turned to gold as the sun began to go down. They watched it from the top of an outcropping as it dropped beneath the horizon, and Ardenai flipped a hand back toward camp.

"There's not much twilight here. Not the best for seeing, at least until we're on the flat again."

Everyone had been avoiding the question of how long the family was going to stay, but as they angled down the slope and back into the meadow Kehailan's curiosity got the better of him and he ventured, "Who is keeping for you, Grandsire?" Short term the tenant families who traditionally shared

Sea keep and Canyon keep would care for the homes and horses. Longer term, someone would probably be brought in. "Anyone we know?"

"Would I leave our home with strangers?" came the cryptic reply.

"Gideon," his father said, reining his mare a little closer to the buckskin, "I asked you earlier about your school work, and I think you dodged the question. I ask you again, Son …."

"I have enough work with me to last until I have sons my age, if I were to have sons. Believe me, I have more than enough assignments and some suggestions for learning in motion, so I'm good. Criollo has work, too."

"So much for keeping that a secret," Criollo muttered, rolling his eyes.

"I trust you're taking time each day for schooling?"

"You're joking, right?" Gideon snorted. "Dad, look who I'm with. Of course I'm taking time every day for school. I caught my grandsire reading to me while I slept one night."

"I will ask no more questions," the Firstlord laughed. "We are just going to make it back to camp before dark. Maybe we should pick up the pace a little."

They were just unsaddling when they heard an aggravated hiss and Pythos' voice drifted down. "I feared I wass being caught in a sstampede," he grumbled. They could see him, barely – draped over a limb halfway up the tree, yellow eyes slightly luminescent, winking from time to time as he blinked. "I cooked for thee, and dinner is sserved at thy conveniencce."

"That's alarming," Criollo whispered, and another hiss from up in the branches told him the old dragon's hearing was still sharp.

The women went ahead to check out Pythos' story and make any necessary repairs while the men brushed and turned out the horses. They washed up and came trooping in to find three lounging women, the kitchen lit with hanging lanterns, the table set, and a full meal in the warming trays – no sign of tree toads or wood rats.

Everyone was suitably impressed until Ardenai observed that the flowers on the table were Menorquin Shore Lilies. "Not that I am in any way attempting to undermine our good physician's story," he laughed, "but I do smell more than lilies in this case."

"Thee hass been too long, too deep in the politicss of thiss placce," Pythos chortled, appearing to take his seat at the table. "Pleasse, enjoy thy dinner. Gallioss ssent the food when he ssent the ssugar melon Kehailan sso kindly requessted for thiss unworthy reccipient."

"You brought me my family," Kehailan replied. "The least I can do is see if there are sugar melons anywhere for you. Besides, what is a warm season holiday without sugar melons?"

"What indeed?" Krush laughed. The lamplight caught the silver in his hair as he turned to pass one of the platters, and in his handsome, weathered face they saw both Ah'din and Criollo.

"I wish you were here forever," Teal blurted, then caught himself and flashed an apologetic smile. "I'm sorry. I know you can't be, of course, but this just feels so good to have everybody around a dinner table again … talking about everything … except what three or four of us most want to know." He laughed and gave Krush an affectionate, one armed hug. "I think we've been exceptionally patient. Out with it, Sire. For how long will we have our family intact?"

Krush put down his eating sticks and prepared to speak. "Well, your mother ..." he began.

"Not your father, of course," Ah'rane drawled.

Krush was not deterred. "She worries, you know. Ah'din has been pining for her husband, Gideon for his sire. That big old house at Canyon keep just seems to get emptier and emptier and Sea keep is already closed. A house needs a family more than a family needs a house." He paused and reached for the pitcher of ammon milk.

Ardenai looked at Teal. "We're going to have to drag this out of him."

"Um hm."

"Let's ask my granddam," Kehailan suggested. "She's a much softer touch."

"I'm getting there," Krush grumbled. "You've been in too many kraaling meetings where everyone speaks without thinking first. So … at the end of three days we are going off holiday and on to work. This planet needs experts, and we have come to offer our expertise. We do not have the first foals due until Latter Omphas, so until First Omphas … we are yours."

"That's nearly two full seasons!" Ardenai laughed. "Really? Please say you're not joking, Sire."

"He's not joking, Sweetheart," Ah'rane said, rejoicing in the happy faces of her family. It had been a hard decision in so many ways, and now it all seemed worthwhile. "Master Darley is overseeing care of the house and horses, along with several others from the Great House who love you, and we're looking forward to doing something different. I am going to be working with the city engineers to develop alternative transit and phase out combustion engines."

"I am going to be working with the anchoresses and the survey teams learning about Lebonathi herbs and herbal medicine," Ah'din said, leaning her head against her husband's shoulder.

Everyone looked expectantly at Krush, who stopped with a bite partway to his mouth.

"Nothing," he said, put the food in his mouth and chewed at leisure. "I'm on holiday. I don't plan to do a blessed thing. I'm going to lie around in the sun, ride these hills maybe looking for a nice little place to keep in the cold months, swim in these wonderful, warm pools and do as little as I possibly can."

"So your comment about all of you going on to work, was overstated?" Teal said. He knew Krush better than to think he had nothing planned. "You're not going to help anybody with horses or anything? Not going to help Ah'ren with laying out keeps, provide her company as she surveys? That is truly amazing."

"I will keep the camp," he said firmly. "I will cook the meals and make the beds. I will make sure the boys keep their noses in their studies. If there is time after that, I may help with other things." He put down his eating sticks and reached for his glass. "The womenfolk had a good idea what they wanted to do before they ever came. I wasn't sure so I thought I'd explore the possibilities after I got here."

"Sounds like you're letting yourself in for the hardest job of all," Kehailan said. "I give you a week of camp duty before you're bored silly."

"Then we'll revisit it in a week," his grandsire said. "Right now, I'm going to finish my dinner, go for a leisurely swim, and then stretch out on the bank and watch the stars and the good ship Belesprit go over."

▲ ▲ ▲ ▲ ▲ ▲ ▲

"How delightful is this?" Ardenai whispered, lying with Ah'ren in his arms, listening to the river sounds outside their pavilion and hearing Gideon's laughter in the distance.

"Your family is here," she said, kissing him where neck met shoulder. "You must be very happy."

"Our family is here," he corrected gently. "And you, you are very good at keeping secrets, dear wife. I had absolutely no idea you'd met them before … other than at Mountain hold, of course, and they don't remember you, because they're not supposed to."

"I suppose it's jaded to say I've had lots of practice," she murmured.

"If you are taking your lives as a collective I suppose it is. But this is a new place, and a new life. Which reminds me, I was asked how old my bride is, and I had no answer. Given we were thrown together that will work for a while, but we do need a backstory."

"According to our contract, I am seventy-three," she said. "As to the rest of the backstory …." she shrugged slightly against him and said nothing more.

He sensed the weight of the silence and rolled so he was looking down at her, and she traced his profile with one finger. "Just a little bump in the nose. Just enough," she said. "You really are a beautiful creature, Ardenai Morning Star."

"Thank you," he whispered. "May I impose myself on you again, or are you tired?"

"I can't imagine being too tired to want to make love to you," she said, sighing with pleasure.

"Tell me something," he said, moving slowly and deeply, lips against the side of her neck, "If it is not too personal a question, how long were you married to my great grandfather?"

"One hundred and forty-eight years," she said, "from the year he rose to be Firstlord until the day he died." Ardenai felt her breath shudder, and realized she was trying not to cry. He started to withdraw and she put her legs around his waist to stop him. "Don't go. Every minute with you is precious. Every minute here on this planet, and with your family is precious."

"Ah'ren, Beloved, please tell me what troubles you," he said, raising up on his forearms to study her by starlight and stroking her hair back from her face. "Are you afraid I'm going to send you back when Io is well again?" She nodded, saying nothing. "I thought that might be it. Remember what I said the other night? As long as I live, I am thine. I meant it. What we have to work out with Io, we will work out with Io. But as to sending you back? Never. I'm the competitive sort. If you were married for a hundred and forty-eight years to the Tenth Dragonhorse, then we will try for at least a hundred and forty-nine."

"Ardenai, be sure you're not just speaking from the euphoria of having your family here. There may be sharp curves in the road ahead."

"There are always sharp curves in the road. Why, do you want to go back?"

"Absolutely not," she breathed. "I love you with all my heart."

"And I love you, Dear Wife. You are beautiful and wise, and I should finish us up here so you can get some sleep."

"I will need my strength, yes," she murmured, moving her lips toward his. "Tomorrow my brother-in-law is going to begin teaching me the intricacies of the Phyllan Wolf Dance."

THE ELEVEN PLANETS OF THE AFFINED EQUI WORLDS (AEW)

Equus
Menorquin
Corvus
Amberia
Demeter
Anguine Prime
Anguine II
Papillia
Phylla
Calumet
Terren

IMPERIAL STORMCLASS TACTICAL CRUISERS

AEW planet of assignation and commanding officer

ISTC XIII "Dragonhorse"– *Equus.* Flagship. Ah'ree Kehailan Ardenai

ISTC I "The Dragon's Teeth" – *Amberia.* Ulric Hamar

ISTC IV "The Dragon's Claws"– *Calumet.* Ah'calla Mecklin Pentro

ISTC V "The Dragon's Hide"– *Corvus.* Cadence Holofernes

ISTC X "The Dragon's Tail" – *Terren.* Marion Eletsky

ISTC II – *Anguine Prime.* Under Construction. Unassigned

ISTC III – *Anguine II.* Under Construction. Offer on table

ISTC VI – *Demeter.* Under Construction. Unassigned

ISTC VII – *Menorquin.* Under construction. Unassigned

ISTC VIII – *Papillia.* Under Construction. Unassigned

ISTC IX – *Phylla.* Under Construction. Unassigned

ISTC XI – *Equus.* Under Construction. Unassigned

ISTC XII – *TBD.* Under Construction. Unassigned (Speculation has it that this ship will be assigned to control Lebonathi space, though no announcement has been made.)

CHARACTER LIST
(Alphabetically)

Ah'brianne – *Equi.* Daughter of Timor and Ah'mae. Love interest of Gideon. Criollo's best friend.

Abeyan – *Equi.* Master of the Equi Cavalry. Ah'riodin's father.

Addur – *Lebonathi.* Deceased. One of Eridu's sons by a secondary wife.

Ah'davan – *Equi.* (Addie) Wife of Konik

Ah'din – *Equi.* (Dini, Din) Wife of Teal, sister of Ardenai, mother of Criollo.

Ah'keena – *Equi.* Wife of Tarpan. Part of the expedition cavalry contingent on Lebonath Tras.

Ah'kra – *Anguine.* Second wife of Abeyan.

Ah'krill – *Equi.* High Priestess. Ardenai's birth mother.

Ah'lauren – *Equi.* Part time member of the expeditionary forces. Wife of Rounce. Mother of twin boys.

Ah'leah – *Equi.* Ah'riodin and Ardenai's infant daughter lost before birth.

Ah'nis – *Equi.* A priestess. Governor of women's Affairs, guardian of Lebonathi Princess Eridi.

Ah'rane – *Equi.* Sister/mother of Ardenai. Wife of Krush. Mother of Ah'din.

Ah'ree – *Equi.* Deceased. Beloved first wife of Ardenai, who raised Ah'riodin in her father's absence.

Ah'riodin – *Equi/Papilli cross.* (Io) Abeyan Ah'riodin Ardenai Morning Star. Wife of Ardenai, Primuxori of Equus. Daughter of Abeyan, mother of Jilfan.

Akadia – *Lebonathi.* Servant who accompanied the Lebonathi delegation to Equus. Wife of Telloh. Naram's lover.

Amir Cohen – *Terren/Demetrian.* Computator Technologist aboard Belesprit.

Ardenai – *Equi.* (Ardi) Ah'rane Ardenai Krush, who becomes Ah'krill Ardenai Morning Star, the Thirteenth Dragonhorse. Firstlord of Equus. First wife, Ah'ree, second wife, Ah'riodin. Fostered by Krush and Ah'rane, birthed by High Priestess Ah'krill.

Aruda – *Lebonathi.* Member of the Lebonathi High Council.

Ashur – *Lebonathi.* One of the five scientists Ardenai finds surviving in the mountains.

Bashkir – *Equi.* Steward of the Great House of Equus.

Basra – *Lebonathi.* One of Eridu's sons by a secondary wife.

Bonfire Dannis – *Phyllan.* Temporary Captain of Seventh Galactic Alliance Science Vessel, Belesprit.

Brak – *Lebonathi.* Standard Bearer. Married to Phaedra. Son is Rakba.

Cadence Holofernes – *Corvi.* Captain of ISTC 5, "The Dragon's Hide" Wife of Merrilina.

Catrio – *Equi.* Member of the Horse Guard of the Great House of Equus. Girsu's companion and lover.

Chirion – *Androtech.* (Master Darley.) One of the most ancient Androtech beings. He spends most of his time away from Mountain hold in various guises, guiding the Dragonhorses and their associates.

Cornwallis Mettenger – *Terren.* (Wally) Seventh Galactic Alliance Observer.

Criollo – *Equi.* Ah'din Criollo Teal. Only son of Teal and Ah'din. Nephew of Ardenai.

Cutter – *Equi.* Communications officer on temporary assignment from the Great House of Equus to Dragonhorse Ten.

Dagan – *Lebonathi.* High Council member.

Dresh – *Amberian.* SGA trooper. On special assignment from Ardenai.

Elam – *Lebonathi.* The youngest of the male scientists hidden in the mountains. Father of Umma, Husband of Larsa.

Ellsbeth – *Demetrian.* SGA trooper. On special assignment from Ardenai.

Ensharra – *Lebonathi.* (Anchoress). The priestess of the ancient city, who befriends the Equi.

Eridi – *Lebonathi.* Princess. Child of Eridu and Lulana. Given to Ardenai as a flesh-gift.

Eridu – *Lebonathi.* Ruler of the Lebonathi Worlds. Father of Eridi. First-wife, Lulana, Eridi's mother.

Etana – *Lebonathi.* The older of the two women scientists Ardenai finds surviving in the mountains.

Gallios – *Menorquin.* General Manager of the terraformers turned farm ships.

Gerritson – *Amberian.* SGA trooper. On special assignment from Ardenai.

Gideon – *Declivian/Terren/Coronian/Equi.* Gideon Ardenai Morning Star. Adopted son of Ardenai.

Gidran – *Equi.* Teal's father. Husband of Ah'clare.

Girsu – *Lebonathi.* Came with the Lebonathi delegation to Equus and is given political asylum. Uncle of Jasreth.

Halaf – *Lebonathi.* Secretary General. Flamen.

Hamazi – *Lebonathi.* Flamen.

Harrier – *Androtech.* One of the most ancients of Mountain hold. Chef extraordinaire.

Hassuna – *Lebonathi.* Servant who accompanied the Lebonathi delegation to Equus.

Hunter – *Equi.* Serving aboard ISTC Dragonhorse Thirteen.

Isin – *Lebonathi.* One of the five hidden scientists Ardenai finds.

Jasreth – *Lebonathi.* Niece of Girsu. Love interest of Criollo.

Jilfan – *Equi/Papilli.* Son of Ah'riodin by Salerno. Grandson of Abeyan. Ardenai's stepson.

Karum – *Lebonathi.* Member of the Lebonathi High Council.

Karun – *Lebonathi.* High Council Member.

Kehailan – *Equi.* (Kee) Ah'ree Kehailan Ardenai. Eldest son of Ardenai. Captain of ISTC Thirteen, "Dragonhorse."

Kestrel – *Androtech.* One of the most ancient of the Androtech beings. Supervises much of what goes on at Mountain hold and beyond. Roundly disliked by all who have to deal with him.

Konik – *Equi.* (Nik) Ah'ria Konik Nokota. Senator from Anguine II. Married to Ah'davan.

Krush – *Equi.* Foster father of Ardenai. Husband of Ah'rane. Father of Ah'din. Father-in-law to Teal.

Lagash – *Lebonathi.* Member of the Lebonathi High Council.

Landais – *Equi.* Master Smith for the Great House of Equus.

Lark – *Androtech.* One of the most ancient and beautiful Androtech beings who inhabit Mountain hold.

Larsa – *Lebonathi.* The younger of the two women scientists Ardenai finds. Mother of Umma, Wife of Elam.

Liadin – *Papilli.* Stable Master for the polo fields on Jocundome Three.

Lornak – *Equi.* Sexual class N-Gen. Expert on dioecious date palms.

Lulana – *Lebonathi.* Firstwife of Eridu. Mother of Eridi. Sister of Phaedra and Naram.

Marion Eletsky – *Terren.* Former Captain of SGASV Belesprit. Currently captain of Imperial Stormclass Tactical Cruiser Ten. "The Dragon's Tail."

Mecklin – *Calumet.* Captain of ISTC 4, "The Dragon's Hoof." Brother of Ah'nora, who carries Ardenai's son.

Merrilina – *Calumet.* Technologist aboard ISTC 5. Wife of Cadence Holofernes.

Nagar the Zealot – *Lebonathi.* Flamen.

Naram – *Lebonathi.* Nuntius d'Affaires to Eridu. Later Lebonathi Regent.

Nika – *Lebonathi.* Wife of Nagar the Zealot.

Oona Pongo – *Terren.* Communications Officer aboard Belesprit.

Phaedra – *Lebonathi.* Brak's wife. Mother of Rakba, sister to Lulana and Naram

Pyron – *Papilli.* Gate Keeper of Jocundome Number Three.

Pythos – *Achernarean.* One of the serpent physicians of Achernar, personal physician to Ardenai and his household, and one of his closest advisors.

Rakba – *Lebonathi.* Small son of Brak and Phaedra.

Robin – *Androtech.* Sent from Mountain hold to be Teal's hetaera and companion.

Rounce – *Equi.* Part time farmer/member of the expeditionary forces. Husband of Ah'lauren.

Salerno – *Equi.* Ah'riodin's first husband, killed in battle. Father of Jilfan.

Samarra – *Lebonathi.* Anchoress who comes with the Lebonathi delegation to Equus.

Sardure – *Telenir.* Right hand to Sarkhan until replaced by Konik.

Saremanno – *Telenir.* Father of Sarkhan and Sardure, stepfather to Ah'cora.

Sarkhan – *Telenir.* Deceased. Sought to overthrow the government and kill the Thirteenth Dragonhorse.

Tarpan – *Equi.* Commander of the expedition cavalry contingent assigned to Lebonath Tras.

Teal – *Equi.* Ah'clare Teal Gidran. Former Master of Horse, now Master Captain and Ardenai's closest advisor. Married to Ardenai's sister, Ah'din.

Telloh – *Lebonathi.* Husband of Akadia.

Timor – *Equi.* Ardenai's neighbor. Ah'mae's husband, Ah'brianne's father.

Timothy McGill – *Demetrian/Terren.* (Tim). Botanist aboard Belesprit. Kehailan's friend and lover.

Ulric Hamar – *Amberian.* Captain of Imperial Stormclass Tactical Cruiser One, "The Dragon's Teeth."

Umma – *Lebonathi.* Infant daughter of Elam and Larsa.

Winslow Moonsgold – *Declivian.* (Winnie). Chief Medical officer aboard Belesprit. Pythos' sidekick.

Wren – *Equi/Androtech.* (Ah'ren.) Ancient and beautiful Androtech being from Mountain hold, who is Ardenai's hetaera.

OTHER NAMES OF IMPORT

Eladeus – the Equi name for the Creator Spirit

El'Shadai – the Declivian name for the Creator Spirit

THE ANCIENT LINES OF THE GREAT HOUSE

Equine – From which most of the Dragonhorses have come, including Ardenai

Waterfowl – More ancient than Equine. Teal is from this line

Aviarium – More ancient yet. Represented mostly by the ancient beings of Mountain hold

Arboranthus – An early line which has fallen into obscurity, but is still represented

Achernarean – Represented by the venerable and powerful sea dragons

HOW EQUI NAMES WORK

A woman carries her father's name first, then her given name, then her mother's name. For example: Ah'din was Krush Ah'din Ah'rane before her marriage to Teal, at which time she took his given name to become Krush Ah'din Teal.

A man carries his mother's name first, then his given name, then his father's name. This does not change when he marries. Hence Ardenai was Ah'rane Ardenai Krush. When he rose to become Dragonhorse his name became Ah'krill Ardenai Morning Star. Morning Star being the designate of all the named Dragonhorses.

Ah' prefaces nearly all women's names. It is an ancient designate meaning, "lady, woman or female."

ABOUT THE AUTHOR

Showandah S. Terrill is an award winning speaker and storyteller, as well as a lifelong writer and equestrian. Steeped in Native American culture, she was raised as the only child of an itinerant cowhand on sprawling ranches in Southern California during the turbulent 1960's.

She is currently writing two extended series: the epic science-fiction *Dragonhorse Chronicles* and the fictional autobiographical *Peter Aarons'* novels.

www.ingramcontent.com/pod-product-compliance
Lightning Source LLC
Chambersburg PA
CBHW030553310726
48979CB00011B/2135/J

* 9 7 8 1 7 3 2 8 0 5 2 9 3 *